I0643403

THE
FIRES
WE BECOME

Manu Dhawan is a New York-based business leader, serial entrepreneur and former private equity professional who found his true calling in storytelling. He lives with his wife and two wonderful daughters, who keep his world grounded and inspired. When not navigating business decisions or parenting puzzles, he can be found experimenting with stories, life and coffee.

His debut novel, *The Unprodigal* (2019), was an instant bestseller. *Business World* described it as 'Poignant, Exciting, Stirring' while *The Times of India* called it 'Dramatic'. Actor Ayushmann Khurrana termed it 'intricately woven like a wonderful spell'.

The Fires We Become is his much-awaited second novel—a noir-soaked, emotionally charged literary thriller brimming with heart, fire and unforgettable characters.

You can connect with the author via:
Instagram: @author_manu_dhawan
Email: manu.dhawan25@gmail.com

Also by Manu Dhawan

The Unprodigal

THE
FIRES
WE BECOME

MANU DHAWAN

RUPA

Published by
Rupa Publications India Pvt. Ltd 2025
161-B/4, Gulmohar House,
Yusuf Sarai Community Centre,
New Delhi 110049

Sales centres:
Bengaluru Chennai Hyderabad
Kolkata Mumbai

P-ISBN: 978-93-7003-662-8
E-ISBN: 978-93-7003-294-1

First impression 2025

10 9 8 7 6 5 4 3 2 1

The moral right of the author has been asserted.

Printed in India

To the most spectacular women ever—
Nidhi, Myra and Kimaya.
Thank you for the love and smiles.

'We are all in the gutter,
but some of us are looking at the stars.'

—Oscar Wilde, *Lady Windermere's Fan*

Contents

01 Unnamed and Unmarked

◦ Johnny ◦

Living had turned out to be such a huge waste of time; going out, I reckoned, would at least be with a bang. There were a million ways to go, yet not one was perfect. Not just that— there were unanswered questions. For instance, would death be a comma or a period after a short sentence littered with nothing but passive verbs and pathetic nouns? The potential answers were merely opinions—at best, aggressive credos falsely polished by time and religion. I suffered from none of them; time hadn't made me better and religion—no one had bothered to choose one for me.

But they did choose for me an infinite number of names. The children in my orphanage called me 'Bauna', 'Chhotu', 'Giddu'. My classmates in med school were more creative: 'Minivan', 'Chhota Coke', 'Half Piece'. Some even called me a mini mutant. The quack I now assisted in his rundown clinic called me 'XS'. My neighbours and drinking buddies at the shanty awarded me names wrapped in a patronizing veil: 'Boss', 'Raja', 'Tiger'. But the name that had really stuck over these 32 pointless years was the one given by the nun who'd found a crying baby in a vegetable bag outside the orphanage: 'Johnny'.

Polyonymous or not, I knew I was as unnamed and unmarked as the cobbled bricks I walked on—eroded by a million feet, yet inconsequential to any of their destinations.

It was past midnight as I pounded my nightly sales beat, selling antidepressants. Thick as thieves with all the dark corners, cracks and secret turns these old streets of Kolkata possessed, I walked on dauntlessly. The streets were empty, lined only with rusty tram tracks and crooked lamp posts. Distant barks and the ill-timed chirps of crickets filled the balmy darkness. Tottering trucks left behind slimy fumes that refused to leave, but every now and then cool river gusts pierced through them and took away the deathly stillness.

It was just like every other night. But tonight, I hoped, would be the last. A dozen pills would do the trick. In the morning, I'd be found by a reluctant garbage collector whose first instincts would be to check my pockets. Not much of a bang, I suppose.

As I turned a corner, lost in thoughts of a wasted life, rough hands grabbed me from behind and hauled me towards them, my legs dangling in the air. I couldn't turn and see who it was. In retaliation, I only managed a muted squeak. Loud footsteps trailed behind my invisible abductor. Maybe he was a junkie trying to rob me of my pills. Or a new peddler in my area stamping out the competition, his team closing in to help.

He turned me around and glared. Squinted eyes. Blood on his face and in his hair. That's all I remember about his appearance as I wrestled to free myself. I couldn't see the people closing in on him—the corner wall cut off my line of sight.

'They killed my sister,' he whispered. His hands quivered, making me shake with him. 'I have information that'll bring everybody down. You have to tell everyone. If I die, promise me you won't. Promise me you won't die!'

My mouth, wide-open as it was, couldn't form any words.

'Say it!' he screamed.

'I…I won't…die!' I managed to get out.

'Now hide!'

'What?'

'Hide, you motherfucker! Use it when the time is right.'

'Use wh—'

'There he is. Catch the bastard!' The footsteps were now just a few metres away.

My abductor flung me behind the trash cans next to the wall. Lying in the filth, I watched him through two bins as he barely trotted—it seemed he had decided my life was now more important than his. Two men caught up with him within seconds. One grabbed his collar while the other bent over, wheezing.

Collecting myself, I tried to stand up but realized those men were police constables. Happy with the presence of law but uncomfortable with the copious amount of illegal antidepressants in my bag, I stayed where I was. A police jeep slowed down and stopped next to them. Another cop, clearly the one leading this witch-hunt, jumped out. The second he did, the out-of-breath constable joined his colleague and held the stranger. They were all missing their name plaques.

The newly arrived cop raised his arms and strolled towards the captive. 'It is better that 10 guilty escape than one innocent suffer.' He stopped in front of the man. 'Tell me who said this, and I'll let you go.'

The stranger looked away from him.

The cop sighed. 'I thought as much. It's pointless to run from me. This is the last time I'll offer you a deal—your life for what I want. Take it.' He squeezed the man's throat. 'If not, I'll cut off your balls and feed them to rabid dogs.'

I shivered. Not just at the words but the way they were said. It made me question my morbid inclinations and incorrigible ability to find myself in other people's bloody soups. A fat, fearless rodent scurried over my hand. I was uncomfortably far from civilization. The kind of distance that wouldn't allow my potential shrieks to reach anyone in time.

I didn't feel like dying much.

The senior cop had star-pinned lapels and paan-stained lips. When the stranger refused to talk, he landed jabs and blows generously on the man's already-bloodied face. Blood seeped down his tattered shirt, and when that was completely soaked, it trickled on to his trousers.

The cop tirelessly beat whatever little living daylights were left in the almost-dead man. One nausea-friendly threat followed another. He pulled his nails, broke his knees. I flinched; in fact, I peed a little in my pants. It also made me promise myself that if I made it out of this alive, I'd gorge on dark chocolates every single day for the rest of my life—without guilt—and I wouldn't die. At least not voluntarily.

The dying stranger finally spoke without looking at the cop. 'I don't believe you. You'll kill me once I tell you everything.' His head hung down, and blood dripped from his drenched trousers into an overflowing drain clogged with cigarette butts, burnt matchsticks and clumps of hair. If not for the constables holding him up, he would drop dead on the ground the second his broken knees realized the weight of his mutilated body.

Those constables were playing the role of nails in this crucifixion.

'Every man must do two things alone: he must do his own believing and his own dying,' the cop said. The audience remained unstirred, clearly having no affinity towards Lutheranism or an understanding of spiritualism and theology. I found it shocking that the cop did.

'You know what?' he continued. 'I don't find too many stubborn fuckers like you in my trade anymore. You're right—

let's not play this game. Here's the real deal, and I swear on my demented mother I'm telling you the truth: you will die today.'

He let out a squeal of laughter. The kind I'd heard only in my darkest nightmares—the ones where people see me naked and guffaw. Shaming and morbid at the same time; shrill, yet like a lullaby that puts you to sleep forever. It almost choked him, but he liked it, so he laughed again like a rat in pain. And again. His colleagues followed suit, out of professional courtesy, but couldn't come anywhere close to his ghoulish squawks.

He stopped laughing and yanked the man's head up by his hair, forcing eye contact. 'But you can buy yourself a quick trip to hell or die one cell at a time. Give me what I need, or I'll do things to you they shudder to talk about in torture prisons around the world. If you talk, I'll put a bullet in your head. Trust me—you won't even know you died! What do you say, huh, old friend?'

Another shriek of laughter. More pee down my pants.

'Go fuck your demented mother.'

The stranger bore the look of a man who was no longer afraid of dying. I couldn't blame him. How much worse could dying be than this? But making the cop squeal again was entirely his fault. He shouldn't have done that. For the good of mankind, he shouldn't have.

By the time the cop stopped laughing, he had already pulled another nail from the man's fingers. No shrieks ensued. That didn't please the cop, so he removed a few more only to earn himself muffled grunts. I ran my thumbs over my fingernails, never more thankful for them being where they should be.

The cop looked around, motioned to one of the constables to keep holding the man, and asked the other to step aside with him.

The two of them walked towards me.

Had they seen me? Had my breathing been too loud? Had my shivering legs gave me away?

They stopped close to the trash cans and I heaved a sigh of relief.

'Does he have any family? Wife? Parents? Kids? Girlfriend?' the cop whispered to the constable, throwing an arm around him.

'No, sir. He lives alone and jerks off to hero comics in his free time.'

The cop gave him a slow, considering look, then let go of his shoulder, distancing himself from him. 'While your interest in his sex life is very intriguing, stick to what I ask you. Is there anyone he cares about? We could kill that person in front of him. That might help.'

I found myself agreeing with the cop's logic.

The constable turned towards the prisoner, then shouted, 'Yes!'

The cop's eyes lit up.

'Yes! Yes! Yes!' the constable continued.

Annoyed by the barrage of yeses and nothing more, the cop swung hard, sending the constable sprawling into the overflowing drain. 'Stop orgasming and tell me who it is. And dial it down; we don't want anyone else turning up and dying for no reason.'

A vague form of cognitive empathy did exist in this man. Did that mean I had a slim chance? Not really. Because if I did 'turn up', I wouldn't fall into the category of people not turning up. So that was that.

'There's a street dog,' the constable said from the ground, wiping the blood trickling down from the corner of his mouth.

'A dog?'

'Yes. Chandu.'

'Chandu?' The cop's mouth hung open for a few more seconds till a glob of paan juice dripped down his chin.

'Yes, Chandu. A street dog.'

The cop stood still, pondering. He wiped his stained lips with his sleeve. 'Where can you find…uh…Chandu?'

'He's usually outside his shanty. I can go get him.'

'Go. And get back here in five minutes. Or I'll make Chandu do things to you.'

Chandu. The dog would pay for his loyalty. But what was my crime? Did I take one turn too many? A turn I wouldn't have taken on any other night while selling my pills?

Assisting a quack as a male nurse had its perks. I had access to large quantities of painkillers, sleeping pills and antidepressants—cheap substitutes for cocaine, crack or meth. I stole them from the clinic, swapped them for fake sugar pills and sold them at half price on the streets every night. My only accomplishment? A loyal customer base for a poor man's narcotics.

My customers called me 'Mini Painkiller'—another name on my distinguished list. For a drug peddler worth his salt, a nickname—any nickname—was equivalent to an 'MD' after a doctor's name.

Most of my med school classmates would be MDs by now. I would have been one too if I hadn't run away after they made me lick their footwear. I was the only one targeted—because I was a dwarf. So I sneaked into their dorm that night and laced their whisky bottles with a magic potion. Not enough to kill them, but enough to make them want to die.

Then I left that godforsaken place. One city after another, until I found a place I could finally call home: Kolkata.

And now, on a night that was meant to be my last, my life was changing forever. I closed my eyes, wishing this would disappear and I'd wake up in cold sweat. No such luck. The paan-chewing law-keeper went back to his entertainment for the night. The tortured stranger was now just a blood-soaked rag, barely held up by the constable, on the verge of slipping into the drains.

The cop walked over and yanked his head up again. 'Couldn't you find anything else to love? A beautiful girl? A fat whore from Sonagachi? A fucking man, for all I care! Did it have to be a dog?'

He shook the man's head to keep him conscious and continued. 'You know, I have three of them. Beautiful boys. No ticks. No rabies. Healthy. Only eat meat. Fucking spoiled fuckers. Pasco, Rancho and Pedro. I bathe them, feed them, talk to them.'

He paused and peered into the man's eyes. 'Oh, I can think of another good one: if you eliminate smoking and gambling, you will be amazed to find that almost all an Englishman's pleasure can be, and mostly are, shared by his dog.'

Then, another ear-piercing squeal of laughter. 'Listen, please don't make me kill Chandu. Just give me the information, and we'll go our separate ways. I kill you, you go to hell, and, well, I go back to my own hell. Let's not get other species involved. It's not right. What do you say?'

I smelled a grain of humanity but quickly dismissed it.

For the first time, the half-dead stranger smiled. 'Everyone's going to know what you bastards did. And everyone will pay the price, including the—'

'I found Chandu!' The constable came running, clutching a confused-looking stray in his arms. Wide-eyed and panting, the dog wagged its bald tail and sniffed the air.

'Okay, smart-ass. Here's the new deal. You get to save the

only thing you care about in this world. You give me what I want, and I promise I won't hurt him. If you don't, I'll rip his heart out in front of you. And then I'll rip out yours.'

He walked to the whimpering dog and caressed it before quickly moving away and wiping his hand violently against his trousers. The dog had remnants of a drain and its erstwhile citizens clinging to its matted fur.

'Son of a—'

'Come close to me,' the stranger suddenly whispered. His voice sounded feebler every time he spoke, and it was becoming difficult to hear him. The blood spewing out of his mouth didn't help much either.

The cop walked towards him, smiling. Maybe the dog had done the trick.

'I want…the dog's…ripped out. That's my…last wish,' the man said. I could only catch a few words but knew what it meant.

The cop stepped back and peered at him. I felt bad for Chandu and sick for myself. Cringing, I looked for escape routes. There were none.

'Tie his mouth and hold him tight.'

The constable holding the dying man pulled a handkerchief from his pocket and moved to gag him.

'Not you, you dumb idiot.' The cop pointed at the one holding the dog. 'You, you fucking moron. Tie the dog's mouth!'

The cop strode over to the police jeep and retrieved a shiny machete. He watched as the dog struggled to free itself. It was clear he wouldn't have hesitated to kill the man, but with the dog, he took his time. Pacing, he muttered to himself, swinging the machete in the air while the dog squealed, sensing what was coming.

'Last chance. Or Chandu pays for your stupidity.'

The man stared at the cop but didn't say a word. The cop turned around and drove the machete down in one clean thrust. Blood sprayed across his face, blending into the paan stains. The dog whimpered and wriggled, until it didn't.

'I've never regretted killing anyone in my life. But you made me do this. My humanity is dead, along with Chandu.'

He stood still, looked up at the dark skies, then let go of the machete, which clanked on the ground—a death knell concluding the gore show.

For a few seconds, nothing happened. No dogs barked in the distance. No trucks rumbled past. Even the rodent had retreated. There was an absolute and eerie silence.

Then the man laughed loudly. A guttural, grisly laugh that sent blood bubbling down his mouth and neck. A 'muhahaha' of a man who didn't give a damn about anything but his last hurrah.

It was contagious. The cop smiled at first, then matched the man's laughing lungs with his subversive squeals. This time the constables didn't join the laugh riot.

When there was nothing left in him, the man stopped, looked at the cop and said, 'That wasn't Chandu.'

The cop looked at the dog, then at the constable still holding it with trembling hands. He picked up the machete, ambled towards the man and slowly pierced his stomach.

The dying stranger was now dead. And in the cold silence that ensued, they heard my helpless whimper.

02 Only Dirty Hands Make Money

✦ Katherine ✦

'Are you psychic, Katherine?'
I did a lot of odd jobs, but writing fortunes for cookies in restaurants run by the Italian mafia in New York was the only one that made people stop talking, listen to me and feign interest in my life. Questions like these were usually accompanied by wide eyes and raised brows, followed by equally weary reactions: 'Fascinating. Does it pay well?'; 'You're like a Linda Goodman rolled into a sentence!'; 'Do your predictions come true?'

My blind date was no exception. We were in a loud bar in Lenox Hill, and I was on my fourth drink. He was buying, so I answered with just a mysterious smile—any words out of my mouth at this stage would end this conversation rather quickly. And with that, my promising supply of whisky.

But he was persistent. 'Don't you need to be good with words for that? I've barely heard you speak the whole evening.'

Crapola. I'll have to stop drinking and talk nice to him.

'You do need to be good with words. I used to be a copywriter. And a damn good one before they...' I trailed off, remembering the day I got fired. Waving to the bartender, I hoped my date's quota of curiosity had tapped out by now.

I was a copywriter in a major ad firm before they caught me making out with the janitor in the storeroom. Yeah, go ahead and judge me. If my mom could, you definitely would—even are expected to. Once I lost my job, it was mostly a downward spiral from there. Smaller apartments. Shorter relationships. Heavier mail.

But it was okay. All I had to do was turn 27, and the pumpkin carriage would permanently transform into a golden chariot.

Twenty-seven. That's when I'd be finally allowed to enjoy what was mine. An eventuality filled with riding horses and flying jets. Seaside mansions. Vintage cars. Ravishing butlers. I'd have it all.

My father, Arthur Gladwell, believed that by that age, I would be a complete woman on her own two feet, ready to be responsible for the legacy. But who was he to be the judge of people and circumstances? He ran away from his own when he couldn't handle them. So, instead of standing on two feet, when I was found on all fours with the janitor, my mother—the great Samantha Gladwell—thought it appropriate to cut off the monthly stipend my father's trust allowed me.

Why? Because she could, according to some perverted clause in the trust. Because I dug sweaty sex. For the love of Jimi Hendrix, what was wrong with that? For one, it was exclusive—no one seemed to claim sex-goddessary in that domain.

Anyway, back to my failing date.

'What are the chances of meeting someone who actually wrote those? My destiny is about to change.' Curiosity officially dead, he went back to focusing on himself.

Chances of any action tonight seemed bleak. I gulped the remnants of my fifth drink.

'I could never be one. Grammar has never been my strong point,' he said.

'Well, apart from the ability to juggle multiple low-paying jobs, you do need a degree and very good grammar and punctuation skills. You definitely don't want a fortune cookie to read, "Use aggression when hunting women will make you happy tomorrow."'

'Huh?'

'The missing period? After "hunting".'

'Huh?'

Definitely no action tonight.

If you were to ask me if I'd ever used that same example of limp grammar in a similar conversation before, I wouldn't answer. I found it an absolute waste of time to look into the past. There wasn't much there anyway—cold money and lonely riches apart.

I was the only child, heir to the Gladwell fortune, built over five generations of American railroads since the 1840s. When I was little, my dad used to tell me bedtime stories—except instead of fairies or knights, they were about our 'rich lineage', meant to wire me into being a 'true Gladwell'.

'Kathy, the railroads are in your blood,' he used to say.

My third great-grandfather, William Gladwell, was a legend in the American railroad industry. He built the longest stretch of track in the country, from Iowa in the east to the Bay Area. An immigrant and an erstwhile mine worker, he made his wealth from the dust in the Wild West. His knowledge of the vast western wastelands, his deep friendships with the natives and the loyalty of thousands of Irish workers—in an otherwise slave-dependent industry—helped him set up his railroad company, one ballast at a time. Angry tornadoes, vicious earthquakes and frequent floods—he had seen it all. The newspapers called him 'The Railman'.

'Only dirty hands make money,' he used to say. But he knew the real money wasn't in laying the tracks—it was in the land grants the government handed out in return. The railroads were critical not just to grow the economy of the country but also to win the Civil War. Supplies, information and ammunition reached Union soldiers just in time to crush the Confederates.

And those barren lands? They would soon be worth a hundred times more when they became towns and cities. When they could be reached from faraway Chicago, sitting in the comforts of a first-class chugging coach, reading the *New-York Daily Tribune* while sipping coffee, as galloping Cheyennes waved fleeting hellos outside the window.

William Gladwell was the real gold sniffer. And sniff, he did.

By the time my father took over the business, the Gladwell Railroad Company was already valued at a gazillion dollars, and the momentum was clearly on our side. He created his own niche, quadrupled the firm's net worth in a few years, and then did it again. And again. Until the Gladwell Railroad Company became the biggest railroad empire in the country.

Only dirty hands make money.

Long story long, I was filthy rich, and then I was just filthy. Those stories—the legend of the Gladwells—were sung to me by my father every night. They intoxicated me like a magic potion, thick with the fumes of bravery and hustle. I dreamt of being a driver of a locomotive that tugged all the 50 united states behind it. Then I pictured myself behind a mahogany desk, signing cheques until the cows came home. But those dreams stopped when my father disappeared. Those stories... departed with him, never to return.

Now I was just Katherine. 'Gladwell' was just a leaden name on my PhD that cast me down. I indulged in exotic jobs—writing fortune cookies, running courier gigs and hacking websites. But the dullest of them all was forensic cleaning. I arrived at the crime scenes long after the interesting stuff had been taken away. Left behind were nothing but the remnants of overfull intestines and, if I was lucky, the unbearable stench of death.

I encountered too many worried landlords and covertly happy widows to see how hope—a drug everyone wants to be high on—tantalizingly hung on a delicate thread of tomorrow. No, that drug didn't blow my skirt up. I chose a more reliable one for my quota of sunshine. Cocaine. White powder. Snow. Blow. Stardust. Mojo. Nose candy. Or whatever ingenuous name the street hatched an hour ago.

I never understood why they gave it such a bad name. Or names. It was the most reliable medicine available to mankind, and it kept me accountable for all the knowledge I didn't want to possess. Like a river trickling over shiny eroded stones, it washed away all the dirt. The baggage. The loneliness and the unseen corners. It filled me with life—a transient hunger to see the world without its ugliness. Cocaine narrowed the corridors of my eyes.

That was my thing. My weapon. The fuel that made me win medals and accolades. Attend top universities. Know things a kid my age had no business knowing. High IQ and A pluses. At first, I was celebrated as a Gladwell trophy. Then, when they found out the Gladwell girl was on coke, I was labelled as the failure of success. Guess I too had 'ballasted' my own niche.

Some Gladwell.

Predictably, my date was a disaster. I left and made my way home through the cold streets of New York, grabbing a sandwich and a bottle of Jack on the way. My apartment was on the Upper East Side, a small place I could barely afford and rarely used. Most days, I worked 16–18 hours, running on snorts and coffee. When I did go home, I'd toss and turn in the bed for a few hours, trying to convince myself I'd slept. When that failed, I stepped out on to the emergency-exit, hang on the metal bars and do a 100 pull-ups until exhaustion forced sleep upon me.

Olav woke me up on the fire escape.

At exactly 5.30 a.m., just like every other morning, my neighbour's black cat rubbed his fur against my face, his golden eyes staring at me as I came back to life. A cold shower and an overripe banana later, I cycled my way through the early-morning streets of Manhattan.

The city wore an interim jacket of calm at this time of the day. Reversing trucks. Steaming drainages. Upright doormen. It gave me time to imagine what other citizens of this godforsaken city might be doing while I slipped mail into sleepy post boxes. Stretching their unsure hands into warm showers, checking if the temperature was perfect for them to get in.

Next up: a beer-launch gig where I was supposed to stand on an avenue, wearing a sexy office suit and getting drenched in beer.

In the vestibule of a residential building, I sniffed a line and got ready for the action. Passing men (and women) cracked open their cans, took a sip, then sprayed the rest on me and a bunch of other girls. One was dressed as a librarian, another as a firewoman. One was practically naked. Some passer-by suits displayed a 'What has the world come to?' bewilderment, while a few participated with glee.

But most didn't care, whizzing by with their heads buried in screens, programmed to look up only for stop signs and planes crashing into buildings.

YokoMan Beer, the taste of man.

A 100 bucks and a six-pack later, I changed and dropped in at the city library to finish the copy for an ad. Only when I overheard someone whisper 'She smells like shit' did the constant frowns from my fellow readers make sense.

I reeked of stale beer, but couldn't care less. Many happy returns for those with the urge to purge—I had a deadline to meet.

I also had other things I had to do today. I had to shop for a nice dress.

Mom had called after two years. 'Let's crack some lobsters at Manhattan Grill tonight. I managed to get a table. Wear a nice dress.'

Click.

Hearing her voice always reminded me of her warm, safe smell. Memories of her were always accompanied by the fragrances of her exotic perfumes and skin creams. She'd place her hands on my forehead, gently playing with my hair and combing it with her moisturized, manicured fingers. I'd relish that lingering scent for as long as I could until there was no more.

For her, important things were important. And she pursued them aggressively.

The smell of hands. The missing rumples in a dress. The flow of rich cloth. The whiteness of a virgin paper. The little molecule of paint outside its boundaries. The perfect yellow in her lamps. The freshness of linen. The floral notes in her merlot—or lack thereof. The lack of scratches on her bag zippers. The absence of soil in her tyre treads. The perfect sizzle in her steak. The imperfect melee of wildflowers. The right place for everything and the wrong place for nothing.

She was a woman who had everything—money, time and nuance. Not many understood her unbridled, uncompromising, pernickety passion for the smaller things. The things that, according to her, made up life.

I thought it was fucking baloney.

A lot had happened in the last two years. And now, here we were, meeting after ages, and I knew I couldn't go like me.

'There's nothing sadder than not embracing your womanhood,' she used to say.

I had to buy a nice dress.

Which essentially meant a $1,000 debilitation of an already dried-up coffer. I could buy a lot of powder with that money, but the potential benefits of playing the part of a 'changed woman' far outweighed the cost of a few missed snorts.

The idea that my mother's heart had thawed and she wanted to welcome me back into her tasteful luxury sounded heartening. I could do with my monthly stipend from my trust. And some nice dresses. I was getting tired of the tattered-cowgirl-meets-city-junkie look.

Hell, I could do with some life. Even if it meant being puppeteered by my loving mother's manicured hands. I guess I'd reached the biblical threshold of not giving a shit, but I wanted to give a shit. I'd take lonely riches. I'd take the cold money. Yesterday.

'God, did she just swim out of a brewery tank?' someone whispered behind me, breaking my thoughts.

I smelled my armpits. Holy mother of Jimi! It was imperative that I stopped at a store and stole a hair conditioner and hand cream. I texted my dealer for what would be my last stash for weeks.

What had made Mom call after all this time? Was she finally marrying again? A queue of suitors would line up outside the Gladwell mansion if she ever decided to remarry, but she never did. She cocooned herself after Dad left.

But I wasn't going to ruin today thinking about that day. I had a thousand bucks of retail therapy ahead of me. And a potential crevice that led to the Gladwell mansion—a crack in Mom's armour, a way to get my life back.

There was no time to waste on self-pity or misplaced adulthood. It was time to get what was mine. Tonight, my third great-grandfather's playbook on dirty hands wouldn't work.

Or maybe it would.

03 A Rung-less Ladder

.→ Johnny .←

'If he wants it, ask him to come see me, look me in the eye and ask me. Nicely,' I said.

I knew it was a wet dream.

What else could it be? In which version of my inconsequential life could I affront that lanky cop's messenger with an open invitation to a machete-carved death—while swinging on a hammock made of antidepressants?

I could see myself there, happy and content, empty chocolate wrappers fluttering around the swaying hammock. I was a witness to my own dream, drifting between the corridors of the conscious. My dream-self had stronger arms and longer legs. Whiter teeth that eclipsed those in any toothpaste commercial and a stubble just like those heroes from the movies. That's all I ever wanted—to look like a man. To say what I really wanted to say.

For some that was everyday life. For me it was a hard-earned dream.

Just when I thought I deserved the dream, the cop appeared out of nowhere. His squeaky laughter echoed, growing louder by the second. Colours faded, and my ears rang with a deathly, perpetual buzz.

He was looking at the girl. *The girl.*

She was back again to haunt me, tears rolling down her cheeks, asking me for help.

The hammock shook. So did the ground beneath it.

I tried to flee, but like always, I couldn't. I clawed at my consciousness to wake me up but couldn't find it. I was stuck in a prison of my own device, and there was no way out.

The cop's laughter and the girl's wailing kept getting louder, until I couldn't take it anymore.

I opened my eyes to find Jhansi and Laxmi cooing and pecking on last night's leftovers.

'Hush!'

My unwanted, yet daily guests flapped aggressively and escaped through the small window of the small room I called home. It was really just four asbestos walls that allowed me to stretch my short legs—yet it felt larger than a football stadium.

Always cold, though. Like a surgeon's theatre.

In one corner was a small table with missing drawers, books, a gas stove and empty jars. Scattered clothes and chocolate wrappings covered the otherwise-bare floor. A flickering bulb fought against the erratic surges of electricity stolen from the main power line that ran outside the only window.

The window hadn't been closed in forever. On the rare occasions I tried, like when it rained hard or the heat became unbearable, it groaned loudly, refusing to meet its pane.

Humans weren't the only creatures of habit.

But the window had its advantages. I could quickly unhook the jerry-rigged cable from the main lines whenever the electricity department paid one of their surprise visits. And this 'feature' alone was enough, according to my landlord, to counter all the other minor discomforts and justify a premium on the rent.

I planned to get a legitimate connection one day and install an air conditioner to rid the place of its wretched humidity.

The humidity.

It had been three days since that muggy night I almost

died—when that squeal-spewing, quote-thrusting, paan-chewing cop had driven his machete into that stranger.

I'd let out a helpless whine that was miraculously drowned by the constable's retching.

They didn't hear me.

The cop yanked the bloodstained knife and stepped back. He gaped at his corpse-cradling peers as blood trickled from the machete to his fingers. 'I am in blood. Stepped in so far that, should I wade no more, returning were as tedious as go o'er,' he said.

His aides—already established as non-lovers of Martin Luther—also weren't big fans of Shakespeare. They just stared at him.

For the longest 15 minutes of my life, I trembled as they ripped the dead man's clothes off, rolled up his naked corpse in a plastic sheet and gingerly loaded it into the back of the vehicle—like it was a newly purchased Persian carpet. Then they cleaned up the mess, swishing thick blood into the drain.

'Burn his clothes in the trash can,' the cop whispered to the constables.

The trash can. This was it.

As the aides walked towards the bins, I had to make a decision. I turned around, got up, and ran with all I had.

Seconds later, I heard them shouting. Heavy footsteps pounded the ground behind me. I didn't look back. There was no time. I had only one shot: the dark serpentine lane across the main road. The one I knew inside and out.

If I could make it there, I had a chance.

But first, I had to cross. And their strides were twice as long as mine.

As they closed in, my medical dorm, the orphanage, the

mocking jokes, the fire, a bullet leaving its chamber—all flashed in front of me. They made my life more precious—like everything I'd ever seen was worth making sense of. Like there was more. And better. I couldn't give up on my ebb tide. There had to be more. Those bits of my life—my past—made me run harder.

I made it to a dark alley, then another. As I buried myself deeper into those lanes, the abusing cops started fading away—until they were no longer there. I found a crevice between two buildings, just big enough to squeeze my body into. I waited for them to find me, but they never did.

I'd saved my wretched life yet again.

Eventually I lost consciousness and woke up around dawn. Before the city stirred, I pushed myself out and hurried back home.

For a few hours, I felt alive. I had escaped certain death. Maybe it was fate. Maybe I was destined to become the greatest drug peddler in Kolkata. My size would no longer be an impediment to my achievements; I'd set up my own factories and sell my unique drug. The 'Mini Drug'. No—better, 'Johnny Pops'.

I'd no longer be deluged with obligatory smiles and insipid questions.

Then reality assailed me.

I was a dwarf. Even if the cops hadn't seen my face, they would've noticed that. Life exited my veins, fear filling the vacuum. What was I thinking, getting up and running like that? When would I stop thinking of myself as a normal human being? I had to start thinking like a little person, reminding myself every second of my handicapped life that I was a mutant with no powers of the ordinary.

I slammed my fists against the walls. Threw things. Ripped off my clothes and hurled them out of the window, as if that could rid me of my burdens.

It didn't.

Every minute of seeing a man slowly lose his life replayed in my mind, sending shivers to forgotten corners and ends of my body. The machete. It was waiting for me.

I holed myself up in the shanty for three days, gourmandizing on dark chocolates and talking mostly to pigeons. I expected the cops to show up any second. I knew there weren't too many dwarfs ambling the dirty streets of Kolkata in the middle of the night. And it wouldn't take too much time for them to figure that out.

I couldn't leave. I'd stand out like a dog's balls at any bus or train station. My only chance was to get to Babughat at night—the crowded wharf on the Hooghly River—and catch the infamous weekly boat to the Bangladesh border. From there, I hoped to cross over and disappear forever, leaving behind my life in Kolkata.

I checked my stash of pills and cash. They were still there. Before leaving the shanty for what I thought would be the very last time, I'd left them as a parting gift, along with a letter, for my only friend and neighbour Rampal. That rangy bastard would have to wait longer; I wasn't ready to die yet. The money and pills were enough for me to start over.

I tiptoed to the window and looked out to an uproarious, wet neighbourhood teeming with hand-pulled rickshaws and hurried pedestrians. On one side of the street, old women sold stale vegetables, fanning away a persistent plague of flies with drenched newspapers. On the other side, a bunch of kids smacked crooked sticks into an overflowing drain, creating their very own wave pool.

A wayward yellow Ambassador cab honked its way through the crowded street, the driver hopeful of making it across without getting water up the vehicle's exhaust or rowdy kids on its hood. I thought he was ambitious.

Beyond our shanty was the modern world, sprinkled with cricket stadiums, shiny façades and roads so wide they could afford faded lane dividers. A little farther still, the Hooghly River flickered in the distance, peeking through cracks in the concrete and smoke.

I lived on the third floor of a shanty that stood on iron rods, asbestos sheets and bent hope. The place was in the heart of Hazaar Basti—'the thousand slums'—an illegal, sprawling ghetto in the northern part of Kolkata. Each level had five more rooms like mine. A wooden ladder, missing more than a few rungs, ran through the middle of the structure. Walking on the upper floors was frowned upon; too much movement caused the whole structure to shake, straining the rusted rods.

Whenever hapless couples copulated, tremors made the neighbours pant with equal fervour. Weary about waking up in a rubble, they'd wait for the fornication to conclude before going back to their well-earned sleep. The structure had miraculously survived all human recreation, including guilty husbands fleeing epiphanic wives. Case of the Missing Rungs explained.

My neighbours were usually friendly and minded their own business. But curiosity about my size always led to questions like 'How big were you when you were born?' or 'Why don't you work at the circus?' The most frequent, and oddly endearing, question came from my mystified male neighbours after a few glasses of hooch: 'Do midgets have humungous dicks?'

Aside from questions weirder than the names they gave me, my neighbours mostly treated me like a human. Which was more than I could ask for. So I'd made this place my home for the last five years, shaky shanty and humungous genitalia notwithstanding. I liked the insignificance of the place. There were no demands for a better life or criticisms of a failed government. People were happy to have made it through the day, quietly bracing for the inevitable: tomorrow.

A loud persistent banging on the door brought me back to my dire circumstances. I was too late. The filthy cops had found me. My guts would be macheted, and my body, rolled in a plastic sheet, would be left to rot somewhere by the river. Mini Painkiller was ready to face his doom.

The banging continued.

'Johnny! Open the door, you lazy dwarf!'

The good news was it was Rampal; the bad news was that he'd never knocked on my door before.

Ever.

Jumping out of the window would result in the same outcome as opening the door. So I opened it halfway.

'Were you having an orgy in there? Dr Verma is standing downstairs, cursing you and making all our lives miserable,' he said.

He stood in his trademark lungi, which was brighter than a halogen bulb. Rampal was a human beanpole, with bones sticking out of places where there weren't meant to be any. It contrasted disgustingly with his stomach, which protruded like a semi-deflated football. I was sure his saggy glob of skin had been surgically implanted on to his skeleton.

His black-framed glasses, broken and repaired multiple times with obtrusive patches of white glue, perched on his nose. Behind them, his bulging eyes, framed with thick, curled eyelashes like those of a girl, lay partially hidden. His fat, pouty lips barely concealed a large set of surprisingly white and perfectly aligned teeth, creating a striking contrast with his dark skin.

The first time I'd met Rampal was in a police station. I'd been picked up by a beat constable for refusing to part with pills for free—you do it once, you have to do it every time. So I spent the night on a cold bench with three other occupants. Next to me was Rampal, who'd been caught in a mall with five stolen phones, stealing his sixth. After an uncomfortable, sleepless night on the bench, thanks to his acicular bones stabbing every part of my body, I opened my eyes to find him smiling at me and asked him what was so funny.

He grinned. 'Never slept with a dwarf before.'

For reasons still unknown to me, I paid extra to the cop to let him go along with me. He took me to his shanty for a round of hooch. And I never left.

'Are you alone?' I asked him through the half-opened door.

'No, you half man. I have the army of Akbar with me.'

I pushed the door ajar and found no cops behind him. Were they waiting for me downstairs, too lazy to climb a rung-less ladder?

I stepped out to check and found the quack, Dr Verma, looking up and shouting my name.

He was a middle-aged man, fat as they come, obsessed with his ill-designed wig that slid off every time he shook his head. And he shook his head all the time. Ever since his medical license had been revoked, he had evolved into a full-time conspiracy specialist, convinced the universe was colluding to bring him down.

According to him, the 'parasitic doctors' running million-dollar hospitals were part of a 'doctorhood'—a secret society of mobsters engineering new diseases in unknown labs. Shake of the head.

The 'soporific lawyers' devised legal maxims in Latin and 'polysyllabic gibberish', only to put their hapless clients into a state of legal trance—it was their 'hypnosis kit,' he'd say. Wag of the head.

The 'pretentious' old-age homes were actually ground zero for mutant drug experimentation. The 'conceited' institution of marriage was just a devious tool used solely to manufacture an indefinite demand for real estate. And his 'vampiric' ex-wife, whose family was from Chinatown? She had left him because she was a spy. Shake and wag.

I had listened to, sometimes even secretly relished, these and a thousand other machinations while assisting him. Dr Verma trusted no one.

'Johnny, what the fuck? Why haven't you been coming to work? I'm going crazy with all the patients! Is this a scheme to destroy my business? Who put you up to this?'

'No one. I haven't been well, that's all.'

'Come down now unless you want me to give your job to someone else.'

'I'll be there in an hour.'

I disregarded his threat, knowing no one was going to work for that prick—except a drug-peddling, semi-suicidal dwarf.

'Be there in 10, fucking XS.' Dr Verma left.

Rampal smacked the back of my head. That smack again. Like he had a right to do it. My bet was he thought of me as a small boy who had stopped growing—physically and mentally. I was at least five years older than the moron. But he was the closest thing I had to a friend, so the smack was acceptable. Even comforting at times.

'All okay, partner?' he asked.

'Yeah. Just been—'

'Unwell. I heard. You look like shit.'

'I feel like shit.' My thoughts flashed back to that night.

'Did anything happen?' he pressed.

'What do you mean?'

'You didn't turn up for our weekly binging. You never miss that.'

I shrugged. 'I had some work.'

'You just said you weren't well.'

'I had work and I wasn't feeling well. Now go. I have to get ready to treat bleeding noses and fissured asses.'

Rampal's eyes narrowed. 'You're up to something. I can always tell. Anyway, give me a few of those shiny pills, will you? The cops banged me up again. My shoulders are crushed.'

'Serves you right, stealing all the time.'

'And you get those pills from the government of India? Maybe I should tell Dr Verma about it.'

'Will you stop shouting? I'll get you some later. I'm out of stock. Now fuck off.'

'Fucking stingy midget. I'm striking you off our drinking sessions.'

Offensive as 'midget' was, I never found it insulting coming from Rampal. He had privileges I wouldn't give anyone else, and I hated myself for it. One day I'd give him a diarrhoea-inducing pill and make him wait outside the common loo. We'd see who the midget was then.

'Okay, do that. Now get out,' I shouted.

Rampal fled instantly. I wasn't sure if he was stunned by my booming voice—something he'd rarely heard—or the fact that I was okay being taken off the prestigious invite list. Probably both. I likely wouldn't survive till the next one anyway.

I had no idea what was going to happen but decided that staying inside a hole forever wouldn't solve it. I had to get on with my life, whatever little was left of it. After a hundred push-ups and pulls-ups, I was ready to go. I still hoped the pull-ups would help me grow taller by some miracle.

I stood in front of the mirror, combing my short spiky hair. I hated my fat nose, which covered most of my face. One day I'd get it surgically corrected. Keeping my three-day stubble, I put on my white coat, slipped a blunt knife into the inside pocket and left.

Down the ladder and into the clamorous street, I walked cautiously, scanning for strangers or faces I'd never seen. But there were none. 'The thousand slums' was the same as any other day. It still had a million more slums than a thousand, and it still smelled of cardamom and fish—an open book to its residents, a labyrinth to outsiders.

The 90-year-old woman I fondly called 'Naani' sat outside her door, chaffing pulses. She smiled a toothless grin and waved at me, like she did every day since I'd moved in. On festivals, she brought me leftover *prasad*. Maybe that's why I was still alive.

Five non-paying customers stood outside the general store next door, waiting for their daily rice, unaffected by the proprietor's usual rant. It always began with a mumble about bad debts and ended with high-pitched vociferation on inflation.

Down the street was a small temple—one that could just as easily be called a church or a mosque. A frog leapt out of a dilapidated, supposedly haunted, concrete structure and hopped towards the safe chaos of the streets. An empty rickshaw, pulled by a boy not more than 14, passed by. The ambitious yellow cab was still stuck, honking and inching forward against an infantry of children slithering on its wet hood, clicking selfies.

Good. Life at the shanty seemed the usual so far.

'Hey, Johnny. Stop!'

I turned to see Radio, another member of our esteemed

drinking club, running towards me. Did he know? He knew everyone's secrets and traded them for anything that had monetary value. He would have been an easy detainee for the cop.

'Hey, buddy. How about a pill, huh? For your good friend? Haven't been able to sleep lately.'

'You have the money?' I asked.

'Radio never pays with money, Johnny. You know that.'

'I have no interest in your gossip. Save it for others. Come back when you have a purple Gandhi.'

'Did you hear what happened a few days back, just a few blocks down?'

'Yes, the raid on the hooch shop. It was bound to—'

'Who cares about a raid on a booze shop? They're looking for a boy.'

'A boy? Why?' I asked.

Radio knew he had an interested customer. He extended his open palm towards me, his wide smile advertising his tobacco-stained teeth. Something made me take out a pill and discreetly hand it to him.

He leaned in close. 'The cops say he killed a man in front of them. A small kid. Killed him with a machete. Can you believe what the world has come to?'

'A...boy?'

'They chased him, but the fat fuckers couldn't catch him. I'm going to find out who this boy is and hopefully get a reward.'

'The man who was killed...who was he?'

'No one from our area. Apparently he was a respected journalist. Amitav Banerjee. His disappearance is all over the news.'

'So...a boy killed a journalist?'

'Yes, a boy.'

04 A Bearable Sense of Nothingness

✦Katherine✦

'That's a pretty dress. You seem to be doing well for yourself.' Mom sipped her merlot, letting it sit in her mouth for a moment. In front of her, a giant Maine lobster lay, ready to be relished. She was almost 60 but didn't look a year over 45. Sharp curved brows and sparkling moss-green eyes pulled attention away from her crow's feet—a pity, really, because they were the perfect set of crow's feet one could hope for. It was as if all those years behind her endorsed her unequivocally. Like it was time's gift, not curse, to her.

A tiny dimple perched comfortably on her left cheek. Her wavy blonde hair brushed her slender shoulders, allowing only occasional glimpses of her five-carat solitaire earrings. She wore a champagne-coloured satin wrap dress that made mine look like tattered rags. I instantly regretted spending all my money on the dress; I should have bought coke instead.

I looked down at my plate of risotto. 'Thanks. The money isn't bad. And the satisfaction of creating meaningful ads is—'

'You mean writing fortune for cookies at restaurants of questionable repute.'

She twisted and pulled at her lobster, crushing the tail and pushing the meat out.

Son of a Jimi. I should have known better. In fact, I should have expected it. My bad.

So the middle-aged guy with thick glasses who kept popping up at coffee shops and movie theatres wasn't just an old pervert with a fetish for coked-out girls. Did he click pictures of me buying powder? That wouldn't go down too well with Mom. But if I'd noticed him more than once, he couldn't be that good at his job. Mom wasn't paying top dollar for the spy job. In other words, she didn't think it was critical. Hope still floated, and all I had to do was piggyback on it.

We sat across from each other in an upscale restaurant where cutlery didn't clank and people discovered taste buds they didn't have. Where discerning sips carried subtle notes of wild berries followed by the bitter aftertaste of buyer's remorse. Tucked napkins and silky shoulder straps were strewn across an intimate dining space that overlooked a sparkling city from a thousand feet up. Some talked insomnia, while others learnt how to cultivate it. The warm glow from the lamps hung above the tables tangled with city lights that crawled in uninvited through the glass walls. Grinning chefs, drenched in white, mingled with guests, while waist-jacketed waiters sauntered between tables, balancing shining trays on their fingertips.

'Are you here, Kath?'

Her soft yet firm voice made me turn to her. In all the years I'd lived with her, I'd never heard her raise it—she didn't need to. Her voice was delicate but orotund; people listened when she spoke.

'Hmm? Of course. The fortune cookies…it's just something I do as a favour to a friend.' I turned to flag the waiter. 'Can I get a refill, please?'

A trip to the restroom for a snort would be too soon—I'd already used that escape route minutes ago. As my gaze wandered across the restaurant, I hoped this conversation would kill itself.

A whiff of coffee, a sizzle of burnt meat. Americanism at its 19th-floor zenith.

I watched the circus play out in front of me as I narrated an economic essay in my mind. The hedge fund manager had made a fat bonus selling junk bonds. Then, to compare dick sizes with friends, he'd bought his third boat and hired an overpaid captain. His captain—let's call him Captain Sanders—sat several yards away, a dress cap occupying half his table. Captain Sanders's salary paid for his son's college and compensated for a semi-existent fatherhood.

The college's dean, an old, lean man with dishevelled grey hair and a dean's list next to his plate, sat at the table next to us. He seemed like a Dean Mitchell. His overweight wife patted her hair and shifted in her chair for the millionth time. The names on the dean's list underwent 'minor changes' to accommodate the captain's son, and Mr Mitchell finally paid for an old-age home for his ailing mother.

Thriving on lonely, Baby Boomer parents and their distant Gen X children, the old-age home hired a janitor who also cleaned up behind the restaurant's bar.

Peter, in his day job at the old-age home, pawned misplaced hearing aids and lost mobile phones to buy a fake Victoria's Secret negligee for his girl. As he wiped the lipstick off champagne glasses, he planned to gift it to her tonight and hoped she'd wear it for him.

Funny how it all came down to janitors.

'Kath?'

'Yes, Mom?'

'Getting beer sprayed on you in the street—who is that a favour for?'

She cracked open the lobster's claws and pulled out the meat.

My fork dropped to the plate with a clang. Murmurs halted momentarily as people glanced at us before returning to their designed grunts and controlled laughter.

I decided to play the role of an aggressor in my quest to get back to the Gladwell mansion. 'I wouldn't have to do that if you didn't—'

'If you didn't get fired from your job.'

'And it always comes back to that.'

I snatched my glass before the waiter finished pouring my third. Wine sloshed on to the pristine white tablecloth. I gestured for him to leave the bottle.

'You can't blame me for that.'

She leaned forward and dabbed at the stain with a napkin, averting her gaze.

'Yeah, I fucked a cleaner. You can say it. It doesn't bother me. I liked it. I'd do it again. You can keep spying on me as much as you want.'

Unmoved, Mom returned to her lobster, pulling slender slips of meat from its legs. *Play the victim card, bitch.*

'You really think it was that? That you're on your own because you made love to a stranger?' she asked.

'I didn't make love to him, Mom. I fu—'

'Stop.' She finally stopped eating and placed her cutlery on her plate, carefully, without a clink. 'I don't want to hear it. I didn't raise you to—'

'To enjoy my body?'

'You know it's not that, Kath. Where is the beauty you used to see in the world? Why don't you get attracted to smiles? Where is that girl who could play with a pup the whole day and decided she wanted to become a vet and save thousands of dogs?'

I sighed. 'She ran into people, Mom.'

'That's what people usually do. They meet people, invest

in meaningful relationships, build a life.' She patted her lips gently with a napkin.

'Easy for you to say.' I drained my glass and refilled it with whatever was left in the bottle. No amount of alcohol was going to be enough to drown this conversation into oblivion.

'No, it isn't easy for me to say. Trust me. You think I enjoy seeing you like this? Snorting away your life to a wasteland? Do you think I want you to sleep on fire escapes and clean up the remains of criminals? I don't. You need to start talking care of yourself. Be on your own. This...this stint was supposed to make you stronger. To get you used to what's coming. But I'm afraid it's working the other way.'

'What exactly is coming?' I asked.

'You know...life. And you want to—what? Zombie away your life on drugs and sex? What do you think happens when both ends of your candle melt into a bottomless pit? Where will you find the light then?'

It was her turn to call for a refill.

'Then let me have it...the light you see,' I urged. 'The world you live in. The world that's rightfully mine as well. Let me in.'

'Soon you will. But Kath, you have to be ready for anything. Show me you can build a life for yourself. It would mean so much to me.'

'If by being ready, you mean not being selfish or entitled, I'm never going to be ready. The fact that I think the money is rightfully mine, regardless of whether I deserve it, proves that. I'm not my father. I have no mission or passion or drive to prove anything. And I'm not you. I don't find beauty in the right spot for fucking roses and paintings hung just right.'

'Stop punishing yourself for something you aren't responsible for. Stop hating yourself for discovering parts of your father in you. There are so many things you don't understand. Stop hiding behind disappointments. Everyone has them. Agreed, you had them too early. But woman up and face them. Come out and live in this world. You have to, before…'

'Before what, Mom?'

'Before it's too late. You're precious, and you need to know how to handle that.'

'I have no idea what you are talking about.'

'You do. You always have. You have more than an idea about everything that has happened so far. An idea of who you really are. Embrace it.'

'This makes for a good poem but doesn't pay my bills. You weren't left alone in a treacherous city to fend for yourself. You were given the proverbial diamond spoon on a platinum platter.'

'I know more than a thing or two about fending for myself. I've given my life for it.'

'Why can't I be a spoiled brat for just one day? Just for a moment, why can't I not be what you expect me to be and still be accepted?'

'Soon you're going to have all the wealth you need; you know that. Question is, are you ready to handle what comes with it? Kath, don't be afraid of your own shine. It won't dim if you burn it brightly. I promise you. Remember my words: don't be afraid to shine.'

'Don't talk like you have cancer or something.' I looked at her and she looked at me; an unbearable tingle ran down my spine. 'Do you?'

I couldn't let my eyes shed a single tear. I couldn't let her know how much I loved her. That, while lying sleepless on my bed, the only thing that made me look forward to the morning was knowing she existed. That somewhere, she was still there—

cleaning her archery sets, humming her favourite song. That her warm hands were still warm and, someday, would caress my forehead again. I couldn't let her know that.

The thought of cocaine came to my rescue, wrapping me in its bearable sense of nothingness, holding me back from breaking down.

'I don't have cancer. I'm not dying.'

'That's a bummer.'

I picked up my glass and sipped slowly, watching her through its gloomy translucence. When she wanted, Mom could be an inscrutable closed book. I had no idea what was going on inside that beautiful head of hers.

'You would have cried if I hadn't spoken for a few more seconds.'

'That's bullshit,' I said. 'People die. It's a fact of life. And I understand that.'

People lie to others all the time, acutely aware of their transgressions. But when they lie to themselves, they seldom know it. Even so, this was an exceptional moment of clarity— one in which I knew, without a doubt, I'd just lied to myself.

Dang, I could never be friends with endings. Goodbyes, like hellos, never came easy to me.

She leaned forward. 'You also understand love. Yet you run away from it. Why?'

'Because it's scary. And I can't handle it.'

Like me, Mom seemed taken aback by my honesty. It was funny how startling the truth sounded when you expected to hear its dressed-up cousin.

She smiled. 'That's the first time you've spoken the truth to me this whole evening.'

'It's the first time you asked nicely.'

'There's something else I'm going to ask nicely.'

'Here we go again.'

'Listen, because it's for your own good.'

'I'm listening.'

I waved towards our server for another bottle.

'I'm leaving.'

'What?'

Did this mean I could sneak back to the Gladwell mansion? Was this my lucky break?

'Well…for a while.'

'Like a vacation?'

'Like…something I've waited all my life to do. I'm going to India.'

'Are you asking for my permission?'

'I'm going to be there for a while. I'm going to Kolkata to help set up and run a charity for underprivileged children.'

'So the guilt finally showed up?'

'Guilt for what?'

'For the largesse. For…having it all. Guilt for—'

My mother raised her hand. 'Shut up and listen. This is the last time you'll interrupt me with your fake indifference. After I'm gone, use the time to decide who you want to be before the burden of being a Gladwell is upon you. Get rid of the drugs. Get healthier. Get a job. Find love. Something to lean on. Life is full of bumps and surprises. You need to be strong enough to go through them.'

'Ooh. Mother knows everything.'

She nodded. 'Mother does.'

'And I thought I was the genius.'

'Why? Because you have multiple masters, read papers by NASA while pooping and hack mainframes for extra cash?'

'Because you used to call me that when I was a kid… Hold on a second—Jimi Hendrix and his mother—have you got cameras in my bathroom? I think I'll have to sue you.' I leaned forward, grabbed her glass and gulped a big one before she could protest.

'I don't need cameras to tell me who you are,' she said. 'The better question is: what have you done with it?'

'See? Therein lies the problem. Who wants to do anything with it? It's mine. I internalized it. I enjoy it. My brain cells love it. The accumulation of knowledge, and my opinions born from it, are for my personal consumption and conclusions. Not for external validation. Not even yours. Why do I have to build another transcontinental railroad to prove I have Gladwell blood running in me?'

'Clearly it's not my validation you're looking for. Since the day your father left—'

'Stop. I don't want to talk about this.'

'When would you want to talk about it, Kath? When I'm dead? Won't it be futile talking to a dead person?'

'*Au contraire.* I might like a one-way conversation.'

'Like the ones you used to have with your father after he left?' I gulped her glass dry. 'I was a child.'

'I bet you still have them.'

She definitely has cameras in my house.

'Kath, you can't camouflage anger with failure.'

'Those are just big words.' I looked at my untouched risotto. Like all my meals back in the apartment, it was cold and dry. 'I have no anger, and I'm certainly no failure.'

'I leave soon.' She led my gaze for a few seconds. 'Now let me order my last peach tiramisu. Don't know when I'll get to eat one again. After that, we need to buy you new clothes.

This one won't last you a lifetime.'

'What I need is another drink.' There were no shortcuts to the Gladwell mansion. I was going to be in my hovel for a while.

'That's the last thing you need. One more thing, Kath: I paid for the stuff you "forgot" to pay for at the grocery store and apologized to the manager. I suggest you don't do that again.'

'Sure.'

I had to do that again.

05 Liquid Courage

⋅⋅ Johnny ⋅⋅

'I want it all,' I said, and drained the last sip from my glass. Rampal and I sat on top of a water tank located on the terrace of a five-storey building, looking out at a quiet Hooghly River. My quack doctor's clinic was on the ground floor, and the building's security guard was one of my regulars. For a discount on his pills, he let me have the keys to the terrace door for our weekly soirées with friends from the shanty next door.

'The whole bottle?' Rampal said.

'No, you dimwit. I mean like they say in the movies.'

Shiny dots lined up both sides of the riverbank—mostly anchored boats and riverside motels. Even though it was past four in the morning, the city buzzed with honking vehicles and the distant hoots of freight trains. The air was placid, barring the occasional smoke-laden humid wafts from the river. We sat on our rusty metal chairs, empty packets of chips threatening to take flight any moment. Everyone else had left; we were usually the last ones to finish—I liked the peace after the jamboree had ended, and Rampal liked to finish the leftovers from all the glasses.

'Movies are a waste of time,' he said. 'I only watch porn. Straight and to the point.'

'You're an idiot. You know that, right?'

'Yeah? And what are you? The fucking drug lord of Kolkata, you…you…small man!'

I nodded and peered into my glass. 'That's what I want to be. I've decided there's no point in making yourself small drinks and sipping small. I'll either burn this city or go down in a blaze of glory.'

'Johnny, I just told you I like porn. Stop uttering metaphors and speak simply to me.'

I turned to look at Rampal. 'Listen to me carefully. I know how to become rich and powerful. And I'm offering you an exclusive invitation to join the joyride. Are you in?'

Rampal laughed. 'You're talking like a mafia don. You know you're a dwarf, right?'

'And who says a dwarf can't be a mafia don?' I asked.

Rampal looked at the almost-empty bottle next to him and then to me. 'Have you lost your fucking marbles? Do you have a death wish? Just because you sell some pills stolen from your clinic to street junkies doesn't mean you've arrived. We're all nibblers. We nibble at the leftovers in the dark. I sell second-hand phones. I don't own fucking Pineapple.'

'It's not that.'

'What?'

'The company that makes iPhones. It's not called Pineapple.'

'Fuck off.'

'You steal mobile phones and sell them at the chor bazaar. You get caught once every couple of months and get your jaw broken. The other times the cops take you for a nice flogging and steal whatever money you've made. So essentially you're working for the cops. Tell me now—where are the leftovers? Do you want to die poor, alone and fucking miserable?'

Rampal went quiet. It took a lot for him to shut up, especially when he was drunk. This was the perfect time to sell my pitch. He was the only one I could trust, even if he came with his own baggage.

'What do you have in mind?' he asked.

'I want to sell amphetamines in the city.'

When I'd run from those cops into the dark alleys, I'd promised myself that if I escaped, I'd no longer stay in the dark—I would find the light. I had to count for something. I had to make a dent before no air was left in my lungs. I had no time to be scrupulous, and I was done being an everyday apology.

I'd been destroyed every time someone called me a joker or a retard. Every time I was treated like a handicap. No more. I was way past that. And now that I'd truly escaped from the murderous cops who were out looking for a boy to kill, it was time to live up to that promise. Even life couldn't keep me away from making it count.

'And I want to own a mobile shop in the city. But I don't know how to. Do you know how to, Mr Johnny?'

'I have an idea.'

'Oh, you have an idea?' Rampal scoffed. 'That's fantastic. Then we don't need to worry about anything. We can now live in Victoria Memorial and fly in planes. Why, even drink scotch every day. Your idea is all our miserable lives were waiting for, *chutiya*.'

'Listen to me carefully and don't repeat a word of what I tell you. Deal?'

Rampal picked up the bottle of whisky and took a long swig. 'The little man has an idea, he says. A death wish is what you have.'

'I need your word!'

'Okay, okay. I won't tell anyone. Now spew your fucking idea.'

'There are more than 2,000 fake clinics run by quacks in Kolkata, just like the one Dr Verma runs. They survive on giving fake prescriptions to people who can't get them from a real doctor. Medicines like antidepressants, sleeping pills and ADHD drugs. They sell these prescriptions for hundreds of rupees, sometimes more.'

'So?'

'We take it a step further.'

Rampal heaved a sigh. 'Like I said, stop the riddles and tell me in simple words. One more metaphor, and I'll bash you up.'

'I know someone who gets ephedrine from Myanmar and can manufacture amphetamine here in Kolkata.'

'What the fuck is ephe—'

I snatched the bottle from him and poured myself another drink. 'It's the chemical required to make amphetamine—a medicine doctors legally use to treat ADHD, depression and sleeping disorders. But it's also sold illegally as a brain and memory enhancer. High school and college students, workers, drivers—there's a huge demand. It isn't fatal and is more sought after than recreational drugs like cocaine and heroin. Lower risks and higher margins. It'll be popular here.'

'That's nothing new. You are talking about meth. Who are you trying to fool?' Rampal seemed to have a rudimentary understanding of drugs. A good start.

'No. Meth, ecstasy or speed, although derivatives of amphetamine, are chemically synthesized. Meth is more potent, more dangerous. They're all clubbed under a group called amphetamine-type stimulants or ATS. Basically, they're stronger, psychedelic and addictive—like cocaine—and damage the brain. They're absorbed faster and take longer to break down. They're entactogens, not stimulants. I'm not talking about selling those.'

'Ugh. Can you speak my language?'

I passed the bottle to him and leaned back in my chair. He

was right; I needed to break it down. 'Think about meth as a ferocious tiger and amphetamines as a domestic cat.'

'One bites and the other doesn't?' he said, taking a swig.

'One kills and the other doesn't,' I said. 'Meth makes you feel good, like you're the king of the world, but it also fries the brain. But just amphetamines—or dextroamphetamine, as they're medically called—are stimulants. They make you more focused, give you energy and keep you awake. They don't kill you, just like the cat. Worldwide, they're sold as branded medicines like Ritalin and Adderall, made by big pharma companies. You'd have to take them for decades to get the same side effects and damage meth causes in months.'

'So this am-whatever is like a superman drug—much less harmful and legal to sell?'

'Yes, but only with a prescription.'

'Go on…'

'We tie up with these quack clinics that are barely surviving and supply them with amphetamines at a huge markup. They sell the pills directly to their clients. They make money; we make money. Everyone goes home with filthy pockets.'

'How much?'

'That's up to us,' I told him. 'No one has done this here before. We set the price based on demand. And trust me, there's infinite demand.'

'But if people stop buying cocaine, won't the cartel come after us?'

'Unlikely. There's room for everyone, my friend. Besides, we won't be competing with cocaine sellers. People who use cocaine have already gone beyond what amphetamines can do. The kick they need will soon kill them. They need tigers, not our cats. Our users are the masses—students, drivers, watchmen.

People who need to work 20 hours a day to make ends meet. I'm talking about selling a legit medicine to the right buyers.'

'Forget the students,' Rampal said. 'In this country, the parents will source it for their kids so they can go to a college abroad and become rich bankers.'

I grinned. 'Exactly.'

'Tell me, Johnny.' Rampal leaned in close and whispered. 'I could take one and go on all night?' He made fists in the air and bobbed his pelvis.

No, you dimwit.

'You could say that,' I said as I got up from the uncomfortable chair and stretched. The darkness was easing up on the city. Soon the sun would be out.

'I am saying that.'

'Yes, you are.'

'So you aren't really talking about being a drug lord or a mafia don. Just a medicine man.'

'Exactly.'

'Then why did you say you wanted to be a mafia don?'

'Because...I feel like a movie star when I say it.'

'Chutiya.'

'Any more intelligent questions?'

Rampal nodded. 'Why would the manufacturer not sell the pills directly to the clinics and keep the fat margin?'

'Because...' I paused for a second, 'he's a manufacturer and not a distributor. He needs people who can move the product through a channel that's reliable and sustainable. You're either a batter or a bowler in this business. You can't be both. Think of the manufacturer as a bowler, swinging the product to us, and we smash it into millions of pieces across the boundary to everyone in the stadium!'

'How do you know this manufacturer? Why would he trust you?'

He was asking the right questions. I ambled along the edge of the water tank looking down at empty swings and flickering lights. 'I've done business with him before. He knows me. Don't worry about him—I'll be the only one handling him.'

'And the clinics?'

'I've sold antidepressants and sleeping pills to them on and off. I know most of them. They'll come in hundreds. The ones I don't know will come once they find out what the others are doing. Who doesn't want to make money?'

'So we buy the product from this guy,' Rampal said. 'How do we get the money to buy it, at least in the beginning?'

'Good question.' I turned and walked closer to Rampal, who now had an empty bottle in his hand. 'See? You aren't that much of a bonehead. Means we have a chance of surviving.'

Rampal flashed his gory white teeth, then snatched my glass and drank whatever was left in it. 'So how do we do it?'

He was on board. His eyes were hungry, like mine. I sat down. 'That's where I need your help. We need to borrow money from the street to purchase our first shipment. It won't be too big, but once we start circulating, we'll multiply. And then there's no looking back.'

I knew Rampal had friends in the cash-lending business. The kind who kept your neck as collateral.

His smile vanished. 'Johnny, you know I'll do anything for you. You're my only friend in this sewage called life. But you don't know these guys. I do. If you can't move the first batch and pay them back in time, with interest, there's no looking ahead or back. You know why? Because our eyes will be floating in this river. Along with our burnt balls.'

'Rampal, imagine. Just imagine.' I leaned in, placing my hand on his shoulder. 'We can be out of this shithole. We can make a life for ourselves. For the people here, by giving back to them. Are there risks? Sure. You think the rich got rich without taking risks? Either we rot and die like rodents or we steal what's ours. It's our idea—no one else has thought of it. Why should we not gain from it? Sooner or later, someone will figure it out. It's either us or them.

'Listen, if you don't have the balls to do it, I understand. But if you're in, you have to be all in. No half measures. We either succeed or die trying.'

Rampal stared at his empty glass for a moment, then turned to me. 'All this ambition... Where does it come from? I mean, you know you have limitations. You're a half man. You—'

'I know what I am. And that's exactly where it comes from. I'm no half man, and I'll prove it to you. All I need is your trust and loyalty. We go in as equal partners. What do you say?'

Rampal stood up, looking down at me. 'I knew you were trouble the day I met you in the police station. Fuck it—let's do it. Worst case, we die right? Big shit!'

I didn't know if it was liquid courage or just plain stupidity, but he bent down and we shook hands. Orange flares painted the sky as the sun crept over on the horizon, birds hustling across the smoke-filled morning.

Just like that, we became partners in what I hoped would become an enterprise worth millions.

❖

Over the next two months, we did everything we said we would. Rampal raised the money from the mob for our first purchase and we paid them back, with interest and on time. No floating eyeballs or any other balls in the river.

I established relationships with clinics run by bankrupt quacks and ensured we had the finished product from the pill manufacturer—'the Maker', as Rampal called him. I stashed our weekly stocks in Dr Verma's clinic until we made our deliveries. Soon we were criss-crossing the city on buses, carrying bags full of amphetamines and cash. We sat separately to minimize risk and it also allowed one to watch over the other.

We had just started and were already making over ₹50 lakh a week—money we needed to hide somewhere safe. Soon we found the perfect place—inside the water tank on the terrace of our party pad, which got cleaned once in never.

Before our drinking buddies showed up each week, we wrapped wads of cash in black garbage bags, sealed them with tape and dropped them in. It made sense logistically too—we were right in the middle of the city, right next to our shanty.

We were diligent about the money we spent on ourselves; I was careful, and Rampal was—at best—reluctant. We both knew we couldn't afford any unwanted attention. There were a few instances of him walking into our shanty with a 70-inch television or feasting at a five-star restaurant, but nothing that raised enough smoke. I purposely overlooked these aberrations; Rampal had to feel happy about what he was doing.

'What good is money if I can't taste it?' he'd say.

These occasional carrots kept him focused and motivated.

Soon the two of us weren't enough; we needed more hands. So we built a team—a small batch of nobodies and underachievers like us. People who truly wanted more from life and were willing to risk life itself. Each had their own reason for it.

Shamshu was our muscleman—the silent rock that wouldn't budge. Years as a dance bar bouncer had earned him little more than tenners and a life that was mostly about patting down drunks and fending off aggressive escorts. In his new avatar, he handled security—moving large amounts of cash or pills, collecting from delinquents, and protecting our employees from petty thieves and miscreants. Baby-faced but with the body of a hulk, he was perfect for the job. Difficult to hate or love.

Then there was Rakhi—Rampal's girlfriend. An accountant at a local lingerie manufacturer, she smelled a rat with Rampal's impulsive and expensive acquisitions. We didn't exactly hire her out of choice, but it turned out to be serendipitous. Very serendipitous. A woman of few words but many strengths, Rakhi was not only great with numbers but also had a knack for cleaning up the money.

She kept the noise out and was logical to the point of being irritating. She created partnership firms, opened multiple bank accounts, and soon, we were collecting cheques and wiring money online but eventually converting everything to cash. And that's how we found our chief money washer.

We also brought in a few packagers and courier boys—people we could trust, those who were grateful for their new-found riches. They were trained well in keeping our enterprise discreet and having credible backstories.

We didn't need an army. We weren't dealing with hardened criminals or cartel bosses who needed to be shepherded. We were transacting with people who thought themselves doctors—'respected' by hapless patients, fake degrees notwithstanding. They truly considered themselves a part of the civilized society where rules were followed and smiles exchanged. But when opportunity knocked, very few could walk away. They paid on time and didn't hustle the system. These clinic owners had no men to go to war for them. Nor did they know mobsters who could help them gain an edge over us. We doled out the pills and their cash drawers stayed full. Win-win.

In three months, we acquired more than 700 clinics, with new ones joining daily. Our weekly trips to the water tank became daily visits. Not only did we now need a better, safer and more efficient distribution system, but we also needed a much bigger and safer place to hoard the incoming cash.

Travelling in city buses with bags full of money and pills was also getting too risky. The building's security guards were watching. Residents were getting curious about 'the dwarf nurse and his friends'. It was only a matter of time before someone figured out our operation. We needed a solution, and no one had come up with an idea that could actually work.

That was before I sat down on a bench in Hazaar Basti on a sultry afternoon, munching on my favourite chocolate, watching bees' nests hanging from the large reservoir atop a water tower at the edge of the shanty. Like black pearls around a fat woman's neck, they encircled the old ellipsoid tank, protecting it from evil eyes.

But not mine.

The 70-metre tower, managed by the municipal corporation, was meant to supply water to the nearby areas. It stood inside a walled enclosure, its gate well-guarded. On one side of the campus, large water pipes—once the city's lifelines—lay dried and rusted, like the ruins of a forgotten empire. Not a drop flowed through them anymore. Instead, a dozen water tankers lined up beside them, filled to the brim with fresh water that would be sold to the Richie Riches for a premium.

As the tankers rolled out through the gate, I knew where our money was going.

It was safe, discreet and a little tongue-in-cheek.

06 Whapatcha

✦Katherine✦

New York City. I never understood the fuss about it. I'd grown up here and was numb to it. I saw only the everyday in the everyday chaos. The cacophony was as unobtrusive to me as the sound of maracas in Latin music. And I was certain it was the same for my fellow New Yorkers.

Every day, people bounced over wobbly manholes and subway ventilation grills while caffeinated voyeurs sat behind the shiny glass walls of jazz-filled cafés, pretending not to look at them. Pies gleamed behind lit-up pizza counters and bagels flew off the street vendors' carts. The luggage store owner stood outside his shop, smoking, hoping to find his first bag-less tourist of the day. Sirens blared, the square dazzled.

Virgin tourists, freshly seduced by the city, tried to blend in, walking fast to keep up with the natives, furtively glancing at Google Maps, hoping no one saw them, lest they be treated as outsiders.

The notion that we, the natives, looked down upon them, that we resented the millions who thronged our streets with their dangling cameras, was a myth. We, or at least I, believed they were as much a part of this jungle as its indigenous animals. Who else would buy the overpriced cocktails in hidden speakeasy bars that were no longer hidden or, for that matter, speakeasies? Who else would put food on the table of the luggage seller hawking bags that barely lasted long enough to spell the word?

Only them.

Because we slugged cheap drinks in neighbourhood bars that were easy to find—on the street and on X. There was no romance in it. You bought one, you got enough real estate for your glass. Bought two? You might get the bartender's fleeting attention for a second. Good luck knowing exactly what to order in that underprepared second.

I preferred making louder conversations in a loud bar, hoping to catch some of the tourist whapatcha to take home. Most nights, though, all I took with me was a hangover in the making and, if I was lucky, an average nightcap who left before I woke up.

So, on an evening just like any other, I sat alone, drinking bourbon in a loud bar, reading a *Nature Nanotechnology* journal. It had been a tough week at work. Crack was all I could afford, but it just wasn't my thing. Made me cranky. So I decided to wait, keeping my wandering mind busy with knowledge of the atomic kind. I wasn't a qualified addict, but I'd be a fool not to know I had all the makings of one.

Mom left for India four months back. I thought about our conversation often. We hadn't had anything more meaningful than that in ages. She seemed genuinely worried about me, but there was all the time in the world to make good on what she wanted.

I enjoyed my loneliness; and my escapades with the powder; and the aimlessness. No lover to endear. No boss to impress. No one to give back to except myself.

Mom had no choice but to let me in when I turned 27. And until then, I could afford to have nothing to lose.

'Helluva song!'

Disturbed from my world of atomic manipulation, I looked

up. A tall man in his early 30s stood next to me, holding a drink. Thin, sharp lips. Protruding blue eyes—not the kind you would read about in a book. His were big and mournful. Expensive suit, no tie. The cufflinks and carefully waxed blond hair told me he was doing better than me.

My grandfather had gifted my dad gold cufflinks on his 40th birthday; they were exquisite. I was just four at that time, but I still remembered every single detail on it—intricate little replicas of rails and crossties, crafted in 24-carat gold. The letter 'A' embossed on one and 'G' on the other. I'd secretly hoped my father would pass them down to me. And preferably earlier than *my* 40th birthday.

Milestones or not, birthdays at the Gladwell home were grand affairs. My mother ensured they played out like a majestic orchestra—days of planning and preparation culminating in a perfect celebratory crescendo. While music played and people danced and laughed, it was the kitchen where battle lines were drawn. An army of chefs, amid furious war cries and clinking silverware, made magic happen.

Freshly uncorked champagnes filled crystal glasses, golden bubbles rising with their ubiquitous pops. Dad would surreptitiously let me have a sip or two before Mom swooped in.

I missed that taste in my mouth.

I missed his soft linen jackets and formal dinner suits; the way we'd jump on my bed; the smell of fresh flowers we plucked from the garden each morning; his harsh, unshaven cheeks and his sharp aftershave that smelled like coffee and vanilla.

'Miss?'

The blue-eyed stranger was infringing on my thoughts, and I hated him for it. He was probably smirking while I dreamt about my childhood. I didn't care; it was routine to find rich bankers after a good or bad day of trading, cooling off with their buddies, talking bonuses and dick-sizing. Most usually looked for some quick action before catching the last train back to suburban wives and bubbly children.

'Sorry,' I said. 'I wasn't listening to the music.'

'What are you reading?'

'Something I'd like to keep to myself.'

I was usually an easy lay. All a man had to do was not be a dick. But tonight I just wanted to sleep, with the whole bed to myself. And his timing sucked; he'd pulled me out of one of those rare instances when I travelled back to happy memories.

'Hey, you don't need to be mean. I just wanted to buy you a drink,' he said.

'You could still do that. And then leave. Would that work for you?' I wondered where all that venom had come from.

The guy pondered, then smiled. 'Okay. I'll leave. Seems like whatever you're reading isn't fun at all.'

He turned around to the bartender. 'Hey, Danny. Give this beautiful lady a 10-year-old Michter's, will you? On me.'

He turned back to me. 'It was nice meeting you.'

Rule number one for measuring power and influence in the city: if the bartender gives a shit, you had to be someone—the kind that goes unfettered into all terrains.

I warmed up. But not enough to leave nanotechnology. 'Thank you for the generosity.'

As I pretended to go back to my journal, I faintly heard his friends booing him.

Before the bartender could pour the Michter's, I asked him to get me three Basil Hayden's instead. 'Rocks. Thanks.'

The three Hayden's led me to a couple more, which I reluctantly bought on my own. Soon I was back in a happy place. And when you're blithe, you need a bump even more. Nanotech left my mind. My eyes wandered, scanning the room, hoping to find an equally generous snow donor.

'Do I get any points for being persistent?'

I turned. The guy in the suit had returned, hoping I was primed. I was.

'Some,' I said.

'Great. I'm Edgar. You can call me Eddie.'

'Hi, Edgar. I'm Katherine. And you can call me Katherine.'

Decide, girl.

'So, *Katherine*, wanna come hang with my friends? We're heading back to my pad to indulge in some...candy.' He leaned in and whispered, 'Do you...partake?'

Hell, I partake. You are a godsend!

'Um...occasionally,' I said. 'Although never with strangers. Especially not ones in suits!'

'I'm no stranger. We met an hour ago, remember?'

'You mean when you tried to buy your way into my panties?'

'Hey, that's not fair,' he said, crossing his arms. 'I liked what I saw and came to have a conversation. And I left like a gentleman when you asked me to, didn't I? That should count for me not being a rapist serial killer, right?'

The bartender placed his drink on the counter and walked away.

'In a normal world, it should.'

'Last I checked we still hadn't been invaded by aliens.' He sipped his drink, then slid the glass away. 'Come on, let me introduce you to my friends.'

Taking my hand, he dragged me over to his table full of whisky bottles and expensive car keys.

'Guys, say hello to Katherine. She likes nanotechnology.'

'Let's not be judgy here, guys,' I said, settling in. 'Pass me a drink, will you?'

We drank till we were the last ones in the bar. Edgar passed me a generous helping of coke, which I consumed in the ladies' room. It was the best I'd ever had; I couldn't let more of it pass me by. Edgar and his friends seemed harmless. He lived alone in a penthouse down on Seventh. So much for a banker from the burbs.

He was mildly attractive; I was little more than indifferent but a little less than disinterested. But a promising stash of coke was reason enough to hook up. He had more to worry about than me anyway.

Edgar and I drove to his place and settled in a dimly lit living area with double-height glass walls overlooking the city's night-time sparkles. He opened a bottle of Michter's, pulled down the remote-controlled blinds, played Bob Marley and took out his hidden stash from the oven.

We slid to the floor by the couch, kissing and necking a bit. He scooped out the white powder on to a glass table and cut up a dozen lines with a credit card. We pulled all of them. And then a few more.

Till my tongue went numb.

Till I flew beyond care.

My mind levitated, blissfully untethered from my body, no synapses to contend with. Every pore opened up, breathing in the cold, comforting air.

I was exactly where I was meant to be.

I talked about my mother, my golden-eyed neighbour Olav, and railroads spilling into the Pacific. I rambled about Dad's cufflinks. Unusual for me. The coke helped, but I blamed that night's walk down memory lane.

Then I slept the most peaceful, dreamless sleep I'd had in a long, long time.

Good thing I got that sleep.

Because when I woke up, my life changed forever.

A plunge into *Sturm und Drang*, where lack of sleep would be the least of my worries. A time and place that would demand the very best of me—just to survive.

If waiting for my trust had made my life rough, I was in for some tough rows to hoe. Because when my eyes opened, the afternoon sun streamed through the half-closed blinds and fell on a very dead Edgar lying next to me.

07 Masterstrokes

⋅→ Johnny →⋅

We'd made it.

Rampal and I ran the business with an efficiency that would make even heart surgeons proud.

Identify and procure a much-needed product that no one else had? Check.

Distribute it without hiring an army or bribing the entire government? Check.

Don't kill people with overdoses or wreck societies by brewing monsters? Check.

More than 2,000 clinics now bought pills from us, reaching tens of thousands of people who wanted the upside of a sharper, more focused brain—without the downside of addiction.

College exams meant high season, with kids popping pills every night, cramming millions of words into their frenzied brains, rote learning be damned. Just as Rampal predicted, it wasn't just students buying our memory enhancers. Parents, worried their kids might turn them into social outcasts, lest they failed *them* by failing their exams, queued up for a miracle drug.

And what was wrong with that? It's no secret that this country spawns and exports an army of engineers and doctors high on cram to all over the world. Those who go on to own three-masted yachts and private pilot licenses. We were making the world a better place.

Could I have been one of those doctors, sitting in an Aspen spa home, next to wood crackling in the fireplace, had I not dropped out of medical school? Yes.

Could I have withstood the ragging sessions meant only for me? Not sure.

Could I take jokes on how a crowded elevator smelled to me? Not really.

No.

Anyway, word of the magic pill spread fast. One kid told another, whose mother whispered to a hundred more. Through laws of limited and equal supply, Rampal and I created a near-perfect market, ensuring no quack would undercut another by lowering prices or flooding a locality. We could have sold far more, but I knew we couldn't overspeed.

Dr Verma also bought and sold our amphetamines in his clinic, without knowing who he was buying from. It was downright stupefying, given his distrust of the world. I tried hard not to smile—while he hid a small stash of amphetamine pills from me, our entire supply was hidden right under his nose, in his own clinic.

His clinic was the perfect hiding place—the pills stayed close to me, camouflaged among the regular medicines. I confess it was difficult to blame him now for his conspiracy paranoia.

We kept our regular jobs as a cover, managing things remotely during the day. While I administered tetanus shots to wailing kids and Rampal stole mobile phones, pills were dropped and cash was collected. We spent our nights handling supplies, new accounts, operations and cash flow.

Our strength was staying under the radar. We were quiet, and our small size kept us nimble. Grow too big too fast and we'd get eaten up either by the mafia or the cops. Or both.

Our weakness? No relationships on either side of the law. The kinds that were required to enter a league that mattered.

Without those ties, we couldn't scale. Sooner than later, we'd need to share our secret with a bigger fish and leverage their size to become a big fish as well.

Dada, as they called it in Kolkata. If you weren't a dada, you were chicken soup for the lurking monsters. It was only a question of when.

Notwithstanding things to do, we had achieved a lot in just a few months. We were moving serious cash. And now we had the perfect place to hide it. It was right in front of everyone, belonging to the public and managed with taxpayer money. The last place where any suspecting cop or rival would think to look.

The municipal corporation's water tower was the first of our masterstrokes.

Rakhi had set up a water tanker shell company, and we bought mobile water tanks mounted on mini trucks. A few visits to the municipal corporation and more than a few greased palms later, we secured a trade license to operate water tankers in the city. Twice a week, these tankers rolled into the water tower campus just before the indifferent government employees shut shop and left for their respective homes for watered-down teas and TV reruns. But one hard-working employee—our amigo— would stay back. He was happy to get home later to a beaming wife and a large LED.

Late at night, our team arrived to take out large packets of cash, wrapped and sealed in black plastic covers, from the mobile water tankers. Then they'd take it on a long, dangerous journey all the way up to the reservoir via a 70-metre iron ladder, dodging thousands of bees. Once at the top, they'd drop the packets in the reservoir and lock the hatch. Like antacid tablets in a big, heartburned belly, those black packets were swallowed by the reservoir with no hesitation.

I'd been to that reservoir more than a few times—a strenuous climb but so very worth it. I loved standing at the top at night, gazing at the smoke-laden city. Cool, dry gusts washed my perspiring face as I waited to hear the sweet sound of cash being plopped into the water. I felt taller. Taller than ever before.

Hazaar Basti had been good to me all these years, and I promised myself to take care of its people—the hard-working rickshaw pullers and the frail old women working on their lice-ridden grandchildren. I was their treasurer and gatekeeper. We had decided to give away half the money to them at the right time. But the residents would have to wait for their lotteries a little more; it wasn't time yet.

♦

Rampal, Rakhi, Shamshu and I were the only ones at the local McDonald's, slurping vanilla cones and talking next steps. Rampal, who was in charge of everyday ops, had just informed us that some of the bigger clinics wanted their supplies to be doubled.

'We first need to find protection, then bigger partners to increase distribution,' I said.

'We have protection,' Rampal replied. 'Shamshu and his men—'

'It's not enough.' I turned to Shamshu and said, 'No offence.'

'Some taken,' Shamshu muttered, licking his ice cream.

Not one for talking, Shamshu preferred listening. With endless shoulders and hands the size of steaming irons, he was usually calm and still. But when he moved, you wouldn't want to be in his way.

'Guys, we need to stop thinking like a mouse,' I said. 'We can't nibble anymore, even if want to. How long do you think it'll be before the sharks smell blood and come for us? We have to protect ourselves and what we've built.'

'I know a few constables,' Rakhi spoke up.

She hailed from a small town near Kolkata, and had escaped to the city as a young girl when her parents tried to marry her off. She had big eyes, a chubby face and always wore a big red bindi and colourful salwar kameez. But nothing else was traditional about her.

She lived alone, knew how to handle the frequent and unsolicited attention, was adept with eye sprays and a revolver, and enjoyed her scotch—two fingers, no rocks. She had worked as a welder's assistant to pay for college before joining the lingerie shop as an accountant. Rumour had it she'd given birth to a baby girl years ago but gave her up to an orphanage. No one dared ask her about the child. Or the father. Least of all Rampal. She wore iron pants in the relationship—and he was rather relieved she did.

Rakhi had done well cleaning up the money. Apart from the water tanker company, we had invested in real estate and gold to manage the volume of cash and make it legit. More importantly, it was her idea to take up a franchise of a leading pizza chain to help wash the money. We improvised on that idea, using the delivery scooters to distribute the pills and collect cash.

That was our second masterstroke—the Blue Bees. Our delivery scooters and crew buzzed around the city and blended in with its madness, adding a little more to it. The clinics ordered 'pizzas' per their delivery schedules, and the Blue Bees arrived, within 30 minutes or less, delivering more than just happiness. Soon we had five such franchises across the city, operating right under the noses of the cops, pollinating the pills and collecting the nectar.

'Rakhi, aren't you full of surprises?' I smiled. 'Constables won't help, but let's try and get information about who are the right people to tap.'

She nodded.

'Johnny, I'm okay about not increasing our supplies,' Rampal said.

'But you just said the clinics want their supplies doubled.' I knew he was worried about Rakhi. It was good to see him worried about something.

'I did. But getting cops involved... How big do we want our bites to be? Let's stay where we are, make as much as we can, and before it blows up, share our treasure with the guys at the shanty, then run away from this godforsaken life. Our share of the money would last a lifetime. Let the four of us disappear from this city, never to come back. Buy a farmhouse somewhere, grow crops and live as friends for the rest of our lives.'

'And when you get bored of milking cows and chaffing wheat, when you get that itch to hustle again, what will you do? Sell milk to the cows? Steal your own wood? Make babies?' I said.

'I could do with that, half man,' Rampal said, taking a big swing at his ice cream with his tongue before glancing sideways at Rakhi. She didn't look at him, but I caught her lips curling up—just for a second—before she pulled them back into her melting ice cream.

'Well, I can't. I didn't sign up for that, and I've told you before: we go big or—'

'Or we die. You're willing to die at the drop of a hat, yet somehow you survive everything despite—'

'Despite being a dwarf?'

'Despite being a stubborn motherfucker. Who wants more ice cream?' He got up.

'Rampal, please sit down. The ice cream can wait,' said Rakhi.

Rampal reluctantly sat back down.

Turning back to me, Rakhi asked, 'Even if we identify the cops we want on our side, how will we make them protect us? They don't need our money; the biggies pay them well.'

'Even if we did, sooner or later, word about what we do—and how we do it—would leak, and the whole world would know. Small fish eats smaller fish,' Rampal said.

'Then we'll pay the cops just to take us off the kill list when we're on it,' I told them. 'Look the other way. Ignore us like harmless flies.'

'On one hand you say you don't want to nibble; on the other you hope they'll treat us like flies. This is wishful thinking,' Rampal said.

He was surprisingly right. I wanted the best of both the worlds. Stay small, and people will let you feed on the leftovers—but you'll stay where you are. Grow too big, and people will shake your hand just long enough to understand your secret sauce—then squeeze it out of your bottle along with your sorry life.

I had to find a way to overcome this conundrum.

We stood at the starting line of a big race. We had a shot at the podium—if I could find a way to secure us a safe racing lane. This was how empires were built—by men who thought of solutions others couldn't.

I understood that.

I just couldn't think of one.

08 Screw the Odds

✣ Katherine ✣

A dreadful comedown followed one of my finest highs; the dead body next to me didn't help.

Was this some kind of a spillover hallucination? Or just a dream? All signs pointed to reality. There was no unexplained haze, no sleep paralysis. I had full control of my body, and it followed my commands. I raised my arms and bent down to touch my feet; I created waves with my hands and made a dolphin jump from them. I pinched myself—several times. It hurt every time.

No, this wasn't a dream. This was the real deal.

Edgar was dead.

The dried froth on his face pointed to an overdose. My body ached and my head reeled. There were no signs of a break-in or struggle. Nothing broken. The couches sat undisturbed, dabbed perfectly. There were unused lines of cocaine on the glass table and a curled-up dollar bill on the carpet.

I exhaled, relieved to conclude I wasn't a murderer.

Mr Blue Eyes must have gotten excited about his nightly catch and snorted more than he could handle. Or had I made him have more than he could have handled? Tempted to snort a few lines just to think clearly, I picked up the dollar bill—then tossed it aside.

As clarity seeped in, I knew I had to call someone. I phoned the family lawyer, Mr Elenburg, who told me to call the cops and said he would meet me at the precinct.

While I waited for the cops to show up, I imagined Mom's disappointed face. She wouldn't say much. She'd call me from Kolkata or whatever godforsaken place she was in, making the world a better place, and ask if I was okay. Then she'd hang up.

Would this be the final nail in my coffin of embarrassments and failures? This surely would top fucking the janitor. In fact, it would make front-page news: 'Third Great-Granddaughter of The Railman Charged with Drug Use; Boyfriend Dies of Overdose'.

Well done, you jerk-off junkie.

I felt sorry for Edgar. Maybe he would still be alive if it weren't for me. Maybe he would have gone home alone and slept off, thinking of how to improve his icebreakers in a bar. Did I make him overdose? Or did he overdose because of my company? More importantly, was there a difference?

I shed the weight of 'almost guilty' when the cops arrived. I told them exactly what had transpired the previous evening. I was then taken to the precinct, where I took a Breathalyzer and a blood test.

Mr Elenburg was there, waiting for me. Loyal and fierce as they come, he has been a trusted family aide and our lawyer for more than 30 years. Before that it was his father, who had been hired by my grandfather. Mr Elenburg wasn't much of a talker. At the Gladwell soirées, he usually spent most of his time in a corner with a glass of malt. He had an oval face and a shiny bald head, with stray hairs spouting from his ears. His body sagged like that of old bear, as if gravity had finally won.

By the time he finished the paperwork and came to sit next to me in the questioning room, it was early evening, and I was as sober as I ever had been. He passed me a cup of coffee, put the papers on the table, and said, 'You're lucky, Ms Gladwell.

Seems like you're looking at a misdemeanour.'

'What does that mean?'

'It means if the prosecutor agrees, you'll just have to pay a fine and maybe do some community service. In any case, the drugs weren't yours. Correct?'

'They were Edgar's.'

'Good. If all goes well, there won't be a possession charge, which would be a felony. And the autopsy should establish the cause of death as OD. Correct?'

'Jimi fucking Hendrix, I didn't kill him, Mr Elenburg.'

'Ms Gladwell, it's my job to ask you.'

'When can I go home?' My head pounded with the makings of a ghastly hangover. An empty stomach didn't help.

'Right after I'm finished talking with you, Ms Gladwell. You can't leave the city till the police determine their position and clear you of any potential charges. If they file for a felony, then there might be a trial. I'll try to see what I can do on my end.'

He put on his glasses and skimmed through the papers.

'Please call me Kath, Mr Elenburg. You've known me since I was a kid.'

I knew he wouldn't.

'You knew the man who died?'

'Not until last evening. I told you.'

'And you just decided to…hook up with him?'

'Yes,' I replied. 'That's how 21st-century dating works. Is it illegal?' I wasn't going to take disdain lying down.

'Ms Gladwell, if the police find any wrongdoing, they'll push very hard, given your family background. I need to know if there's anything else.'

'There's absolutely nothing else. We pulled a few lines and talked. Maybe kissed a little. That's the last thing I remember.'

'Okay. I'll start to work on this and pay the fine. You should go home and catch some slee—'

'I've already missed my morning job,' I interrupted. 'I can't afford to miss the second gig. Thanks for all the help, Mr Elenburg.'

'Of course. I'll do everything I can to make sure you're safe.'

'I know you will.' I stood up to leave. 'Listen, I know you think I'm reckless with my life and I don't give half a Jimi's ass about anything. But I'm very thankful for everything you're doing. Don't take the words coming out of my mouth as an offence to you. It's just my way of…'

'Communicating?'

I smiled. 'Levelling up with the world.'

'Hmm. I think I can understand that. Don't worry; everyone has their edges. I know why you have yours.'

I smiled. 'I doubt that, but thanks for understanding. Will you let my mother know? I don't want to—'

'Sure. I have to call her anyway to sort out the expenses.'

'Thanks.'

'One more thing, Ms Gladwell.'

'Shoot.'

'Do not, uh…pull any more lines. Not even to level up with the world. You can't afford it.'

◆

'I have bad news and worse news,' Mr Elenburg declared.

'They found out I'm overdue on my rent?' I asked.

'This is serious, Ms Gladwell. I want you to sit down and listen carefully.'

We were at the family office in downtown Manhattan that managed the Gladwell estates, investments and finances. I pulled out a chair in the vast conference room rich in mahogany and leather and sat down. It was the middle of a summer day but the office was cold as a corpse, notwithstanding an all-glass wall letting the bright blue sky in.

The last time I was here was eight years back when I turned 18 and was eligible to sign contracts. I had scrawled my name on an affidavit acknowledging receipt of the trust document, agreeing to its terms. Not that I'd ever read them. Like Jimi could care. I did not bother to find out how many zeroes the Gladwell family had accumulated over the years. It was only a matter of time till I got it all.

Mom had been there as well, making sure the trust Dad had set up before disappearing would be honoured. After signing the papers, we ate Chinese takeout down the street and talked about waistlines and menopause.

'Give me the bad news first,' I told Mr Elenburg. 'I can do with some sunshine.' I'd worked hard at keeping my nostrils clean and head down for the last three days, and it wasn't going too well.

'They're pressing possession charges. With the intent to distribute.'

'What?' I leaned forward. 'I wasn't carrying anything. It was Edgar's. This is absolute bullshit!'

'The police spoke to witnesses—Edgar's friends, the bartender, a few other customers at the bar. They told the cops you offered cocaine to him and his friends. This doesn't look good at all.'

My hands went cold, then numb, then shook wildly. I clasped them together, but it was futile. I tried to understand the implications of what he'd said, but my mind refused to let any of it in.

'Ms Gladwell, don't worry. We'll fight this. You have to keep yourself together.'

'What's the worse news? They found out I have cancer?'

Mr Elenburg paused for a long moment. 'Your mother is missing.'

'What?'

'Mrs Gladwell—'

'I know her fucking name! What do you mean she's missing? What happened to her?'

My hands stopped quivering as a rush of hot blood passed through them.

'Settle down, Ms Gladwell. I know it's a lot to take in, but we need to stay calm.'

I shot up from my chair. 'Don't tell me to stay calm. What happened to her? Lay it out!'

The door opened before he could respond and Charles walked into the room.

Charles Morrison, the CEO of the Gladwell company, was another loyal friend of the family. A numbers whizz-kid and a Wall Street specialist, he had joined the firm as an analyst but quickly grew to earn the family's trust. He soon became a part of the inner circle, taking more and more financial responsibilities and delivering on them. He was unlike any of those Wall Street animals, always ready with a joke and a candy for me at those dreadful parties. Now in his 50s, he had thin, unkempt hair, an overgrown blond moustache and long, droopy cheeks. Gold-rimmed circle glasses sat low on his nose. Dressed in loose, colourful shirts and baggy trousers, he could easily be mistaken for a retired farmer or lazy professor.

'Hey, Kath. I'm so sorry about what's going on.' His hug was warm and welcome. He sat down next to me. 'I promise we'll do everything in our power to get you and your mother out of harm's way. Have you briefed her on the state of affairs, Mr Elenburg?'

'We were in the middle of it, Charles.' Turning to me, Mr Elenburg said, 'Ms Gladwell, here's what we know so far. Your mother set up a shelter in Kolkata to help abandoned street kids—mostly addicts—by providing them with rehabilitation, education and job skills. So they could reintegrate into society as self-sufficient citizens. Over the last three to four months, they've taken in more than a thousand kids.'

'So how is that a bad thing?' I asked, rubbing my thumbs over my fingers beneath the table.

'Turns out these poor kids were being given free drugs by the local mafia. In return, the mafia would get their dirty work done through them—murder, extortion, trafficking, distribution. You name it, they were doing it.'

'What kind of world does that happen in? Where's the government, the laws—'

'The cops are probably in on it. Happens everywhere, including here,' Charles said. 'The only difference is, no one wants to see the underbelly. Everyone's too busy eating their Wagyu steaks and drinking their oat-milk lattes to notice. I lost my sister to the street, so I know. It's as dirty here as anywhere.'

'So where's my mom?'

'I'm sorry, I digress,' Charles said. 'What our informants have found out so far is that Mrs Gladwell was causing significant problems for the mafia by taking away their junkie army and rehabilitating them.'

'Did she know that?'

'Difficult to say,' Mr Elenburg said. 'But knowing your mother, even if she knew, it wouldn't have stopped her.'

'And? What did they do to her?' I asked. 'Where do you think she is?'

'We don't know,' he admitted. 'All we know is she went to bed two nights ago, just like any other night. She wasn't there the next morning. The police found crude paintings of fish all over her bedroom wall. The shelter's manager called me yesterday, and we hired a local detective to find out more.'

'And you're only telling me this now?'

'We wanted to make sure it wasn't a false alarm. We just got confirmation this morning,' Mr Elenburg said.

'Kath, I just got off a conference call with the US ambassador to India and the city's police commissioner,' Charles said. 'We won't leave any stone unturned to find your mother. Whatever it takes.'

'But you just said the cops are dirty. How will they help?'

'Cops across the world are mostly fence-sitters. Based on my professional experience, I know that if you put the right kind of pressure on them, they'll do what they are told,' Mr Elenburg said.

'And we'll apply as much pressure as we can,' Charles added. 'Not just that, we've also hired the best possible private investigator and extraction specialists to find her. Trust me, Kath—we will find her.'

'I have to go find my mom.' I looked through the glass at the empty sky as a lone eagle glided across.

'What?' Charles asked.

'I have to go to India... I...I have to find her.'

'Ms Gladwell, you cannot do that,' Mr Elenburg said.

I slammed my hands on the table. 'I can do whatever the fuck I want. I won't let her leave me like my father did.'

'I don't think you understand. You *cannot* go,' Mr Elenburg said. 'The prosecutor will press felony charges against you very soon. If you're convicted, it'll carry a jail or prison term. You aren't even allowed to leave the city, let alone the country.'

'I don't care.' I got up and paced the room.

Mr Elenburg took out a folder from his bag. 'You *should* care. If you leave now, you'll be declared a fugitive. I'd call it a certain suicide.'

'Kath, I know the pain, and I'm with you on this,' Charles said. 'But we have to think through this clearly. Right now, you're between a rock and a hard place. Doing nothing seems to be the worst alternative, but trust me—it's the best. Think about it. Even if we set aside the fact that breaking the law will destroy your life, you'd be walking into a country you don't know, searching for your mother, who has likely been taken by a violent criminal organization. What are your chances of surviving that? Do the math; those odds are not in your favour.'

I nodded. 'They aren't, but I never made my life decisions based on math.'

'And look where we are,' he said.

I froze. 'Excuse me?'

Charles sighed, took off his glasses slowly and set them on the table. His wrinkled eyes narrowed as he said, 'I'm sorry; I don't mean to be rude, but someone needs to hold up a mirror for you. I've known you since you were a kid—and to me, you still are one. Wasn't it you who did drugs with a stranger and woke up next to a dead one? Those decisions didn't work out too well for you, did they? Look at where you are in life. You have everything most people dream of, yet you squander it all away on drugs and aimless pursuits. Why?'

'Speaking of having it all,' Mr Elenburg chimed in, turning the pages of a copy of the trust, 'I also need to bring up a few applicable clauses of the trust.'

'That has nothing to do with this. I just want my mother to—'

'I respect that, Ms Gladwell, but this is important. The trust clearly states that when the beneficiary—you—reaches the age of 27, ownership of all assets will transfer to you, provided you're of sound mind and have not been convicted of a criminal offence in a US court of law. If you are convicted, all assets will be transferred to a third-party family office, with only basic upkeep and legal expenses allotted to you.'

Charles put his glasses back on, stood up and moved closer to me. 'Kath, there's too much at stake. You have an entire life ahead of you. Don't make a hurried decision. You'll lose everything if you go.'

I turned away and walked to the glass wall, peering at the world outside. Amid all the noise, one image pushed its way to the front. My mom's glowing, smiling face as she moved gracefully through the house, always with a bagful of instructions for everyone. A fangirl had once followed her everywhere, wanting only to be just like her. Where did she go? When did those memories fade into a bad mash-up of seething anger and self-destruction? When did I forget to show my love for her? When did I forget to show anyone love? And why?

'Ms Gladwell?'

If there was ever a time in her life that she needed me, it was now. If there was ever a time that I needed her, it was most definitely now. Someone had attacked my family. A rush of blood flooded my face. Thinnest odds, implied risks and all the money in the world couldn't stop me from going.

I'm coming to get you, Mom; you hang in there.

'I'm a fucking Gladwell. No amount of money, or the lack thereof, will ever change that.' I turned around to face the men. 'Screw the odds, gentlemen. I'm going to Kolkata.'

09 Sanitary Morals

.⋅ Johnny ⋅.

Dr Verma's clinic was the dirtiest place in the city. Cracks in the damp walls oozed with moss, barely concealed by second-hand pictures of freedom fighters and pharmacy ads. The green privacy curtain for patient examination had holes bigger than the black hole. Impotent mousetraps, placed years ago, lay idle, serving only to boost the doctor's sanitary morals. The examination bed's rubber mat had never been washed, let alone replaced.

I'd bet my spiked hair that entire new civilizations of bacteria had emerged from this eternal filth spring over the years.

In my early days with Dr Verma, I frequently, yet reluctantly, offered to clean up, but he would have none of it. I eventually figured out the filth served the doctor well—patients came with the common flu, then came back again with swine flu; and then, maybe, with cancer. Customer loyalty wasn't pursued at this cesspool—it was guaranteed.

Most of our patients came from the neighbouring shanties, including Hazaar Basti. They couldn't afford private hospitals and public hospitals were the worst. So private fake clinics like this one—run by college dropouts and failed medical students, and charging one-fifth of private hospital fees—did brisk business throughout Kolkata.

A patient was suffering from fever? No problem—prescribe antibiotics. Pain? Antibiotics. Headache? Why, antibiotics. People were prescribed quick fixes even if it killed them slowly.

And they took it, oblivious and grateful. How was my business worse than theirs?

Also, in my experienced opinion—as a medical college runaway and an assistant to a quack—healthcare and fashion in this country were very similar. You could buy amoxicillin, a common penicillin antibiotic, for ₹10 *and* for ₹150. Just like a shirt woven on the same loom but branded differently, cheaper brands of medicines, with exactly the same salt, were sold alongside its more expensive counterparts. So the rich paid fifteen times more for it, while the poor bought the cheaper version. Why? Because they could.

Were we selling our pills too cheap?

'Take amoxicillin twice a day after meals. Do you understand? You can buy it from our medicine shop in the next room. We have the cheapest one,' Dr Verma said.

The doctor then wielded his occupational sword on a plain piece of paper, scrawling in purposefully incomprehensible handwriting. Like battle wounds for a soldier, bad handwriting was a trademark of a good doctor. Quack 101.

'Come and see me next week, else you'll have problems.' He announced his verdict and dismissed the poor sod.

I stood behind his desk, emptying and rinsing the emesis basin.

'Next!' he shouted.

A middle-aged woman entered, a scrawny teen in tow. She sat down while the kid stood next to her.

'Doctor, please cure my son. He's addicted to this wretched pill. He doesn't sleep for days. If he isn't running non-stop around the colony, he's staring into thin air, grinding his teeth like a zombie. He doesn't eat at all and has lost so much weight. He beats up other kids and steals their money to buy this crap.

He'll die, Doctor. Please do something.'

'What pill? What are you taking, boy?' Dr Verma asked.

'I don't know what it's called. I bought it from your clinic. The guy in the medicine shop sold it to me. I—'

'What nonsense are you talking? Clearly he's lost his marbles. Don't worry, ma'am. I'll prescribe some antibiotics. It'll help him sleep.'

There was no doubt the kid was on my amphetamines. They shouldn't have been sold to him. Worse, he was definitely taking more than he should and didn't have an outlet for all the extra energy.

These were surely stray cases; I would think one in a hundred. And he only had himself to blame. We were absolutely clear in our instructions to clinics about the dosages. If they sold to underage kids and gave doses larger than they should, it wasn't on me. I couldn't afford to be morally upright in this business; I had a promise to keep—to myself.

I stared at the boy for as long as he was there. His eyes were red from constant rubbing and blinking. The woman and her son left after receiving an incorrect prescription. All he needed was hot water and honey for a week and he'd be fine. I turned back to the sink, cleaning the rusted tongue depressors.

With his back to me, Dr Verma muttered, 'The lies kids tell their mothers these days. Poor sod is probably on some street drug and doesn't have a clue what he's talking about, blaming us for it.'

'Yeah, must be.'

His voice faded as I wiped the instruments, lost in the wretched memories of *that day*.

'What has the world come to? Who sells these disgusting things, ruining the future generation of this country?'

'I shouldn't have left her behind!' I shouted, shocked at the words coming out of my mouth.

'What? Left who behind?'

'Sorry. I was… The kid…he was inconsequential.' I turned away. 'He'll die inconsequential.'

'You've lost it, Johnny.'

'You're right. It's disgusting.' I got back to the sink.

I hadn't factored in greed. The age-old enemy of prosperity.

We had intended to sell the pills to people who could do with that extra push—an extended rope to help them tie the knot before life slipped away. The truck driver who drove all night, dreaming of buying his own rig; the security guard grinding through three shifts so his kids could learn English; the call-centre employee who spent their nights listening to racial slurs to keep their family afloat; the student who couldn't take the humiliation of not acing his degree. But apparently the clinics had expanded the market by preying on new, hapless customers and suggesting dosages that were dangerously high.

Could I blame them?

Who was I to draw a line?

Someone famous once said, 'Art, like morality, consists of drawing the line somewhere.' But the real difficulty was to know *where*. How far was too far? The lines were ambiguous and lightly drawn. And with every passing day, they moved further away, becoming thinner and inconsequential.

If global corporations could get away with selling food with MSG and drinks with aspartame, did a line need to be drawn at all? On the contrary, maybe we could become a case study on business success in prestigious schools. Maybe we could be the legend talked about in corporate elevators and during smoke breaks. Maybe we were mainstream and just didn't know it yet.

Either way, I couldn't afford to go back and find those lines. For now, all I could think of was our planned visit to the top of water tank later that night.

◆

'How far are we?' Rampal whispered.

On a moonless night, we climbed cautiously, step by step, up the rusty ladder to the reservoir. I, for one, always found the hike exhausting.

Seventy metres up involved a lot of rungs, and we were only halfway. Moments like these reminded me of my physical limitations—my small arms, bowed legs and short chubby fingers made it exhausting for me to get to the top. The late nights and overnighters needed to keep the business going weren't helping my fitness either. I'd missed my workouts and promised myself to get back to them.

Even though we'd been on top of the reservoir multiple times, this would be the first time we are all there together. The venue was my idea. Ever since we'd moved our cash hideout here, I'd missed our meetings close to where the money was. God is everywhere, yet temples and churches thrive. For our new-found religion, this was our sanctuary, and it was only fair to pay homage to the floating wealth by coming together and raising a toast.

I'd made it up alone once, in the middle of an equally balmy night, with nothing but a hip flask and a yearning for the quiet of the city. As I sat by the edge, a few tears had rolled by and I wasn't sure why. Was it pride? Maybe. Shame? Probably both. Regardless, I had descended the ladder with a smile.

For the moment, I was winded. And since I led a pack of four—Rampal, Rakhi and Shamshu below me on the ladder—

my slow pace was a bit of an irritant to them. Maybe this wasn't such a great idea after all.

'Can you move your dwarf ass faster? I can't take this view any longer. You should've been the last to start climbing,' Rampal muttered behind me.

'I'm doing the best I can. You have an exclusive view of a dwarf's ass. Not many people...' I had to stop to catch my breath.

'Shut the fuck up, Johnny. Save your breath and climb faster. Unlike you, I'm not a big fan of dying.' He looked down and added, 'Although falling and surviving would be worse.'

'Let him take a moment, Ramu. You don't need to catch the metro. And don't look down,' Rakhi said.

'This is taking forever. If those bees smell us and come for us, we're fucked,' Rampal hissed. 'If someone down below sees us, we're fucked. So yeah, I need to catch the metro.'

'It's the middle of the night and pitch-dark. No one will see us. Relax,' Rakhi reassured.

'Bees have five eyes. Even then, they can't see images like we can. They only sense light. And at night, any unusual light is considered predatory,' Shamshu, who was last in the line of medicine monkeys, said in his baritone voice. I was surprised he had it in him to speak at length about anything. His answers, opinions and retorts usually consisted of one or two words.

'Your timing sucks,' Rampal grumbled. 'No wonder you don't speak much. I told you, Rakhi—we're fucked. Agreeing to this midget... Who the fuck wants to party with bees?'

'Shut the fuck up, Rampal. We are not fucked,' I said.

'Chutiya.'

I ignored him and turned to Shamshu. 'How do you know so much about bees, Shamshu?' I asked, hoping to hear more from him, a welcome respite from Rampal's sissy tirade against everything.

'I was a beekeeper in my village,' he replied. 'Thirty thousand beautiful bees gave me the purest honey. But that was many years ago.'

'A bouncer who loves honey. Very interesting,' I mused.

'I love bees. The honey is a bonus.'

'How can you love those monsters? The farther I'm from them, the better,' Rampal whined.

We climbed higher, passing the level where the hives hung in dense clusters, low-pitched hums emanating from them.

'Those hard workers are fanning their cells with wings to turn nectar into honey. How are we any different?' I asked.

'The only nectar I can care about is the bottle of whisky I'm going to glug down the second we reach the top,' Rampal said.

'Shh. Don't talk now. If the bees hear us, it'll be a disaster,' Shamshu said.

Thankfully that was enough to shut Rampal up. We continued our slow, silent climb—until the flashlights found us.

Voices screamed from below. 'Who's there?'

'Get down, you fuckers.'

'Catch them and bring them down. Fucking mongrels.'

We froze. The only way out was down and down didn't seem very welcoming. The noises amplified; it was clear more men had joined the mob. We heard clangs that soon became vibrations rushing up the iron ladder and into our cold fingers. The men were hitting the ladder with rods, making it difficult for us to keep our balance and hold on.

'Johnny, what should we do?' Rampal shouted.

'Climb up and—'

Before I could finish, thick swarms of bees buzzed out

of their homes, preparing to flank us from all sides. For a few seconds, we could only hear their deathly buzzing in the darkness. I decided we should climb down as quickly as we could. Armed angry men definitely would be easier opponents than mad bees with their stingers up.

'Climb down!' I screamed.

'What? Make up your mind,' Rampal said.

'Now! Do it.'

We scrambled down the rungs, skipping a few, to escape the aerial onslaught. A few bees hovered close to us—the aggressive front liners that led an invisible, determined army of thousands right behind them. If we made it alive through this, our stories had to be consistent to avoid any suspicions about why we were headed to the reservoir. We couldn't afford to lose the money.

'We came here to have a drink and have a good time,' I told the others.

'You've lost your mind. Just climb down as fast as you can if you don't want to be killed by those winged assassins!' Rampal said.

I looked down while my small legs tried to find the next rung and then the one after it. The distance between my cohorts and me was increasing. I was the weakest link in the chain and, thankfully for the other three, at the right end this time.

'We should all stick to the same story. We were here to have a few drinks and have a good time. Do you guys understand? Don't mention the money.'

No one replied. They were busy not dying.

'Do you understand?' I shouted.

'Yes!' they yelled in unison.

Just then, a million burning needles pierced the back of my hands, shooting waves of unadulterated pain through my arms.

I lost my grip and my foot slipped. As I slid down the ladder with my head tilted up, my chin hit every horizontal step.

The last thing I saw was a dense cloud of black vengeful devils right above me.

The last thing I heard was Rampal saying, 'You bastard.'

10 Words on the Street

✢Katherine✢

'Please fasten your seat belt, ma'am. We'll be landing in Kolkata in 10 minutes.'

I put aside my musings on why they had flotation devices under the seats instead of parachutes as a pleasant yet assertive flight attendant flashed me a robotic smile and moved to the next row.

This was the farthest I'd ever been from home. As a child, my travels outside America had mostly been to Europe and Latin America—protected, luxurious and short once-a-year sojourns with Mom and Dad. We flew first-class and stayed in the finest hotels—those pockets of neutral territories with a consistently cold culture, meant to cut out the one that thrived right outside. The hotels behaved like my parents—shielding me from the city's slug and slime. Its grind and grime. Its life and death.

I never really saw any life outside of the hotels. I never dipped my hands in cold, unknown waters or warm chocolate fondues. I never smelled people or eavesdropped on their conversations in languages I didn't understand. I never found the air thinner or thicker. I never spoke to strangers in a foreign land, bereft of my societal tag.

I never lost my way. Tourist booklets and maps never confounded me. We always had a smiling chauffeur, an accommodating boat captain or a polite host leading the way for us, showing us only the clean and befitting. There were chartered flights and stately parties. Luxury boats and gold-splashed banquets. But never a walk down a street where nothing happened. After all, I was a Gladwell.

As an adult, every once in a while, when passing an office lobby or using a bar's restroom, I picked up a familiar fragrance and remembered a city—like Prague, which I'd seen only through a hotel window; a distant sea of red roofs that I longed to leap on to and, through the chimneys, listen to people sing, argue, pray and mourn. Make love. Take turns doing dishes and diapers. Then spy on a stout kid on the streets fixing his guitar. An estranged lover drinking his fifth. A baroque angel coming to life in the still of the night. That would make for a real city. But all I'd heard in Prague was the banal hotel lobby music and the doorkeeper's candied greetings.

Over the years, my travels were so uneventful that I started disliking them, avoiding them whenever I could. But that was surely about to change. If losing a gazillion dollars of family fortune and being a fugitive weren't exciting enough, rescuing my mother from the local mafia in an unknown country would surely do it.

Why would the police press wrong charges against me? Was Mom's disappearance connected to it in some way? Who would want me behind bars? Was it a conspiracy? Or just shitty luck?

'Ma'am, please wear your seat belt.' The flight attendant was back and not so polite this time.

'Sure.' I clicked it on.

Leaving New York wasn't short of an escape. In less than a day, Mr Elenburg—against his and Charles's wishes—had arranged for a fake passport, much-needed funds and a Gladwell safe house to keep me hidden until my flight. I had dyed my long red hair blonde and cut it short. I hated it; I looked a stranger to myself but a lot like Mom. Even so, my chances of being recognized at the airport were far less. I went to my apartment in the middle of the night, packed my clothes and kissed Olav goodbye. I also picked up a stash of powder from my dealer, airport security be damned.

Mr Elenburg briefed me on where to go and whom to meet. 'Pay for everything with cash. Don't use plastic or electronic money.'

My backstory was that I was a writer researching global slums and had come to Kolkata for it. That would allow me to stay in a guest house close to Mom's shelter home.

I expected to be petrified. This was my lowest low. My darkest dark. But I wasn't. Yes, I was afraid, but I rather liked the way my heart pounded—one lively beat after another. I had a new name and identity. I could be anyone. With the drawing board all to myself, I could dab it with any colour. Grey. I wanted lots of grey.

Elene McCarthy.

Mr Elenburg had chosen the name. 'It's a seventh-century, Old English poem that lays out the first account of the search for the Holy Cross. I think it's an apt name, given what you're setting out to do, Ms Gladwell,' he'd said.

I found the name's similarity to 'Elenburg' a little more than just coincidence. He could be full of himself sometimes.

I had other ideas for Elene McCarthy. The short-tempered, absent-minded girl next door. Or a docile, happy-go-lucky type who thought the world was full of magentas and knit yarns. Maybe an alcoholic with an epileptic disposition. Or a lesbian with a penchant for black magic and pyromania.

I could be anyone.

Or I could truly be myself.

But before all and any of those, I had to be the daughter willing to do anything to find her mother alive.

◆

I stepped out of the airport, relieved I hadn't been selected for a random customs check. The amount of coke I carried would have earned me a long stay in an Indian cell, with only the tiny possibility of diplomatic extraction. Outside, the heat and dampness hit my face. The air was so humid it was wet—like invisible rain had devoured every molecule of oxygen available and disguised itself as air. I could dip an empty glass into this thick wetness and fill it with water.

Rows of shiny windows displayed unlit pictures of burgers, sandwiches and local food I didn't know the names of. The fumes of coffee mingled with a mild-smelling floor disinfectant, freshly applied by a frail old man wearing wired headphones. He stretched just enough to make his mop reach the corners he didn't need to see. Going about his business in merry cadence, he made the same soapy swirls he had made all his life.

I got rid of my layers and waited at the pickup zone for the man from the security company Mr Elenburg had hired. A million taxi drivers accosted me in an English dialect difficult to understand, offering free rides to random 'royal hotels'. One even promised a grand tour to the Taj Mahal, which was only a thousand miles away, per *Lonely Planet*.

Through the crowd, I spotted my chaperone in the departure area, holding a placard with my new name. Long shanked and broad shouldered, he had curly locks that covered his ears and most of his forehead. Bright, sharp eyes contrasted with his coffee-coloured skin. He ticked all the boxes for a mysterious guy next door. A bodyguard, though? I wasn't sure.

He smiled and asked, 'Can I selfie, madam?'

Definitely not a bodyguard.

It wasn't much of a request, and before I could answer, he raised his phone and clicked. Maybe it was his way of welcoming guests. Maybe I was his first white guest. It was invasive, yet oddly endearing.

'I take that,' he said, snatching my bags.

I let him, deciding I wouldn't be like those tourists in New York, unsure and sore like a thumb. We reached his car, which looked like an overgrown male version of a Volkswagen Beetle. Luckily it was air conditioned, and I settled into the back, welcoming the dry, cold air. I reached out the window and banged on the car twice—according to a tourist guidebook, that was how the locals instructed the driver to start driving. All it got me was an amused glare from my driver. Clearly I had to find better tourist guidebooks.

The drive to the guest house was a torrid initiation into a world of whizzing scooters, persistent hawkers and rumbling trucks. New York was busy, but this was a medieval battle. There were people everywhere; companies of soldiers ran into one another, collided bloodlessly and disappeared into the enemy's phalanx as traitors. Hundreds more followed, and the battle continued.

Heaps of vegetables lined the roads as sellers negotiated with a hundred buyers and a thousand flies. Buckets of water were splashed over the produce to give it a brief respite from dogged gnats but, more importantly, it secured a window of opportunity to close deals.

Music played in the open and changed every 20 yards down the road. It reminded me of country music back home, albeit with more melody and more vocalized singing than words. Still it was country-ish.

There was colour. Lots of colour. Anfractuous words in pink and purple sprawled across yellow signboards, their edges skirted with flowers painted in hues yet to be named. Doors were washed with blue and red, while rust gnawed on windows with virility. If walls weren't cloaked in layers of colourful posters of movies and circuses, they were adorned with psychedelic murals of magenta pigeons and bony fists. A rickshaw puller in yellow shoes bobbed by, jangling his bell in a rhythmic pattern. Black umbrellas snapped open everywhere; those wavering, weightless droplets would soon turn into fat, silvery goblets.

My taciturn driver sped through lanes the vehicle barely fit in, his meek car horn sounding like an itchy-throated owl, heard only by the two of us. Yet he found success on the roads as the pedestrians and the driver expected the worst and thus evaded each other. Motion sickness apart, I loved it. I was relieved to discover I wasn't a lily-livered white tourist in a world of fearless pedestrians and angry drivers.

Yet there were contradictions. A little ahead, beyond the colourful signboards and through the dust-hazed air, gleaming towers and shiny offices stood tall. The long patches of rusted shanties gave way to unoccupied pavements, smooth tarred roads and still intact road dividers. Mobile phone ads on billboards and neon-splashed malls. Bass-spewing German cars roared by. Girls walked in clothes that would put a fashionista's wardrobe to shame, and boys walked right behind, wearing dark glasses and hidden smirks.

It was as if two worlds existed within one city and let each other be.

As we drove deeper into the heart of Kolkata, the urban modernity was replaced by a honky-tonk town. It was the old city—everything curved and domed. Two-coached trams rattled along the middle of the road, stopping frequently for everything: passengers, pedestrians and strays. I smelled a river; the fish stench was unbearable yet welcoming.

'Are we close to um…the Hawgli?' I asked.

'What, madam?' Smiling, the driver glanced at me through the rear-view mirror.

'The river. Are we close to it?'

He chuckled. 'Ah! You mean the Hooghly. Yes, it's very nearby. You stay close to one of the ghats, you can see the puja.'

'Puja?'

'Prayer. Worship. People do that in the river.' His smile widened.

'Oh, interesting.'

I recalled pictures of semi-naked men with long hair dipping themselves in the river. Definitely not the view from my balcony I wanted; I'd take those red-roofed houses of Prague.

'My name is Imaan, madam. I will be close to you. You call me anytime to go sightseeing or shopping. I know people. They like me. I get you inside Fort William. Anywhere you want. No one else can.'

He smiled every time he spoke.

'Thank you, Imaan. My name is Ka…Elene.'

'I know, madam. I wrote your name on the placard. I can write a little in English. My son teaches me.' He glanced back briefly, armoured with that smile. 'I see you coming out of the arrival section, but you did not point at the placard. I then go to departures, thinking you might be lost.'

I had been looking for the wrong name. *Shift gears, Elene McCarthy.*

'You like the weather, madam?'

'No!'

He laughed as he swerved the car around a sharp bend. 'Good! You are honest. It is rain season here. Gets very wet. And floods.'

'Is it this humid all the time?'

'Always. You wear cotton. Get rid of the jackets.'

'I definitely plan to. Does "Imaan" mean anything? I read somewhere Indian names usually have a meaning.'

'It means "honour",' he said. 'I am...very honourable.'

I laughed. His simplicity was refreshing.

'Sorry, my English is not very good. But I mean it.'

'No, of course. I believe you, Imaan. I didn't mean to disagree.'

'No problem. Is this first time to Kolkata?'

'First time to India.'

'India is great,' he said. 'I will show you.'

He thrusted his palm on the horn, making the car whimper. Rolling down his window, he stuck his hand out and waived it in the air to threaten an indifferent cyclist who had just escaped collision and a certain death.

'I'm afraid I won't have that much time. I need to finish my research and get back home quickly.'

'Americans always in hurry. Now, even Indians. They work in office and make money, I tell them, "Spend for your happiness." They don't understand. They say, "Later."'

'How do you spend your money, Imaan?'

'I don't have many money. But what I save, I spend on my son. He is eight years old. He goes to the school. Speak better English than me.'

I noticed a small picture of him with a woman and a child on the centre console.

'That's awesome. And what does your wife do?'

'She off long time back. He was only four then.'

'Off?'

'She died,' he said. 'Pneumonia.'

'I'm so sorry.'

'It's okay. That was long time back. I have my son. He wants to go to space. Can I ask you question, madam?'

He looked at me in the rear-view mirror, smiling as usual.

'Sure.'

'Why do you need security? I don't mind. I protect shady men and running politicians. But why are you afraid of anything? Is it the many people here? New country?'

I smiled. 'No, it's not that at all. I love the vibe of your city. It's so vibrant and happy. It's just that…the research I'm doing doesn't make some people happy.'

He raised an eyebrow. 'Secret work?'

'Something like that.'

'Are you a spy?'

'Do I look like one?'

'No, you don't. You look like a heroine from a *Rambo* movie.'

'I'm hurt now.'

'No, sorry! I don't mean it that way.'

Another sharp cut and we entered a narrower lane, leaving only a few inches between us and the oncoming traffic.

'I'm kidding. No, I'm not a spy. Let's just say I need to find something quickly.'

'Don't worry. I'll find it for you,' he said. 'If that *thing* is in Kolkata, it cannot escape me.'

'Clearly it cannot. Thank you, Imaan. You're very sweet.'

He was.

While he meant well, I needed the help of the professional investigator hired by Mr Elenburg—the one I was set to meet the next day. I'd called Mr Elenburg the minute I landed. The word on the street was that my mother was alive. But there were too many words on the street.

Some said she was a covert drug dealer and had gone into hiding when her cover was blown. Others said she was taken for ransom. Or an orphan from the shelter had killed her. All those words made me sick.

Mr Elenburg had advised me, more than once, not to get involved with the investigator's work and, at the most, be an observer. He said I'd hinder their process and put myself in danger. Jimi bullocking Hendrix, he should have thought about that before naming me 'Elene'. I planned to visit Mom's shelter home as soon as I could. Hopefully there I would find a clue to what had happened to her.

We stopped at a traffic light and, within seconds, rattling hawkers and peeking beggars blanketed the car windows, dimming the interior. Paying no heed to the semi-invasion, Imaan turned around.

He wasn't smiling when he asked me, 'Madam, it's not a *thing* you are looking for, right? It is someone.'

'How do you know?'

'It's in your eyes. I can see.'

11   Just Johnny

Tied to a chair in a dark room, I writhed in sharp pain. A lit cigarette had just been stubbed out on my right arm.

A bald man stood a few feet away, barely visible on the periphery of a bright spotlight. He lit another cigarette.

My head pounded. My chin throbbed so badly I couldn't open my mouth. My hands were swollen—thanks to the bees. I tasted blood and sand in my mouth, but it hurt too much to spit them out.

The image of the battered journalist, held by two constables and drawing on borrowed breath, flashed in my mind. Now I truly knew how he had felt. If this was my end, I was happy I at least had done something that mattered, even though it was for a very short time. I was sure my friends faced similar fates in rooms close by and I felt sorry for them. If not for me, they would have carried on with their sorry lives.

Then there was the money in the reservoir. I prayed our captors—whoever they were—hadn't found it. That some poor water tank cleaner would stumble upon the floating packets of a bright future and use them for their family's betterment. There was enough there for a few generations.

Chances were they hadn't found the money yet—otherwise, I wouldn't be alive. And Rampal hadn't peed in his pants and spilled everything the second someone questioned him unpleasantly. That was refreshing.

'You know,' the bald man said, stepping into the spotlight,

'they say you should focus the spotlight on your detainee during torture. So they don't know when or where the next ounce of pain will enter their body. Expecting pain anytime and therefore experiencing it all the time.'

He paused before saying, 'Interesting point of view, but I say that's just a noisy set of wall clocks. I like the lights on me. I don't get my hands dirty too often these days. There was a time, though, when I was sure to crack a bone or two every day. As sure as the hands that move in a watch. *Tick tock. Tick tock.*'

He smiled, revealing a set of nicotine-stained, crooked teeth. 'So when I do get a chance, I love to show myself to my prey. They have earned the right to know where death is coming from. Just like the bringer of death has earned the joy of seeing it flow from his hands into another body. Can you see me, my Lilliputian friend?'

He was all I could see. His shiny, bald head gleamed under the light, scarred with stitch marks. Sharp black eyes, a clean-shaven face, his double chin slick with sweat. Tattoos of fish in varying size populated his semi-existent neckline.

He was obese, obnoxious; his pants hung low on his short legs. His feeble, wheezy voice made me want to clear my own throat. He scratched himself often—the back of his neck, then his chest, then, lazily, his earlobes.

He came closer and took a long drag from his cigarette. Before it stopped smouldering, he crushed it into my thigh. I shrieked and thrashed, desperate to break free of the restraints. The chair I was tied to toppled, taking me along with it.

'Pick the shit up,' he said.

Footsteps approached from behind. A pair of hands grabbed the chair, hoisting me upright again.

The dark room juddered.

At first, I thought it was just my head playing tricks on me. Then the tremors grew stronger and I knew we were moving—and gaining speed.

'I apologize for this,' the bald man said. 'I like my office to keep moving. No fun stagnating in one place.'

The spotlight swayed with the increased motion, casting erratic shadows on the walls. He disappeared.

Shuttered, slit windows lined the walls. Street lights peeked through them, vanishing just as quickly as they appeared. Cool air seeped in.

Metal squealed. Rail joints clacked.

We were in a tram.

'Don't worry.'

He was still there in the darkness. As the tram steadied, the spotlight found him again, like a faithful pet.

'After a while the pain seems distant. Transient. Like it's not even yours. Just borrowed. Like time. So…let's talk business. My associates tell me you've been stealing from me.'

'I haven't stolen anything from anyone. I don't even know you.' It took everything in me to force out the words.

'Incorrect. And correct. You *have* stolen from me. And you don't know me—because I don't like to be known. Especially by inconsequential street rats.'

He stepped close again. 'I must admit, I'm a little impressed—you built a thriving business in a world that doesn't let outsiders in. And with a handicapped ass.'

He laughed and scratched his chest. 'Now, listen to me carefully. Your little medicine business is hurting my business. My soldiers think those pills are medicine, and coke isn't. They're not very different, you know. Cousins, really. But one is a sissy tied to a chair, legs dangling, and the other is the alpha—the father of all fathers—the one that makes you forget the ticking of the clock.

'Here's the deal: I want you to take your fucking Ponzi scheme and disappear. I'll spare your life for it. If not, you'll find your balls stuffed in your mouth and those pills shoved up your ass.'

'I'm just a doctor's assistant.'

His slap cracked across my face. Pain exploded in white-hot flashes, and my cheek throbbed, heat radiating from where his hand had been. 'Look at me, you bloody miniature.'

I did. The tram lurched, making my tilted torturer from hell appear in front of me.

'Tell me you understand. Or you'll join your friend in his grave.'

'What? Which one?'

'That big, burly bodyguard of yours. Seemed to be a handful for my guys, so they shot him and left him to rot in the drains. Would you like to lie next to him?'

They had taken Shamshu down. How could I not see this coming? I should have died by the hands of the cop that night. Shamshu would still be collecting tenners from patrons of a dance bar, but at least, he would be alive.

I didn't answer fast enough. The bald man yanked me closer. 'Should I get another grave dug up?'

I shook my head. He slapped me again. This one hurt less, but warm blood dribbled from the corner of my lips.

'Answer me.'

'No!' I shouted.

'Good. Now we have an open line of communication. I don't care whether you were planning an orgy up there on the tower or to jump off it. Listen carefully—leave town in a week. If my guys see you, you're dead. And so are your other friends. If your product turns up on the streets, you're dead. If you go to the cops, you're dead. For the losses you caused me, I took all your fucking pills. Hiding them in a clinic is rather ironic, isn't it?'

'Yes, it is. That's why I hid them there.'

He slapped me again. 'Seven days, smart-ass. Not a minute more. When the clock's hands move past that, pray I don't find you.'

He turned, stepping into the darkness, but quickly came back to stand under the spotlight.

'Sorry, I didn't tell you my name. Bad manners not to introduce myself like a gentleman. I'm Rafiq Chowdhury. They call me "RC". You know why? Because they can't decide if I'm a Rafiq or a Chowdhury. I am neither, but it helps to stand right in the middle of the fence... Remember who threw you out of Kolkata—RC did.'

'I'm Johnny. Just...Johnny.'

Scratching the back of his neck, he said, 'People like you pop up every now and then like wild weeds. And we uproot them well in time. This is nothing new for my guys; they do it day in and day out. I wouldn't have come to say hello to you, but thank your stars I did. I was really curious to see the dwarf drug peddler running a racket right under our noses for so long. I'm sparing your life because you're a handicapped piece of shit. Remember that. I won't be so merciful if I see you again. Now go fuck yourself off from my city, Just fucking Johnny!'

He faded into the darkness. The tram stopped. Someone got off; then it jerked forward again.

It was a few hours before they let me go. I stayed tied to that chair, moving through the city in what seemed like the middle of the night, given how quiet it was. Drifting in and out of consciousness, I thought of what might have changed in the world outside. I wasn't sure how many days it had been since the night at the water tower. I was hungry but not starving, which meant it couldn't have been more than a day.

The chair felt wet. Sweat? Pee? Maybe both.

I moved my hands and legs to check if anything was broken, but the bones seemed to be where they should be. I only had cuts and bruises. Surprising, given the fall. I was making a habit of escaping death. I just hoped my friends had the same fortune.

I'd never heard of RC or his cocaine business before. But he seemed likely to be sitting somewhere at the top of the food chain. He thought we'd climbed the tower to party—that was a lucky break. We could afford to lose a week's supply of pills but not the money. It was almost all we had.

I had a choice to make: fight or flight. Tail between the legs or fists pumping the chest.

I was aware enough to know I wasn't thinking straight. Now wasn't the time to decide. My mind was in a cold, hazy near-space, somewhere between pain, pride and greed. And shame. Guilt for getting caught and putting my friends at risk. Greed for the power that kept eluding me, no matter how hard I tried. I was still an inconsequential dwarf. Pride pricked me, commanding me to find requital, to go against the whole world and win. But pain led me to incomplete thoughts. All roads led nowhere, and this wasn't the time to pick any. This was a time to bear it quietly and make it out alive.

But the mind, like always, decides without letting you know. You, a slave controlled by nerves and impulses, only come to know of it when it's time to act.

✦

Sometime before dawn, two guys dragged me off the tram, threw me in a van and dumped me on my street. I lay there for a while, till I heard footsteps. I opened my eyes to find Rampal and Rakhi running towards me. I'd never been happier to see anyone in my life. In the lowest lows, I realized I'd found friends. Real ones. Ones who didn't run away with the money. Ones who gave a fuck about a stupid dwarf. Ones who waited for their friend to come back.

And just like that, I knew what had to be done. All the adrenaline and power weren't worth their lives. Significance had consequences. We were lucky this time, barring poor Shamshu. I was tired of fighting the world; giving up felt like a happy place to be.

I decided I'd give them half of the money and distribute the rest in our shanty. Then leave town. Having the ability to sniff out new adventures, I was pretty sure I'd quickly make friends with disaster somewhere else. I could be Mini Painkiller elsewhere. It didn't have to be them. It didn't have to be here.

I forced myself up and started wobbling towards them, but my legs had other ideas. Exhausted, I collapsed into a puddle. The cold, earthy water felt refreshing to the wounds on my face. Parched, I couldn't help but open my mouth to drink but it tasted like shit. Probably was.

They reached me and picked me up. Took me home and put me in bed. Rakhi cleaned my wounds while Rampal wiped my face. His forehead was bandaged and lips swollen red.

He smiled. 'Welcome back, brother. You're no half man, Johnny. You're more than any of us will ever be. You're one stubborn motherfucker.'

And just like the last time I lost my consciousness, Rampal's words put me to sleep.

◆

'Just keep walking and don't ask questions,' Rampal said.

Rampal, Rakhi and I walked through a hospital corridor, past endless benches lined with patients. They sat glued to their mobile phones, awaiting verdicts and unwanted prescriptions. Rows of dirty tube lights flickered above, playing with the insistent insects around them. The air reeked of cheap sanitizers—the kind that reminded me of public loos.

It had been a week since I returned home. Today was my last day in Kolkata. I'd recovered well from my wounds, thanks to the daily warm soup made by Rakhi and the involuntarily funny ones by Rampal. But my body was still sore, my chin swollen and red. I was lucky my jaw wasn't broken. The fall from the water tower hadn't been as bad as I'd feared. Apparently, I'd slipped down the ladder, crashed into Rampal, who fell on to Rakhi, and we all dominoed into our rock, Shamshu. He had held on to the ladder, despite the three of us slamming into him and breaking his ribs.

We had been about 50 metres up, and a clean fall would have been conclusive. Somehow, Rampal and Rakhi had regained their balance, and the three carefully made their way down, with Rampal holding me in one arm. I'd already heard about it more than a few times from him as part of my recovery regimen and was certain there would be many more retellings in the near future.

When we reached the ground, eight armed men, their necks tattooed with fish, greeted us. We were no match for them. Even though Shamshu was injured, he offered a brave resistance against RC's men before being shot.

He saved our lives. No relationship, no control, no power made him do it. Every second I lay on my sickbed, I whispered an apology to him. The weakest link in the chain had given in, and the strongest one had paid for it.

They had bashed up Rampal and Rakhi too, when they tried to stop them from taking me away. They never expected to see me again, but a day later, Radio had informed Rampal that he'd seen some people throw me out of a van outside our shanty.

I'd told them about my meeting with RC and the deadline I was given. And how dead I'd be if I didn't adhere to it. I told Rampal to get the money out and leave town. He scoffed and said we'd talk about everything once I was up on my feet. I knew it couldn't be good news.

Now, as he dragged me through the hospital corridor, I tried again.

'Is the money safe?' I asked.

'Yes.'

'Where the fuck are we going? I don't need a doctor, Rampal.'

'Shut up, chutiya. I have a surprise.'

Rakhi smirked, despite the cuts on her face. We entered a crowded room lined with eight occupied patient beds. All of them had visitors hovering around, barring one.

Shamshu's.

12 The Maker and the Boy

.→ Johnny .←

'You're alive!' I shouted.

'Barely,' Shamshu murmured, trying to sit upright.

'Fucking hulk, you're alive!' I stood frozen next to his bed, even though a dead whale had been lifted off my chest. I wanted to cry, but the high likelihood of Rampal using it to rag me later stopped me.

'Yes, he's alive,' Rampal said. 'Are you going to say something else, or just stand here blabbering like an idiot? Our rock star took two bullets. We wanted this to be a surprise for you.'

I attempted to hug Shamshu but found the bed to be higher than my liking. I had to make do with stretching out my short arms, which barely reached his massive chest. 'Thank you for being alive.'

'Very welcome,' he said, smiling.

Rampal and Rakhi laughed.

As we gathered around Shamshu's bed, he seemed embarrassed with all the attention, his eyes pausing for a fleeting second on one of us then moving to the other. He had bandages on his forehead, arms and torso. An IV dangled from a white pole and snaked into his left wrist. An oxygen tank was pressed against the wall behind his bed.

Loud chatter from the other beds filled the room. Some patients were smiling, a swarm of visitors sitting around them, with boxes of sweets and flowers beside their beds. Others found it hard to smile as they held their lone visitor's hands. A sheer curtain separated the beds—each section was appointed with a long downrod fan that hung precariously from the ceiling and clanked while spinning sluggishly. Newspapers plastered on the windows filled in for drapes. The place was uncomfortably warm and smelled of surgical spirit and phenol.

'Why didn't you tell me earlier? I would have at least gotten some sleep,' I said.

'Then we wouldn't have seen you smiling. An event that takes place only when a friend comes back from the dead—or when we add more clinics to our distribution,' Rampal said.

That had to be an incorrect observation; I was sure I smiled more often.

'But seriously,' Rakhi said, 'we wanted you to get better and see him yourself. We got him here just in time. The doctor says he's very lucky. Whatever we decide—we do it together.'

'Okay, here's some bad news to go along with the good,' Rampal said. 'They've destroyed our pizza franchises and burned many scooters. They even bashed up some of the delivery guys in broad daylight. Now everyone's afraid to come back. Your doctor's clinic is gone and so are the pills. Nothing's left—except the money and the investments.'

'Ramu, let's go slow. We just got here,' Rakhi said.

'There's no time. For all we know, we could be killed today. We need to decide. Now,' Rampal said, scanning the ward out of the corners of his eyes.

'Who are these guys?' I asked.

'They are called the Mandal. They run the streets. The city. The biggies. Merciless and dangerous. Nothing moves without them knowing,' Shamshu said.

'You wanted to know the biggest fish in the pond? Well, they're the sharks. There's no one bigger than them,' Rampal said.

I pulled a stool close to the bed and sat down. 'I don't think it's worth it, guys. We almost lost Shamshu. And these guys are ruthless. I was a fool to—'

'What happened to not being afraid of dying?' Rampal cut in. 'RC made you a chicken?'

'I'm not afraid of dying. But I'm not looking to take credit for another death,' I said. Flashes of a burning orphanage clouded my mind.

'What do you mean? Shamshu's alive. No one died.'

'That's…not relevant,' I said.

'What is relevant is how we respond. I say we go all out. They tortured and threatened you. Took what was ours. The only way to respond is by becoming bigger and stronger—then fucking their backsides!' Rampal said, his voice rising.

'Keep your voice down! People can hear us,' Rakhi hissed.

'Respond?' I said. 'You will die responding. That's what will happen. Have you ever come close to death, you retard? In any case, they have bad blood only against me. Take the money and go. There's more than enough for all of you. Buy a house somewhere and start a mobile shop with legit phones. Shamshu, go back to your village and your bees. Nothing is lost yet. We've been lucky.'

'Don't mention those fucking bees,' Rampal muttered.

'Nothing has been gained yet, Johnny,' Shamshu said, trying to sit up straighter. 'Rampal got injured, but I came very close to death. I know what it's like, and I'm telling you, we can't run like chickens. We've been chickens all our lives. I don't care anymore if I die. It's time to make a stand.'

I knew what he meant, having escaped death more than once in the past few months. Shamshu had just joined the club.

For some people, evading death can be cathartic; it makes

you fearless. It's as if death, that dreaded drawback of living, has been taken out of the equation. Even though you don't die, coming close makes you as misguided as an immortal.

'I agree,' Rakhi said, putting an extra pillow behind Shamshu's head.

Something shifted inside me. In that instant, I'd never felt more confident, complete, safe and wanted. I belonged.

Here was a man in pain, far away from his home and bees, who had just cheated death—yet he exuded the brightest courage I'd ever seen. Here was a woman who had only known life's rough edges—yet showed more balls than most men. Here was a brother who trembled watching horror flicks but was raring to go against the dreaded mafia because they had tortured his friend.

Who was I to stop that verve? Who was I to question the ferocity of an unlikely, yet determined, force? They say when a highly unlikely event occurs, all bets are off. The naysayers take a holiday and the pigs fly. Stones bleed and the rivers surge. Phoenixes rise and the sun doesn't care in which direction it sets.

They were right. All bets were off.

We had to make it count. We had to make *us* count.

'What do you suggest we do?' I asked.

'We build muscle and protection. Shamshu will get us the right guys. He has friends in the coal mines of Dhanbad who are experts with *katta*—country-made firearms—and are loyal to him.'

'How many?'

'A dozen. Maybe more,' Shamshu said, his voice gaining strength.

'We'd need much more than just muscle. How much cash do we have up there?' I turned to Rakhi.

'About five crores. Our assets and investments should be worth another three,' she said.

'We need to triple our pill production,' I said. 'We also need more clinics, provide them with security against RC's men and halve the prices. Double the commissions of our delivery boys. We'll need weapons too. But not to go on a head-on battle; we'll lose that no matter what. We'll use them only to protect what's ours and hurt the mafia by taking their customers. RC told me people prefer our less-harmful medicine over cocaine and meth. We have to flood the market with amphetamines. Cocaine needs to disappear from the city—that'll kill them. We'll need informants. Be ready for anything.'

'So all this you thought of just now? You fucker, you already had a plan ready,' Rampal said.

'I did. But I'd decided not to put it into action.'

'What changed?'

'Us,' I said, looking at Shamshu. 'But please know this—this is a one-way street. There's no coming back from here.'

'I love big fish,' Shamshu said with a grin.

Rakhi poured lemonade into paper cups and handed the first one to him.

'Will the Maker be able to produce three times more for us?' Rampal asked.

'Yes, he will.'

Rampal's eyes narrowed. 'How are you so sure? Everyone in town knows we have been marked by RC's men. He might chicken out.'

'Guys, it's time to let you in on a secret. I am the Maker,' I said.

'What the fuck!' Rampal sprang up. Shamshu leaned forward with great difficulty and Rakhi stopped pouring the second round of lemonade.

'I make the amphetamines. At least some good came out of medical school.'

'Stop fucking around,' Rampal said.

'I'm not. It's me. It's always been me. That money we borrowed from the street wasn't used to pay an advance to the Maker but to buy a small storage unit and set up the lab in Taltala. I've been making those pills every night from chemicals smuggled out of pharma factories across the border with the help of some people I know.'

'So that's the reason you weren't getting any sleep?' Rampal asked.

'Among other things,' I said.

'So much for all that spiel about specialist batters and bowlers. You cunning all-rounder! Why didn't you tell us? Chutiya!' Rampal said.

'What you don't know, you can't tell.'

'Wow. I'll call you Dr Johnny now,' Shamshu said.

'No, don't. Call me Johnny…Just Johnny,' I told him.

'So…Just Johnny,' Rampal smirked, 'let's get on with it then!'

I put a hand up. 'Not so fast. Now, more than ever, we need the blessings of the police. We can't do anything without them. They're as much the mafia as the mafia is. We need to find out who their man is on the force.'

'I have some good news. I spoke to the constables I know since we last discussed it,' Rakhi said. She pulled out a folded newspaper clipping from her purse and handed it to me. 'This is Deputy Commissioner Indraneel Debroy of the Port Division, Kolkata Police. He controls what comes in and goes out of the port. Moved up the ranks fast and is influential. Considered extremely ruthless and kills for fun. He's the Mandal's man and its conduit to the ministers and government corridors. We need him on our side.'

I unfolded the clipping, which showed a picture of the same cop I'd witnessed killing Amitav Banerjee, a journalist.

'What's wrong?' Rampal asked.

'Huh?' I looked up.

'You look like you have seen a ghost. What happened?' Rakhi said.

'Nothing. He just…looks scary,' I said.

'He is,' Rakhi confirmed.

I let out the breath that had been stuck in my lungs. 'Can you arrange a meeting with him?'

'You can't just waltz in and shake his hand. He works for RC—the man who shook you up. Debroy will cut you and feed you to him,' Rampal said.

I smirked. 'I have a feeling he might not.'

'No more secrets and riddles, Johnny. What's going on in that big head of yours?' Rampal asked.

I pulled my stool closer to Shamshu and beckoned everyone to huddle around the bed. 'Did you guys hear about the boy who killed journalist Amitav Banerjee near Hazaar Basti and ran away?' I whispered.

'Yeah. Radio told me…for a wasted bottle of whisky,' Rampal said.

'That boy was me,' I said.

Rampal stood up. 'Okay, first you're the Maker. Now you're the boy who killed a journalist. Next you'll tell us you're RC himself. Your head isn't in the right place.'

'The boy didn't kill the journalist. I mean I didn't. It was Debroy. And I saw him do it. When I ran, all they saw in the dark was a *boy* escaping. They couldn't catch me, so they made up the story Radio told you,' I said.

'So that's why you were holed up in your home for days?' Rampal said.

I nodded. 'Until I heard the story about the boy.' I turned to Rakhi. 'We need to find out more about Debroy. Where does he live? What's his daily schedule? Likes and dislikes? Weaknesses? Any family? Anything that can help us. He's the only way we'll get the Mandal's blessing to keep doing this.'

Rakhi nodded.

'Once we know enough, set up the meeting,' I told her. 'Also, pass the word around that I have information about Amitav Banerjee's murder.'

'Johnny, I'll set it up, but please be careful. This guy is afraid of nothing. If you're thinking about blackmailing or bullying him...well, he's an animal. He won't think twice before cutting you in two. I know his kind,' Rakhi said.

'I've seen what that animal can do, but we don't have a choice. Debroy is our only way in. There was a reason I witnessed that murder. And now is the time to use it.'

'So what will happen when you see him?' Rampal asked. 'You think he cares that you saw him? It's your word against a police commissioner's. Who do you think the cops will believe? You'll be dead within an hour.'

'I'll threaten to go public with the evidence,' I smiled.

Rampal's face lit up. 'You have evidence? Johnny, you champ! Well done! What is it? A video on your phone?'

'I don't have any evidence.'

'I told you guys—his head is inside his ass. What the heck will you blackmail him with?'

'With the evidence that doesn't exist,' I said.

Rampal dropped on to the bed and smirked. 'We're definitely going to die.'

13 Zero Choices

✦Katherine✦

I shared everything with Imaan on our way to the guest house—my mother, the mafia, the facts, the fears, the uncertainty. Maybe more than I should have. But he surprisingly understood most of it. If it wasn't my unexplained trust in him, it was my need to speak with someone. *Anyone.* I needed to dump how I felt into words. Gain perspective. And I found a surprising ease in doing so with Imaan. There were no judgments. He wasn't a contrived bigot, a conceited banker or a cocky bartender. He heard everything I had to say and promised to find out more through his connections. They were probably just words to make me feel better, but they did their job.

He parked a few metres away from the guest house and said, 'Madam, I come with you. It's not good idea to be lonely.'

As he stepped out of the car, I noticed a pistol tucked under his T-shirt. Maybe he'd turn out to be an effective bodyguard after all.

'It's a guest house, Imaan, not the trenches,' I said as he unloaded my luggage.

'I don't know what that mean. What I know…people taking your mother are dangerous. They kill for nothing. I am sorry, but there is little chance she live.'

'I know she's alive,' I said, and walked inside.

◆

The next day, the investigator stood me up. No messages, no calls, no contact. I spent the next few days calling him but to no avail. Mr Elenburg eventually phoned and told me the investigator was deep undercover and I'd have to wait for him to call.

My plans to visit the shelter home also turned out to be more difficult than I'd imagined. A crime scene sealed by the police, the home was out of bounds for everyone. My request to visit as a journalist was rejected.

The city kept me busy. I walked its endless streets and breathed its wet, balmy air. Met its people and learnt its beautiful words. Maybe it was too early to decide, but Kolkata ended up being way above my misguided expectations. People treated me with a certain kind of biased kindness. Little girls on the street wanted to play with my blonde hair. Some clicked selfies with me. Chirpy adolescent boys thought I was an actress and coyly showed me their pirated collection of Hollywood movies.

Never for a second did I feel unsafe.

All I got were unsure handshakes and well-meant namastes. Maybe it was the colour of my skin; maybe it was because I was an outsider; maybe it was because Imaan hovered over me all the time. To them, I was just a girl who had turned up in the middle of the city's ruins to write about stuff that didn't matter to them. All they had was curiosity for me.

More days passed. Tired of waiting for things to happen, I decided to bend the rules. I convinced Imaan to drive me to the shelter home, promising I'd only look from the outside. Ignoring his request to sit in the back, I climbed into the front seat of his bloated Beetle, much to his discomfort.

'Your mother, madam,' Imaan began. 'The mafia has her.'

'I already know that, Imaan. Tell me something I don't know.'

'It is no small drug cartel. They are…the Devil. They are called the Mandal. They don't make small money. They take away everyone's land for almost free. Their soldiers…they are murderers. The Mandal doesn't stop till they have taken your house. You should leave the country.'

'So they take away people's homes by force?'

'No, they pay for them.'

'That's not so bad then.'

'They pay only so much for your bus fare to leave city.'

'I don't understand.'

'I make you understand,' he said and looked at me momentarily. 'But don't speak about this to anyone…for your own good.'

'For the love of Jimi Hendrix, will you just tell me?'

'Okay. I try… So…you live in this house.' He pointed to a large iron gate with a lush green driveway that led to a grand old bungalow with a mossy facade and an external spiral staircase. 'Number-one locality. House is for a lot of rupees. Maybe five crores.'

'What's crores?'

'Crores, madam…lot of zeroes.' He made circles in the air with one hand.

'Okay.'

'The Mandal come and open the gutters,' Imaan continued. 'They leave snakes in the house. Drainage choked, sewers opened. Walls painted with *gaalis*.'

'Gaalis?'

'Um…warning…threat. Tea shops crop up outside the house. They have parties in the night; make it difficult to sleep. They cut electricity. Water even. If it doesn't work, they make slum around your house and throw cow shit inside. Some homeowners don't give up easily. For them, the Mandal send their special cocaine soldiers who harass and rape ladies, kidnap children, put fire in the house. It never stops. Until you are ready to sell for nothing.'

He then mumbled something under his breath. I didn't understand exactly what he said but I was sure they weren't pleasant.

'Not just this, madam. They take bigger areas by creating new slums where their soldiers live.'

'And what do they do with the real estate?'

'They make buildings. Expensive buildings. Modern India.'

'So who runs this Mandal?'

'They don't have faces. No names. It is a big burden to carry. Makes life short.'

'And the police?' I asked. 'Why don't they intervene?'

'They are all doing this together. Please don't tell anyone I told you.'

'How do you know so much?'

'Everyone who…' he thought of the right word to use, 'lives off the street knows. No one talk about it.'

'So why are you telling me?'

'You are…nice person, madam.' He looked at me. In his keen eyes, all I saw was repressed affection. Maybe there was more but that's just what I wanted to see. 'I see your pain. Same pain I had when I lost my wife. You should go. Before it is dirty.'

'Do you have any information on my mother?'

'If someone dies, the streets know quickly. Your mother, no one knows about her. It's a big secret.'

'I'll go with the working theory that she's still alive. That's the only one I can choose.'

Tears fell, wetting my cheeks.

'Madam, don't cry. You have to be strong. Thousand times strong.'

'Yeah, I know. Sorry.' I wiped my tears and looked out of the window. 'Your wife, she didn't die of pneumonia, did she?'

'No...the Mandal kill her. When she stop them from taking over our house in slum. My son was with me. I gave up the house to save him. But...it never ends.'

'Why do you do this risky job?'

He stopped at a traffic signal. Tapping his fingers on the wheel, he smiled and looked at me. 'For him, madam. I pay for my son's private school. He wears new uniform. Only he matters now...only he.'

'You realize there's no one for him after you?'

'Zero choices, madam.' His eyes were moist, but his lips curved into that winsome smile.

We crossed the traffic light and stopped at the next corner. The road narrowed, making it impossible for us to drive through it.

'We walk from here.'

As we stepped out, I said, 'I'd suggest you carry your gun, Imaan.'

'You know I have gun?' he asked, sounding surprised.

'I have eyes.'

'Sharp eyes, madam.'

'Suggest you take it.'

'Not very sharp.' He looked around, pulled his pant leg up and smiled. He had his gun stuffed inside his sock. 'I change location every day. Now we go.'

A few minutes later, we arrived at the shelter home, located in the heart of an open market. It was nothing like I'd imagined— just an old, unassuming two-storey structure in a busy market square. Three-wheeled mini taxis, locally called 'autos', belched smoke into the already thick air, weaving through a road filled with people. Colourful streamers hung across the road and swung wildly, indicating imminent rain. They were also the first signs of celebration of the upcoming festival season.

The lower section of the buildings had small shops that sold everything from books to mops. Brightly coloured umbrellas on the road, put up by industrious hawkers, had shiny toys dangling around them. Bamboo scaffolding, laden with bare-chested painters, stood precariously next to a few old buildings. A flute seller, with long, dishevelled hair and a sunburnt tawny face, carried a long wooden stick that rested on his chest and shoulder; several flutes bloomed like stick-thin flowers on the end. A haunting melody trickled through his flute, overpowering the sounds of the clamorous vendors.

I turned to Imaan. 'I have to go in and see for myself.'

'Madam, the home is sealed by police. You promised me... We can't go in there.'

'Zero choices, Imaan.'

I climbed the steps and shoved my shoulders against a rundown door. It refused to budge. I turned to him. 'You told me you could get me anywhere I wanted. I don't want to get inside fucking Fort William; I want to get inside this place. Now help me.'

He dragged himself to the door and pushed it open without much effort. Those broad shoulders proved useful.

'What do you expect inside?' he asked.

All I could see was darkness. 'A couple of managers and teachers were working with my mom. If I can find an address, a way to get in touch with them, maybe I can track her down somehow.'

I entered and Imaan reluctantly followed. Even though the door wasn't completely shut, the noise of the market outside died in an instant. All that remained was the sound of hollowness. My eyes adjusted to the darkness as we walked cautiously. The dusty interior emerged slowly. We were in what probably was the reception area. Shattered furniture lay in ruins—mangled chairs, splintered desks, scattered papers. Broken glass crunched beneath my shoes. Needles of dust-laden light pierced through cracked windows. A splintered frame with a map of the city hung precariously on a single nail. On one wall, big words in the local language were painted in red.

'Don't come here,' Imaan translated for me.

I switched on my phone's flashlight to discover a narrow door in a corner leading to a small courtyard. It was covered with dirty asbestos sheets; a narrow, open corridor lined with doors ran along one side. Sprinkles of light pinched through the crevices on the sheets but weren't enough to chase the darkness away. Dust swam in thin, still layers as far as I could see.

A faint rasp and a flare of fire—Imaan had lit his lighter. He bent down to pick up a half-melted candle and lit it.

Suddenly there was so much more to see. In the centre of the courtyard was an elevated concrete planter with a sole shrub, almost leafless. Red ribbons and trinkets were wrapped around the planter. Some doors along the corridor were open, while others lay on the ground. The shelter home had been thoroughly ransacked. My hopes of finding anything useful dwindled.

Then—a sound.

A door creaked at the far end of the courtyard. Imaan pulled out his gun. My first instinct was to duck. When nothing happened, I got up and darted towards the noise.

'Stop. Don't,' Imaan whisper-shouted.

The footsteps weren't far. They moved fast, darting through the rooms on the other side. The rooms were possibly connected, and they were trying to escape. I entered the closest room and chased the noise through the darkness.

A muffled cry, followed by a gunshot a few rooms ahead, then absolute silence. I raced through the connecting doors until I reached the last room and found a motionless body lying face down on the floor.

It was a woman with blonde hair.

I froze. My faculties started to fade. First it was my ability to move. Then my eyes, blanketed with haze, let visions of my mind take over: a shining, smiling figure walked gracefully on clouds, then fell into a throbbing pool of lava. She waved goodbye at me, before fading away. She was here and I was a minute too late.

Gunshots jarred my fading consciousness back to life. The room exploded with flashes of light. A man collapsed to the floor.

'Are you okay?' Imaan came from behind and held me as I sank to my knees. I looked at him but couldn't find my voice.

'Madam? Are you hurt?' He patted my cheeks.

'She's dead. They killed her. They killed my mother.'

Imaan looked at the woman, then back at me. 'Hold on.' He got up and walked past the woman and to the fallen man. He pressed a finger to his neck. Courage flowed back to my legs. I got up and walked closer to Mom's body.

It wasn't Mom. And the woman wasn't dead.

'He's dead,' Imaan announced.

'She's not. She's breathing. Come here and help me.' I picked her head up and put it on my lap. My hands became sticky with blood. 'Can you hear me? What's your name?'

Her eyes fluttered open for the briefest second.

'No! Please don't die. Please wake the fuck up!'

'They took her away,' she mumbled without opening her eyes.

'Where? Where did they take her?' I shook her gently, and her eyes opened.

'Mrs Gladwell.' She smiled, then grimaced. 'I'm so glad you're back. I thought you'd never come back.' She squeezed her eyes shut again.

'No, no, no. I'm not Mrs Gladwell. Where is she? Who took her?'

'They destroyed everything, Mrs Gladwell. They took all the children. I came back to look for you... Sorry, Mrs Gladwell.' Her eyes found mine, then froze. She lay still, her body trembling with my shivers.

Imaan squatted next to me. 'Madam, let her go. You can't help her. She is dead. We have to get out. That man almost shot you. They were waiting for you.'

'We can't leave her here.'

'If we stay, they come back. That man I killed was the flute seller. There must be more. If you want to find your mother, get up now. Only one time, madam, listen to me.'

I gazed at the dead woman's face. She reminded me of my mother. Next to her, half-buried in the debris, a picture of my mother and me peeked at me. This must have been Mom's room. I reached into my pocket, pulled out my pouch of coke and tore it open. After scooping out some of it with my fingers, I inhaled the cold stupefaction in.

14 Lions, Swans and Owls

-•- Johnny -•-

Feeble sprinkles of daylight filtered through thousands of clay idols lined up one after another. Shamshu and I had entered a potter's workshop in Kumartuli—the 300-year-old potters' colony located along the northern bank of the Hooghly in Kolkata.

Dark as a coal mine, the workshop was a cavern of shadows. A high, tarpaulin ceiling, wired together with bamboo, loomed above, and ash-coloured mud walls absorbed what little light dared to enter. The earthen sculptures of Durga stood unfinished—the potters had a little over a month to complete them for the festival season.

The place smelled like a farmhouse—a faint stench of cow dung and fertilizer floating atop a strong current of dried grass. The semi-wet clay idols devoured all the heat they could find to fortify their new identity, making the air eerily cooler than the outside. A thousand undone eyes of the ochre goddess watched us as we walked deeper into the darkness and down a narrow aisle, our footsteps squelching against a wet, muddy floor. Despite the dimness around us, the idols remained vivid and stark, almost luminous in the gloom.

Soon, they would leave this darkness, carried away by eclectic devotees and installed across the city for a grand, 10-day religious spectacle. Streets would transform into dazzling arenas of worship and revelry. The 10-armed goddess, sent to vanquish the mighty Mahishasura beyond the reach of man or God, would reign over a city pulsing with song, dance and devotion. But for now, this dark, unending tunnel showed no affiliation to dance and merriment.

As we moved deeper inside, small halogen bulbs dangling from a high asbestos ceiling took over, gradually replacing the faint sunlight. The idols grew in size and ferocity—more intricate in the depiction of their stories and more powerful in their bearing. These larger idols had bamboo meshes supporting them, soon to be populated with Durga's progeny and an army of lions, swans and owls—the celestial entourage accompanying her on her yearly visit. Some idols smiled at us, while others roared silent battle cries, their 10 hands clenching invisible weapons and their third eye, unblinking in the centre of their foreheads. Some wore unfinished crowns, yet to be adorned with sparkle. Some were partially painted, with bright colours peeking out, draping the bodies in reds and golds—a promise of what she would become.

Shamshu and I quickened our pace. At the centre of the workshop—a spacious amphitheatre of sorts—stood a giant idol, about 30 feet tall, its arms fanned out and forming a halo.

Unlike the others, this pièce de résistance had already been armed—not with clay but with steel—the shiny trident buried deep inside the chest of the fallen demon at her feet. His face, frozen in defiance, bore witness to his own doom.

'Are you sure this is the place?' Shamshu asked.

'Yes, this is the address Rakhi gave me.'

'It's very, very quiet.'

'Looks like the potters left in a hurry.' I pointed to the open paint buckets next to the idol's base.

'God-makers,' Shamshu said.

'What now?'

'They call them God-makers. Feared by the locals. Legend has it—'

'Let's just focus on one problem at a time, okay?'

It had been a fortnight since we decided to fight for what was ours. RC's men hadn't made a move yet. Maybe it had been a hollow threat. Maybe it had been a hollower calm. Either way, we were ready for anything.

I spent most of my time in the lab, making pills day and night. Every hour pushed us closer to resurgence. I had brought Dr Verma into the fold and taught him how to make amphetamine. Guess he was my apprentice now. We tripled our production and increased our distribution.

Shamshu, fresh out of the hospital, refused to rest. He followed me everywhere I went and had hired a team of strong, fearless ex-miners for transportation and protection. I don't know what I'd done to deserve his loyalty.

Rampal, meanwhile, expanded our network. Every day he signed up new clinics and even managed to revive Blue Bees and water tank operations. He'd found a shrewd businessman within himself; he was everywhere he needed to be.

Rakhi moved the money faster and bought real estate across the city. She also dug out useful information on the deputy commissioner through her network of constables and set up this meeting.

Deputy Commissioner Debroy joined the police force late. His brother had owned a bookshop—where he spent most of his time—until a rioting mob ransacked it, leaving his brother dead. Debroy disappeared after that; some thought he had killed himself.

Six years later, he returned to the city as a ruthless and ambitious police officer. Making up for lost time, Debroy shot through the ranks. He was feared by the street and loved by politicos. He didn't arrest criminals—he organized them. Nothing moved in the city without his nod. His way was simple: you were either valuable enough to be an ally or disposable enough to be eliminated. No loose ends. No fuss.

People said that he couldn't be killed—because he was already dead. That he'd mutter weird literary quotes out of the blue to a constable mid-piss or as an icebreaker in an interrogation. I knew at least one of those rumours to be true.

No one knew how he had met RC or how they had formed the Mandal, which now ruled every corner of the city.

Debroy lived alone, except for his three dogs (about whom I knew, of course) and stacks of books. He led a simple life; whatever wealth he had amassed didn't show up anywhere in his lifestyle. My bet was it wasn't money he was after. And men not lured by money were always dangerous. But I wasn't doing all this for money either. So there.

He was religious. *Very* religious. He prayed three times a day, and had a private worship room in his office where he spent hours in silence. On most of his weekends and holidays, he went to temples and on pilgrimages. Given his ledger of sins, I guessed he'd surely need to double down on penance. But his piety was also the weakness we had been searching for. He found it hard to kill a God-fearing man. He never touched a weapon during Ashwin, the seventh month in the Hindu calendar—a holy month, which had just begun. Holy places were off-limits for violence.

Hence the choice of this venue. We'd have preferred a temple—which was more populated and definitely much brighter than an empty and eerie idol-making workshop—but he wouldn't agree to that. It would be too public for him, they said. I just hoped this was holy enough for him not to unveil his machete.

'I don't like this. We should get out of here,' Shamshu whispered.

'This is our only chance. I can't leave. You should go. I'll be okay.'

'I'm not leaving you alone in this cave.'

Then we heard footsteps. Soft, deliberate. Squishing through the mud behind the big idol.

Then more. Multiplying. They came from the darkness beyond the rows of deities. Shamshu took out his gun, aiming at nothing and everything. 'Take it out!' He pointed at my still-holstered gun.

I had never used a gun, but Shamshu had taught me the basics: point and shoot. Simple instructions that usually meant the difference between life and death. But not today. When you aim at everything, you hit nothing. Also, I was sure a dwarf with a gun wouldn't be enough to stop an invisible army; words were our last hope.

'I form the light, and create darkness; I make peace, and create evil: I, the LORD, do all these things. Who approaches my altar in these dark hours?' A familiar and repugnant bellow echoed behind the idol as the spear held by the goddess swung on its own. What followed was that unmistakable, nauseating, raucous squeal of laughter.

I had the meeting I wanted.

'My name is Johnny. I have information on the boy who killed the journalist.'

Silence. Then—

'Johnny Johnny?' the voice behind the idol called out.

I stayed quiet.

The voice repeated the words, this time louder and more assertive. 'Johnny Johnny?'

'Yes…Papa,' I played along. This wasn't the first time I was subjected to such lame humour. Shamshu looked at me, unsure what was happening.

'Eating sugar?'

'No, Papa.'

'Telling lies?' The spear swayed again.

'No, Papa.'

'Open your mouth.'

'Ha-ha-ha.'

Debroy emerged from behind the idol with a squeal that made my toes twitch. Several cops surfaced from the dark aisles, stepping into the light, their guns pointed at us.

'Good boy, Johnny,' Debroy said. 'I like people with a sense of humour. Even when they're about to die.'

'I can help you,' I said.

'I don't need your fucking help.'

'Then why did you come here, quoting the Bible and playing God?'

'Humour *and* intelligence. Seems I didn't waste my time after all… Let's just say I was curious to witness a fucking dwarf threaten me. It would make for a great story. Plus I've never killed a dwarf.'

He picked up a machete placed at the idol's altar and ran his thumb lightly over the blade.

I should have spotted the machete earlier. Much earlier. So much for a religious place. This guy clearly had no rules. He made and broke them as he pleased.

'I'm thinking of an interesting story for this massacre.' He twirled his idle hand in the air, writing an imaginary headline.

'"Midget Terrorist Gunned Down by Kolkata Police"... No. Something more exciting... "Gay Midget Kills Burly Boyfriend, Then Himself, in a Gory Crime of Passion."'

His hideous squeal followed.

Flashes of that horrid night interrupted my thoughts as I stepped closer to him, making the cops adjust their aim.

Debroy was a tall, lean man—not the usual picture of a veteran cop with a bulging belly bursting against overburdened buttons. His uniform fit rather well. There existed no imminent threat of unwanted fat popping the buttons open.

He had long ears that hung down to his jawline. They appeared longer given my view of him was a few feet below his face. His lips were thin and red, stained with the juicy concoction of tobacco he frequently choked on. As he was darker than the average Bengali, his grey stubble stood out—ignored rather than cultivated. His irises were bright white and squinted, and his long arms were hairier than a Shih Tzu.

'How about "Decorated Deputy Commissioner Stabs Journalist Amitav Banerjee to Bury His Crimes"?' I traced the imaginary headline in the air just like he had.

The squealing stopped. 'Tread very carefully, midget.'

'The boy you were looking for but never found...it was me. I saw you stab that poor journalist with the same machete. And I have evidence to prove it.'

Debroy's thin brows arched like crescents. Paan dripped from his mouth. He wiped it with his sleeve and studied me carefully. 'The ways life surprises you. Who would have thought it was a dwarf?' He turned to his team and barked, 'It was a fucking dwarf! And you idiots were looking for a boy!'

'Yes, it was a dwarf,' I said. 'Did you know the journalist's sister was pregnant and his father had Alzheimer's?'

'Humour, intelligence and stupidity.' It was Debroy's turn to step closer to me, making Shamshu point the gun at him.

'Put the gun down, soldier,' he instructed without looking at Shamshu, but Shamshu wouldn't have it. 'Kill him,' Debroy ordered his men.

'Wait! Shamshu, put the gun down. Now!'

Shamshu reluctantly obeyed.

'I've always wanted that kind of loyalty,' Debroy said. 'Unfortunately they never come like that these days. To get work done, I either have to feed them or cut their intestines out. You're impressive, my little boy, to have people ready to give their lives for you. But like I said, you're also stupid. You see, evidence has no value if you're dead. I'll cut you generous deal, though. Whatever you have on me, pass it on. In return, I'll give you two days to leave the city.'

'Why does everyone want me to leave the city?' I asked, turning to Shamshu, who shrugged. I turned back to Debroy. 'Including your boss, RC. Are you all scared of a little person?'

Debroy stepped even closer. 'How do you know RC?'

'He tortured me, destroyed my businesses and said he'd let me go if I left the city. Big mistake.'

'So you're also the dwarf with that pill business! Small world. I'm privileged to meet you. But I'll be more privileged to chop off your balls. Take the deal and get the fuck out. You already have a death warrant on you. You're alive because it hasn't been acted upon yet. That's how small you are. Oh, wait, but you already know that.'

He squealed, nearly piercing my eardrums.

'You don't want me added to the list of people who want you dead. Because I won't serve any warrants. And since we're being cordial, I'll let you in on a secret—RC isn't my boss. No one is.'

'He surely looks like your boss.'

My riposte didn't go down too well with Debroy. In a flash he lunged, grabbed me by the throat and lifted me off the ground. He smiled as he choked me. 'Last chance. Give me the evidence, and I'll give you two days. Or you both die here.'

I tried speaking but couldn't.

'All my life, I've been threatened by more people than you've met in yours. Don't think I'll cow down and become your pussycat. I haven't reached where I have by giving in. And I won't go down to a fucking lousy dwarf.'

I was out of breath, and my vision grew darker by the second.

Then Debroy hurled me to the ground. My forehead slammed against the floor, splitting open. Blood trickled through my eyebrows as I gasped for air. I wiped the blood off my face.

'If I don't return home in one hour,' I said, 'a video showing you killing the journalist will be emailed to every media channel, newspaper and the entire police force. From a hundred email accounts. If anything happens to me or my colleagues at any time, the result will be the same. If my business operations are hampered—the same.'

Debroy stood still, glaring at me.

I caught my breath, brushed the mud off my clothes and touched the open wound on my forehead. 'I'd be careful doing that again.'

The deputy commissioner squatted in the wet mud and thrust the machete into the ground. He pulled it out and plunged it again. Over and over. Muddy water splashed on to his face and mine. He then smiled and said, 'What do you want?'

'I want in.'

'What?'

'I want police protection for my business. And I want a meeting with RC for a potential partnership. I want him to partner with me and sell amphetamines through his channels.'

'Careful, my friend. Be careful what you wish for. You have no understanding of what the business is and who RC is.'

'He is the Mandal. I figured that one out.'

'And what does this Mandal do, my small friend?'

'Drugs. Cocaine. Meth. I'm a peddler. I know.'

He let out another of his ear-splitting squeals. 'Oh, so you know, do you? Very well. I will fix a meeting with RC. I'll give you the protection you need. But how long do you think you'll last? You have a death wish, and it will be granted very soon. I won't have to do anything. Others will.'

He pulled out his handkerchief and handed it to me.

I dabbed my wound and said, 'Well, that's why you have to make sure I live. If I die, that video comes out.'

'I can't protect you from RC or others like him.'

'I'm very sure you can. Unless you want to be the most infamous cop in the country, hanged for your crimes.'

'The truth is incontrovertible. Malice may attack it, ignorance may deride it, but in the end, there it is,' Debroy said, getting up.

'Fan of Winston Churchill?'

'A true one. The steeliest man who ever lived.'

'Some say he suffered from depression.'

'Some also say, "Make everything as simple as possible but not simpler."'

I smiled. He and Albert Einstein made a good point.

Pleased with his moment of intellectual supremacy, Debroy turned and walked back towards the idol. Facing the goddess, he pressed his palms together and bowed.

'Do you know why it smells like shit in here? Because the clay with which Ma Durga is made is mixed with cow dung and urine.' He turned back to me. 'Shows you how important things that people hate and despise are. Behind everything beautiful is the grime and muck that makes it so.'

'Did you know the clay also has soil collected from a brothel?' I said. 'It's considered sacred. It holds the virtues and piety men abandon at the doorstep before stepping into the world of carnal sins. Without this soil, you can't make an idol. And what's more interesting is when these thousands of idols are later immersed in the river, it's that same soil that flows ubiquitously through its holy waters. Men come back again, this time dipping into that river, hoping to regain their purity—like a lost pair of trousers. I am that soil, Commissioner.'

'It seems Johnny boy knows Hindu mythology well. I assumed you were Christian because of your name.'

'I have no religion.'

'Good for you. Demons won't haunt you then.'

'Demons gnaw on the guilty mind, Commissioner, not on a religious one. Unfortunately, all of us have guilt.'

The little girl in the fire.

'Well, then,' Debroy said, 'get ready for some more demons. Starting with RC. Now fuck off before I change my mind.'

'Next week—on the 14th. At 11 a.m. We'll meet at my shanty, and you'll personally ensure our protection. Ask RC to be there on time.'

Debroy didn't respond; he simply started walking away. The cops also disappeared into the same darkness they'd come from.

'And Commissioner Debroy...'

He stopped but didn't turn.

'The quote about making everything simple? I know you

think Albert Einstein said that, but I'm afraid you're wrong. It's just someone who romanticized and ironically *simplified* Einstein's Constraint—a rather complicated set of equations.'

He stood there for a moment, then blended into the stillness of a dark aisle.

15 The Devilled Chasseur

❖Katherine❖

We left the dead woman in the shelter home, along with the flute-selling assassin. Imaan expected more to come, now that the Mandal knew I was there.

We rushed towards Imaan's car but stopped short. It was trashed. The tyres were slashed in multiple places, and the windows smashed. While the street hustle continued across the marketplace, the space around the car, six yards on either side, was oddly vacant; not a soul sniffed close to the wreckage. I attributed it to the freshly painted words on the car, along with a picture of a strange-looking fish.

Imaan grabbed my hand and pulled me into a narrow alleyway, then let go and bolted. 'Run! And don't look back!'

I did exactly as he instructed. I sprinted past indifferent ice cream sellers and scooter riders, painting them in my mind as snipers and assassins. I stumbled into school kids and stray dogs, but forced myself not to look back. But I imagined them—our invisible pursuers—teeth grinding, jaws clenched, weapons in hand, waiting for a clean line of sight. Every second that passed without a blow to my head or stomach was a transient appeasement. The cocaine helped. Yet each second was laden with terror.

Imaan was a few metres ahead of me. I took pride in my running, but he'd had a healthy head start. My uncomfortable sandals didn't help. Neither did the oncoming onslaught of humans and animals I had to weave through while he cut through them more deftly. So much for protecting me.

We emerged into a busy main street and crossed. I jumped over a fence and landed on a pavement so packed that running wasn't an option. The crowd swept me along in its tide— unfortunately, in the wrong direction.

I couldn't see Imaan anywhere amid a gazillion bobbing heads; everything in front of me was a constant, clamorous blur.

For the first time since I'd landed in Kolkata, I was alone. And afraid. Out of breath, I treaded on legs that begged me to stop. I lowered my head and walked as quickly as I could. *What have you got your pretty little fingers into, Mom? What have I gotten myself into?*

'Get in!' Imaan's hand shot out from a moving hand-pulled rickshaw and yanked me inside.

'Where did you disappear to? I thought you were here to protect me!' I shouted. I'd never been happier to see another human in my life, fatuous temper notwithstanding.

'I can protect you only if you listen to me, you…spoiled American girl!' Turning to the rickshaw puller, Imaan said, 'Hundred rupees. *Taratari chalao,* go faster!' Motivated, the boy swerved through the street, hopefully losing our devilled chasseurs.

After a bumpy 15-minute ride, we pulled up in front of a colonial structure with the word 'Babughat' written on it. Hawkers selling marigolds and coconuts stood in front of most of its pale white facade. A few saffron-draped sadhus sat on the marble steps leading down to the Hooghly River. We were at a wharf.

Next to the steps, an empty iron footbridge covered with thick and intricate steel arches emanated from the banks. It ran a few metres above the marshy land and ended at a jetty, where a ferryboat hooted, preparing to depart.

'We are late. We catch boat!' Imaan said, pulling me towards the footbridge. The last passengers were boarding, some leaping across. As we hurried across the footbridge, I risked a glance back.

I shouldn't have.

Three men, no weapons in hand, wore untucked white shirts and trousers: angels of death. Even though they were about 50 yards away, they seemed calm and less hurried than us, confident of catching their prey. They knew we had nowhere to go. No crowd to vanish into. No rickshaw to hide in. Our only chance was to make it to the jetty and jump on to the ferry at the last second—just before they could follow. That, or jump into the river.

Imaan and I ran with everything we had.

They started running too, their footsteps clanking loudly on the bridge. A nearby cop whistled vehemently and joined the chase. Whistles and hoots emitted from the ferry as well, its occupants seemingly entertained by the commotion. Our pursuers shouted, asking us to stop. It seemed they were open to a non-violent mode of communication, but Imaan wouldn't have any of it.

'*Thaamo*, stop!' he shouted, waving at the ferry captain. I was right behind him as the ropes were untied from the bitts.

We got off the bridge, on to the jetty and then jumped into the ferry right before the door pulled up. A few crumpled bills were exchanged in the next few seconds. The ferry parted from the jetty just in time for our pursuers to ill afford an ambitious leap on to the boat. As they stood there, helpless and overwhelmed, I caught my breath and gave them a one-finger salute.

'We made it! We didn't die!' I hugged Imaan tightly. He embraced me back. It was a warm, safe feeling that lasted only a few seconds. When the rush from our narrow escape settled down, I let him go, awkwardly and reluctantly, adjusting back to the reality of human equations—unsolved and unequal.

'Let's go inside. Not safe here,' Imaan said. We walked inside the ferry and found an empty corner.

'Relax,' I told him. 'They aren't gonna send fighter drones.'

'Don't underestimate the Mandal.'

I smirked. 'They seemed rather amiable.'

'They were the Mandal. The fish on my car—it was a warning for you to stay away.'

'Why do they want to harm me? It's my mother they had a problem with. They have her. What threat do I pose?'

'They think you come to restart shelter home. You should go away.'

'If they wanted me dead, they had enough opportunities. They weren't carrying any weapons—at least not that I saw. Even if they did, they didn't use them when they easily could. We were easy targets on that footbridge.'

'Maybe they want to kidnap you. It is not safe to live in that guest house. We go to other side of river, to Howrah. We stay there for a day or two; you buy a plane ticket and get out.'

'I'm not going anywhere, Imaan. Not until I find—'

'You will die! They will kill you. They will kill everyone! You not listening to me. Every time I ask you to do something, you do opposite. This isn't movie—'

I pulled him close and kissed him. Till he gently pulled away.

'Madam, I...' His face turned as pink as a kitten's tongue.

'I'm sorry. I don't know why I did that.'

I wasn't sorry. I wanted to kiss him and stop only at the Greek calends. But Imaan was shell-shocked by my effusiveness. The gawking onlookers made the moment slip away in just a few seconds.

'It's okay. Happens.' He smiled sheepishly.

'Thank you for saving my life.'

'Not till we get to Howrah and—'

'Imaan, I appreciate why you're asking me to run away. But I can't. Would you run away if it was your son?'

He turned and gazed out at the river. I looked out too. The ferry glided beneath a massive bridge suspended over the river, connecting Kolkata to Howrah; it was certainly one of the longest I'd ever seen. Horizontal metal trusses, shining faintly against the setting sun, rose to form two enormous vertical suspenders at either end of the bridge, holding the steel giant steady over the holy river. A little farther ahead, just below the bridge, bare-chested men plunged into the water from concrete steps. The faint sounds of temple bells filled the balmy air.

'I agree,' I said. 'I need to be somewhere safer. Let me check into a decent hotel in the city. I assume the Mandal won't shoot me in a hotel lobby in broad daylight. I doubt I'm that important to them.'

Imaan thought about it for a moment, then said, 'Okay. But I choose hotel and you listen to what I say from now on. Otherwise I leave.'

It was an empty threat. I knew he liked me; he wouldn't leave me alone.

'Agreed. The minute I check in, I have to call my people back home to update them on my adventures. I also need to find out where that bloody investigator is.'

'Investigator?'

'We hired someone professional to help find my mom.'

'You don't need any investigator; I know more than them. Trust no one.'

'I trust you.'

'I...thank you, madam.'

'Are you embarrassed I kissed you?' I asked.

'Yes. No! It's just...I can't do this now.'

'Do what? Don't worry—I'm not falling in love with you. I just think you're awesome. With your perpetual smile and country-style gun that finds a new place to hide every day.'

'Thank you, madam.'

'See? That's something no man would say back home.'

'Thank you, madam.'

'God! Come give me a hug. I won't bite you.'

Imaan hugged me half-heartedly and said, 'We get off here.'

◆

We took a cab back and checked into separate rooms in a hotel located in a posh, modern part of the city. Imaan went to the guest house to get my stuff; thankfully, it hadn't been ransacked.

I called Mr Elenburg to check if he had spoken to the investigator.

'Not yet. The best we can do is wait,' he replied.

'Wait? They tried to kill me. Twice! If it hadn't been for my bodyguard, I'd be in a coffin on a flight back to New York. Or worse, floating up to some holy man's prayers on the banks of the Hooghly. I can't afford to wait anymore, Mr Elenburg.'

'I'm sending you tickets for the next—'

'Jimi fucking Hendrix! I'm sick of saying this to everyone.

I'm not moving my ass from here until I find her!' It was unfair of me to fly off the handle with Mr Elenburg. He was the only one I had, besides Charles. 'I'm...sorry, Mr Elenburg. It's just been—'

'I understand. Now tell me exactly what happened.'

I did.

He promised to contact a senior executive of the investigation agency to find out about the investigator and also beef up my security.

'I have no leads, no starting point,' I said.

'How are you on money? Do you need me to arrange for more?'

'No. I have enough. Thanks. Just find me that investigator. Or hire another if this one is MIA.'

'I'll try my best, Ms Gladwell.'

'Thank you.'

There was a pause before Mr Elenburg spoke again. 'I'm afraid there's more to share.'

'I bet Jimi's Fender there is.'

'A warrant has been issued for your arrest. The cops are looking for you. Your court date is in five weeks. I can file a motion for continuance and try to push the date a bit, but not much. If you can't make it back within two weeks, plead not guilty and fight your case, you'll be declared a fugitive and lose your family's inheritance. And you'll also be facing years in prison. Now...I'm not going to ask you to come back anymore. But you need to know what lies ahead.'

'If we can't find her within that time frame,' I said, 'I guess I could sell coconuts by a river somewhere in India.'

'I'll call you the minute I have an update.'

'Can you do me another favour, Mr Elenburg? Can you...

can you arrange for some…snow? Not much. I just want to—'

'I'm not going to do that, Ms Gladwell. This is not the time to drown in drugs. We need you to be your best version.'

'I just had a woman die in my arms. I need… It helps me be sharper. Can you do it?'

'I'm afraid I can't. Your mother wouldn't have it.'

'Okay, I understand. Thanks again. I gotta go.'

'Good night, Ms—'

I disconnected and used up almost all the powder I had left. Then I changed into a negligee, opened the mini bar, grabbed a bottle of wine and knocked on Imaan's door.

'Madam, everything okay?' He was only in his jeans, just the right amount of hair on his well-built chest. He looked at me, held my gaze for a moment, then dropped his eyes.

'No, it's not. Can I come in?'

'It is late. You don't look okay. What happened?'

'Do you like wine?'

'What?'

'Do you?' I lifted the bottle.

'Um…yes.'

'Then what's the problem?'

Imaan sighed. 'You should go and sleep, madam.'

'I can't sleep. Please, Imaan…' I stepped closer. 'Let me come in.'

He opened the door to let me inside, then shut it. Maybe it was the tears rolling down my cheeks. Maybe it was the negligee. I didn't care.

When I opened my eyes the next morning, I was naked under the sheets, and there was more than one empty bottle on the floor. My head pounded and my lips were parched. Waves of bright light edged my vision even though the drapes didn't allow the morning sun in. Imaan wasn't in bed. I reached for a bottle of water on the nightstand and noticed several missed calls and a message from Mr Elenburg on my phone: 'Ms Gladwell, call me immediately. The investigation agency found your bodyguard's mangled body in an alley yesterday. The man with you isn't your bodyguard. Run!'

16 Annus Mirabilis

⋆ Johnny ⋆

Rampal, Shamshu and I stood on a busy cobbled street beside the tram tracks. Accompanying us were Debroy and his plain-clothed policemen. A little farther away, more of his men sat in police vehicles, studying the crowd. It was just another sunny and humid day in Kolkata.

'How long?' I asked.

'We are not now that strength which in old days moved earth and heaven, that which we are, we are; one equal temper of heroic hearts, made weak by time and fate, but strong in will to strive, to seek, to find, and not to yield,' Debroy said.

I smiled. Despite all his monstrosity, I could effortlessly paint him as a prideful librarian, at peace with the weight of words and their play. 'Old man contemplating life's end is hardly a way to shake on a partnership, the greatness of Lord Tennyson notwithstanding,' I said.

It was his turn to smile. 'You're taking the joy away from me, Johnny. I promise you the next one I quote will be unknown to you. It'll baffle you and confuse you. Might even show you how this all ends.'

'I look forward to it. But you haven't answered my question.'

'As long as it takes,' Debroy said.

'This wasn't the venue I asked for, Commissioner.'

'Be thankful you're still breathing.'

'I am. I'm also thankful for your personal security. But I asked for a safe public space to meet, not a tram stop. What is the guarantee that nothing untoward will happen here?'

'You have my word.'

Rampal laughed loudly. 'Your word? We all know what your word is worth.' Turning to me, he whispered, 'This is a bad idea, Johnny.'

So far, we had faced no threat from RC or Debroy. We had expanded our operations over that last few weeks, raking in millions every day. At some point, I was certain, there would be more money and gold in that water tower than water. But problems of plenty could wait.

'A good idea would be me slicing your throat. Who gave this rodent the permission to talk to me, Johnny?'

Rampal stepped behind Shamshu who, as usual, was unmoved by the unnecessary chatter.

'It's okay, Ramp,' I said. 'You know our new friend will take care of us as long as—'

'As long as I know you're not lying to me,' Debroy cut in. 'If you are, you'll be sorry you were born.'

'I'm getting tired of your threats. And I'm not lying to you. You think I'd risk my life—and my friends'—on a lie? I'm not an idiot.'

Every time he threatened me, I became surer I was an idiot. Debroy would never just stand down and let me blackmail him forever. He hadn't even asked for a copy of the video yet. My prepared answers to that—'I'll show you when the time is right' or 'Trust me, it's buried safe somewhere'—didn't even convince me. So a ferocious, murderous interrogator, willing to swing his blade just because he could, would be the last to believe them.

Debroy smiled. 'It would be so much easier if you were, though.'

'Let's not get emotional now,' I said. 'While you mull over the next literary flex, you'll be happy to hear what I have to say to RC. Our partnership is going to make much more money than coke ever could.'

'You think *all* this is running on the money we make from coke? You have no idea what we do. And you want to be a part of it. The day your leverage runs out—'

'Enough!' I barked. 'You'll speak to me with respect. And no more threats. Don't force me to send that video out. I don't really care what happens to me.'

Debroy was startled. He searched my face, sniffing for bullshit. 'All right, fine.'

Thankfully, I'd covered the stench well. Just then a red-coloured tram with two coaches hummed towards us and squealed to a stop.

'Get in,' Debroy said.

'What?'

'Get in the tram. It's safe.'

Notwithstanding my previous, torturous journey on a tram, I got in. I entered the first coach, followed by Debroy, Shamshu and Rampal. Debroy's men got into the second coach. Inside, RC sat in the middle row, the only one with seats facing each other. A cigarette in one hand, the other lazily scratching his chest over his shirt. His bald head glistened with gigantic beads of sweat, ready to trickle down his fleshy face any second. The tattoos on his neck were partially hidden by layers of fat hanging from his chin. Half a dozen armed men stood behind him, a fish tattoo inked on each of their arms. The tram car had no other passengers.

'Welcome, Just Johnny!' RC rasped in his throaty, feeble voice, smiling as the tram lurched forward.

It felt familiar to those lonely train journeys I'd made as

a boy to run away from the orphanage. With no certainty of making it to an unknown destination, I gave up and came back every single time. The caretakers, relieved to have one child less to feed and educate, were disappointed every time I returned—a dwarf bathed in dirt and scum.

While I was an unwelcome sight for most at the orphanage, I was also their coveted public relations trophy. The local papers interviewed me several times: the child dwarf, orphaned and left to die but taken in by Good Samaritans who took care of people with 'special abilities'. My biggest curse was also what had afforded me an education, thanks to all the goodwill and fat cheques I acquired for them. Guess that education was finally counting for something. I didn't end up opening hearts, removing prostates and skiing the slopes of Aspen, but I did get to open minds, one pill at a time.

Shaking off those memories, I strutted towards RC as the tram gained speed. 'Thank you.'

'Come, sit with me. How do you like my mobile office?'

As I sat down across from him, legs dangling in the air on an uncomfortably warm, iron seat, Debroy sat next to RC. Shamshu and Rampal stood next to me.

'Nice. Although it's not the first time I've had the privilege of being in one of your...offices,' I said, rubbing my hands against the rusted metal.

'It's not nice,' RC corrected. 'It's hot, uncomfortable and rickety. But the trams of Kolkata are among the very few things in the city that move with the precision of time. It also helps me stay close to the city...a part of it. It's very easy to forget how it smells, how it talks, how it runs, sitting inside an air-conditioned office in a high-rise and looking down on it. After all, it's the city that feeds all of us, doesn't it?'

'It does. I live in its dirtiest labyrinth. You should come visit me to really know how it smells and talks.'

RC smiled. 'I'm so pleased about your hospitable offer. I promise you I will. But I'm not sure Debroy Sir will. He's very unhappy with you. Says you don't trust us.'

'He's right. After your last round of hospitality, you can't blame me.'

'Please accept my apologies for my...unsocial behaviour the last time.' Then, turning to Debroy, he said, 'See, I told you, Debroy Sir: he's a fearless tiger. Don't be fooled by his size. It was destiny that you thought it was a boy who saw you cut open that journalist. Destiny that you couldn't catch him. Not your fault. It was destiny that he didn't die falling from that water tower. And it is nothing but destiny that I did not kill him. He's meant for bigger things, this destiny's dwarf.'

RC was making a habit of coining names that I liked. 'That's what I've been trying to convince Debroy about.'

'Why, he calls you by your name, sir!' he addressed Debroy. 'Very bold. Just Johnny, not many people do that and breathe. He's "Debroy Sir" to me, but some also call him the "Machete Man". Without him, we're nothing. I'd be careful what I address him as.' He put a hand on Debroy's shoulder and patted it.

His words didn't frighten me a bit. 'As you know, I've had the privilege of seeing the machete show in person,' I said. 'Now, can we talk business?'

'What business? I thought you were here to hand over the evidence, and in return, I'd think about sparing your life. Again.' RC's smile had disappeared.

I glowered at Debroy, who gestured for me to calm down. He then whispered something to RC, who was scratching the back of his neck.

'Debroy Sir,' RC said, 'I've always hated mobile technology. Everyone's watching noisy screens everywhere, laughing at forwarded jokes and memes and making videos when they deem fit. There's no privacy anymore.' He crushed his cigarette on the seat, leaving a burn mark. It made me twitch.

I nodded. 'I agree. All the more reason to be extra careful while slicing someone open in the middle of a street. Especially if you're supposed to stop others from doing such things.'

'Hmm. This dwarf is more of a man than you guys are,' RC muttered, looking at his cronies. He turned to face us again. 'And who are these jokers with you? Laurel and Hardy? Your partners?'

To be honest, I thought it was rich, coming from RC, a flowing blob of fat, and Debroy, shiny bones on red skin. 'They're my brothers,' I said.

'The rangy one looks like he's peed his pants. What's wrong, my friend? Are you scared?' RC smiled again; his fingers were back on his chest, gently abrading the cloth.

Rampal didn't answer, although I was sure he was aching to make a cocky reply. Thankfully, for once, he was following my instructions. The tram stopped at a busy station but soon moved without picking any passengers.

'RC, last time we met, you said you don't like stagnation. Let's not do that then. Either we get on with what we came here to talk about or you take your chances and kill us. Either way, I'm sure all of us have somewhere better to be,' I said.

He shrugged. 'I'm still deciding. I'd be careful not to rush me; the pressure of time makes one do things in haste. And I don't like time on my wrong side.'

'He was there. He's shared enough information about that night—things he couldn't have made up. We can't afford to let that get out,' Debroy said.

RC lit up another cigarette and took a drag, exhaling as he looked out of the window for a few seconds. 'Hmm… Mr Just Johnny, what do you think our business is?'

'You run the Mandal,' I said.

'Debroy, the streets come up with some fancy names, don't they? Too much TV, I think.' He looked at Debroy, then turned back to me. 'Very good. And what does the Mandal do?'

'They sell drugs. What else?'

'Yes, what else.' He took a deep drag. 'Okay, what's your proposal?'

'Word on the streets is your product sales have dropped by over 50 per cent since my amphetamines hit the market. And it's getting worse. My product is easier to make and distribute. It isn't on anybody's radar, has higher margins and a wider market. It's also not fatal like cocaine. No one else is making it in Kolkata, but soon they will. I'm offering to sell the pills to you at half our retail price. You're free to sell it at any price you deem is right for you and control the market before others try to come in. My calculations say that you'd triple your turnover within a month. The market is infinite.'

RC leaned back in his seat. 'That's very generous of you, my friend. But I believe in other means to stop anyone from entering my market. I find it gives me better control.'

I resisted the urge to gulp.

He continued. 'And what would you like in return?'

'I want an exclusive territory, assurance of no harm from you and protection from the police. We should be able to carry out our business in peace.'

'Peace is very expensive, my friend. *Very* expensive. But that isn't really what makes you poor. What makes you poor is that you don't realize the price you paid for it until it's too late.' He took another long drag and blew a dense cloud of smoke in my face; it was turbid and earthy, a transient ghost. 'A million pills every week at 30 per cent of current market price. And you'll have to teach our guys how to cook it. You can have the territory Debroy is in charge of. You will sell more than you can dream of in that part of the city. Deal?'

RC didn't take much time laying out the offer; I wasn't the only one who had done his homework.

'Forty per cent of market price. And I won't teach anyone how it's done.'

'Debroy Sir, he is a hard negotiator, this dwarf. Where did you find him?' It was the back of his neck that got the attention of his nails this time.

'Well, he found me,' Debroy said, seeming a little embarrassed.

'Of course he did… Okay, I'll agree to your deal on one condition. When the time is right, you'll have to convince your neighbours and friends from your shanty to move out.'

I raised an eyebrow. 'Move out where?'

'To the other side of the river. We'll provide them with better homes there.'

'Why?'

'Did I ask you why you wouldn't part with the know-how of cooking your pills? That's your secret sauce; this is mine. I can use force to throw them out. But it's easier this way. If you keep your part of the deal, you might get a chance to lead one of our companies in the future. Did you ever imagine you could do that?'

I tried hard not to think that far ahead. 'What will you do with the shanty?'

'Let's just say they'll have new inhabitants.'

'Why not let these inhabitants be?'

'Why not slit your throat and toss you into the gutter? Nobody would care.'

I'd reached the end of the road as far as asking questions was concerned. I looked at Rampal and Shamshu, who wore blank expressions. 'Okay. I don't think it'll be a problem if they're moving to better places.'

I knew it would be a problem, but I just didn't know *how*. I figured that would be the right time to give my neighbours the cash I'd kept reserved for them. That would help them settle down comfortably in the new place. Some could hopefully buy a decent house somewhere away from the dirt.

'Perfect,' RC said. 'We have a deal. My guys will figure out the details with you later.'

'Sure. Rampal and Ra—'

'Mr Just Johnny...' RC leaned forward and whispered. 'Please keep in mind that if you falter on your part of the deal, I won't care what you have on my friend Debroy. I won't spare your life again. Is that clear?'

His mundungus breath was unbearable. I nodded, holding my breath and waiting for the air to be breathable again.

He leaned back again and put his arm up as the tram came to a stop. 'It was a real pleasure, Mr Just Johnny.' He looked at Rampal and Shamshu. 'And you, Mr Laurel and Mr Hardy; I suggest Laurel change his pants after he gets off the tram.'

I got up and motioned for Rampal and Shamshu to move, but Rampal didn't. He walked closer to RC, making his men cock their guns.

'Can I ask you a question, sir?' Rampal said, as I tried to pull him away. He couldn't help himself; he was going to undo everything we'd just achieved.

'If you're going to ask where to buy diapers...' The men behind him laughed.

'Why fish?' Rampal said, pointing to his neck.

He looked at Rampal for a second, then said, 'This motley crew is full of surprises! Another excellent question.'

Rampal smirked, awaiting an answer.

'Get the fuck out of my tram!' RC scowled, pointing towards the exit. It was the first time he had raised his feeble voice. It was enough for our feet to move in the right direction. As I got down, I caught a glimpse of RC whispering something into Debroy's ears, making the deputy commissioner sneer at me. Those frontbenchers at my medical school had worn the same smirk as they coined new dwarf jokes at my expense.

But certainly, dwarf jokes weren't enough to make these gentlemen's lips curl up. Either I was a tough negotiator, or the deal meant little to my new partners. In a complicated flowchart that ran smoggy in my head, all assumptions led to worrying conclusions. But for now, I was more than pleased with my *annus mirabilis,* however short-lived it might turn out to be.

17 Unseen Pits and Unknown Traps

I wasn't sure if I'd been officially kidnapped or was just being babysat. So far, the man pretending to be my bodyguard had shown no signs of coercion or violence—at least none I could anticipate.

'Are you going to kill me?' I asked.

'If I have to,' Imaan said, gazing out of the lone window in his hotel room. The low hum of the air conditioner filled the silence.

Though last night now seemed distant and ludicrous, he didn't repulse me. He did not even seem menacing. Just aloof and quiet. All I could sense in him was a raging pain, a conflict. A dilemma that begged the question of what he was to do with me. Strangely, deep in my bag of pity, I found more for him than for myself. But then again, I'd been wrong about almost everything since landing in Kolkata.

An hour prior, within seconds of reading Mr Elenburg's text, I'd scrambled into my clothes—well, a cloth really—and searched the room for my missing shoe. I hadn't prepared for subterfuge when I'd walked into the room the previous night.

My mind had raced through the options that lay in front of me. I wasn't ready to answer questions like 'Why?' or 'Who?' yet; no matter the *who* and the *why*, I had nowhere to run. Maybe the US Embassy? No, Katherine Gladwell would land up in a US prison. Call Mr Elenburg and ask him to charter a private jet to smuggle me out as Elene McCarthy? Maybe. Life on the run could be exciting, although quite certainly penniless and short-lived. For now, a question like 'what next' was way higher on the list of questions I wanted answers to.

So much for not being afraid to shine, Mom.

Every failing day, her face blurred a little more. Her smell, her warmth, the brush of her fingers on my head—everything seemed to trickle away. I'd pinched out the last few granules of cocaine from the pouch, snorted it and rubbed my nose clean.

Shoes in hand, I had opened the door to leave the room only to find Imaan right outside.

'You leaving?' He had asked, smiling.

'Yes. I thought I should get ready and go…find that investigator.' It was my turn to drop my eyes.

'I got breakfast.' He dangled a brown bag, oil-soaked in patches.

'No…I…don't feel like it.' I sniffed. 'I think I'll skip it.'

I advanced slowly, hoping he would give way.

Reluctant and confused, he stepped aside. As I crossed him, I saw the gun tucked behind him. I decided to pull it out and take him head-on.

It had been a mistake.

Imaan spun, catching my wrist before I could grab the weapon. Before I could shout, he'd shoved me back into the room and locked the door behind him.

'What do you want? Who are you? And where's the real Imaan? Where's my mother?'

He continued looking out the window. 'I don't do this because I like it.'

'What then? The money was too good to look away? A stellar show you put up—against your will, I'd say. A simpleton with a smile and a gun. The milquetoast with manners. The doting father to a son. Turned out to be enough.'

'No acting, madam. I did this to save my son. And I will do it again...and again. I stop only when I know he is safe. The world can burn and die—I don't care. I'm sorry you have to be in it. I am.'

'You can drop the act now and get on with whatever you have to do with me.'

Imaan turned and squeezed my throat. 'They have my son. Do you understand me? I'll do anything to get him back. It is truth. It is truth. It is...'

He finally let go, and I coughed back to life.

'I'm sorry. I—'

'Get the fuck away from me.'

He obeyed, retreating to the window. 'Let me go, Imaan. I promise I'll leave this place.'

'I cannot. It is my job to make sure you stay with me,' he said, looking outside again.

'Who sent you?'

He didn't answer.

I moved on from the 'What next?'—which seemed beyond my control for the time being—to the 'Who?' Was it Mr Elenburg? If so, why would he tell me to run? It didn't make sense. Nothing made sense. 'Is my mother alive?' I asked.

'I don't know.'

'Tell me, goddamn it!'

'They kidnap my son from school the day before you land. Then they tell me I meet you as Imaan at airport. Be your bodyguard. They wanted proof of you with me. I clicked selfie with you for that. They told me to be with you and report every day. If I didn't, they would kill my son.'

'Why you?'

'After they took my house, they give me jobs sometimes. When they want outsider.' He raised his arm. 'No fish tattoo.'

'And you do anything for them?'

'No. But when I said no, they took my boy.'

'And who are "they"?'

'The Mandal.'

'The story of your wife being killed?'

'No story, madam. They killed her. But I saved my son.'

'And sleeping with me…was that part of their instructions too?'

Imaan turned sharply, his voice firm. 'I didn't come to you, madam. You… You are the most beautiful lady I ever see. I have never been with any lady after my wife. You cried. I don't like that. I don't want to harm you. I told you how dangerous the Mandal is. I thought you would get scared and leave. And I get my son. But you are so idiot.'

That was the sweetest thing a man had ever said to me. I brushed aside my meandering, ill-timed, warm-puppy thoughts. 'The men chasing us? Were they part of the Mandal?'

'I don't know. Maybe security agency. I can't let anyone find you. They will punish me. And if they are Mandal men, it means they don't need me anymore and want to take you. I have to get my son back first. I will use you to get him back.'

'Who killed the flute seller in the shelter home?'

He glared but didn't answer.

'And the woman? You killed an innocent woman as well?'

'She couldn't tell you anything. I just push her; she fall down and hit her head.'

'Who smashed your car?' I asked.

'Not my car. They give it to me. They ask me to beat the car to make you afraid. I pay the street children to do it.'

'They don't want me to leave. They don't want me poking

around. What the hell do they want from me?'

He shrugged.

'All this because my mother rehabilitated some kids? It doesn't make sense.'

'I just do my job to get my son. No more. No less.'

'So now what?'

'I call them.' Imaan turned to stare out of the window yet again. Was he looking for something—or someone?

'What if those men weren't the Mandal and someone else also knows who I am? And were trying to protect me? Then you are useless to them; they'll get rid of you.'

Imaan stayed quiet, but I saw the fear in his eyes. There was an opportunity here. It was the first time I sensed an inroad— an unknown turn on a dark highway that promised to take a hungry traveller through a forested path to a cosy cabin with smoking chimney. The path was replete with unseen pits and unknown traps, but it was the only one to take. So I swerved.

'Can I call you Imaan?'

'*Only* Imaan. I am nobody else.'

'Look, I feel your pain.' I approached him and placed a hand on his shoulder. 'I want you to get your son back. But what if you got him back *and* helped me find my mother?'

'How?'

'The investigator. My lawyer told me he's deep undercover in the Mandal, trying to locate my mother. When they call you, chances are they'd only be doing it to get me and then get rid of both you and your son. But you offer them something else. You tell them you know of an infiltrator in their ranks who's looking for my mother. Tell them you know where he is. Offer him in exchange for your son. Tell them you'll bring him in, and take me along with you.'

'What happens to you?'

'Don't worry about me. Get your son and disappear. I'll think of a way to get my mother out.'

'You and I, madam...we are the same. Out of our mind.'

'I know. Will you help me?'

Imaan thought for a while and asked, 'Where is the investigator?'

'I...I don't know. I've been trying to get in touch with him since I landed.'

'Then there is no plan. You are thinking of telling them a lie, then getting my son and your mother? And run away from most dangerous people?' He clenched his fist and pulled an imaginary line of snow off it. 'The coke you have... I think it is bad quality.'

'Was. I finished it.'

He stared at me.

'I know there is no plan without the investigator. We have to find him. Mr Elenburg is close. Once we locate him, we tell him and you take both of us as captives. Hopefully we'll both find what we are looking for. Then we use the element of surprise to escape.'

'Lot of hope in your plan. And no idea where investigator is. How do you know your mother will be there?'

'It's the only chance we have.'

'Only chance *you* have, madam. All I have to do is—'

'Kill my mother!'

'What? I don't kill your mother. I just take you and get my son back.'

'Doing that will eventually lead to her death,' I said. 'And probably mine. Will you be able to live with that?'

'I told you...I do anything to save my son.'

I leaned forward. 'What happens when your son asks you for the truth?'

'This isn't the first time I've done something like this for him.'

'Then go ahead and do it. Line up more graves for him to walk on.'

'I will!' Imaan snapped.

'They'll kill you and your son once they realize you're not useful to them,' I said. 'Imaan, do this for whatever little pain you felt for me. Please. Give me a chance to save my mother. I beg you.'

Imaan didn't speak for a long time. He ambled across the room, switched the TV on and off, opened a bottle of water and drank a sip from it. 'Find your investigator. No plan without him. Then I call the Mandal.'

'Thank you! I have another request.'

'We don't go out of hotel,' he said.

'I need cocaine. Can you source some for me?'

'Yes. But you should not do it. You need to be—'

'Here's the money. Please get me the best quality you can find.'

18 A Million Slithering Snakes

Cocaine was just powder.

Yet it brought consequences; every pouch that exchanged hands, every snort that travelled through stormy nasal caves, every prick that broke down a helpless brain barrier, every shade of white that a rush of dopamine painted—it changed lives. It blurred the line between right and wrong, carved out perspectives that never existed and justified everything.

Insurmountable power or a bottomless void—one of them would choose you, depending on which side of that thin white line you stood.

Back when we only sold amphetamines and hadn't partnered with the city's largest cocaine outfit, no one opened doors for me or dusted off padded chairs for me to sit on. But everything changed when cocaine was added to the menu. Now people, not just from the shanty but from across the city, knew me. Talked about me. Loved me. Hated me. They smiled and waved at me from across the street. I was no longer trivial; I represented the eventual totality of what the powder brought.

No, cocaine wasn't just powder. It was power. Sheer and shameful.

I wanted neither, yet I looked the other way. The Mandal had made it clear—if I wanted to keep my amphetamine business, their cocaine had to flow through my supply chain. And with that power came surprising dollops of helplessness. I was winning wars but losing the battle against myself. A sinewy body that barely covered its mutinous organs, each one trying to break free every day. I could barely see myself anymore. Maybe that's what I wanted—a parapet that stopped me from falling deep down into myself and seeing who I really was, what I had done.

In the last few weeks, Rampal, Rakhi and Shamshu had moved out of Hazaar Basti and into apartments a few blocks away. I stayed behind but bought an air conditioner. And an official electricity connection. I also purchased a mini fridge to stock my chocolates, but the shelves were soon used for the safekeeping of neighbours' baby milk bottles and half-cut cabbages. So I bought fridges for all of them. Along with microwaves and washing machines—and anything else they needed. White goods from money that was as black as the fish tattoos on the Mandal's men.

Everyone knew who we were now. And we were okay with that, given the police's blessings.

Rampal bought an expensive car and cheap suits with extra padding on the shoulders. I forced him to buy a new pair of specs, to which he reluctantly agreed. Rakhi continued managing the books, the money and Rampal. We also hired a team of accountants to help her launder the staggering amount of cash we churned.

Shamshu now had an army of coal miners from the neighbouring state working with him, though he still refused to let me out of his careful watch. On the rare occasions he couldn't watch me himself, he deployed his men—camouflaged as shanty residents—to do it for him. I hadn't yet been able to identify them yet, so he knew what he was doing.

The water trucks multiplied, and we had a monopoly over the sale of public works' water. We couldn't afford having others come in and sniff around. More government officials were on our books. Mobile tankers came loaded with cash, which was discreetly dumped into the reservoir at night. Then they were filled with water and distributed to our shanty for free. To most of our men, the water truck company was just another shell business to wash money. The fact that we literally washed the money there was a secret known only to a few. Soon we were supplying free water to neighbouring shanties as well; there was too much of it. Friday nights in our shanty became pizza nights, delivered free of cost by the Blue Bees.

The only thing keeping RC and Debroy from wiping me out was that 'evidence'. I had no doubt they were using every resource they had to find it. The only reason they hadn't was because it didn't exist. And Debroy hadn't spent enough time finding that out, given he was on his annual pilgrimage. And therein lay my biggest worry: the day he found nothing, there would be *nothing* left.

'Do you think we'll die soon, Johnny?' Rampal asked.

Rampal and I were the last ones left, finishing off the surviving bottle of scotch after a day-long house-warming party at his new apartment—a cosy nook on the seventh floor overlooking our shanty and the sprawl beyond.

It was the drinker's hour—that liminal time when the horizon clung to its shiny carpet of stars but knew it had to surrender to the great glob of fire that would soon birth through it. The earth below waited to welcome life, fresh from another completed lap.

Shamshu had left a few hours before, keen on getting sleep before another busy day tomorrow. Rakhi had given up an hour back, leaving just the two of us to waffle—a ritual now reduced in frequency but deeply missed.

The jamboree had been a riot; over 50 friends from the shanty had crammed into the apartment with food and drinks. Rampal and Rakhi's erstwhile neighbours had nothing but love and awe for them—not a single finger pointed to a clock ticking the late hours of morality. They looked at me expectantly, confident that soon we'd make them enough money to let them have their own homes, away from creaking asbestos and open gutters.

Naani, the 90-year-old grandma who smiled at me every single day since I'd moved to Hazaar Basti, had sat next to me, smiling, as I watched the merrymaking from a secluded corner. The list of things to worry about was long, and I'd just started reading it in my mind. Struggling to chew her pizza with her new set of teeth, she said, 'Never be ashamed of who you are, son. That's the quickest way to die.'

I didn't know if the advice was for my obvious indignation towards my physical shortcomings or my meteoric and questionable professional rise. What I did know was the advice had been practised for years before it was preached; it was backed empirically.

Now I pondered her words as I sat by an open French window, legs on the pane, gazing at a city draped in a quiet blanket.

'No. Why would we die?' I said.

'Because our hands are inside the tiger's mouth. It's only a question of when he will be hungry enough to chew them off, along with everything else. That's why.'

'Is that regret I smell on you?'

He pushed his new glasses up the bridge of his nose. 'Nah. I don't do regrets. Never have.'

'Really? None?'

'They give me diarrhoea. I do what I think is best. Then

I don't care. It might turn out to be wrong later, but in that moment when I do it, I'm as right as our prime minister. I stole my first phone inside a police station. Did I regret it? No.'

'Not even when the cops thrashed you for it?'

'Yeah, mastermind, maybe a little then. So what?'

'Regret is a loyal friend of mine,' I said. 'She keeps me company most nights.'

'Just because you didn't become a doctor? Who cares about those things?'

'I never wanted to become one. The nuns decided that for me,' I said. 'So no regrets there.'

'So what? Did you kill someone? You wouldn't be the first.'

'It's worse.'

'Spill it out, dumbass. You'll feel better.'

'I've tried...my whole life. I can't.'

'You and your fucking philosophies.'

Rakhi walked in, half-asleep, muttering something in Bengali that didn't sound pleasant. She went straight to the fridge and grabbed a bottle of water.

'I can't sleep. Our damn bed is too soft. Johnny, you were smart not to move into one of these,' she said, gulping big sips.

'Try the floor. I slept like a baby last night,' Rampal said.

'I don't like this, guys.' She stood in front of the open fridge, its light casting deep lines across her chubby face. 'We're growing too big, too fast. Maybe we should get out while we're still winning. I don't know if I can live with the Mandal using our channels to sell cocaine.'

'Don't worry. I'll find a way to stop it,' I said.

There was no way to stop it.

'I know you will, Johnny. You always do,' Rakhi said. 'Maybe it's just the bed Rampal overpaid for. I'll give it one more try. If it doesn't work, I'm going to butt into your party with a glass of whisky.' She shut the fridge door and walked off, muttering some more Bengali.

'When are you getting married?' I whispered.

'Married? To whom?'

'Shamshu.'

'Chutiya. Fucking half man.' Rampal smacked the back of my head. I laughed loudly, choking on my whisky.

'Shh… Let her get some sleep. It's been a lot for her these past few days.'

'See? You're practically married to each other. You probably sync your snoring patterns now. "Honey, it's my turn to hit the high note. Can you lower your octave?"' I laughed again. 'Why not make it official?'

Rampal smiled and sipped from his glass as he looked out of the window. 'Someday, my friend. When you decide we've made enough and you're ready to leave with us.'

'We'll never make enough. Because, honestly, we aren't doing this just for the money. You know that.'

'Yeah, yeah. You and your fucking claptrap about being counted. You know what I'd like to count? The wads of cash floating in that water tower.'

'All I can tell you is there's more paper in that reservoir now than water. Ask your wife. She knows exactly how much is up there.'

Rampal waved a hand in the air. 'Nah, no fun. There's something deeply satisfying about counting every goddamn note we've earned. I can't wait to do that.'

'I agree. But you remember what happened the last time we all tried to get up there. Better leave it to Shamshu and his men.'

'When you put it like that…'

'It *is* like that,' I said. 'I don't think I can survive another fall from that tower.'

'You mean you can't survive falling your lame ass on to me.'

'Yeah, that too.'

Rampal didn't smile, which was unusual; I was nearly offended.

'Johnny, how long before you think they find out?'

'Find out what?'

'You know exactly what.'

'The commissioner still believes I have something on him.'

'Which is why we breathe. Do you have a plan for when he finds out the truth?'

'Yes. It's a very simple plan. Unlike our complicated lives right now.'

'And what is that?'

'We run,' I said.

'If we can.'

'If we can.'

I finished my glass and poured another, promising myself it was the last.

Rampal looked at me and swigged his glass empty. 'The guys at the shanty want you to run in the municipal elections. Ready to become a *neta*?'

'I'm no politician. It's just their way of thanking us for the free water and pizza parties. You would make a much better one than me. You can talk until the cows come home and drink until they go back.'

'Huh. Soon, when we ask them to leave their houses and move across the river, they wouldn't be so cordial. This is their home. Their jobs, kids' schools…their life—it's all here. They will trust us and leave because we will promise them something better. You and I both know that they will get nothing.'

'Uprooting them pains me as much as it does you. If there was any way to stop this, I would. You think if we refuse to help the Mandal, they won't throw them out? It'll be worse. They'll use other tactics. All we're doing is making life peaceful for our neighbours and saving time and money for the Mandal. With this arrangement, at least they'll have another home.'

The non-existent evidence against Debroy wasn't my only problem. The more time we spent hobnobbing with the Mandal's men and chatting up the bottom feeders, the clearer their real business became.

Debroy had been right to call me a fool for believing they had grown so big and powerful just by selling cocaine. That they had their hands dipped deep in the political sauce of the city, churning it just right, only with the powder business. They were far more entrenched and invested in power corridors at the top floor.

The Mandal was more than a city mob; it was a real estate mafia. An enterprise with a land bank that would put dictators and monarchs to shame. If there was any piece of land worth owning in Kolkata, you could safely assume it belonged to them—or soon would. Thousands of hectares bought almost free of cost, taken from hapless owners through a sophisticated extortion process.

'Stop fooling yourself. They'll get nothing. You think I don't know why you do so much for the people in the shanty? It's your guilt, Johnny. And it isn't going to get washed away with a few washing machines.'

The Mandal had mastered the art of making people *want*

to sell—and for a price that wouldn't even buy them a grave anywhere in the city. Families who had owned and lived in their homes for generations suddenly found their localities turning into waking nightmares. Temporary slums of illegal immigrants sprung up where parks and playgrounds once existed. Sewers overflowed and dead dogs appeared in front of doorsteps. And if that didn't work, the molestations would start, followed by old men being beaten up in dark alleys and children being snatched from bus stops. Until the families were left with no choice but to leave.

Then came a seemingly unknown, small real estate company, happy to help the helpless by buying out their houses. The properties changed hands a few times and paper trails blurred. Eventually, the houses were owned by one of the biggest real estate companies, primed for overpriced, high-rise apartments in a couple of years. These 'oases in the city' or 'urban heavens' were part of a carefully controlled supply of residential units making high real estate prices an unwanted, yet legitimate, son of India's booming economy. They were eventually bought by a callow generation that thrived on gigabytes and 52-week highs.

Everyone went home happy.

Except those left without one.

I'd underestimated the Mandal, and my deal with RC had come back to haunt me. We didn't have a plan B. The shanty residents would be replaced by the Mandal's people, who would infiltrate neighbouring localities that currently had a high-price sticker on them. And the churn would begin. While I didn't care about the Mandal making billions and corporate junkies overpaying for their sliver of skyline, I shuddered to think what would happen to my resettled neighbours. RC wasn't going to cut them a fair deal; that much was clear. He hadn't gotten to where he was by honouring deals.

'Debroy is back from his pilgrimage. Says he has good news and will meet us soon,' I said.

'Maybe they're going to give us more territory once the shanty is cleared. Like RC promised. We're doing more than their cocaine business in the city.'

'I doubt that very much. At some point, the scales will tip and they'll take their chance to call my bluff. I'm hoping by then we'll become valuable enough to them—a necessary evil.'

'That's wishful thinking, my friend.'

'It is,' I said. 'But it's all I have right now.'

The life I'd left behind—that of the 'Mini Painkiller'—was simple and linear. I had lived in the shadows that were small and inconsequential. But I had grown tired of that; like Rampal had said, I wanted to be counted. So I chased potency and found myself tangled in knots—a million slithery snakes entwined together. These knots, and the decisions I had to make to untie them, as well as the significant implications they had on everyone, cast an unparalleled inebriation on me.

One that was impossible to sleep off. A spell I wasn't ready to break.

Because sobriety revealed a different monster. A coward who ran.

Rampal leaned back and scratched his forehead. 'Maybe we're just overthinking it. Maybe we finally have arrived on the big stage.'

'Debroy was unusually pleasant on the phone. He's usually full of doom and threats, frustrated that he can't cut me into pieces.'

'If he's finally figured out a way to do that, make your peace with the machete. You'd be half the work for him anyway.'

I chuckled. 'Glad my physical limitations will finally be of some use.'

'I'm telling you, keep away from that rascal. You never know when he'll lose his patience.'

'You know we can't afford that.'

Rampal sighed. 'Then what should we do?'

I drained my glass and stood up. 'If things go south, remember our *simple plan*,' I said, turning towards the door. 'Goodnight, my friend. Go snore with your wife now.'

19 A Sliver of Hope

⁑Katherine⁑

Imaan and I spent days anxiously waiting for the investigator to call. We ordered room service and watched HBO reruns. I spent minutes staring at myself in the mirror, a toothbrush dangling from my frothy mouth, and hours giving up, only to pull myself back together again.

Imaan confiscated my phone but allowed me to send several texts to the investigator and one to Mr Elenburg that just said, 'I'm okay.'

Even if I could have told Mr Elenburg where I was and what I planned to do, he'd call it suicide. But I was beyond that. My plan had holes, but it was the only one I had. And it beat doing nothing. I wasn't just a daughter searching for her mother. I was on the greatest hunt of all: the quest to find myself.

So far, I'd failed with every leaden step I took. I had to find the will to leap. And pray gravity would turn a blind eye to me, busy dragging others down.

The days were long. I snorted most of the coke Imaan got, waiting for the damn phone to ring. It was one of the worst blows I'd ever had, but it was enough for me to find and hold on to a sliver of hope. Imaan was polite but firm—a departure from the ever-smiling, unassuming and charming man he'd started off as. But he still had *honour*. He was still Imaan, as far as I was concerned.

We slept in separate beds and talked mostly about his son, Akhil. How he was the sharpest kid in his class but the laziest at home. How Imaan wanted him to see the world and read 'thick books' and speak English like the news anchors did. Simple dreams of a love so strong.

Why didn't I deserve that kind of love? Why did my dad leave me?

I cried myself to sleep every night. And every time Imaan heard me, he offered me a glass of water and dropped his eyes when I didn't take it. He couldn't sleep either; I heard him grunting and tossing most nights. With no call from the investigator or the Mandal, I was out of hope. *And* powder.

Imaan paced around the room, mumbling in his language. Then he turned to me. 'I cannot wait anymore. I'm taking you to them.'

That's when my phone rang. It was Bijoy, the investigator. I arranged a time for him to come to the hotel, and then waited for him to turn up.

When he did, I unleashed a barrage of questions on him. 'Where the hell have you been? Why haven't you been taking my calls? Where's my mother? Is she okay?'

Bijoy seemed unaffected by them. He slouched comfortably on the couch while Imaan and I stood next to him. 'We were supposed to meet a couple of weeks back. Do you have *any* information?'

Still no answer. Instead, he sank deeper into the couch and crossed his legs, resting his face in one hand. I sat down on the edge of the bed while Imaan moved to the window. Bijoy was a well-built, middle-aged man, as serious as they came, with a receding hairline and a thick, silver-grey moustache that added body to his narrow, pale face. Oversized, thick-framed glasses covered a slight squint; a diamond-studded earring glistened on his right ear.

'What do you do for a living, madam?' he finally asked.

'What?'

He cleared his throat. 'What is your profession? How do you earn your bread?'

'I...write.'

'Write. Fantastic. And tell me...' He cleared his throat again; these recurring interjections were longer than a playful 'ahem' but briefer than a sickly hawk. Just long enough to make me think he was about to read aloud the Declaration of Independence. 'When you are in the middle of writing, do you reach out to agents, publishers, interviewers, claiming to have a finished manuscript?'

'What news do you have about my mother?'

Bijoy looked at Imaan, then back at me.

'It's okay. He's on our side. Go ahead,' I said.

He chuckled. 'I'm sure he is...' Another throat clearing. 'The good news is your mother is alive. The bad news—'

I stood up. The room warped. Shiny oversized heels; scattered shoe trees; stolen apple pies and burnt tongues.

'Hold on,' I said, then rushed to the washroom and broke down. I couldn't control the tears that had been patient with me so far. But I had to pull myself together; there was no time to waste. I washed and wiped my face, and stepped back into the room.

Imaan was staring at the floor while Bijoy, now sitting upright, was observing the ceiling.

'I'm sorry. I just... How do you know she's alive?' I asked, sinking back on to the bed. Imaan handed me a handkerchief, which I grabbed without looking at him.

'I got myself recruited into the Mandal—the fish gang, as some call it—posing as an illegal immigrant from Bangladesh.'

Rolling up his shirtsleeve, he showed us a tattoo of a fish on his forearm, similar to the one I'd seen on Imaan's car. 'For the past week, I've been trying to get deeper into their operations, obtaining whatever information I could about your mother. There's enough chatter, but the credible version is that they have her in custody.'

'Do you know where?'

'Yes, the House of Dolls.'

The place sounded sickening.

'Can you take me there?'

'Madam, this isn't a local band of jokers we're dealing with. I would strongly suggest you leave the city. I got out at the right time. They'd started getting suspicious and would have found out who I am.'

'Good,' I said.

'Good?'

'You don't have to go back undercover—you have to go as yourself. I have a plan, and I'll need you to help us.'

Bijoy listened silently, his fingers grinding against one another the whole time. It took me a few minutes and the promise of lots of money to convince him. But he still seemed worried.

'Madam, while I'm impressed with your courage and fearlessness, I must tell you'—he cleared his throat—'chances are you won't make out of there alive. If I smell trouble, I'll find a way to escape—with or without you. Why don't you just leave?'

'Don't worry,' Imaan chimed in. 'I'll protect her. Just do what she asks.'

'If I were you,' Bijoy said, looking at me, 'I would be very worried.'

'Jimi and his holy mother, I'm very, very worried. But you aren't me.' I turned to Imaan. 'Imaan, make the call.'

20 The House of Dolls – Part I

✦Katherine✦

The next day, we drove to the address the Mandal had given Imaan. Dark clouds loomed overhead, carrying thunderous reminders of inevitable rain. Shopkeepers hurriedly withdrew their wares from the streets and shut shops. A uniformed worker pried open manhole covers, readying the drains for a sold-out show. At turn signals, child hawkers darted between cars, selling transparent raincoats identical to the ones they wore. It was children like these my mother had tried to help before she was taken.

Imaan sat in the front seat next to Bijoy, who was driving. He fiddled with the car lock and rolled the windows up and down. Each time he did, sounds of grumbling engines and insistent horns seeped in like waves. I wanted to shut it all out and float on my own waves, but I was out of snow.

Maybe that was a good thing.

'We need you to be your best version'—Mr Elenburg's words rang loudly in my head. I hoped the version of me without coke in her bloodstream would be enough. So far, I was surprisingly calm, almost confident that my plan, perforated with question marks and cul-de-sacs, would somehow work.

'Mr Bijoy, remember—we don't make any moves before I see my son,' Imaan said.

'And my mother, Imaan,' I corrected.

Imaan turned to look at me. 'Don't worry, madam. If she there, we go back with her.'

I still believed him.

'I know my part well, and it's not the first time I'm doing it, friends.' Bijoy cleared his throat and shot me a look. 'The question is, are you ready for it? We can't afford mistakes. If they smell something fishy, they won't ask us questions; they will just kill.'

'That helps,' I muttered.

'Just remember your mother's face,' Imaan said. 'I do same with my son.'

I smiled. 'Thanks.'

Bijoy pulled into a narrow street and parked. 'We are here. Imaan, please lead the way.'

'No, you both go ahead of me. You are my prisoners,' he replied, taking out his gun. 'Mr Bijoy, please hide your gun; use when time is right.'

Bijoy nodded and tucked it away.

Flashes ran amok in the sky, pursued by distant rumbles. We entered a lane lined with unfinished clay sculptures of a goddess with a million hands and beautiful wide eyes. Left outside to bake in the sun, they had now been hastily covered with blue tarps. A little farther down the lane, we reached a set of concrete steps that led to four old wooden doors. Only one was open.

'We are here,' Imaan said, stopping to make a call.

The doors were carved with intricate floral designs and framed by hollow arches. Between them, bare-bricked columns jutted out. They were skirted with capitals and bases that had Roman, maybe Tuscan, insignias. Three of the doors had long since fused into the wall, their hinges rusted shut. On top of the three-storey building, a crumbling Romanesque statue—draped in a fustanella—gazed down at us, flanked by equally ruined statues of naked women. Some had their arms…bitten off?…while others had half a head missing. Like shadows from the erstwhile, they watched over their unwanted, fidgety visitors.

'*Pratima Bari*,' Bijoy said.

'What?' I said, still staring up at the statues.

'The name of the building. Locals call it'—he cleared his throat again—'the House of Dolls.'

'Sounds haunted,' I said.

'It is. It's a heritage building, abandoned years ago after the last owner was found dead on the terrace.'

'So the owner haunts this place?'

'No, it's the dolls.'

'What dolls?'

'The ones on top of the building,' Bijoy said, pointing. 'There are more inside.'

I followed his gaze, then turned back to him. 'Is that what they tell the children?'

'This building is over a hundred years old. It was once a warehouse for spices and silk, servicing a nearby port. Legend has it that the wealthy babus, traders and sailors brought women here for their carnal callings. When the fun was over, the women were killed and buried here. They say one can still hear their screams and howls at night. The statues you see on top of the terrace, and the ones you will see inside, are a constant reminder of those dead dolls.'

'You seriously believe all this? All I see is an English architect in love with Roman architecture.'

'Partially. The intricate Roman architecture, the elaborate design and the overall grandeur couldn't have been for just a warehouse. It was a bordello, all right.'

'So an abandoned brothel and warehouse, right in the middle of the city, is now used by the city's underworld? Isn't that a bit too cliché?'

'Truth is the biggest cliché, madam.'

I couldn't disagree with him.

'There were three other historical warehouses and structures down the street,' Bijoy continued. 'Most of them, except this one, were gutted by mysterious fires and have been redeveloped into glitzy modern spaces by private companies. Some still have a touch of colonialism left in them.'

'Thanks to façadism,' I said. 'I noticed them on the way. You know your history and architecture well.'

'And by the sound of it, you do too.'

I smiled. 'I do. But nothing beats seeing it with your own eyes.'

'Then you should also know—this building has no owner, yet the government hasn't touched it, let alone preserve it or redevelop it. Few know about it. Even fewer talk about it. What does that tell you?'

'Perfect address for the Mandal.'

Bijoy smiled. 'The mafia. Dead people. A haunted house. A strange country. Aren't you scared?'

'Witless and shitless.'

'Then why not go back? You still can.'

I shrugged. 'Guess I like it.'

'You should walk away from all this.'

'Appreciate your concern,' I replied, then tried to shift the conversation. 'Is this where you were undercover?'

'No, I was stationed on the other side of the river.' He glanced at Imaan. 'What's taking him so much time?'

We turned to Imaan, who had just finished speaking on his phone. He looked at us and said, 'Time to go inside.'

I stared at him for a second, wishing we were still driving through the streets of Kolkata. My toes felt cold.

He held my gaze and said, 'I'm sorry for all this.'

'I'm not.'

We stepped through the open door and into the darkness. As my eyes adjusted to the dim light seeping in through a small, meshed ventilator, I spotted a staircase ahead, its banister carved with rectangular patterns.

'Up,' Imaan instructed. He had his gun out.

As we climbed, the mezzanine level revealed a row of doors with the same rectangular woodwork as that on the wall. They were well camouflaged, but for the heavy locks that hung on them like shiny, sleeping vampires. The wooden stairs creaked loudly beneath our weight, each step announcing our arrival to whoever was waiting for us on the other side.

At the end of the stairs, a gush of grey daylight greeted us, streaming in through an open door. Beyond it lay a courtyard, encircled by a staggering gallimaufry of Romanesque pillars. Intricate arches similar to the ones outside but far more elaborate connected them in an eerie arcade. Carved into each keystone above the arches was the identical face of a bearded man with fearful eyes; a fountain of flowers, leaves and vines cascaded from his hair.

Some columns had eroded, revealing the cracked bricks beneath, while the fortunate ones still bore their fluted shafts intact. The floor overlooking the courtyard had a colonnade, whitewashed carelessly, and wooden blinds, half-hanging from the ceiling in a state of arrested decay. Behind them were doors that lined the corridor like shuttered storefronts on a promenade.

The three of us stood in the middle of the courtyard, trying hard to look beyond the arcade but finding only darkness. A white cat darted past, slipping behind a column just as a thunder cracked.

'Dark, dark! The horror of darkness, like a shroud, wraps me and bears me on through mist and cloud.' A voice echoed beyond the columns, hollow and theatrical. 'Ah me, ah me! What spasms athwart me shoot? What pangs of agonizing memory?' A revolting squeal followed—high, unnatural—swelling before fading into silence.

Drops of water landed on my goose-bumped arms. Moments later, they were followed by an army of giant fury that had turned weary of being a dark cloud.

From the darkness beyond the pillars, a lanky figure emerged. Gaunt and dark-skinned, the man approached us, water dripping from his long ears on to a narrow face split by a smile stained red with tobacco. Four men followed, stone-faced and armed.

'Miss, it is an utter pleasure to finally meet you,' he said, stepping forward and extending his hand. 'I'm sorry that it is under such circumstances.'

I obliged reluctantly, wiping the water from my brows. 'Who are you?'

'That's not relevant. The better question is—who are *you*? Elene McCarthy or Katherine Gladwell?' He smiled. 'I believe you're quite a scholar, adept in languages and such. Always a delight to meet such people. I thought you'd find this venue rather fitting. And the timing is perfect; even the rain gods agree.'

He folded his hands and tilted his head back, letting water splash across his face. 'It's one of my favourite jaunts; so much history stored within its walls. A lot of it even created by us.' He let out that high-pitched squeal again.

'I'm sure,' I said, forcing a smile.

'I hope our friend here didn't trouble you too much,' he added, gesturing at Imaan without looking at him.

'Where's my mother? Release her now and we'll leave this place—'

'Stop talking,' Imaan interrupted.

This wasn't how it was supposed to go. I stopped. Rain pooled around our feet, forming puddles that threatened to grow into a pond.

Imaan continued. 'As I told your men, I found rat in your team and caught him for you.' He pointed at a motionless Bijoy standing next to me. 'Now please let my son go.'

The lanky man looked at Imaan for the first time. 'What exactly were you asked to do, my friend?'

'Be with the girl as bodyguard, not let her find anything and not let anyone find her. I did my best and—'

'She found more than she should have, didn't she?' said the man, cutting Imaan off. Then he turned towards me. 'You're very sharp, Ms Gladwell. My compliments.'

'I cannot help that she find out who I was. I did what you ask me. I also found you traitor. Now give me back my son!' Imaan said, raising his gun.

'I'm sorry, but I can't do that.'

'Then you die. I don't care what happens to me.'

Imaan cocked his gun. I glanced at Bijoy, hoping he'd do something, but he stood frozen, likely mapping an escape route.

'Oedipus!' I shouted.

'What?' The lanky man looked shocked. Imaan turned towards me, looking confused.

'*Oedipus Rex* by Sophocles. The line about darkness,' I said, hoping to distract the man by naming the play and buy us some time before things got worse.

He frowned, as if a prized possession had been taken away from him.

'I seem to be bumping into too many literary geniuses lately,' he said, slowly walking around the courtyard, indifferent to Imaan's gun.

'Please. We don't have anything against you or what you do. Just let them go. And then we'll leave this godforsaken place forever.'

I shivered, completely drenched.

'*We*? Are you now a messiah for all missing people, Ms Gladwell? You shouldn't have come to this city. What were you thinking? That you'd fight evil, rescue your mother and win all your battles? Is that how easy things are in New York?'

'What has she done to you?' I needed to keep him talking until a way out presented itself.

'Why, don't you know? She took our boys away. And we don't like anything taken from us. A lot of blood and sweat goes into what we build. Well, more blood than sweat, but please don't judge us.' He squealed loudly again.

'Then why have you kept her alive?'

'I say there's no darkness but ignorance,' he quoted, lifting his arms to the rain, eyes straining to stay open against the downpour. 'I wish you could see light, but alas—darkness is all you'll see for a long, long time. Another unfortunate addition to the House of Dolls.'

'Enough!' Imaan took a step closer, gun raised. 'My son, get him out! Where is he?'

The man still looked unperturbed.

'Imaan, back down,' I said as calmly as I could.

'You know why we chose you and not one of our men to *assist* Ms Gladwell? Because you're like a hapless dog, desperate for love and affection. That works well with the ladies.'

'My son!' Imaan screamed.

'He's gone!' the man thundered. 'Forever. Never to come back. You have to pay for your mistakes. We'll make a soldier out of him.'

Imaan lowered his gun and turned to me, a tragic smile ghosting his lips. 'Zero choices, madam.'

He then swung his gun back towards the lanky man, but before he could pull the trigger, a shot rang out. Then another.

Imaan collapsed immediately.

I stood frozen, watching him die as Bijoy lowered his gun, blinking repeatedly to clear Imaan's splattered blood from my eyes.

21 The House of Dolls – Part II

.+ Johnny +.

'Why not make MMDA instead of these amphetamines?' Dr Verma asked. 'They're cheaper, more addictive and—'

'And fatal,' I interrupted. 'You know MMDA crosses the blood-brain barrier faster. And the other toxic chemicals required to make it ensure disastrous side effects.'

We stood in the mezzanine-level room overlooking the laboratory through a glass wall—a place that had started as an artisanal lab but had grown to a medical-grade production shop. Bright horizontal lights skirted the pale yellow walls that enclosed a column-less open hall. Humongous exhausts emerged from gleaming cooking chambers and disappeared behind the walls. Colourful pipes snaked across the floor, vined up the walls and escaped through closed ventilators. Autoclaves, vacuum chambers and stacks of empty amber vials occupied most of the tables, alongside beakers, Florence flasks and tubes.

My friends and I had created this. It was ours.

'Murder is murder,' Dr Verma replied, 'whether you slit someone's throat or strangle them. The messier one doesn't carry a greater punishment. The amphetamines we make are still illegal. Why not expand the menu and make more money before someone else does?'

'We don't sell illegal drugs,' I corrected him. 'We illegally sell legal medicines used for cognitive enhancement in a controlled fashion by the medical fraternity. All we're doing is giving everyone a chance to be more productive and attentive, to live life a little more fully. Even if one is addicted to it, it is easily reversible. And the side effects are manageable, unlike meth and its other cousins.'

Dr Verma shook his head, his wig slipping slightly to one side. 'That just helps you sleep better at night, doesn't it?'

'No, Dr Verma, it helps me stay awake. *This* is my amphetamine,' I said, pointing to the lab below. 'Everyone has a right to chase their dreams. I had a right to be someone, and I grabbed the only opportunity I had.'

'And I respect you for that. But you have to be ambitious. You can't have one foot in and one foot out. I closed my clinic and committed fully. Now it's time to go to the next level. The Mandal is already using our distribution to sell cocaine. Why not sell it ourselves and make ten times more? Ten times more, Johnny!'

'That will never happen. If you have a problem with that, you're free to leave. I can find another assistant.'

He waved his hands in the air. 'No, no, you misunderstand me. I was just suggesting ways of multiplying the money. The whole world is doing it anyway. Business requires protection from unknown conspirators. You never know where they'll come from.'

'I'll ask you if I need any business advice. Now, did you replace the boiling flasks and the gas cylinders?'

'Yes,' Dr Verma replied. He adjusted his wig and walked out slowly.

Just then, Rakhi and Shamshu barged in.

'Rampal's gone!' Rakhi screamed. 'They took him!'

'When? Where?'

'I don't know. I don't... He said this would happen. We should have run away. This is my fault...' She collapsed and I rushed to catch her before she hit the ground.

'Rakhi, listen to me. When did it happen? Did they say where they were taking him?'

'He was on his usual run to the clinics. He called to ask me about a new TV he liked. Then something happened. I heard him shouting, cursing, muffled sounds. The phone disconnected. It's been off since then. It's them. I'm sure it's them. Do something, Johnny!'

'Don't worry. I'll get him back. Shamshu, did he have protection?'

'Yes, as always,' he replied. 'But they're nowhere to be found, and their phones are also off.'

I guided Rakhi towards a couch and got her some water, using the time to understand what could have happened.

'Johnny, they came to the shanty this morning and raided your house,' Shamshu informed me.

'Stay with Rakhi. I'm going to call Debroy.' As I was about to walk out, I turned to Rakhi and said, 'We'll get him back. I promise.'

Rakhi nodded half-heartedly.

Shamshu followed me out and closed the door behind us. 'I should come with you. You'll need me if things go bad.'

'You need to protect her more than anyone else, Shamshu. They won't do anything to me. They can't. Just make sure she's okay.'

'Take the guys outside with you.'

'If they mean to harm me, those guys won't stop them. They'll just die for nothing. I'm going alone.'

'Johnny, this is suicide.'

'Then let it be just one.'

'Let's think it through, I might—'

'I've thought about this every single day since we agreed to jump into this,' I said. 'I was a fool to think it was a question of *if.* It was always a question of *when.* I have to get Rampal back, whatever it takes. Stay here with Rakhi, and if you don't hear from me soon, do three things for me.'

'Sure,' Shamshu said. 'Anything.'

'One: get all the money out of the water tank and cash out every stock and investment we have. There's over ₹10 crore there. Split half between you and Rakhi and divide the other half equally among our guys and the people in the shanty. Two: burn this lab down to ashes. Can you do that?'

'Johnny, you are being hasty.'

'Our luck has run out. This is the only way. Can you do this for me?'

He nodded vigorously. 'Yes!'

'Good. Third: wrap everything up and leave town forever. Make sure Rakhi does too.'

Shamshu nodded, his head low.

'Thank you for everything, my friend. You're our pillar. I hope you find peace with your bees in the village.' I held my hand out, but Shamshu knelt and hugged me.

'Try to stay alive,' he said.

'Don't worry; I have a lot of practice,' I replied, pulling myself from his crushing embrace and leaving.

On my way out of the lab, I called Debroy. He picked up on my third attempt.

'Mr Johnny, to what do I owe the honour of hearing from the amphetamine king of Kolkata?' he said.

'Cut the crap, Commissioner. Where's Rampal?'

'Oh, he's just giving me some company while I read a most fascinating play. Your friend, however, is a very impatient listener. The things I have to do to hold his attention.'

'Listen, he's just a kid. If you even look at him again, I'm going to release the evidence, like I told you.'

'That's the thing. I keep asking this gentleman about that evidence, and he seems to have nothing to say about it. Not for long, though. Soon he'll talk.'

'What do you want?'

'Don't ask stupid questions,' Debroy snapped. 'It insults me. You know what I want. I'm almost sure you don't have shit against me. The advantage of being a commissioner is that I get to use all the resources at my disposal. My guys have been watching and listening to you and your friends for weeks, and there's nothing that makes me believe you have anything. But on the off chance that you do, my suggestion is that you bring it along when you come to say hello. And your friend... Well, whatever is left of him.'

'Debroy, I'll—'

'Stop threatening a police commissioner. And remember, Rampal lives only if I see something I like.'

'Where?'

'The House of Dolls, 30 minutes. I'm on the last act of the play, Johnny. Don't be late. Once the climax is over, there are no characters left.'

He squealed and disconnected.

◆

Forty minutes later, I reached the House of Dolls, which looked like it would collapse any day. I climbed a dark set of stairs leading to an open courtyard. Debroy was there, prancing around, talking loudly on the phone while half a dozen cops stood by. I couldn't see Rampal anywhere.

'Don't worry. I know what needs to be done,' Debroy said into the phone before hanging up. Seeing me, he raised his arms and called out, 'Johnny Johnny! You certainly were telling lies. Now where is your ha-ha-ha?'

'I'm not lying. I have the video and you don't look too good in it.'

'So tell me, where is this video?'

'I've instructed my—'

'Stop the circus,' he scoffed, then gestured to his men.

One of the cops pushed out a wheelchair. Rampal, unconscious, was tied to it. His head slumped forward, blood dripping from his temple. His arms were covered in fresh, jagged cuts. He groaned, trying to lift his head, but couldn't.

'Show me the video now. Or he dies.'

I regretted the day I convinced him to be the kings of the world.

'Let him go, please. He's done nothing.'

'Life's but a walking shadow, a poor player. That struts and frets his hour upon the stage, and then is heard no more. It is a tale told by an idiot, full of sound and fury, signifying nothing.'

'Stop the fucking riddles and let him go. I'll give you everything—all the money.'

Debroy smiled. 'I got you this time, Johnny. I promised you the next quote I came up with would be a stranger to you. And it is, isn't it? Now, here is a generous offer from me to you.'

He picked up the machete from a table next to him and wielded it in the air.

'No, no, no. Not him. Please, Commissioner, don't.'

I stood frozen, just a few yards from Rampal. A few men came to hold me, but they didn't need to. My legs had abandoned me. Fear had swallowed them whole, and I was their willing prisoner.

'Okay, I won't, Johnny. But only if you tell me where the quote is from. Name the play, and I'll let him live.'

'What?'

'Ten seconds.'

I shook my head violently. 'I don't know. I don't know. You win. I don't...I don't remember!'

'Okay, do you have the video then?'

'No. I lied, okay? I don't have a video. It was all a bluff. Kill me. Let him go. Please!' I shouted.

Life surged through my legs, and I struggled, kicking wildly, hoping to escape from the clutches of the cops and run to Rampal; but I couldn't. They picked me up like a ragged doll.

'Apart from the video, do you have anything else that doesn't belong to you?'

'No, I swear on my life. I have nothing on you. I was there that night and thought I could use it to protect my business. But it was just me, not Rampal.'

'I believe you now, my friend. I believe you.' Debroy strolled towards Rampal, rested the machete against his throat, and said, 'Last chance. Where is the quote from?'

Rampal finally looked up and gave me a resigned smile.

'I don't know,' I said. 'I fucking don't—'

The machete sliced clean.

Rampal's body spasmed, blood gushing from his throat, soaking his shirt, dripping down the chair and pooling beneath him. Then he became absolutely still and his head drooped forward, lifeless.

My friend was gone.

'I told you to be careful what you wish for,' Debroy sneered at me. He turned to his men and said, 'Get rid of the body. Put Johnny in one of the rooms...and make him speak.'

They dragged me away from Rampal and tossed me into darkness.

22 A Curious Juxtaposition – Part I

✢Katherine✢

A t least a week had passed since I'd been locked in this dark room. May be three; I wasn't sure.

Surprisingly, they treated me well. The lanky man—cold-hearted murderer that he was—and his team didn't lay a hand on me. They provided me with regular meals, bottled water and even the occasional desserts and fruits. It was better than the guest house I'd stayed in. But their real generosity lay in the never-ending supply of coke. I snorted lines every time I neared reality, cocooning myself in tender clouds, careful never to escape it.

The room smelled of wet chalk, and I could hear the rain falling outside every few hours. Each day, a sliver of light seeped in through the bottom of the door and traced itself back before it reached my bed. As I lay there, all I did was stare at a small ventilation window on the wall and hum Indian songs that seemed to come from nowhere. The concrete walls had hand-carved messages in a language I couldn't understand and random sketches of a face throughout—a dreary face with big droopy eyes and a long jagged jaw. The guest who had checked in before me had either been enraged or enamoured by it. *How many days of confinement does it take to carve faces on walls?*

'Kath, come here and help me with the roses, will you, honey?' My mother was in her greenhouse, pruning plants that always looked the same to me.

'I want to do Java, Mom.'

'You can learn computers later, honey. C'mon. Hold these stems and plant them after I loosen the soil.'

'Will Daddy be home for dinner?'

'He should be. Now let's get some of these geraniums done, shall we?'

'But it stinks in here, Mom.'

She smiled. 'Not everything that stinks is bad.'

'But Daddy said he'll—'

'You can ask him when he comes. Now be a good girl. Remember to keep a distance of about eight inches between each stem.'

'How long is eight inches?' I asked.

'Um, the length of my hand.'

Your hands, I miss them.

'Now let's finish planting these so they'll bloom by—'

'Daddy promised to take me hunting on Thanksgiving. He also said he'd take me across the country on his railroad when I'm big enough.'

'He did now, did he?'

A loud slam yanked me back to reality. I thought I'd done a spectacular job of erasing every memory I'd had of my dad. But like relentless ants, every few years they crawled back into my head and haunted me. Remembering him meant accepting that once, long ago, he was there. And then he wasn't. The noise on the other side of the wall had come to my rescue at the perfect time.

I heard someone sob, then drag their body across the floor, followed by a loud thud.

'Hello? Who's there?' I whispered, looking up at the ventilator.

No one answered. The sobs grew louder, interspersed with feeble groans. My new neighbour, it seemed, was hurt badly. Maybe I could sneak in a few pouches of coke through the small ventilator; I had more than enough to snort myself to death.

'Do you understand English?'

Silence; then the sobs and groans stopped. Was the prisoner dead?

'Can you hear me?' I asked.

No reply again.

I drifted into asleep. And dreamt of the lanky man yelling at me.

'Traitors don't last long in our neck of the woods.'

He glared at Imaan, who lay dead on the floor, half submerged in bloodied water rising fast. The walls caved in as the water level rose. Imaan's body turned into sand and dissolved.

I looked down at the furious water but saw no reflection. As the water level reached our faces, the lanky man squealed and dipped his head under, leaving me alone. I took a deep breath and followed, but he was gone. There was nothing in the water except brittle rose petals dissolving into blood.

I tried coming up for air but couldn't move.

Just as water filled my lungs, I opened my eyes and saw the faces on the wall staring at me. I didn't hear my scream, but I was sure that somewhere between my nightmare and waking up, I had let out a helpless whimper.

A flickering yellow light had replaced the daylight under the door. The room was still.

I remembered my new, mysterious neighbour.

'Hello? Are you still there? I've been kidnapped. I need help.'

I immediately realized how stupid and selfish I sounded.

'How are you feeling?' Still stupid.

No response. Maybe the prisoner had escaped—or died, and they had taken the body away.

Why were they keeping me alive?

I gave up and laid out crooked lines of powder on my hand. Just as I was about to snort, a thick, breathy, baritone filled the room.

'Macbeth.'

'What? Who are you?'

'It was fucking Macbeth.'

'What was Macbeth?' Was he calling himself that? Maybe he was crazy.

'I couldn't remember.' The voice grew louder. 'I killed him. I slit his throat. The name of the play was fucking *Macbeth*!'

'I'm sorry; I don't understand. What is your name? Are you hurt?'

And then that deep, sad voice was gone.

♦

A few nights passed. Food arrived every three hours and cocaine every hour. My neighbour had gone silent on me.

I tried everything—'Do you like Kolkata?' 'Do you want some cocaine?' 'Are you alone?'—but all I got were indifferent groans and moans.

Every now and then, I'd hear him move, go to the bathroom, cough feebly, bang on his door, utter profanities and throw objects. I was just happy he was there, even though he wouldn't talk to me. I threw a few pouches of coke through the ventilator and pressed my ear against the wall to hear the sound of tearing plastic or a sharp inhale, but nothing happened. He didn't know what he was missing.

Hours blurred into nothing when he finally spoke again.

'I was never meant to be anything. I should have killed myself that day. To think...we could... My fault...murdered him... I should have remained no one...trying to make my shadow longer... What was I thinking?'

Something shattered against the common wall, making me flinch. I hoped he'd say more but only silence followed.

Sometime later, he spoke again, clearer and louder this time. 'My name is Johnny,' he said. 'And I hate this city.'

'I'm sorry to hear that, Johnny.' My neighbour wasn't too chatty when I asked him questions, so I let him lead a much-needed conversation.

'Yeah, me too...me too.'

'I'm Katherine.' 'Elene' had no use for me; it never did. 'How long have you been in here?'

'Your accent...American?'

'As apple pie. Came to Kolkata a few weeks ago.'

'And what did you do to earn your...luxury suite?' he asked.

'I tried to get my mother back. You?'

'Huh. I tried to be a hero, but wrecked everyone's lives instead.'

'What do you mean?' I bit my lip, having asked a question again.

And just like that, he stopped talking for another day. Time dripped, slow and syrupy. Or maybe it moved too fast, and I'd lost the ability to tell. I now appreciated the merits of drawing pictures and scribbling thoughts on a wall, but wasn't motivated enough to find something to carve with.

Then I heard Johnny scream and struggle against several people who had barged into his room. They dragged him out and shut the door.

I braced for them to come for me next.

They didn't.

Hours later, his door slammed shut again.

A ragged breath. Then—rage. 'Kill me, you fucking cowards! What are you waiting for? I told you I don't have any evidence!' he yelled.

He then walked over to the wall. 'You wanna know why I'm here? Because I tried to matter. Because I wanted to be someone. Because I was sick of how people looked at me. But I guess that was too much to ask for a fucking dwarf, wasn't it? They took everything from me. They killed my best friend. I'll burn this city down…I will burn this—'

He howled in pain, the sound echoing through a ruinous promenade and across a courtyard where men were eliminated without a fuss and rains washed their blood away, forever.

A dwarf.

I could picture him, curled up in a corner, heaving and fidgeting constantly.

Another day in the dark.

A weaker sun seeped in through the bottom of the door. It was overcast outside; I could smell it—the unmistakable whiff of air pregnant with water, ready to deliver. I found a spoon to carve something into the wall.

'I'm sorry. I have no idea what I said to you.' That deep, pained voice spoke again.

'It's fine. Snort some coke. It helps.'

'Huh. Cocaine destroyed everything,' he said. 'Any chance you have chocolates? Dark, preferably.'

'I don't. But I can ask them to get me some.'

His bed creaked, and he groaned loudly. 'How can they get away with this?' he whispered. 'Is it that…easy?'

'Listen, I feel your pain. But for the love of God, I don't

know what you're talking about.'

'It's a long story.'

'Then we're in luck,' I said. 'We have our calendars fairly open.'

◆

Between his daily trips to the torture room, we swapped our crazy chronicles bit by bit. Scraps from the past interwoven with lessons the present had taught us. A new chapter every day, from a thriller with an unwritten climax.

Him—an orphaned dwarf who never got to be a child, who could have become a doctor but, instead, chose to thrive in the city's dark underworld. And then paid for it.

Me—just a fatherless, doped-out fugitive looking for her mother, running into a minefield of mistakes. At the least, I was consistent.

'Seeing a man die…it changes you. I can't explain how, but I feel like I've seen everything there is to see. Nothing can be more helpless, more…moving than seeing life wither away so easily. All that we strive for, fight for, cry for, love and hate—it's all suddenly…meaningless.' I paused and snuffed a line. 'Are you there, Johnny?'

'Yes.'

'They killed him. Right in front of me. A father trying to save his son at any cost—they killed him. Now his son, lost in a world full of animals, will blame himself forever. It's not his fault. It's not his fault!' I wailed. 'I used him. *I* killed him.'

'Seeing someone die is one thing,' Johnny said quietly. 'Doing it is a whole different ball game.'

I flinched. 'Have…you?' I asked. Was I swapping life stories and inner demons with a serial killer?

'How is it in your country?' he asked instead. 'Your life? White picket fences and trash pickups on Fridays like they show in the movies?'

'It's not as pretty as you think.'

'Huh. People just can't stop wanting more. Have security? Great, now let's crave love and happiness. Have that too? Fantastic, let's find peace. Done that? Okay, time to save the world then—icebergs are melting. Zebras are dying. Then maybe that will be enough.'

'What's your point?' I asked him. 'Do you want me to be sorry for you? You wanted more, didn't you? That's what made you create your *empire,* as you fondly call it. You got what you wanted.'

'Guess I'm *people*, after all. But most people I know live every day like it's their last. Ironically that makes them reach the top of this...pyramid of life—if you can call it that. They have their peace; they know who they are. And they do good for others. It's the ugly base of the pyramid—health, safety, a respectful livelihood—that they never get.'

'Respect. That's what you've been chasing, isn't it?'

'Don't we all?' Johnny said. 'Is that offensive to you because I'm a dwarf?'

'Absolutely not. In fact, it's understandable. Even justifiable and relatable. You don't need to be vertically challenged to be a dwarf, my friend.'

'Is that why a genius runs away from glory and respect? Because she's angry with herself?'

'You didn't answer me,' I said. 'Have you taken a life?'

'The more potent question is—have you lost one that mattered?'

'Not answering till you do.'

It was a curious juxtaposition—two stories that were strikingly different, yet they became the same when spoken across a prison wall etched with strange faces. Some answers were, at best, grey, while others were really just more questions, yet they revealed more than answers ever could.

We were reluctant members of the same runaway fraternity, directionless travellers close to our unwanted destinations. Failures in our own rights. Regardless of where we had come from, we belonged to the same goddamn place.

The only question that needed a *real* answer was—where do we go from here?

23 A Curious Juxtaposition – Part II

.•Johnny•.

'**O**kay. I'll answer first,' I said, struggling to get up. My body screamed in protest. My legs were sore, and my arms burned with open wounds. My lips were swollen, and my ears oozed sticky blood. But I wanted to talk, share, possibly for the last time, with another human.

It was the middle of the day. The air was thick, heavy with heat, pressing down like a hand around my throat. I reached the earthen pot, filled a glass with muddy water and slid back against the wall, my knees trembling.

It had been 10 days since Debroy killed my friend. Every day after that, they dragged me to another room, tortured me, and asked how I knew the journalist. My answer was always the same. Debroy visited often, indulging in the torment with fervour. He knew I had nothing, but he didn't stop. Soon, he'd get bored of it all—and that would be the end of my suffering. Maybe hell was waiting for me. Maybe I'd find Rampal there, in his flannel lungi and wretched glasses. Between the pain and the brief spurts of consciousness, I prayed Shamshu and Rakhi had made it out in time. They had to.

'C'mon. Don't keep me hanging,' Katherine urged.

'It was bound to happen. Given where I come from… Damp mattresses and lonely nights. At the orphanage, everything had to be fought for. And fought with. The bread you ate, where you stood in the queue to pee, the candy you deserved for acing your test. There was a broken jaw or a lost tooth every day. Sometimes it was for the bimonthly ride to the hospital that allowed us to see the world outside. Other times, it was because there was nothing better to do. That was the life of every kid in that hellhole. But it was worse for me, given my...illness. That's what the kids and the caretakers called it, despite earnest protests from the lone hapless nun who had brought me in. I was the sick child, so I deserved nothing.'

I gulped the water. I'd never talked about my days in the orphanage to anyone. But my end was near, and the burden would soon be lifted forever. So I spilled everything to the rich American girl searching for her lost mother with an irritating habit of asking weird questions and throwing coke through the vent.

'Sorry,' she said.

'I spent my life running away from that word. Yet it always found me and mocked me.'

'I...I understand.'

'So I had a special quota of rebukes,' I went on. 'I was ragged and beaten up at every opportunity. And those were plenty, given each one of us was angry with—and dejected by—the hand that had been dealt to us. The caretakers ignored it; some even partook once in a while, when no one was watching.'

'How did you survive it?'

'I didn't.'

'What do you mean?'

'I think I was around 12 then.' I remembered that hot, scalding day, similar to this one, and got lost in my thoughts.

'Then when?' Katherine asked.

'When I burned it all down.'

'You set the orphanage on fire? Jimi be damned! That's what I would have done.'

'I remember that day vividly. And I'd do anything to forget it.'

'They deserved to—'

'I chose a Sunday,' I interrupted her, continuing my story. 'When most of them would be at the cathedral next door, away from the orphanage. Except the ones I wanted to stay. I planned it for a week. Waited until after lunch when the kitchen was empty. I sneaked in and opened the gas valves, letting the burners leak. In some twisted version of my juvenile fantasy, I imagined the fire would make the place disappear and I wouldn't have to cry myself to sleep anymore...'

'Go on. Why the hell did you stop?'

'The gas hissed, filling the room. I sat there, still deciding if I wanted to stay there and end my misery or watch the place burn down and then run away. When the air became thin and rancid, I couldn't stay put. I exited through the door, held it shut, struck a match and threw it in.'

'Wow,' Katherine said.

'Wow?'

'Sorry, I meant it like I'm horrified, not impressed.'

'I waited for minutes, but nothing happened. Nervously I opened the door to find that the matchstick had died. The room stank like rotten eggs. I hid behind the door and lit another. The instant I threw it inside, the small spark became the size of the room—a giant glob of fire. An unbearably hot, hard wave of air hit my face, blowing the door off its hinges. It also blew me down the hallway, knocking me out.'

'Then?' Katherine prompted.

'I don't know how long I was out, but when I woke up, I heard people screaming. The door had collapsed on top of me, pinning me down. My face was so hot it felt like it was melting. I pushed myself up and saw the kitchen in flames.

Fire snaked through the hallways, blackening everything. Every breath I let out burned my upper lip, so I forced myself to breathe in through my nose and exhale through my mouth. I ran, past the empty, burning dorms. The rowdy kids and the mean caretakers I wanted to burn in hell had escaped.'

'So all that, and for nothing?'

'As the fire spread, I ran towards the exit. As I was crossing the last dorm room, I heard a whimper. I stopped and peeked in from the window to find a small girl, maybe around three or four years old, sitting on the floor, crying. Curly blonde hair fell across her pale white cheeks; she was the most beautiful child I'd ever seen. Her ethnicity was a rarity, as our orphanage barely had any kids who weren't Indian or Asian. I'd never seen her before; she must have been admitted recently.'

'So you saved her?'

'I killed her.' I picked up my steel cup and flung it against the wall. 'For a precious few minutes in that inferno, I collected all my anger and pain and saw all the people who had hurt me—ridiculed me and kicked me—in that girl's face. Those who had thrown me into an orphanage to die like a diseased animal.

'I smiled at her like a devil, assailed by all my hate, as the smoke seared my mouth and lungs. But then something happened. As the ceiling came crashing around us and smoke swallowed everything up, she stopped crying and smiled back at me. It was the most beautiful yet saddest smile I'd ever seen. I let go of my misplaced anger and realized I couldn't let her die there.

'I kicked the door with all I had, but it wouldn't budge. My short, useless legs weren't enough. Just then, a firefighter burst through the main door. He swiftly picked me up and ran towards the exit. I kept screaming, "Girl! Girl!", but he wouldn't stop; maybe he couldn't hear me. We got out just seconds before the whole place collapsed. No one died that day, except that little girl. So there you go… That's how I took my first and only scalp.'

'Johnny, you didn't kill her,' Katherine said. 'You tried to save her.'

'No, I wasted time, blinded by my own rage against a life that hadn't even started. Until it was too late. No matter how I look at it, I killed her. And I'll take that to my grave. Which, hopefully, is already dug up somewhere close.'

'You were just a kid.'

'No, I wasn't. It's the same anger that made me sell amphetamines and go up against the mob. That's what got Rampal killed.'

Katherine remained quiet for some time. There were no more quips or weird questions for me. Even though she'd never seen me, she had discovered the man I saw every day in the mirror.

'What about your friends who were with you? Where are they?'

'It's your turn to spill your secrets,' I said.

She was quiet for a few minutes. I heard her rip open a pouch, sniff in a long one and exhale loudly.

'That'll kill you, you know.'

'Lately I haven't encountered too many things that won't,' she said, then snorted another line.

'How the hell do you have an endless supply of coke with you?' I asked.

'Excellent room service.'

'Looks like I'm the only one who's going to die in here.'

'How do you know for sure?' she said.

'If they wanted you dead, they wouldn't fuss about you.

Probably the same reason your mother is alive. They want you drowning in powder, Katherine. Throw that stuff away.'

'I don't mind this place,' she said. 'I have everything I need.'

'Except what you came here for.'

'You think I'm a coward?'

'No, just a furious woman who seems to have lost her furiosity.'

'Fury.'

'Does mastery of the language come to your rescue every time?'

'Most of the time. For other times, I have cocaine. It keeps me going.'

'Until it doesn't… How did you lose your father, Katherine?'

Silence.

'You can tell me. I won't tell a soul. I promise.'

'Kath.'

'Huh?'

'Call me Kath.'

'Okay… Kath, it's your turn.'

'He ran away,' she said. 'He picked up his bag and left without saying goodbye. I was 10. I'll never forget that day, even though I tell myself I have.'

'Ran away?'

'He came home and went straight to his study upstairs. Mom and I were planting flowers in her greenhouse. She must have sensed something was off, because she followed him up. A few minutes later, they came down together. They weren't talking or smiling.

'He approached me and knelt down, drawing me into a hug. "Kathy, always know there's someone looking out for you," he said. And then he left. Through the light between the leaves and the glass walls of the greenhouse, I smiled at him and waved, thinking he was just going for a business trip.

'But he didn't wave back. He didn't return my smile like he usually did. He just looked at me through the glass; then he turned around and disappeared. "Where has Daddy gone, Mom?" I asked my mother.

'"Somewhere far away, honey. Somewhere very far away," she said, gathering the remaining stems and dropping them into a box. When I asked her when he would be back, my mother picked me up and hugged me tightly, not allowing me to study her face. "He's never coming back, sweetheart. Your father's gone," she told me. My shoulders were damp with her tears. But I didn't cry. I have never cried for him.'

'Were you close to him?' I asked.

'He was my life. My everything. The only one who called me "Kathy". Mom says—well, she used to say—that I got my indifference from him. And the stick up my ass.'

'Did you ever find out what happened to him?'

'I asked my mom over the years, but never got the answer I was looking for. The papers speculated suicide. After a while I started hating him and shut him out of my mind. So did my mom, I guess. I don't blame her for that. Then Mom and I... We grew apart. She was hardly there. And I liked being alone. I...I don't know when I started liking being lonely.'

Kath and I didn't speak for hours afterwards. The sun disappeared from the cracks of my door. Amid the silence plastered over the ragged walls, we chewed on words we'd spoken earlier. I wasn't sure who had been dealt a worse hand—someone who had been showered with love and then left hollow or someone who'd never come close to finding and losing it.

Eventually, I broke the quiet. 'Seems like you shut out more than just your father.'

'What do you mean?'

'You use your intelligence—or rather, don't use it—to punish yourself. If you keep failing, you can't disappoint yourself with hope.'

'You and my mother will make good friends. Those are all just big words.'

I shrugged, though she couldn't see me. 'True nonetheless. You squander your life like it's a middle finger to the world. You blame yourself for your father leaving. You've pushed everyone away, including your mother. But when she disappeared, you realized you couldn't afford to lose her too. Not even if it meant losing your family fortune.'

'Were you studying psychology at your college before you ran away? Cause that would explain why you suck so goddamn much at it.'

I chuckled. 'No, it's just that I've had the luxury of a similar life. After the fire, everything changed. *I* changed. I replaced my anger with a burning desire to be something more than just a half man. Books were my only escape; I became obsessed with them. The nuns helped me, getting me as many as they could. That's when they decided I had to become a doctor. Now I'm no highbrow, but I worked very, very hard. Made it to college.'

'And then you threw it all away because someone didn't treat you well.'

'Sounds familiar?'

24 Runaways

⋆ Johnny ⋆

The familiar smell of ash ran up my dry nose and woke me up. Dark smoke and a simmering light seeped in from under the door. Footsteps scrambled across the passageway, leaving hurried shadows flickering beneath the gap. Distant, confused voices echoed loudly, mingling with splashes of water.

I turned over, trying to go back to sleep. It was just the same nightmare again in a different avatar. No matter how hard I tried, the girl in the fire would always be my nocturnal torturer. Then the smoke reached my lungs, making me cough. That's when I realized this wasn't a dream. There was definitely a fire outside. Judging by the clamour, the flames were winning.

I shot up, ran to the door and yanked the handle. It was hot and wouldn't budge. I looked all around the room, trying to find an opening, but there were none.

'Help! Help me! Open the door!'

Suddenly, an epiphany struck me—this was the right way to go. What could be more poetic than dying the same way she did? I'd finally found my perfect death.

Smiling, I walked back to my bed and finished the last few drops of water from the cup, easing my throat for the last time. Then I lay down and closed my eyes, arms folded under my head. Everything made sense now.

I thought of the orphanage, the nuns, the medical school. The day I arrived in this city of despair with nothing but a well-earned stamp that said 'runaway'. I thought of all I'd been through—rejections, disappointments, ridicule, shame. The names I'd collected. The friends I'd made and lost. Running from corrupt cops. Making pills out of nothing. Falling from towers. Being tortured by the mob. Gaining love from my neighbours. Hating Debroy with every ounce of my being.

I'd moved the needle; so what if the pointy end eventually landed on my back? My life had been life enough. But if I could choose to be greedy, I would have wanted to end the commissioner's life before being done with mine. He had no right to live. But then, neither did I.

The noises outside grew louder and the air in the room thinned. Every breath became faster and shallower than the previous one. The bed felt like a hot pan, growing hotter by the second. I opened my eyes momentarily—saw nothing but a thick cloud of smoke hovering above me—and shut them again.

Then, just as my lungs reached their limit—

BANG.

A loud crash at the door. Then again.

BANG.

With the third bang, the door smashed open. A face wrapped in a blanket emerged from the smoke.

Shamshu.

'Get up and move!'

I stared at him, dazed. Maybe it was the smoke. Or maybe it was death.

He shook me hard. His hands were uncomfortably hot. This wasn't a dream.

'What's wrong with you? Get the fuck up! We have to get out before this place burns to the ground.'

'What... Why are you here? I told you—'

'You want to discuss that *now*? You wanna die or live?'

'Tough choice.' I sat up and looked up at him as he towered over me, smoke curling behind him like a halo of ash. 'Rampal... He's gone. I couldn't... I asked you to leave me alone.'

'Listen to me. You know why I took that bullet for you? Why I stick to you like bees to honey? Because I can't make the same mistake twice.'

'What?'

'I had a brother. Paarth,' Shamshu said. 'People threw stones at him. Killed him. Because he was a dwarf. I just stood and watched. I won't let that happen to you. Drown in self-pity later. Now let's go.'

He grabbed my arm, yanking me to my feet. He then picked up the water pot and dumped the contents over my head.

'Helps against the fire,' he muttered.

We stepped out of the room into a million-watt, blinding dazzle.

Below, the courtyard burned like a molten reservoir, yellow flames gobbling everything unapologetically. The blaze crawled up the façade and reached the terrace, melting the dolls into hot oblivion.

Shamshu led the way down the backstairs, out into an alley. A mob roared on the other side of the building and a police siren wailed in the distance.

As we got inside the car and it started moving, I shouted. 'Stop! I have to go back.'

'Are you out of your mind? There's nothing to go back to. Why are you so hell-bent on dying? The cops are going to be—'

'Stop the fucking car, Shamshu!'

The second he braked, I jumped out. 'Wait for me here.'

I wanted to instruct him to leave if the cops came before me, but I knew better. He wasn't going to budge. I covered my face with my forearm and ran back into the inferno.

Not this time, Johnny. Not this time.

Upstairs, the corridor was barely holding together. Tall flames rolled across the ceiling; walls charred and black. I hurried past rooms till I made it to Kath's. The door gave way on my second attempt. A thick cloud of smoke punched me in the face, forcing a cough up from my lungs.

'Kath? Katherine?'

'I'm here!' came a weak voice.

I stumbled forward, arms outstretched, eyes burning. She was curled up in a corner, coughing, her face smudged with soot.

'Of course. Blonde hair. It had to be blonde hair.'

She blinked at me in stunned confusion.

'It's not my real colour. I'm a redhead.'

'Let's get the hell out of here.'

I extended a hand to help her up. As we ran towards safety, the ceiling groaned—columns splintering, flames licking at our arms and ears, heat clawing at our lungs. By the time we reached the back exit, we were out of breath and found it completely blocked by burning debris.

'Take off your shirt,' she shouted.

'What? Why?'

'Do it. Now!'

'Why do I have to do it? You Americans shout about equality, yet—'

'Because cotton burns faster than denim,' she snapped, tugging at her collar. 'Don't be a pansy.'

I took off my denim shirt and gave it to her. The heat instantly slapped against my bare skin. Kath wrapped the shirt around her hands, grabbed a seething log and smashed the nearest window. The glass shattered and we jumped out. Then we ran to Shamshu's waiting vehicle and got in.

'Thanks for coming back for me,' Kath said.

She had my incorrigible habit of jumping into other people's bloody soup to thank.

'Kath, meet the pyromaniac bee lover and my...brother, Shamshu. Shamshu, meet the poorest billionaire with daddy—'

Shamshu hit the accelerator before I could finish, the torque slamming me against the seat.

Through the rear windshield, we watched the House of Dolls come crashing down, the fire swallowing it, till it became a heap of black rubble.

'Well, at least now, there'll be no more dolls wailing at night,' Kath said, as the swaying flames disappeared into the distance.

25 Two for the Price of One

⊹Katherine⊹

Johnny's friend Shamshu drove us to an apartment. The grey sky slowly gave way to the sun, which peaked in through a giant French window.

No matter how much one sees the dark of the night, the sun has nothing to do with it. It comes with no hangovers of the nocturne. Fresh and sprightly, it's ready to bake the world into an oblivious happiness. And it was here again.

Cuts and burns covered my body. My face throbbed, radiating heat. I blinked incessantly and washed my eyes for what felt like forever, but the soot still clung to them. The pain was there, the shock too—but only in the way one feels them for a stranger—distant and detached.

They gave me the bedroom and first rights to a much-needed bath. Rakhi, another friend of Johnny's, was quiet yet carried herself with a steady confidence. She was probably in her early 30s, and a generous host. She brought a dozen popsicles, skin cream and a change of clothes for me, drew the curtains and filled the bathtub with ice. I tried to remember the last time I'd done so much for a stranger.

'Do you mind if the curtains are open?' I asked.

'No problem,' Rakhi said. 'I thought you'd want some privacy and quiet, given what you two went through.'

I glanced at the golden light spilling into the room. 'The sun. I forgot how beautiful it is.'

She smiled, drew the curtains back open and left.

After an ice-cold bath and too many iced candies, I walked into a bustling living room. Suitcases lay open on the floor, heaps of clothes spilling over them. A stack of pizza boxes that seemed larger than usual sat on the coffee table. Maybe they loved their pizza more here than back home.

Johnny and Shamshu sealed the last pizza box but not before I caught a glimpse of what was inside. They had vials full of pills. Johnny had told me everything about them back in that hideous prison. Wads of cash lay beside the pizza boxes, along with a couple of pistols, a few mobile phones and scraps of leftover food.

'Are we planning a heist?' I asked.

'On the contrary, we're going to run and hide,' Johnny said, offering me a Coke. 'They'll be here sooner or later.'

His face was similar to mine—sprinkled with cuts and bruises. But unlike me, he had a big forehead, spiked hair and a strong jaw. A little under five feet, he had muscular arms that ended at his stomach and fleshy hands. But his lack of height and his small limbs weren't a thing. If anything, I found him taller than me in more ways than one, and there weren't many others like that to me. Even though all he could do was feel angry and sorry about his 'stature' and do everything to compensate for it, deep down, I knew, that when he wasn't so caught up trying hard to be ordinary, he actually liked himself.

'Is this your apartment?' I asked him.

'No, I prefer the cold harshness of my shanty. Although I'm sure there's nothing left of it anymore. This is Rampal's place…used to be.'

The pieces clicked together. I turned towards Rakhi and hugged her. 'I'm so sorry, Rakhi. I just realized… How are you holding up?'

She smiled, her eyes tired and weary. 'I'm okay.'

'Kath, can I speak to you for a moment?' Johnny said as he bit into a chocolate bar.

'Sure.'

We walked back to the bedroom. I sat down on the edge of the bed.

'May I?' Johnny asked, pointing to a couch next to the bed.

'Of course.'

He pulled himself up, legs dangling and chocolate in one hand. 'Listen, I have to disappear and figure out what to do next. I had the guys find the earliest flight back to the US for you. We'll drop you off at the airport and wait till you're on that flight.'

'They took my all my belongings, along with my passport—passports, actually. But it helps that I have no plans to go.'

'What are you going to do? You know what these guys are capable of? You won't survive another day. Get to the US embassy and—'

'What worse can they do? I have nothing left to lose. I was good to go when you barged in and spoiled my plans.'

'You weren't the only one. Trust Shamshu to ruin many such welcome moments.'

I grinned. 'He's a true friend.'

'He is. I wish you could have met Rampal too. He was a few clowns short of a circus, but that wisecracker put smiles on our faces. We could do with some right now. But the moron had to die on me.'

'How is Rakhi holding up? She doesn't look well.'

'I haven't found the courage to look her in the eyes and tell her how sorry I am. I promised her I would save him... She hasn't slept for days. I can tell. They would have gotten married soon.'

'I feel for her. She's a kind and strong one. But you have to stop thinking of yourself as a superhero.'

He sighed. 'I'd settle for just being a man.'

'Self-pity is exhausting. Trust me, I know. I've been doing it all my life.'

He shifted on the couch. 'We're wasting precious time. What's your plan?'

'There's nothing for me back home. I'm a fugitive there. I don't care about it anymore. But my mother, Johnny. I have to find her. Even if it's the last thing I do. I also need to find Imaan's son and get him out of this mess, and if I'm being ambitious, bring that son of a bitch cop down.'

'For a girl alone in a city full of monsters, that's quite a laundry list.'

'You wanted me to find my "furiosity". Well, I found it. Where's yours?'

'Oh, trust me, I have it well placed and preserved. Debroy will pay for Rampal. Or I'll die trying.'

'Looks like we're both running with scissors in one hand and a death wish in the other. We're after the same people, Johnny. Help me find my mother. If it's about money, I can ask Mr Elenburg to—'

'Kath, the only things money got you in this city are a fake bodyguard, an undercover agent working for the Mandal and a few dead people. I made a fortune selling those pills. How much do you think I spent on myself?'

I shrugged. 'Given the gleam in your eyes and your self-satisfied smirk, I'm guessing not much.'

'Just enough to buy a fridge, an air conditioner and every single brand of dark chocolate I could find. So no, I don't need your money, Uncle Sam.'

'Uncle Sam is, by definition, a male—'

'One doesn't need testosterone to be called that.'

'Touché.'

'I don't mean to be insensitive, but chances are your mother was in the House of Dolls when it burned.'

'No. She's alive, Johnny. Will you help me?'

'You'll greatly reduce your chances of staying alive and finding your mother if you're with me,' he said. 'I have a huge laser dot on my back, like the ones in your movies.'

'Which means the shooter is close.'

'So now I'm bait?'

'No, my friend,' I said. 'You're my only hope.'

'This city,' he muttered, 'sucks in all the reluctant renegades and helpless fugitives.'

'There's a reason we met in that shithole. We're the missing pieces in each other's puzzles. Don't you see it?'

Johnny studied me for a few seconds, then licked the last of the chocolate off his fingers. 'Then let's put those pieces together. I'll help you get your mother back. But first things first. We survive. Regroup. Figure out our options.'

'Thank you. I have...one more request.'

'Cocaine?'

'No, rather the opposite. I'm quitting. Forever. I know it's going to be difficult, nearly impossible. I need a friend to see me through it.'

He went quiet again, crossing and uncrossing his legs. 'Your timing sucks. You want to go against the world and yourself at the same time? Why?'

Because I'm not afraid to shine anymore. 'Because it's killing me.'

I knew it was too much to ask from myself. To let go of

the only place where I lived and smiled and floated and cried. I knew I'd concoct reasons and extend timelines in my head, renegotiating my promise to myself. But if I ever were to find a place beyond it, this was it.

'Living is dying, Kath.'

'No. Dying is dying.'

Johnny clapped loudly, like a kid. 'Good news—you passed the first test, Ms Gladwell. Better news—I know how I can make it easier for you.'

'How?'

'With my pills.'

'Are you serious?'

'Amphetamines do what coke does, but in a way that isn't a one-way street. Coke is like a fancy car—zero to a hundred in four seconds. My pills make you cruise at 50. The highs don't border on psychedelic, and the lows are bearable. It keeps you sharp and awake, similar to what coke does. We lower the dosage, wean you off. No coke, no pills. Just you.'

'So you'll help me?'

'I thought you'd figured that out by now.'

'Figured what out?'

'I'm getting two for the price of one. You're my chance to save that girl from the fire. And hopefully myself...'

'But you already saved that girl from the fire,' I said.

Johnny shook his head. 'Not yet. She still burns. I can see the flames around her.'

I looked at that big face, his eyes beaming with resolve.

'Now let's get the hell out of here.' He jumped off the couch, grinning.

It was the first time I'd seen him smile.

'I'll ask Rakhi to pack for you. We'll buy whatever else we

need on the way. Get ready for the ride of your life, Kath. It might be your last.'

Like I wasn't already on it.

'First, go hug Rakhi. Let her cry. And cry if you have to. I did a whole lot of that in that freezing bathtub. Helps get the crap out of your eyes.'

Johnny stopped smiling. Nodding, almost imperceptibly, he dragged himself out of the room.

That very second, I knew we were going to be the best of friends.

We'd burned in the same fires all our lives, waiting for them to eventually engulf us. Little did we know, those flames we reluctantly carried inside all these years, were now the very fires we had become.

26 Heavier but Better

⋅→ Johnny ⋅→

'This is where the magic happens…or at least, it used to,' I said, as we walked down an aisle. Shiny apparatus and steel pressure vessels peered at us from both sides.

Kath picked up a rack of glass tubes, the faint clinking echoing through the space. 'It's a slick lab, all right.'

Her hands still shook, albeit much lesser than a week before when we all moved into the lab. She'd been off coke since then, but this was the first time she'd made it out of her room. The struggle was real, but she was determined. Although the amphetamines were helpful, she wasn't out of the woods yet.

There were moments of weakness, when all she wanted was a 'little sniff'. Nights when she pink-clouded, then screamed and cried, pleading for coke. She sobbed in her sleep; other times, she cursed, calling out for her father. But with every passing day she looked stronger and more resolved.

I kept her engaged with stories of the Blue Bees and pizza deliveries, torture trams, a water tank that barely had any space for water, the 'lanky man' and his love for books and his machete, and my encounters with RC—the ghost who roamed in trams, never seen or heard anywhere else. And the evidence that never existed.

Meanwhile Shamshu, Rakhi and I spent the week thinking, planning. But we hadn't moved an inch. The Mandal would find us sooner or later. We could leave Kolkata—there was enough money for everyone—but no one was willing. Debroy's loud squeals echoed in my ears no matter how hard I tried to drown them out. Rampal's smile, right before he was cut open, floated on walls that caved in an inch a minute.

Between discussions of money and product, who we could trust, how we'd scoop out all the floating money and how we could hit the Mandal where it hurt, I finally got through to Rakhi. She'd wept silently; I found her a place she hadn't allowed herself to be in years—yet one she needed to be. Years that had taught her to take it on the chin and move on. I found her broken and sorry and regretful. And willing to show it.

'There wasn't a single morning Rampal didn't think of running away,' she'd confessed. 'But he could never desert you. "How can I let him die alone?" he used to say. I told him it was fine. That there was time.'

Tears rolled down her soft face.

'I'm the one to be blamed—'

'We aren't children, Johnny. We knew the risks. *He* knew the risks. I don't blame you. But we could have gotten out when there still was time. We had planned to adopt my own girl, who's now five and lives in an orphanage in Hati Bagan. We would have given her a good life. Maybe, just maybe, we could have found happiness... And kept it. Guess it wasn't meant to be.'

'I'm so sorry, Rakhi. You still can give your daughter that life. I swear we'll get her back to you. I know you've lost more, but I lost the only friend I had and—'

'I'd officially like to take offence to that,' Shamshu said, standing in the doorway.

'I'm sorry, my brother. You are and always will be the biggest blessing in our lives. I take it back. Without you—'

He put up a beefy hand. 'Okay, enough. I didn't mean to hijack your conversation.'

All Shamshu wanted was an unspoken assurance that he mattered; he got embarrassed when it was said aloud. He was an unobtrusive anchor willing to sink into the blackest of depths to keep us moored. But if weeds snaked on into the chain, he'd dredge the water without hesitation. And dredge he did. Silently, from the wings of the stage, he watched the action unfold.

'Rampal went out smiling,' I said.

Rakhi wiped her cheeks and sat up straight. 'He did?'

I told them how it happened. How, even when there was no light left between the machete's blade and his neck, Rampal smiled. He was strong. Unworried. At peace. Maybe just a shot at happiness had been enough for him. Maybe *this* was enough. Maybe he had lived.

Or maybe that was just Rampal—the rangy rascal from nowhere. The gauche phone thief who loved big ugly TVs. The jittery relief in our lives. The excited motormouth. The one gifted with the art of perfectly timed abuse. The one who had jumped into fire because his friend had asked him to—and paid the ultimate price for it. My best friend.

'Do you want to know the last words out of his big mouth?' I said.

'Let me guess. "Fucking half man"?' Rakhi said, a smile trying to make its way to her moist cheeks.

'Chutiya.'

The three of us laughed—nitrous laughter that still echoed through the narrow aisles and cold walls of the lab as we walked through the space, showing Kath around.

'Very few know about this place, so it's probably the safest. And in case there is trouble, there's a pier next door to catch a boat and escape.'

'What happens to all this now?' she asked.

'I don't know. Maybe it's time to let go of it. Maybe it's done what it was supposed to do.'

'Make your shadow grow longer?' Kath asked.

'Now who's being a psychologist?'

She shrugged. 'It doesn't take one much to see why you did what you did.'

'I regret telling you so much in that cell.'

'I don't. Thanks for everything,' she replied. 'I know I've been more than a handful.'

'Handful? How come you call a spade a spade but conveniently reserve all the euphemisms for yourself?'

She threw her hands up in the air. 'Okay, fine. I'm a monster!'

'See? The sobering up is helping.'

'Maybe they think we're dead and have stopped looking.'

'Doubt that. They wouldn't have found any bodies in our cells.'

'So what's our next step?'

I sighed, brushing dust off the boilers. 'We don't have one. I don't know any way to hurt them—or Debroy, for that matter. They've taken over our entire distribution network. The clinics are now true-blue coke centres. Amphetamines are off the menu since no one's making them. Most of our guys have been threatened or injured. The few who remain are with us. Interestingly, a lot of their own guys took the fall for losing you.'

'I don't understand. Why? What am I to them?' She hoisted herself on to a counter, making the test tubes clink.

'Figuring that out might be our way in. But we haven't got anything so far. Rakhi has been winding up most of our businesses and liquidating what she can. Shamshu is trying to find a greedy insider who could be stuffed with cash in exchange for information.'

'Like that asshole investigator, Bijoy,' Kath scoffed. 'Everyone is up for sale.'

'He never was an investigator. He's one of their trusted assassins. A master of disguises. At some stage, they must have realized Imaan wasn't going to be enough to keep you tethered, so they sent him out to bring you in—peacefully, if possible. And you took the bait.'

'Jimi's fine ass, I made the bait. I literally begged him to take us there. He must be rolling on the floor, telling his colleagues about my pathetic plan—the sadistic glee he would have derived from it... Where's the real investigator? Maybe he can still help.'

'Probably lying next to the real Imaan,' I said. 'And the fake Imaan.'

'So many bodies piled up to keep me alive. It doesn't make any sense.'

I heaved a sigh. 'Nothing does. For instance, why keep me alive? Once they knew I had no proof against Debroy, why torture me, ask me what else I had? Why are they so scared of me?'

'Maybe I should just go back home,' said Kath. 'Try to salvage whatever is left.'

'You're just saying that to yourself so you can reject it and be even more sure of what you're doing.'

'Now I regret telling you more than I should have in that hellhole. Have they found Imaan's son? It's the least I can do for him.'

'Shamshu found out Imaan's real name was Akash. He lived a few blocks from our shanty. Did odd jobs for the Mandal every now and then. Akash's son, Akhil, is still missing, but we're trying our best to locate him. Shamshu found one of their "training camps", where they get these kids addicted to coke, then induct them into their so-called army.'

'Imaan… Let's just call him Imaan.'

'You do know he was from the enemy's camp, right?'

'He took the job to protect his son. He didn't deserve to die for it.'

'None of them did. Yet here we are.'

Kath hopped off the counter, dusting off her hands. 'They have to pay for this, Johnny. They have to.'

'They will.' I started walking and she followed. 'I don't know how yet, but they will. I'll find a way. But for now, I have to make sure I lose no one else.'

Kath nodded. 'I'm gonna try to get some sleep. Your pills have been keeping me wide awake at night.'

'Trust me, coming off coke would have been worse without them. And with the dosage going down, you are at least getting a few hours every night. That's good.'

'I'm feeling better,' she admitted. 'Heavier, but better.'

After Kath went to back to her room, I walked around the ammonia prep table, running my fingers over the flasks and funnels. Before everything had come crashing down, I'd sometimes stand here alone, put on my lab coat and pretend I was a scientist. I'd set up the apparatus to synthesize volatile compounds like we used to back in college. I spent hours running experiments and relishing the pungent smoke that came out of those slender tubes. I loved directing the liquids and gases, watching them dance to my recipes, changing their identities forever. And after I had my fill, I'd drain them away and watch them disappear into a dark hole to nowhere.

I smiled, remembering our latest jaunt to the water reservoir. It was probably our last. We'd climbed the wobbly iron ladder, past the beehives, and I had shown Kath what we had achieved— our score. It had been good while it lasted, and there was enough to take care of everyone. It was the only thing left to do. The only right thing.

'Holy mother of Jimi and his guitars! There's barely any water! Is that all cash?' Kath had gasped, peering through the open latch. 'You're a gangster, Johnny!'

'You think a dying man would lie to you? I just don't know how to get it to the right people.'

'What do you wanna do with it? Build a city?'

'Build hope. Apart from what the team needs, I want those guys to have it all,' I'd replied, pointing at the dimly lit shanties of Hazaar Basti below.

A sharp click behind me snapped me back to the present.

'You are a difficult man to find. Even for me,' a voice rasped from behind.

I turned around to find a lean, muscular man with a thick duck-tailed beard, wearing a driving cap and a camel-coloured overcoat. He had a pistol pointed at my face.

'Who are—'

'Not important.' He took forever to clear his throat. 'You have one last chance to give up any evidence against Debroy—no more torture, no more questions. Yes or no?'

'I don't have anything. Tell that paranoid commissioner to go to hell.'

My sickening indifference to a gun that meant business and the words coming out of my mouth shocked me.

The man sighed. 'I knew this was a waste of time. Before I kill you—' he cleared his throat again—'I was instructed to ask you if you got a chance to read *Macbeth*.'

'Go fu—'

'Whatever.'

A gunshot rang out.

His neck burst open. Blood sprayed onto the table of beakers and flasks as he collapsed.

Kath stood in the doorway, pale and blank, my gun in her trembling hands.

'Truth is the biggest cliché,' she muttered, staring at the fallen man.

'Lower your weapon, Kath.'

She paid no heed to me, seemingly shell-shocked. Then she leered.

'Johnny, meet Bijoy—master of disguises…and now a permanent resident of hell,' she said, lowering the gun.

I struck number four off the nine lives I was now sure I had.

27 Flinch and Shake and Tremble and Cry

Katherine

I had no plan, no path that led me to my mother. Nothing to bring down those who had taken her. Losing my family fortune and name was a foregone conclusion. Yet I was okay; my steps were surer, lighter.

Cocaine hadn't touched my blood in 12 days. Mornings promised eternal hell, but it was the cold, desolate nights that delivered it. I flinched. I shook. I trembled. And I cried. I begged for release and howled at the walls. But I took the blows. Slowly and painfully, my wings grew back.

Only a fool would think I overcame it on my own. And a fool I was not. It was because of them that I survived—Johnny, Rakhi and Shamshu—my new-found friends from nowhere. Their lucidity. The things they did and the things they refused to do. Their longer smiles and louder laughs, even as the darkness around threatened to swallow us whole.

I survived because I knew every time I woke up in a pool of cold sweat, they'd be there, willing to just sit and talk. About how they missed their dreary lives, when they could complain about cold water and roaches. How they'd built castles in the air and how Johnny had made them real. How their dreams were small yet sometimes daunting. Their shanties and the things they wanted to do for their people.

They didn't pity me when I shook unbearably or begged

Johnny to let me have some snow. Johnny wouldn't have it. Unmoved, he stood like a rock between me and myself, refusing to let me give up. He saw through the darkest in me and pulled me out of the abyss. He was no dwarf, this man. He couldn't be. He stood taller than anyone else in my life ever had.

But my emancipation came, unexpectedly, in the form of Bijoy. The instant I pulled the trigger, I was free from my perversions. I felt more blood in my veins than any high had ever given me. The rush of electricity down my spine burned away all the shame, the loss and the misery. I felt *right*. For the first time in years, I liked the sound of myself. Despite all I had lost, I was a finally a winner.

After Bijoy's intrusion, we moved our base from the lab to a house on the outskirts of Kolkata. Shamshu managed to find Akhil and set up a discreet meeting but warned us of the risk. So, to meet Imaan's son, we entered the lion's den—Taltala, an old neighbourhood where the Mandal trained new recruits.

The cabbie dropped us off at Curzon Park, a few blocks away from our meeting place.

'We walk through the park and avoid the streets. They'll be crawling with the Mandal's men,' Johnny said.

We entered the park, disguised as a mother-daughter duo. I wore one of Rakhi's salwar kameez and covered my head and face with a dupatta. Johnny was my little girl in a loose frock that hid his legs and hands and a bow turban concealing most of his head. He had hated the disguise the second Shamshu suggested it. We had rolled on the floor laughing while he scowled.

'This is why you aren't my best friend,' Johnny had grumbled to Shamshu.

It was Shamshu's way of punishing Johnny, who had agreed to my 'ridiculous' suggestion of going out to find Imaan's son.

'It's as good as suicide,' he had declared.

The park was an overgrown, unkempt oasis in the middle of the city's toxicity. As if we had stepped through a time warp into an old, forgotten world, untouched by modern excess. The roots of ancient trees meandered across the ground until they ran out of space, cut off by concrete drains that skirted the park. Dry leaves carpeted most of the ground, while patchy grass struggled to find sun beneath the dense green canopy. Vines camouflaged the rusted, twisted railings that were once meant to surround a jogging track.

Rain was imminent. The winds carried a strong petrichor and the sky flashed frequently, its growls uncomfortably close. Beyond the swaying trees, faint outlines of civilization flickered—cars rushed by, bus drivers honked impatiently and machines clanked and tore into the earth, digging for an underground subway.

As we walked deeper into the park, I stumbled upon columned structures guarding sleepy statues. One such statue stood inside a covered marble pavilion, its four motif-carved pillars joined by cusped arches—an unmistakable Mughal imprint. Steps leading to the structure were submerged in a sea of leaves, cracked open in places by virile roots. I stopped, gazing at the monument, concocting ruinous tales of love and struggle from a hundred years ago.

'It was a drinking fountain built by some lord to honour another,' Johnny said. 'Now it's just leaves and wild cats.'

'It's spectacular.'

'It's just history. People drowning in mobile screens and left swipes are too worried about their futures. History has no place for anyone.'

'For a non-believer, you know a lot of history.'

'I told you, I didn't have any friends growing up, except for books.'

I switched gears. 'By the way, how did Bijoy find us?'

'Dr Verma. I got intel that he sold us out to the Mandal in exchange for his own coke territory. I should have known better than to trust someone who doesn't trust anyone.'

'Where is he now?'

Johnny shrugged. 'Don't know. Don't care. There are bigger battles to fight. Let's keep moving. We don't want that fountain turning into a tomb.'

We emerged on to a loud main street, the wet, earthy scent giving way to acrid stench of smoke. A blue-and-white street sign read: Chowringhee Road.

Across the street was an enormous colonial-era building with golden domes in the corners, one doubling up as a clock tower. Baroque in its style, its pale-yellow façade was dressed in arched and recessed windows, partially hidden by swaying trees and insurance billboards.

'This city never stops surprising me,' I murmured.

'Keep your head down and walk slowly. No need to run and catch anyone's attention.'

I realized I was almost jogging. 'Finding it tough to keep up with me, are you, little girl?' I said.

Johnny rolled his eyes.

'Laugh at yourself once in a while,' I said.

'Yeah, now's the perfect time to get in touch with myself and work on my humour.'

'It is. In fact, there's no better time to do it.'

'Okay, Mommy,' he smirked.

We walked a few more yards. Johnny's disapproving glares did little to stop me from looking everywhere but down—there was too much to take in. Manhattan's hurried verve was home and always would be. But this was different—a crash course in colour and cacophony, an endless reservoir of shocks and reverberations. I was a hungry kid in candy land, overdosing on strangers and strangeness. On my first day here, I had been a mere spectator of possibilities, peering out of a car window. Now, I was one of them.

We crossed an under-construction pergola, its flapping canvas and wooden beams leading to a massive structure ahead. Made with bamboos and prefab sheets, it looked like a replica of a temple and was at least 20 metres high. Underneath, a tight lattice of bamboo stalks and jute ropes held a stage, half covered with metal sheets.

Drum paradiddles and cymbal clangs filled the air. About 50 men wearing white vests hammered, pulled and drilled in unison, while boys jumped around them, hoping to learn their trade. I couldn't help but stop and take in the splendour, snapping pictures on my phone. I had turned into a virgin tourist just like those in New York City.

Johnny gave up on trying to make me blend into the crowd and decided we could afford a breather.

'The puja season begins soon,' he informed me. 'Here, and in a thousand other places like this, the goddess Durga's idol will be placed and worshipped under bright lights and amid triumphant music. Thousands will gather every day to celebrate, pray, dance and seek blessings from the warrior goddess.'

'And you find this city boring? There's so much to see and do! And feel.'

'I never said I found it boring. I said—'

'Of course you said you found it boring.'

'I said I hated the city,' Johnny corrected. 'It's a lot of

things…but certainly not boring.'

'You don't hate the city either. It's just crap you keep telling yourself.'

'Keep moving.' He lowered his sheepish eyes and started walking.

A little farther ahead, we crossed the street and entered a stuffy indoor marketplace selling sporting goods. A narrow aisle lit with white tubes and twinkling LEDs snaked through the space. Shops on both sides spilled over with colourful jerseys, soccer shoes and badminton racquets—most of those with misspelt brand names like 'Mike' and 'Badass'. The place smelled like moist wine corks, a low-tide beach with no air.

Chatty shop owners leaned behind narrow counters, watching us from the corners of their eyes, hopeful of closing a sale on a slow day. Could any of them be from the Mandal? Had someone noticed my blonde hair peeking from my scarf? Or Johnny's waddle? Was that smiling shopkeeper we just passed picking up his phone to call in the cavalry? Was death waiting for us right around the bend?

'Of all the places, you figured this to be the safest?' I whispered without looking at Johnny. Each breath felt heavier than the last, as we walked deeper into the retail labyrinth. Early raindrops pattered on the asbestos roof above.

'It's the only place in Taltala that doesn't belong to the Mandal. And we're away from prying eyes.'

I heaved a sigh. 'Feels like a trap to me. Is the way in and out the same?'

Johnny didn't answer. He ambled along, wearing that sheepish look again. 'Keep walking. We're close.'

He was much calmer than I was; he was calm escaping fires and almost getting shot at but fidgety and jumpy when nothing happened. As if the rush of adrenaline kept him grounded.

As we reached the end of the aisle, Johnny stopped in front of a desolate shop with no signboard, its shutter rolled down, and knocked. The shutter was opened by Shamshu. Inside sat a small, scruffy boy, about eight or nine years old, on a stool, completely immersed in a phone, oblivious to his surroundings.

We hurried in and Shamshu pulled the shutter down behind us.

'We don't have much time,' Shamshu said, looking at me.

'Hello,' I said, kneeling before the boy.

He looked up momentarily before turning back to his phone. He was Imaan's son. He had his father's narrow face and that same hair—curly on the sides, straight at the top. He wore an oversized shirt and dirty jeans. He was fairer, probably had his mother's skin, his eyes droopy, and I knew why.

'My name's Katherine. You can call me Kath. My friends call me that.'

He didn't look up, but his eyes darted across the floor. I knew he was listening.

'Your father was my friend.'

'Akhil.'

'You look just like your father, Akhil.'

He finally looked up and glared at me. 'Where's my father?'

I sighed, trying to hold back tears, but a few rowdy ones still escaped. 'He's...with God now. But he...he asked me to come and meet you. Be your friend. And take care of you. He really loved you.'

He went back to his phone, pretending not to believe me.

'You were lucky to have a father like him. I never had one.'

He looked up again; his glare had mellowed.

'He said you speak great English. And I can see that now. Which school do you go to?'

'I used to,' Akhil murmured. 'Now I don't. They say I don't need to. They will teach me everything.' He rubbed his eyes. 'But I want to sleep. And I can't.'

'Don't worry. I promise you will sleep. I couldn't sleep for years. I know what you're going through. I'll help you sleep. And go to school. Will you come with me?'

The boy sprang up, ready to go. His eyes were wide and glassy. As I stood up and extended my hand, a sharp knock came at the shutter. And then another. Johnny gestured for us to stay quiet while Shamshu took his gun out. The knocking quickly escalated into loud, frantic banging, accompanied by threatening voices.

Akhil clutched me and I looked at Johnny, who glared back at me. His eyes were the same ones I'd seen in the smoke when we'd escaped the fire—fiery and afraid.

The shutter rattled violently. It would give in at any second.

'I promised him I wouldn't die!' Johnny shouted suddenly. 'I have to tell everyone. Yes, I can save all of us! I can save your mother, Kath!'

'What?' I asked.

Everyone has their breaking point. When, after all they've seen and done and endured, the reservoir of calm dries up. I was sure Johnny had just reached his and finally gone off the deep end.

But, like so many times these past few weeks, I was wrong.

28 Under a Mountain of Sludge and Mire

.•Johnny•.

My house felt different. Not because it had been ransacked and lay in dark ruins—it just didn't feel like home anymore.

A full moon poured in through the lonely window. Water from the evening rain dripped from the corners, tapping softly against the floor. I kept the flashlight off, lest it woke up the neighbours in the middle of an unreasonably quiet night. They'd be happy to see me, but I couldn't risk who else might be alerted in the process. Surely the Mandal would have men planted nearby, sleeping under a pulling cart or hiding inside the darkness of an auto.

Jhansi and Laxmi, my fluttering friends, were gone. Maybe they felt the same way about the place. Or maybe they missed me too much.

Shamshu, my loyal, persistent, sometimes irksome giant glue, walked quietly behind me as I looked around. Clothes lay scattered. My new fridge had been gutted, melted chocolate having made its way through the cracked door. They should have left my chocolates alone.

The kitchen shelves had been torn down, canisters smashed— jagged necks lay abandoned, their plastic caps still intact. We trudged over broken glass and rice.

A passing vehicle cast a brief wash of lights on the walls—

they were painted with threats in red, fish swimming in imaginary waters.

My study table lay shattered in the middle of the room, its drawers open and empty. If there had been anything worth finding here, they would have found it. The largest crime syndicate in the city—maybe even the country—was desperate to find me. Or what I had. Smiling, I breathed in the familiar scent of fish and sat on a creaking chair to think.

Back in Taltala—inside that shuttered shop—cornered and without help, I had been sure we wouldn't make it out.

I pictured armed men forcing their way in while shopkeepers gathered around them, ready for a gory show. The only way out was *through* them.

I also imagined Debroy outside, ready with a literary quip and paan-stained smile. He'd have a hearty squeal, seeing me dressed like a girl. That's when I realized the journalist, Amitav Banerjee, must have slipped something into my pocket when he'd picked me up: 'You have to tell everyone. Promise me you won't die. Use it when the time is right.'

It.

Why hadn't I realized earlier? Maybe I would have actually had something to threaten the Mandal with. Maybe Rampal wouldn't have died if I'd remembered. Maybe I could've saved him.

Eventually we found the courage to pull up the shutter. Not that we had much choice. It was futile to stay inside; they would have broken through in a few minutes anyway. But when we did, we weren't met with armed men.

We only found a vexed mob of shopkeepers, led by one in the centre who looked the angriest. The shop belonged to him, and we were the usurpers of his only asset. We explained to them that we weren't interested in the store. Turned out Shamshu had paid the shopkeeper's slap-happy son for using the space for a few hours. While the boy was off spending the money on his girlfriend, we had an unsuspecting, angry father to contend with.

A few wads of notes helped him see our point of view, and Shamshu's gun convinced the remaining non-believers. We were out in no time, with a boy who rather enjoyed the commotion. And hearing a dwarf girl with a man's voice. The poor kid's puffy eyes barely stayed open, thanks to the all the cocaine injected into him.

On our way out, Kath bought him a soccer jersey against my strong advice on not fooling around with the fickle-minded shopkeepers. But when had my advice ever stopped her?

She looked happy, victorious. If it weren't for her constant insistence on finding the kid, he would have been lost forever, swallowed by the city's underbelly. Maybe one day he'd have stood behind a corrupt cop, helping him cut someone's throat.

So yeah, we'd done something good.

Shamshu's voice broke my reverie. 'We should leave. There's nothing here.'

'The clothes I wore the night the journalist was killed. They have to be here.'

'If they were here, the Mandal would have found them.'

Then I remembered. They weren't in the house. That night, when I'd reached home, panic stricken, I'd removed them and thrown them out the window. Straight into the garbage below.

I stood up. 'I threw them out!'

'Out? Where?'

'Into the dump below. I was scared they might recognize me by my clothes.'

Shamshu walked over to the window and peered down. 'Do you think they're still there?'

I joined him, looking at the unfriendly pile beneath. I imagined it teeming with used condoms, cigarette butts and soiled diapers. Maybe worse.

'They have to be. It's a pile of garbage no one ever touches,' I said.

Shamshu flinched.

I grinned. 'C'mon. How bad can it be, beekeeper?'

We took the rustic ladder with the missing rungs to make our way down. I still had my muscle memory, but Shamshu slipped a few times, causing the rickety structure to shake. For once it wasn't me falling down the steps.

Midway, a light flicked on. A window creaked opened. We froze.

The grizzly light sleeper on the second floor mumbled something, then shut the window and switched off the light. We waited a few beats before continuing our climb down, then hunched into the crawl space below the building. Invisible, giddy mosquitoes welcomed us warmly.

'It smells like shit,' Shamshu complained.

'It probably is.'

We hopped into the dump. While all it did to Shamshu was cover his calves, it sucked me right in, up to my chest, that wretched quicksand full of unmentionable filth. It smelled of curdled yoghurt and fermented rice. We gave our noses a second to recover, then got to work. Our hands roamed through the moist, sticky muck but didn't find my clothes.

'This is ridiculous.' Shamshu stood upright and looked at his grimy hands.

Just as I was about to give up as well, I felt it. A squishy cloth with buttons, buried deep inside a mountain of sludge and mire. I pulled it out to find my shirt—unrecognizable and layered with fungi. And then my pants.

There was nothing in them.

'This doesn't make sense. There has to be something. I'm sick of this!' I shouted.

I picked up an empty bottle of whisky—Rampal's favourite, probably the last he'd had—and hurled it against the wall. Glass shattered, glittering briefly before sinking into the filth.

'Let's get out of this shithole, Johnny. We don't even know what we're looking for,' Shamshu pleaded.

He was right. I was chasing ghosts. Every minute we stayed in the open, we put ourselves—and our friends—at risk.

Like an unsung hero from an unread comic, I'd hoped to find a magic lamp in the dump—rub away my miseries and undo the deaths. All because I believed a dying man's final words to mean something.

I should have known better.

I should have been caught by Debroy that night in that dark alley and let him put me out of my misery.

The alley.

The narrow passage between two homes where I had hidden from Debroy.

That was it.

If Amitav Banerjee had slipped something into my pocket, if there had been anything on me that night—anything at all— that was the only place I could have dropped it.

The only place left to check.

My only chance to avenge my friend's death. To get Kath's mother back. To bring the bastards down.

My last chance.

'Wait. There's one more place.'

'Johnny, it's going to be morning soon. Are you sure? We can come back tomorrow night. That bottle probably woke up the whole neighbourhood.'

'I have to know. I can't go back without knowing. I have to find out.'

'Of course you do.' Shamshu climbed out of the dump and pulled me up. 'Let's go before someone sees us.'

◆

We drove to the alley where I'd cheated death for the first time.

Where everything had changed. This was where it all had started. The rush of life, the alienation of fear. Maybe, just maybe, this was where it would all begin to end.

Shamshu followed my directions as I guided him deeper into the labyrinth of alleys. I knew exactly where to go.

'Stop here.'

I jumped out.

The nook where I had hidden was seared into my memory, but I couldn't see it. The walls. The narrow opening between them.

Gone.

Swallowed by something large and colourful.

A canopy stretched across the alley—polyester, translucent, shimmering in the weak dawn light. A pandal for the upcoming puja season. I forced my way between the fabric and the wall, finally finding the dark crevice that had saved me. Shamshu stayed back—he was too big to fit without bringing the entire structure down. I gulped a stone down my throat and switched on the flashlight, looking around for anything that seemed out of place on the dusty floor.

There—peeking through a tangle of wet leaves—was a yellow flash drive. I picked it up like it was something fragile, a butterfly. It was wet and mucky, but so was I.

Could it be just another flash drive, lost by a careless boy, swept inside by the rain and rendered useless? Could it just be a collection of porn, tossed out a window by a furious wife? Could it be nothing but a mirage?

No.

I knew it was more than that. It had to be.

29 Halloween on Steroids

✢Katherine✢

We sat around the table, staring at a yellow flash drive like it was a relic in a museum. No one was touching it, talking about it or placing any bets on what it contained. Doing that would jinx it, it seemed.

Bright, dusty morning light pierced through the joints of the closed wooden windows of the safe house. They also failed to keep out the loud, disjointed music from the street—blaring, stopping, blaring again—as the speakers were tested for the festivities about to begin. It was *Shasthi*, the day the grand idol of Goddess Durga would be revealed inside a golden pavilion draped in flowing linens, illuminated by dancing lights and adorned with ice sculptures of slain monsters. The evening's ritual would mark the *Akal Bodhon*—the untimely awakening of the goddess from her divine slumber—signalling the start of the Durga Puja celebrations.

It was almost like Halloween. But on steroids.

I pressed my hands together so they wouldn't lunge for the damn flash drive. What was the point of having it if we were not going to do anything? Sure, I understood the stakes—our lives depended on this—but staring at it wasn't going to make its contents pop out into a hologram and talk to us: *Here, these are things you can use to blackmail the mob. These will get you back your mother. And this button here? This will make your nightmares go away.*

And then I'd wake up in my apartment, after a rare restful

night, as Olav licked my ears. I missed Olav. I missed my
sleepless nights with him. There were no nightmares in them.

The silence was fickle, perforated with bass-puffed Bollywood
songs. Finally fed up, I yelled, 'What in Jimi's blessed ass are
we waiting for?'

'I... I'm just thinking of how to use it against them. We
have to be careful this time, now that we have real leverage.'

Johnny sat across from me, his head barely floating above
the table.

'And what if it just has reruns of *Friends*?' I asked.

'It doesn't. It can't,' he insisted.

'Fantastic. Shamshu, what do you think?' I turned to the
giant teddy bear on my right.

'I'm just relishing the quiet,' he murmured.

I turned to Rakhi.

'Don't look at me,' she said. 'I don't understand computers.
I don't even know what this is.'

I stretched and grabbed the small piece of plastic. Johnny
gasped like I'd just desecrated a holy artefact. His eyes ballooned
to the size of his open mouth.

'It's in terrible shape,' I said, turning it over my fingers.
'Even if it does have dirty secrets and mob stories, they might
be gone forever. The USB connector is rusted and can't be used.'

'I'm trying to find a computer specialist—'

'Jimi be dead, are you kidding me? Get me a jar of uncooked
rice, a functional flash drive, a soldering kit and a laptop. You
already have a specialist.'

'Uncooked rice? We could get you biryani,' Johnny said,
his eyes still wide and blank.

'What's a soldering—' Shamshu started.

'Go. Get me the damn things!'

They scampered like obedient children while I revelled in the absurdity of it all. They were listening to me—a hapless, lost girl they didn't owe a damn thing to.

But by now I knew better. They did it because they were my friends. My only friends.

Once I had my tools, I got to work. I buried the flash drive's memory chip in rice to dry it out. Then I soldered it on to the circuit of the new drive and connected it to the laptop. It took me a few hours, my mind drifting back to the phone call with Mr Elenburg the day before.

He had seemed genuinely concerned, and relieved, when he spoke to me.

'Thank God, Ms Gladwell. I've been worried sick. The investigating company called to tell me their investigator had disappeared. And then I couldn't reach you. I imagined the worst.'

I told him everything.

'I'm so sorry to hear this. I suppose you still don't want to come back, so I won't ask. What can I do? Do you want me to send people from here?'

'I need you to arrange admission to a rehab centre far away from this city.'

'I'm so glad you decided to quit. Why don't you—'

'It's not for me. It's for a child. I need it to be the best in this country. And after that, I need his education and living expenses to be taken care of. Maybe a nice boarding school in the hills, away from this madness.'

'Sure. Text me the details, and I'll find the right place. How are you on money? Do you need me to transfer more?'

'I'm okay. But I lost my passports... Both of them.'

'Leave that to me.'

'When is the verdict?'

'Ten days. Most likely you'll be convicted for possession with intent to distribute. Carries at least five years in jail. Unless you come back to fight it and prove your innocence.'

'Ten days, huh?' My mind went back to that night. I hadn't had any coke on me, hadn't sold or distributed anything. So why these insane charges? Who wanted me out of the way?

'Yes. And needless to say, if you don't show up, you'll forfeit the family—'

'Needless to say.'

'Ms Gladwell, do you have any leads? Any inroads? Any hope of finding your mother?'

'Hope… That's all I have.'

He didn't sound like a man who had anything to do with what was happening. My mom trusted him; my father had trusted him. What possible motivation would he have to harm the family?

Could it be Charles, the CEO? But what would he gain from any of this? If I lost my share of the trust, the money would go to charity.

It didn't make any sense. Nothing did.

The door swung open, cutting through my thoughts. As the trio walked back in, I turned the laptop towards them. 'I have good news and bad news.'

'Bad news-good news,' Johnny and Rakhi said in unison.

'Good news first,' Shamshu muttered.

'The good news is that the content is intact,' I said. 'The bad news—it's heavily encrypted.'

'So…it can't be done?' Johnny asked.

'I need time. And a much faster laptop with at least seven terabytes of computational power. And the right set of software. I—'

'Let's get her whatever she needs,' Johnny said, looking at Shamshu. 'How long will you need, Kath?'

'If it can be cracked, probably a day.'

◆

A day and a million coffees later, we were back at the table.

Still no luck.

The music outside had stopped, replaced by the ceaseless sounds of drums—*dhaak*, according to Johnny—their rhythmic beats rolling through the streets like an unbroken chant.

I rubbed my face, stretched my fingers and exhaled. 'I was hoping the encryption was based on a simpler asymmetric cryptography, but it's AES-256.'

Blank faces stared back at me.

'Um... There's good news and bad news,' I said.

'Good news!' they shouted.

'I have to tell you the bad news first, because...you know... the good news is based on the bad news and—'

'Kath, what's the bad news?' Johnny asked gently.

'I can't crack it. No one can. Not without a key. Trust me.'

They groaned and sighed. Shamshu started pacing like an impatient gorilla, while Rakhi sat staring, completely blank.

'And what would the good news be?' Johnny's face had lost colour but his voice sounded firm, in control.

'Some of the files in here look like account details for offshore banks—mostly in Mauritius, the Seychelles and Luxembourg.'

'Tax havens. Friendly to offshore, unaccounted money. No questions asked,' Rakhi declared, having found a familiar terrain: numbers and accounts.

I nodded. 'Correct. I'm guessing these are account numbers, IDs, passwords, amounts, addresses, money trails, et cetera. There are about 30 such files, each tied to a bank. Then there are other documents, but I don't know what they contain.'

'If you can't open the files, how do you know they are bank account details?' Johnny asked.

'There's a master list matching the random filenames to bank names. It was a simple password-protected file. I could crack it with a simple rainbow table. A rainbow table—'

'So all we really have are bank names from around the world,' said Johnny. 'Not sure how that's even close to good news. This won't—'

'Hold the phone, my friend,' I said.

'How will holding a phone help?'

'I meant hold your horses.'

'Why wouldn't you say that then?'

'Jimi and his blazing guitars…forget I said anything. Now listen. We know these individual files contain important bank information. The money involved has to be serious, given people have died for it. We also know the Mandal is desperate to get their hands on this. Which means they don't have another copy of this. And are without access to their foreign accounts.'

'No, no, no. I tried blackmailing them with an empty threat, Kath, and it didn't work. This won't—'

'I'm not asking you to blackmail them. I'm asking you to hold the key in your hand.'

'I don't understand.'

'We encrypt the encrypted files.'

Johnny looked at me, his eyes gleaming as colour rushed back to his cheeks. 'We can encrypt an already encrypted file?'

'Yes. Then we get what we want from them. We don't need to know what's inside those files. All we need to do is lock them up and have the only key that can open it.'

'So we lock the lock?' Shamshu asked.

'Exactly!' I said.

'But we still can't bring them down,' said Rakhi. 'We don't have any evidence. If we're lucky, we'll get your mother back. But what about Rampal? What about justice?'

I couldn't blame her for that. 'Don't worry, Rakhi. I want the same justice you do. There's more.'

'Go on,' Johnny said.

'We'll set up a meeting. Tell them we have what they need, but we've encrypted it. Ask them to bring my mother and a laptop. I'll connect the flash drive and enter the key to "unlock" our encryption. While I'm doing that, my phone will capture the IP address of their laptop. They'll definitely check the files for authenticity—decrypt them with their key. And the moment they do, an app on my phone will secretly hack their laptop and transfer all the unencrypted data to us. We'll get my mother in exchange for the flash drive, and then we'll bring them down with everything there is in those bank records and other documents. If that doesn't work, we'll suck them dry by taking out all the money. I'm sure that'll hurt them.'

Johnny looked out the window, lost in thought. Then he turned to me. 'So the genius finally surfaced from the sea of powder. All those sleepless nights, listening to your crazy reasons for needing coke, weren't worth nothing.'

'It wasn't, was it?' I smirked. 'And it's a good thing…because no "computer specialist" would come up with this, let alone suggest doing it themselves.'

'Are you sure you can do whatever you said with the IP and—'

'Are you sure you can arrange a meeting with RC and company and hold them long enough for me?' I asked.

'Let's think this through,' Johnny said, sitting down. 'There are a lot of holes in your plan. First, they have to take the bait and meet us somewhere we choose. Not in a tram. Not in a dollhouse.

'Second, our assumption about these documents has to be correct. These files have to contain something valuable. Third, everything has to go according to the plan. What if they catch you stealing their IP? What if they don't check the flash drive right there?

'Fourth, what if the technology doesn't work? Fifth, let's say we give them what they want and get the information we need. What stops them from killing us right there? That's what I would do if I were them. What good will the information be to us if we're all dead?'

'I don't have a better plan. Do you?' I asked him. His sheep eyes resurfaced.

'I'll go to the meeting alone,' Rakhi declared. She stood up, wide-eyed and excited. 'The data from the laptop can be relayed to Kath's phone, and then we can use it against them later.'

Johnny shook his head. 'Not happening.'

'Agreed,' I said. 'Also, you'd need to work the laptop and the phone at the same time. I don't think you'll be able to do it.'

'Let me do it. You can teach me what needs to be done,' Shamshu said.

'No one is dying! No one. Stop trying to be heroes!' Johnny shouted. 'We have to think of a way to get out of this alive. I need you guys alive. I want to see Debroy one last time before he's finished. I want to see the Mandal pay for Rampal. Sacrificing ourselves is easy. Our lives are worth as much as theirs.'

'It has to be a public place,' I said.

'That won't stop them. They don't care if people see. Who

will the witnesses go to? The police?' Rakhi said.

'So then what?' Shamshu said. 'We just go ahead with it, bare and vulnerable? Like Johnny said, there are a million ways this could go wrong. I don't have enough guys to protect us in a public place. And I'm sure they'll have many. Cops too.'

Silence followed. And stayed with us for what seemed like forever. Several questions pounded at the walls of our minds, waiting to break in and play havoc, while a few unsure answers defended a shrinking territory.

This was our only shot. We couldn't afford to screw it up. We had to be the best versions of ourselves. *I* had to be the best version of myself. This was what I had come to Kolkata to do. The world had taken my father; it wasn't going to take my mother. Not if I had any say about it.

We needed a diversion. A way to buy us time to get away. Something chaotic. Something that destroyed—to create... Just like the goddess.

'I think I know what needs to be done.'

The three pairs of eyes turned to me; no one dared to breathe.

'But it's not going to be pretty.' I picked up my coffee mug, taking a long, cold, pungent sip. 'Jimi be damned, it's not going to be pretty at all.'

30 Come an Earthquake

✦ Katherine ✦

It would soon pour.

I stood by Johnny's window, inhaling the cool morning air and remembering the streets of an October New York—strangers from a previous life. Who would've thought I'd end up in Kolkata, standing on the edge of storm, soon to face the mob of a treacherous beautiful city?

Rain under my chin. Courage on my lips.

Courage that, in some distant life back home, would have shocked me. Now it oozed from my pores, feeding off the danger ahead. The odds. The fire. The losses and gains.

'Here. This is the last of them.' Johnny passed me a pill, which I swallowed. 'You're now coke-free.' He smiled.

We were all gathered in Johnny's house, waiting for nightfall. It was pointless to hide anymore, now that they would be here soon. We could only manage a day to prepare, and I hoped it was enough.

Whatever happened tonight would be washed away by the rains and swallowed by the drains and cesspools. One way or another, tonight would change the course of my life…our lives. And the lives of hundreds of others. For some, it would end them.

The dice had been rolled, and the odds were stacked against everything and everyone. Except hope—that cunning, ironic monster that never abandoned the underdog. All we needed were double sixes—a faultless alignment of stars—for the game to turn in our favour.

It was *Ashtami*—the heart of Durga Puja, Rakhi had said. Through the window, I watched people gather at the *pandal*, dressed in their finest, ready to offer Pushpanjali—a ritual offering of flowers accompanied by sacred mantras, performed in quiet reverence to the goddess. The pandal shimmered like a temple of light, and the air felt thick with energy—ancient and powerful. The *Sandhi Puja* would be held soon, at the cusp of day and night, when it's believed Durga became Chamunda, slaying the demons Chanda and Munda in a blaze of divine fury. As the sun set, Ashtami, the eighth day, would give way to *Navami*, another big day of celebration—an inflection point cherished and remembered by this world for over a thousand years.

Could this be our inflection point? Hell, could this be mine?

I closed my eyes and whispered my own prayer.

'It's unbelievable RC agreed to meet us here. I've never seen him outside of a tram,' Johnny said from the floor, his back against the peeling wall.

'It proves we have something of critical importance. He's desperate,' I said.

'She's right. Otherwise he would have sent his dog, Debroy, to do the barking and biting,' Rakhi added. She was pouring lassi into tumblers for us. Rakhi was always feeding us with something. Always.

'Oh, Debroy will be here too, for sure, along with an army of cops. I could tell he was itching to run his blade on me when I spoke to him, given Kath and I escaped his torture chamber. No literary quotes from him this time—only his choicest blessings in Bengali.'

'Let him squirm. We need him angry and out of control. That's the only way he won't be at his sharpest,' Shamshu said, greasing his revolver.

'Did he agree to bring my mother?' I asked.

'I told him there's no deal without her. And that we would rather die. I think he was convinced. Let's hope RC is too.'

'Your tram traveller better show up with my mother. If not, I'm cutting open his throat before he can slice mine. I don't care anymore.'

'Let's focus on what we need to do,' Johnny said. 'Remember, we need to be connected on the phone all the time. Kath, you have to point Debroy towards me. I'll do the rest. He can't be near the flash drive when it's being checked. Otherwise he'll smell a fish.'

'What if he refuses to move his skinny ass?' I asked.

'They'll want to tie up loose ends. And I'm the loosest end. All you have to do is make him sniff my blood. Make him see my scarecrow cut-out.'

'Got it,' I said. 'It should take a few minutes for the drive to be exchanged and the data to be transferred on my phone. When it's done, I'll say "Namaste"—that's your signal, Johnny. You have to make sure Debroy is exactly where he should be. It's the only way we'll be able to vanish into the crowd. If we make it out alive, we'll meet back at the safe house. Hopefully the data will tell us what to do next. I've texted my cloud ID and password to all of you in case things don't go well for me.'

'Are you sure the people of Hazaar Basti will be safe?' Johnny asked me. 'The last thing we want is them caught in the crossfire.'

'As sure as I can be,' I said. 'If my calculations are correct, they'll get paid for it instead.'

'What are we possibly missing?' Johnny said.

Rakhi pressed a glass into my hand, smiling softly. 'Lassi,' she said.

◆

.✦ Johnny ✦.

Kath's plan of diversion was downright outrageous. But it was exactly what we needed.

The fact that I'd doubled it up as a way to avenge Rampal's death only made it sweeter. We'd worked hard to set things in motion, given we only had a day. The plan had a lot of moving parts and 'danger' written all over it. But we'd signed up for it and couldn't afford buyer's remorse. It was the perfect way to end this. Even poetic, if you ask me.

Life had drawn a full, crooked circle. If I made it out alive, I'd go back to being nobody. But that didn't tear me up into a thousand unimportant pieces. If anything, I still felt relevant, strangely content in my own bowed legs.

We were close to bringing the goddamn Mandal down. The same people I'd once cut a deal with. In this twisted mess of shifting fortunes and new alliances, I'd ended up exactly where I wanted to be. A great man once said, 'If you can't beat them, join them. But if you can, knock them the hell down.' Well, he didn't exactly say that, but knock them down we would.

'It looks just like you, only taller,' Shamshu said, grinning at the full-size cut-out of me we'd just had made at a local photo studio.

'Hilarious,' I muttered. 'Now can we please put it in your car without making a scene? It's embarrassing.'

He took his time, walking slowly across the road, holding it up so the children could see and dance around it. And there I was—walking right next to my own ridiculous cardboard twin. Sadist beekeeper.

'How many men do we have?' I asked.

'Not enough.' He loaded the cut-out and we got in.

'Listen. I didn't discuss this with the others, but we need to talk about what to do if things go south.'

'Kill as many as we can before we die. That would be my plan.'

'No, there's more at stake, my friend. Stay close to Rakhi and Kath. Get them to the airport. If we're lucky and Kath is successful in transferring the data, take Rakhi's help to make sense of the Mandal's numbers and send the information to all the media outlets. Hopefully someone will have the balls to run it.'

'You playing a martyr again?'

'Just playing out all scenarios. Chances are I'll be dead, considering I'd literally be asking Debroy to do that.'

'Don't worry,' Shamshu said. 'The caricature will save you.'

'It's not a caricature.'

'Well, it looks like one.'

'Well, it isn't. You got our share of the money from the reservoir?'

'Yes.'

'And the rest is still there?'

'Yes, like you wanted,' he said. 'I have your share. If you don't want it invested in the biggest apiary in the country, you'd better make it back.'

I shrugged. 'I wouldn't know a better way to spend it anyway.'

'You could buy a chocolate factory.'

'For someone who might die, you seem all happy and spry.'

'We aren't dying tonight, Johnny. I know it,' Shamshu said with a smile.

'Great, now you are a crystal gazer as well.'

'Johnny, I have something to ask.' His smile disappeared.

'Shoot.'

'Promise me you won't tell anyone.'

'C'mon. Out with it already.'

'Who the fuck is Jimi?'

'What?'

'Jimi. Kath keeps saying his name.'

I laughed. 'Just a rock star. Don't worry about it.'

✦

We returned to the shanty late in the afternoon, just a few hours before the Mandal's men were due.

They'd meet us at 7 p.m. by the entrance of the puja pandal at the heart of the shanty; by then the place would be swarming with hundreds of people—packed together in celebration—for us to disappear into. Shamshu and his men would be watching over us, hidden in the throngs, ready for action.

The music. The chaos. The drunk, dancing bodies—everything should be enough for Kath to do what she needed. And to push Debroy towards me. We'd be waiting for him just a hundred metres away, me and my 'caricature'.

At the stroke of 'namaste', this shanty would witness the biggest, brightest, loudest and most prosperous Durga Puja it had ever seen.

31 Higher Ground

✦Katherine✦

The Mandal didn't bring my mother.

A portly, bald man stood in front of me, smirking and smoking. His shiny head had more scars than skin. Weird fish tattoos skirted his thick neck, and his pants were so loose they could double as parachutes. Pretty much what I'd been told to expect.

Debroy stood next to him, looking angrier than the last time. Behind him were at least half a dozen men who certainly weren't here to worship. There were more of them; I could feel their invisible eyes watching me.

It was dark now. Behind me, the entrance to the eclectic puja pavilion glowed with bright lights flashing pink, red and blue. Hundreds of worshippers in their most colourful clothes passed by me, hands folded in reverence. Priests chanted in unison, their voices filling the damp air as they prepared for the Sandhi Puja. Soon, 108 lamps would be lit, their flames flickering in unison like a prophecy coming to life, marking the divine intersection of destruction and renewal, rage and grace.

Outside the pavilion, children giggled and clambered on to a mini merry-go-round with Godzillas and King Kongs painted on it. Multitudes of people descended upon the food stalls, preferring the churn of spicy festive grub instead of roller coasters.

The study beats of dhaak echoed through the hubbub. It was accompanied by the piercing *ulu-dhwani* of the women—a rhythmic, high-pitched ulutation that rang out in waves of devotion.

Rakhi told me these sound codes had been passed down through generations, from mothers to their daughters, since medieval times. They were supposed to ward off evil during important occasions and different events had their specific codes. Three breath cycles, or *jhar*, were for worship; 14 for celebrating the fourth day of marriage. But come an earthquake, they would jhar repeatedly, passing the message of imminent danger on to the next village.

I sang my own silent ululation in my heart. If ever I was ready for something, it was today.

'You brought an army to protect yourself from a woman?' That wasn't the way I'd planned to start the conversation, but not finding my mother with them had pissed me off.

'Ms Gladwell, it's a pleasure to finally meet you. Forgive me; I don't do too well in open, public spaces. But since you and…your friend insisted, I obliged. You've been a difficult guest, sniffing around corners you shouldn't.' RC's voice was low and breathy, almost inaudible amid the constant chatter of the crowd assembled at the pandal. He made no effort to speak louder.

'Not as difficult as you've been.'

'Why, I take offence in that. We've treated you like our guest. Guests are God, just like the one inside that pandal. But you burned down the very place of hospitality.' He turned to Debroy. 'Was there something lacking in our hospitality, Debroy Sir? I thought we served Ms Gladwell the best cocaine in the country.'

Debroy ignored him, scanning the area instead.

'Where's my mother? This doesn't happen without her. There's no deal if—'

260 + The Fires We Become

'You could learn some patience from your mother,' RC said.

'I have other qualities I rely on.'

'I'm very curious to know what made you run away with that midget. Did he promise to save your mother?'

I scoffed. 'I promised him I would bring all of you down.'

'You know, Ms Gladwell,' RC sighed, shaking his head, 'with time, promises ripen into conversations...then slowly ferment into lies. It's almost pitiful to see you swim in so many lies.'

Debroy finally spoke. 'Where is that rat?'

'I'll tell you where he is when you tell me where my mother is.'

RC tsked. 'You didn't think we'd bring her out here in the open, did you? She's safe and close, ready to be handed over once we get what we want.'

'Sorry. That doesn't work.'

Johnny's voice crackled in my earpiece. 'Kath, we'll get your mother. We have to get the decrypted data. Don't kill this.'

Debroy took a step closer. 'How do you see this going down? You thought we'd come here, hand over your mother, take the drive and shake hands? Even you can't be that naïve. Now let's get on with it. Give us the flash drive and tell me where Johnny is. You've seen what I can and will do if we don't get what—'

'Here's what will happen,' I cut him off. 'You'll bring my mother here, and I'll give you the drive. We have people everywhere. They won't just watch whatever you have in mind.'

'There is nothing more deceptive than an obvious fact,' Debroy said. 'Do you know who said that?'

'Stop hiding your cowardice behind your stupid quotes.'

'Not true... Not true at all. I live in these quotes. Breathe them...for the world outside is very polluted.'

'And who polluted it?'

'I'm not the first and certainly won't be the last. Anyway, since you don't believe me, I'll have to demonstrate my power to you again.' Debroy waved his hands; within seconds, Shamshu and his team were shoved into the open by their captors, their hands locked behind their heads. 'Like I said, there's nothing more deceptive than an obvious fact. You aren't dealing with street goons, madam. You are dealing with *the street*. Information scores over muscle. And more muscle scores over muscle.'

Tiny drops of rain ghosted down my forearms. Ice cold.

'He's such a show-off, Ms Gladwell. Don't mind the theatrics,' RC spoke up, scratching his neck. 'Even the strongest men melt before it. Now let's not waste each other's time. Would you kindly hand over what we need? Debroy Sir hates killing in a religious space. Don't make him. He'll have to concoct an entire report for it. Too much paperwork. Wastes his time…our time.'

Johnny's voice ripped through my earpiece. 'What's going on, Kath? Talk to me!'

Shut up, Johnny. Let me think.

'So you have Shamshu and others in captivity. That I understand,' I said loudly. 'But I need to be clear: you'll let my mother go after I give you the drive?'

'Of course we will,' RC said.

'The drive and that little rat's location,' Debroy added.

Drops turned into a steady drizzle, but the crowd seemed unaffected, swirling around us in a blur of festival colours and movement.

'You see that water reservoir right behind the puja pavilion?' I pointed beyond the lights, where the water tower stood, strung with decorative bulbs. 'He's up there, waiting for you.'

Debroy's eyes snapped upwards. The shadow of a lonely dwarf could be seen perched atop, through the thin veil of rain.

'There he is!' Debroy squealed. He turned towards me. 'I'll see you soon, Ms Gladwell.'

'I doubt that,' I said.

He didn't hear me—he was already moving, a dozen men following, hands twitching at their holsters.

I turned to RC. 'Give me that laptop.'

RC nodded his neckless head towards a man, who brought me the device.

I opened it as he stood close to me, keenly observing what I was up to.

'Can I have some space? I can't work like this.'

RC gestured at his man, who moved away. I launched the decryption and started tracing the IP discovery. I needed time. I looked up at RC. 'Why did you kidnap my mother?'

'I thought that was pretty obvious. She was stealing our people. We don't take kindly to such things.'

'So why keep her alive? Why keep me locked in a room?'

'You know, I can't leave an opportunity like this to talk about precision.'

'I'm sorry?'

'Ms Gladwell, do you know what "escapement" means?'

I knew it had something to do with watches. 'No. What does it mean?'

'It is the mechanism inside a watch that allows the gears—one tooth at a time. With each movement, the gears push back, keeping the cycle going. That is escapement. But the result of all this is something even more powerful. In fact, there's nothing more powerful than it. Do you know what it is?'

I continued posing as a lost schoolgirl. I still needed time to trace the IP.

'The result is time,' he said.

'And what does that have to do with anything?'

'Everything.'

'So you kidnap people to pass the time?'

'I believe you're sharper than that, Ms Gladwell. Time... It is the answer to all your questions. To all our questions. If only we have the ability to see it. Now, have you decrypted the files?'

'Almost. Give it a minute.' Time... I needed more time. The damn thing was taking forever.

'Take your time. I'm not as impatient as Debroy Sir.'

'How did you find that piece of shit?'

RC smiled. 'He's a lot of things... Depends on which side you look from.'

'From where I'm standing, he looks like a big heap of trash.'

'Now now. Be kind.' He scratched the back of his neck. Again. 'I'll tell you a story I haven't told many people. Debroy... He was just a boy, helping his brother sell books in their little shop. It was next to mine.'

'Let me guess, you were a butcher.' I glanced at Shamshu, who seemed unperturbed by the gun thrusted at his back. His men were equally sharp, ready for what was to come.

RC laughed. 'I used to repair clocks. When the riots happened, they burned our shops and killed our families. I escaped. And pulled Debroy out with me. Since then, he's done everything I've asked of him.'

My phone screen flickered. Time remaining: 50 seconds.

'Who burned your shops?'

He shrugged. 'Hindus. Muslims. I never found out. That's why I named myself Rafiq Chowdhury. Keeps everyone happy. And confused.'

Johnny's voice crackled in my ear. 'Debroy is on his way up. He'll be there in two minutes.'

I was running out of conversation topics with a mobster.

'Do you always talk in clues?' I asked.

'Only when I'm made to.' RC lazily scratched his chest, making me cringe.

'And who makes you talk in clues?'

'Time. Speaking of which—are you done?'

'Yes.' I had the IP address. 'You can now decrypt the files with your key and check their authenticity.'

'No need. I trust you'd give us the genuine drive since you want your mother back. You won't play games like that dwarf.'

'Kath, he can't leave without checking it!' Johnny screamed in my ear. 'We'll have nothing. Make him check it. Kath? Kath!'

'What makes you think I wouldn't have expected you to come without my mother? What makes you so sure I'd give everything over so easily? I told you—there's no deal without her.'

RC studied me, his smirk shrinking. He wiped the sweat off his bald head.

'Check the drive quickly,' he finally instructed his techie.

My phone's screen lit up: Receiving data.

'Okay, he's up on the tower. Time for act two,' Johnny murmured in my ear.

My phone flashed again: Data transfer complete.

RC's techie sifted through the files, checking. Finally he shut the laptop and whispered something to RC.

'It seems everything's in place,' RC said. 'Thank you for your cooperation. I'm afraid you and I won't be staying to partake in the merriment.'

'That's such a pity! The fun's just getting started. Namaste!' I shouted, hands folded.

Over to you, Johnny.

◆

⋆ Johnny ⋆

Debroy and his men climbed the final steps of the water tank, their boots ringing against the steel.

I came out of my hiding spot below the tower and watched them walk slowly around the edge of the structure until they reached my cut-out.

Realizing what it was, Debroy hurled the cardboard figure, which tumbled 70 metres down.

Before he could call RC and warn him, I called him.

'Mr Debroy, sir. A bit of a bootless errand, wasn't it?'

'Where are you, Johnny? Enough of these games.'

'Look down,' I said. 'I hope you have your machete.'

He squealed as he peered down. 'Of course I do. It's been specially sharpened for your thick neck.'

'What? No nursery rhymes for me today?'

'You disappointed me last time,' Debroy said. 'I gave you a quote, you couldn't answer it and your friend paid for it. It's no fun for me anymore. So what's this circus all about? Scared to face me?'

'Humour and intelligence! Seems like I didn't waste my time after all. Let's just say I was curious to see a police commissioner and his dogs standing on top of a water reservoir, looking down at us mere mortals. Plus I've never killed a police officer before.'

'Why don't you give it a try? You want to come up or should I come down?'

'I was there with you,' I said, 'but you threw me down like an unwanted partner. Now here I am.'

'Then wait right there and I'll come say hello to you.'

I heard his squeal floating in the air. Then he instructed some of his men to move down.

'I wouldn't do that if I were you.'

'Why?'

'I'm thinking of an interesting headline for this massacre: "Corrupt Cops Go After Hidden Money in Water Tank and Are Blown to Smithereens." How does it sound?'

He stopped his men. 'Sounds interesting. Tell me more.'

'The water tank is strapped with explosives. It'll blow up if anyone moves.'

'I'm done with your bluffs, Johnny.'

'Don't trust me. Trust your eyes. Check the periphery. Check the columns. They're decorated with the stuff you like to play with.'

Debroy barked at his men. They fanned out, searching.

The water tank looked eerily bare—Shamshu had carefully removed all the bees' nests earlier. Couldn't have the bees getting hurt.

A tense pause.

Then—'What do you want?' Debroy said.

'Life's but a walking shadow, a poor player that struts and frets his hour upon the stage and then is heard no more. It is a tale told by an idiot, full of sound and fury, signifying nothing.'

'You could be a little original.'

'Oh, I will. You know, I read *Macbeth* in school. Never thought words written centuries ago by an English playwright would mean life or death for someone.'

'It was your fault. You stuck your nose where it didn't belong.'

'And you shouldn't have killed my friend. So here's the deal: picking up my phone activated the electronic ignition. The second I disconnect this call, *kaboom*! Your machete will probably be found in the same drain where you spilled the blood of that journalist. And probably a thousand others.'

I started walking away from the tower and towards Hazaar Basti.

'I... I'm listening. What do you want? We'll make you a Mandal leader. Give you free rein and police protection— whatever you want.'

His team scampered around the water tank, trying to figure out if they could dismantle the explosives. Temple bells tolled loudly, as the music from the puja pavilion stopped. It was time for the last *aarti*. The air pulsed with chants and drumbeats as priests raised their hands in prayer, flames from the aarti thalis circling in rhythmic arcs. Soon, the entire city would be swept into the ritual—voices lifted in unison, flowers offered with trembling hands, hearts heavy with awe and devotion. Tomorrow would bring *visarjan*, the final farewell. But tonight, they worshipped the goddess in her moment of fiercest grace.

'I don't need that anymore, Commissioner. I was a fool to chase that mirage.'

A few of his men started descending the ladder.

'Tell your guys not to try coming down. If they do, I'll disconnect the call to show my disappointment.'

'Okay.' Debroy turned to his team and commanded them to stop. They froze in place and looked down.

'Here's what might save you—tell me where Mrs Gladwell is being held, and I'll let you go.'

'I don't know! I don't know everything RC does! This isn't part of our business. I've never asked him, and he's never told me. I swear to God!'

'That's a pity.' I stopped walking and looked up again.

'You were born in dirt!' Debroy spat down from the edge of the reservoir. 'And you will die there!' He flung his machete. 'I've seen thousands of you come and go, thinking they have a right to something bigger. You fucking, inconsequential midget. Come up and fight like a man if you can!'

'Commissioner, we are all in the gutter, but some of us are looking at the stars.'

'What?'

I smiled. 'Yes, I figured you'd find that one difficult to place.'

'What are you talking about, you mad dwarf?'

'Another chance to save your life. Tell me where the quote comes from. If you answer correctly, I'll let you go.'

There was a long silence. I saw him sit down at the edge of the tank, legs dangling, staring at me. It was the same place where Rampal and I had spent hours talking about everything and nothing.

'It's a pity a scholar like you doesn't know that. While you look down at the hell you've created, I'm only looking up to what can be. That, Commissioner, is what I'm talking about.'

'You won't risk it. You won't risk the people in the shanty getting hurt from this. You know what happens if this collapses? This isn't a movie.'

'I know exactly what will happen, and I have Ms Gladwell to thank for that.'

Silence. Again.

'Do what you have to do,' he finally said. 'Tell me where that quote is from. I hate it.'

'I'm sure you do. You weren't the only one keeping an eye on us. Before we met at the idol workshop, I paid a visit to your house in the middle of the night to find out more about you. Pasco, Rancho and Pedro loved me—the irony. Then I checked your library. Pretty impressive. Rows filled with Shakespeare and…Dickens and…Shaw. There was one little guy missing though—Oscar Wilde. Not a single book of his.'

'Gay,' Debroy said. 'He was gay.'

'Namaste!' I heard Kath's voice in my ear.

'I guess your homophobia will cost you more than you thought.'

'Let me go... Please!'

'Did Rampal plead like that with you?'

'Go to—'

'Goodbye, Commissioner.'

I disconnected the call, turned around and ran. As fast as my little legs would take me. They were good at running from death.

✦

✦Katherine✦

'Get the girl. Kill everyone else,' RC instructed, before turning around to disappear into the crowd. His men walked towards me.

Then it happened—like fire had given birth to water in the sky.

A thunderous bang ripped through the night, swallowing the chants and drumbeats, shaking the ground below.

The reservoir exploded into a thousand pieces, shards of concrete launched outwards as a monstrous gush of water roared free. The columns came next, withering into the ground. Pandemonium ensued all around me as I stood still.

The crowd screamed and scurried in all directions. RC's men gathered around him to find a way to usher him out.

The blast was as strong as it needed to be—feeble enough to keep the pieces of the structure from flying towards us and harming the thousands gathered, but powerful enough to make it rain. Not only water. Paper.

Millions of green and grey and white, glinting and fluttering in the dark sky.

The crowd froze. As eyes lifted, panic morphed into awe. The scuffle stilled. Hands stretched towards the sky, catching blessings in the form of currency. Some stuffed their shirts. Others fished with nets. A few simply gazed upwards, hands folded in prayer.

That was my cue.

'Higher ground,' Johnny had said.

I dashed towards the shanty and climbed up the ladder, careful not to miss a step, praying the building would survive the gush of water when it crashed against its shaky foundation. But when it came, it was only a gentle wave.

Laughter. Shouts of joy. People waded through the water, fistfuls of currency in their hands.

And there she stood. The goddess.

Towering over all, eyes unblinking, unmoved by the storm or the celebration, her gaze stretched over a sea of happiness.

32 A Better Story

·⊶ Johnny ⊷·

I woke up unaware of my surroundings—a feeling I'd gotten very used to. My forehead throbbed, my body ached and all I heard was a piercing ring in my ears. My clothes squelched, soaked in water and mud.

I forced my eyes open, expecting a scathing sun, but only cold, damp darkness greeted me. Something clung to my face, blocking my vision. Newspaper? Used toilet paper? I peeled it off with stiff fingers.

It was a decomposed ₹2,000 note.

The memories of last night rushed in. Did everyone make it? Were the people at the puja pavilion okay? Did they get the money? Where was I?

I sat up and remembered. I had been scurrying towards the shanty, a smile on my face, when a thunderous bang pinched my ears. I'd known exactly what was going to happen but still shuddered when it did—the sheer loudness of it.

I'd looked behind me for a moment to see the reservoir burst into flames, a river of shiny yellow lighting up the sky. Then a hot gush of air hit me like an oven door flung open. I stumbled, hit the ground and fell into an open drain. There was nothing but darkness after that.

I could have chosen to be far away from the water tank when it happened, somewhere safe. But it would have been pointless. I had to see Debroy one last time. He had to know what was coming and who was bringing it to him. The price he was going to pay for taking Rampal away. Risking my life for that undiluted moment of pleasure wasn't even a question. But now, the bump on my forehead strongly disagreed.

The ringing in my ears dulled, replaced by the distant hum of earthmovers and the clang of metal. I climbed out of the drain and dragged myself away from ground zero, which was about 50 metres away. I did not bother to look behind at the remains.

I didn't want to know if firemen had sifted through the debris, washed in the red and blue glow of emergency lights. Or the media vans lining the periphery, reporters frantically rehearsing how to break the juiciest news in town. I didn't care which way they would spin it; my job here was done. Debroy was gone. No more squeals, no more machetes. No more dying.

Despite the pain, I picked up my pace. Daybreak was minutes away and I had to make it to the safe house before RC's men showed up, trying to find Debroy or whatever was left of him. Or me. The last thing I wanted was to run into one of them. All I wanted was to get back to my friends. To see them alive and safe.

Then—a click.

'Keep walking and don't turn back.'

A gun cocked behind my head.

The voice was deep and muffled; it sounded odd. I couldn't be sure if it was a man or a woman. I tried to turn against the unsolicited advice, but my latest hijacker thrust the cold metal into the back of my head. From the corner of my eye, I could only catch a glimpse—their head was covered with a shawl.

How many assassins do they have?

'I'm not kidding. I'll blow your head into pieces,' the voice said.

I believed it and obeyed. 'You'll kill me anyway. Why should I not try to run?'

'Because you can barely walk.'

'So why the talk?' I said. 'Just do it.'

'The girl. Where's the girl?'

'What girl? Do I look like a pimp?'

'You know exactly who I'm talking about. Her location for your life... What will it be? I'll find her regardless,' my abductor said. The voice sounded different now, but I couldn't fathom why.

'She would have left the country by now. Her flight was at—'

'You're testing my patience, boy. I'll ask you one last time.'

The cold metal slid to the back of my neck, sending prickles down my spine. I had to choose—either end it here and hope it was worth the sacrifice or play along and find the right moment to retaliate.

'Okay! Okay!' I said. 'I'll take you to her. But you have to let go of me after that. Deal?' If RC's men were still looking for Kath, then maybe she'd made it. Maybe Shamshu too. There was hope.

'Deal.'

I knew that meant nothing; soon my captor would make their move.

We reached Rakhi's apartment and took the lift to the 10th floor. I was still wet—shivering, jaws clenched and knees unsteady. I saw my abductor's shadowy reflection in the shining chrome walls of the elevator but couldn't make much out of it. Their breath was short and fast, much like mine.

We exited the lift and walked up to Rakhi's door. I stood there for more than a minute, doing nothing.

'Ring the bell now,' the voice instructed, and I followed.

Rakhi opened the door, smiling—until she saw the gun pointed at my head. She slammed the door shut. But in that split second, I saw them—Shamshu and Kath—sitting at the dining table; they'd made it.

I prayed there were more of our men inside and my latest captor hadn't seen what I had. I tried to look up, but they shoved the gun harder against my skull.

'Ring it again. Make sure she doesn't shut it this time.'

I did, but no one opened the door. There was no other way out for them but through this door and into the lift. They were getting ready, Shamshu and his men—if any were inside. I was ready to move out of the way when they opened the door and started shooting. That wouldn't go well for anyone, but it was the only play. I tried gulping, but my parched throat wouldn't allow it.

As I raised my hand to knock again, Shamshu opened the door slowly, gun raised. He was the only one at the door. Rakhi and Kath stood behind the kitchen counter, steak knives in their hands. Besides Shamshu, there were no other men in sight. Behind them, peeking through the slightly ajar door of the bedroom, was a young boy—Akhil.

No one spoke for a few seconds, each side assessing the outs. Shamshu had bandages on his forearms; his gun-holding arm trembled. My captor held the back of my collar and pushed me in.

'Move inside.'

As the door shut behind us, Shamshu moved back a few steps, glancing at me and then at the person behind me. Like me, he seemed unsure how this battle could be won without losses.

'Listen, I have money,' I said. 'Whatever they're paying you, I'll give you more. You can—'

'Shut up. And you, lower your weapon,' he told Shamshu. 'You first,' Shamshu replied.

My abductor lowered the gun, but not all the way. 'Don't try to do anything. I'm now going to remove my scarf.'

Rakhi was hidden behind Shamshu, so I couldn't see her, but Kath was in my line of sight. I gestured for her to throw her knife at my captor to create a distraction. Hopefully Shamshu would have enough time to bring them down.

Kath stared at me and then at my captor. I drew an imaginary trajectory with my eyes and raised my eyebrows, but it was futile. She stopped looking at me. So did Shamshu. Clearly my captor conveyed a better story to them.

As the scarf hit the floor, Kath turned white as a sheet. Something was wrong. Maybe my kidnapper had a burnt face. By now, I was sure she wouldn't make any move. Fortunately, I sensed Shamshu was about to take his chance, so I got ready to duck.

In that instant, Kath stepped forwards, her head tilted and eyes wide.

'Dad?'

33 Right of Way

✣ Katherine ✣

My hands were numb, my fingers like icicles.
I stood motionless in front of my father. All I could do was go back in time—to the day he left. Those same eyes, which had peered through the walls of the greenhouse, now were heavy with sadness and pain. Eighteen years had shrunk them; they were dirty and saggy.

I felt nothing. Emptiness, maybe. No love, no hatred. No bouts of anger or surprise, fear or joy.

We said nothing for a long time. He stood there in a wrinkled white shirt, hands pressed together, thumbs running over each other. Maybe it was too much to feel—too many emotions fighting, none winning.

Maybe, like me, he didn't know what could be said to overcome this wretched woodenness. Or maybe there was more to this than met the eye. Was he the one behind all of this—Mom's disappearance, people chasing me, people dying? Had he been watching me? Had he been in captivity like Mom? Where had he been all these years? Was he even the same man I once called 'Dad'? An overwhelming urge to slap him rushed through me but died even quicker, replaced by shaking knees, ready to run to him and hug him.

Would he hug me back?

No. Bad idea.

I'm stronger than that. I can't forgive him. I won't be a

sack of tears. Not in front of him. Not in front of the man who stole my childhood.

All such instructions to myself faded quickly when I spotted the corners of his eyes go wet.

'Kathy,' he finally broke the silence. 'It's... I... You look beautiful!'

And then the tears fell. Down his face, then mine. Uncontrollable, wretched beings with minds of their own. I stood there, unable to move, sobbing and hiccupping like a 10-year-old. I went back in time and didn't know how to come back; I didn't want to. He walked slowly towards me, unsure what to do next.

Do not hug him. Do not—

I lunged at him. He caught me, enveloping me in his open arms. A rush of familiar smells, flashes of a long-ago time. The softest, strongest wall surrounded me again. All I wanted was to stay hidden there.

But slowly the world crept back in. The slow drag of the fan; the city waking up; the open-mouthed gawking of my friends. I remembered where I was.

I sniffed and then wiped my flowing nose before looking up at him. 'You look like shit, Dad.'

He laughed the same laugh. The one that started slow, then built into a guffaw. He wiped his face with his sleeve and said, 'I do, don't I?'

We didn't let go of each other. We had a lot of time and distance to cover. Questions to ask and answers to give. But that could wait. Everything else could wait.

'It's...very...interesting to meet you, Mr Gladwell,' Johnny spoke up.

The three of them had been patient with us, not moving an

inch lest it took away from the moment. I spotted Rakhi wiping her wet cheeks. Shamshu seemed unmoved. Johnny just smiled.

'Indeed it is. This one here is a chopper squad, Kathy,' my father said, pointing to Johnny.

'Did he give you that bump on the head?' I asked Johnny, my arms still around my dad.

'No, only I can be blamed for that. But I did think I'd run out of luck this time.' Then he turned to Dad. 'You put on an unrecognizable accent. Definitely not American.'

'Perks of living like a vagabond across Asia. You learn to thicken it when you need to blend in... Stay in the shadows,' Dad told Johnny. Then he turned to me. 'So Kathy, will you introduce me to your friends?'

'Meet the three musketeers: Johnny, Shamshu and Rakhi.'

'Arthur Gladwell. Pleased to meet you. Sorry about putting a gun to your head, Johnny. I couldn't be sure.'

His voice was softer and thinner, his speech slower than I remembered. His wavy red hair was gone, replaced by a short, receding crop, now lighter and greyer. His square face, bronzed, almost burnt, sported a flock of freckles under his eyes.

'Johnny's getting used to having a gun pointed at him,' I said.

'Along with peeing a wee bit in my pants,' Johnny added.

'Well, then you must be doing something right, son,' my father said.

'I tell myself that every day,' Johnny sighed.

'Let me get something for your forehead,' Rakhi said, heading to the kitchen.

Akhil came out of hiding and walked cautiously towards me.

'Don't worry. Everything's fine,' I reassured him. 'Rakhi has brownies for you in the kitchen. Do you want some?'

He smiled and took off.

The poor kid missed his father. He played video games all night and stared out the window most of the day, unable to understand the withdrawals his body struggled with. He'd soon be admitted to a rehab, where hopefully he'd start a new life. Mr Elenburg had also arranged for his admission to one of the best boarding schools in India.

Dad turned back to look at me, his smile fading. 'Kathy, I'd been looking all over Kolkata for you. One of my men tried speaking to you at the shelter home, but your "bodyguard" killed him. Others tried stopping you at the wharf, but you disappeared. That's when I found out the Fish Gang was trying to keep you in their custody. I dug deeper and followed the trails—the burnt House of Dolls; the water tank explosion; cops found dead, along with members of the Fish Gang. I knew you had to be involved and had paid a visit. That's where I found—'

'That was your man in the shelter home?' I let go of him like he'd turned into a ghost.

'He wasn't trying to harm you, Kathy. He was only—'

'Then why did he have a gun?' My voice rose. 'What's going on? Where have you been all these years? Why are you *here*? Where's Mom? I have to get her back! There's no time for this.'

I stared at him, a stranger again.

'We have a lot to catch up on. If only you'd listen to me.'

'We'll leave you guys to it. I'll get up to speed with Shamshu and Rakhi,' Johnny said, starting to move away.

'No, please stay. This is making me... It's difficult to breathe.' I sank on to the couch. 'I need...someone... Someone I can trust.'

Johnny took a seat at the dining table. 'Absolutely. We're all here.'

'I'm so sorry it's come to this, Kathy,' my dad began. 'I

can understand why you don't trust me. It's a lot to take in. But please give me a chance to explain. Then you can decide for yourself.' He sat down next to me, while Shamshu hovered close by. 'I promise to tell you everything.'

'Let's start with—who the hell are you?'

'Just a father trying to protect his daughter.'

'That's hilarious. Protect me? By disappearing? By not being there? You're a coward.' I could only say that much; anything more and I would have broken down.

'The only answer to that is to start from the very beginning. But you have to be patient and hear me out.'

'I'm not making any promises.'

'Fair enough,' he said. 'About 19 years ago, I realized the Gladwell Railroad Company had rotted from the inside. It had become a front for something much, much bigger and more powerful than ours. And dirtier.'

'Let me guess… Someone had gobbled up all the land the government had granted your railroad?'

'The value of those lands doesn't compare in the least to what I'm talking about. The grants were legit. That's how the transcontinental railroad was built in the first place—how we made our fortune. That's how the country was made. American capital in full bloom. But this isn't about that.'

'So what went wrong?'

'To understand, you need to know a little more about the history of American railroads. In the 1840s and '50s, the railroads flourished—albeit sporadically. Back then, trains ran on pre-set timetables. A highly inefficient system where changes to the movements of trains were relayed to the next station by human dispatchers on horses; there was no other reliable form of communication. In addition to not being able to keep up with an ever-growing demand for rail transport, it often led to accidents and inefficiencies.

'Given the country's need to expand to the Wild West, your third great-grandfather, William Gladwell, who'd already spent a decade creating railroads, knew this primitive system wouldn't work for him. He had to find something that would allow the business to grow unhindered, reach the jerkwater towns.'

'What's a...jerkwater town?' Johnny asked.

I beat Dad to it. 'A town so small,' I said, 'they didn't have stored water. So the train crew had to lug water from a creek.'

'You know your railroads, Kathy.' Dad smiled. 'Anyway, around this time, an invention changed everything: the telegraph. Patented by Morse and a dozen other entrepreneurs, it was faster than anything the world had seen. But back then, no one wanted to invest big money in it yet—too many unknowns. Smaller railroads started experimenting, using it for basic communication.

'William Gladwell saw its potential and collaborated with one of the telegraph companies to relay information between officers of different stations. Using our railroad's right of way, telegraph lines were built along the tracks. Other companies followed, and within a decade, telegraph became essential to railroad operations. The Railman now had a choice to make: build his own telegraph infrastructure or partner with an expert. He chose the latter.

'He signed a contract with the biggest telegraph company in the US, which allowed us to send telegraphs over their infrastructure for free. In return, they used our railroad land to expand their network deep into the West.

'Their investors were shadowy figures from New York and Europe, some known to be...dubious; but this company became more than just a strategic partner over the next 15 years. We had minor stakes in each other's businesses, and more and more of their executives started working from our offices. Some even took key decision-making roles. They connected us with smaller railroads that had once resisted us—now suddenly willing and cheap acquisitions. We highballed to the top.

'That's how we came to be the United Pacific Railroad Company. And soon we were about to be linked to an equally large railroad corporation being built from the West to—'

'To create the transcontinental railroad. I know that. Partnering with a telegraph company makes sense. You share infrastructure. So why was this a bad thing?'

'Good question,' Dad said. 'It wouldn't be a bad thing—if they were just in the business of sending messages.'

'I don't understand.'

Dad leaned back on the couch. 'Tell me something, Kathy. Why do we travel? Why did we need railroads in the first place? Travel is nothing but an exchange of information. Falling in love with a stranger... Smelling wild orchids in Texas... Learning to drive on the wrong side of the road in an alien country... The eeriness of a strange village with no electricity... The roughness of grains and the smoothness of a python's skin. You collect information when you travel.

'But travel and transportation—the business we were in—was the slowest form of receiving information. Before us, it took six weeks for information to travel from California to New York. The railways brought that down to a few days. But the telegraph? It did in minutes, at least on land. Electric impulses through wires running along our railroads, protected by the Railroad Act. Turning into dots and dashes, then words decoded by brass pounders.'

Johnny looked confused. 'What's a brass—?'

'A telegraph operator,' I explained.

'Now,' Dad went on, 'imagine if only a select few controlled that information—political views and strategies; decisions regarding wars and revolutions and the impact they would have on commerce; the price of beef in New York before it became the price of beef in California; information that would affect the value of stocks—the list is endless. They say the US economy grew by billions because of the invention of the telegraph. Guess who pocketed most of it? The telegraph company.'

'And we had no idea what was happening?'

Dad shrugged. 'We didn't care. We were making our fortune ferrying people, black diamonds and silver from the East to the West. Meanwhile, they piggybacked on us, hoarding, leveraging, amplifying and selling information. Growing stronger with every dot and dash. By the 1870s, they controlled 90 per cent of the country's telegraph infrastructure. And with that kind of power and money, they were soon pulling strings in the government.'

'And what became of them?' I asked.

'They dug deeper trenches into our business. During William Gladwell's time, it was the telegraph. When his son took over, it was telephone lines. By the time I joined the company, optical fibre ran alongside the railroads—the backbone of the Internet, carrying virtually every piece of information in the world today. The telegraph company owns it, directly or indirectly.

'Their cables now run along ocean beds as well. The company is the first to know everything—before it becomes news. And they leverage this discreetly, without anyone knowing it. A fraction of a second before a share hits a higher bid, it's bought by offshore companies and sold at an even higher price. They have algorithms and software that leverage a second's head-start—

communications between countries; deals cut with rogue terrorist organizations and failed nations; arms trade; dirty diamonds. You name it, they're the first to know and profit from it. We're talking trillions of dollars.'

'So we've been reduced to an old-world front while they run the biggest mint, away from all the attention.'

'Exactly.'

'So why not make this public? Why not let the world know? And what does this have to do with my missing mother—your wife—who you left years back? Why are you here telling me this now?'

'All legit questions and I'll answer all of them. But the only way it'll make sense is if you hear it chronologically, one step at a time.'

'Let me lay it out for you, then,' I said. 'I was born into a rich family—of men who were smart enough to build and own American railroads but foolish enough not to see what was happening, literally right under their noses. By the time they realized they'd become glorified puppets in the hands of information lords, it was too late. And you left us, probably afraid of the consequences of knowing everything. Did I summarize it well?'

'Not really,' he said, as his gaze dropped to the floor.

'Dad, you left. And that's the truth. The whys and hows can be talked about later. Right now, I have to find her. That's more important.'

'Don't be in a hurry to write me off, Kathy. It's convenient… to try and frame a story that makes sense. But it's not the truth. Far from it. And you need to know the truth.'

'Kath, I think you should hear him out,' Johnny said quietly.

I exhaled. 'Fine. Go on.'

'Years went by. I took over the business in 1988. A decade or so later, I stumbled upon the truth. I was furious. I ruffled the wrong feathers, posing uncomfortable questions and threatening to part ways with them.'

'Why would the telegraph guys still be dependent on you? Why not just throw money and buy land easements independently from landowners across the country? They had more than enough to do that by then.'

'It's never been done successfully in the history of the country. To recreate the railroad's right of way? It would take decades—endless negotiations, lawsuits and public scrutiny; a logistical nightmare. The only reason the railroads managed to get that land in the first place was because of two things: one—America needed them. The government was desperate to connect the East with the Wild West. The economy depended on it. Two—the Civil War. The side that moved soldiers, supplies and ammunition fastest would win. The railroads were the key to both. So, to incentivize entrepreneurs, the government left no stone unturned, doling out rights of way, granting land grants and bonds through an aggressive railroad act. It was a lottery for a few intrepid entrepreneurs back, and lotteries like that are never going to come back.'

'Why won't they just buy you out? Or eliminate you? That would be easier.'

Dad sighed. 'We'd never sell the railroads. We're too proud to do that. And as far as eliminating me was concerned, that wouldn't have worked out in their favour. According to your grandfather's estate and inheritance planning, all assets and ownership would have gone to a rightful heir in case of my death. If I have no heir, it would go to the government. I wasn't married then and had no heir.'

'So?'

'So I lived on, blissfully unaware of the axe dangling over my head, ready to strike when the time was right. And then I met your mother, fell in love and got married.'

Something about his tone was off. It was heavier and choky, a sense of desolation in the way he formed his words. It made the hairs on the back of my neck and arms rise. I squirmed in my couch. 'What does that mean?'

'Your mother,' he said slowly, 'isn't who you think she is. She never was. She hasn't been kidnapped, Kathy. I'm sorry I have to—'

'You're lying,' I shouted as I shot up, an acute head rush blurring my vision. 'This...this elaborate story to have me back in your life—it doesn't make any sense.'

'Please, sit down and hear me out,' my dad pleaded. 'Then decide for yourself.'

I sank back into the couch, but not out of choice. My knees were bereft of any strength. Darkness edged into my vision and a stony lump in my throat rendered me dumb.

34 In Truth We Trust

A loud ringing in my ear accompanied my blurry vision.
What does he mean…my mother isn't who I think she is?

He didn't have the right to say that. *He* hadn't been there. *She*
had. Well, at least she had been present—in her room downstairs;
in the car, leaving the gates; in her nursery, planting exotic flora;
in the darkness of auditoriums, watching me perform. Every day
her voice filled the halls of the house, her footsteps preceding
elaborate instructions to the chef. Every day her soft clucks in
the stables were answered with firm nickers from her horses.

At least she was real, not a ghost. I didn't get any bedtime
stories, but her being there had been enough for me. Or had it?

She hasn't been kidnapped.

The words rattled in my skull like loose change.

'We didn't conceive you for a long time.' My father's voice
finally cut through the noise in my head. The ringing faded.

'I wanted a child, and we tried for years, but with no
success. Eventually I found out your mother was secretly taking
birth control pills; it broke my heart. When I confronted her,
she confessed that she wasn't ready…that she wasn't meant to
be a mother. She pleaded with me not to end the marriage;
said she loved me and begged for another chance. I relented.

'For what it was worth, I still loved her. She was a complete
woman, full of grace and love. Never a shade of malice in her.
We found our way back, and you were in my arms a year later…
and for the next eight years.' His eyes misted over. 'Those were

the best years of my life, Kathy, the ones that help me make it through my days and nights.

'Anyway, I digress. When I found out about the telegraph guys, how the railroads were being used to wash their money, how they'd taken control of our shares, I decided to break ties and expose them. That's when they threatened to kill me and our family.'

'What does Mom have to with all this?'

'I hired security to keep an eye on both of you and investigators to find out more,' he said. 'That's when they came back with pictures and recordings of phone calls between her and them—this information mafia is notoriously known among the upper echelons of power as "The Commission".'

He got up from the couch and walked towards the window, staring out. 'My world was shattered. My wife, the mother of my child, was an imposter.'

'Why?' I asked, but regretted it immediately. I didn't want to know any more.

He turned around. 'The Commission had decided it was time for them to own all the railroads even before I took over the business. They needed an insider—a rightful heir who would own the company after they eliminated me. So they recruited your mother when she was still in college.

'Her job was simple: make me fall in love with her and marry her. All she had to do was to play Mrs Gladwell for a few years; then, once I was gone, sign over the business to them, take her fortune and disappear forever. She was on those birth control pills for the very same reason—an heir would be counterproductive to their plans. They'd been inside our house, Kathy. I had to protect you.'

'You mean—the only heir to the Gladwell legacy.'

'No, I mean *you*. I gave up my life and offered them a deal—your life and safety, in exchange for their continued control of the railroads. I told them I'd go away, never come back, if they promised to not harm you. They took the deal, probably sure they'd eventually find me and eliminate a loose end.'

'Why would they wait for years after you got married?' I asked. 'Why not just get on with it and take you down? Mom would be the rightful heir after that.'

'A prenuptial agreement, forced by my sceptical father, turned out to be my lifesaver. My spouse would receive an inheritance only after seven years of a successful marriage. They couldn't eliminate me till then. And when I proposed to end the marriage, they had no choice but to—'

'So Mom had me out of no choice? She never wanted me? All this…all that I did to save her…it's all a lie?'

'Your love for her isn't a lie, or else you wouldn't be playing hide-and-seek with the underworld in an unknown foreign country, losing billions of dollars in the process. As for her love for you… I don't know. You're her daughter; maybe she does have love for you. Or something close to it.'

'If she did, she would have stopped all this. People have died. I've been held captive. These guys'—I pointed to Johnny and Shamshu—'put their lives on the line to get her back. No, I don't think she feels anything for me. Mrs Gladwell is a myth. A con. And her daughter is just one of her victims.'

'I'm sorry you have to go through this, Kathy. But you deserved to know the truth.'

'Why did you leave me behind? All I ever wanted was a normal life. I didn't care about the money and the glory.'

'So you could live.'

'How? Leaving me alone... How does that help? I'm surprised I still breathe.'

'You live because of the trust I made before I left. It ensured that only a Gladwell could control what a Gladwell built. It was your insurance.'

'The trust? How?'

'It was irrevocable and legally binding,' he explained. 'I appointed Mr Elenburg as the trustee, with you and your mother as beneficiaries. However, the distribution of assets could only happen when you turned 27. Before that, everything remained under the trustee's control. I allocated a minor 0.5 per cent ownership and essentials for your mother—a house in the city and a generous amount to last a lifetime. Most of the other assets, including estates and the ownership of the business, were to be awarded to you. The clauses of the trust also ensured that the Commission couldn't harm you if they wanted to keep using our assets and face.'

'How does the trust ensure that?'

'In case you die or go missing before turning 27, the ownership and control of the railroads would go to the government; everything else would be liquidated and given to the named government-owned charities. When the Commission found out about the trust, they knew that they were in a jam. That even if they found and killed me, it wouldn't change a thing.

'So they gave up looking for me, deciding to carry on with the operations as is, with no threat to them in the foreseeable future. My disappearing had already raised alarms in the corporate and judicial circles, and anything happening to you subsequently would call for a full-blown investigation, which they could do without. So instead of eliminating the heir to the Gladwell fortune, they had to protect you. Because if anything happened to you—an accident, a petty mugging gone wrong—they'd lose everything to the government.

'Samantha's role was supposed to be a short one—that of a young widow. But it turned out to be a lifelong one—that of a mother. She had no choice but to stay and play that role until they figured out a solution. So they watched you and protected you from any harm all this while. I made our enemies protect you more than I could…from thousands of miles away.'

'I turn 27 in a few months. There's still time. I could go back to New York and—'

'The trust protects you, but it also has serious threats to you. To us.'

'Of course it does. How can anything be easy and simple?'

Before my father could respond, Akhil strolled in from the kitchen, wiping the last crumbs of a brownie from his face. He plopped down on to my lap.

'The Commission stayed quiet until they knew what to do,' my dad said. 'When they did, you woke up next to a dead, overdosed stranger.'

'So they set me up? I've questioned that night every single day. It just didn't add up. Why?'

'They found a way out. The trust has a standard clause that at the time of distribution, the beneficiaries should be of sound mind and have no criminal conviction under an American court of law. If any beneficiary fails to meet this condition, then apart from legal expenses and basic upkeep, all assets would be transferred to the family office—where the Commission had installed their own people years ago—and all future profits would be paid out to specific government-sponsored charities in perpetuity. This was the only way they could control and own everything.'

'By making me a drug dealer?' I exclaimed. 'Sorry, Johnny. No offence.'

'Taken,' Johnny relied. 'But it's okay. I'm not a drug dealer anymore.'

'They set their plan in motion a few months ago,' Dad said. 'Your mother disappears in an alien country. A story is crafted about her being kidnapped by a local crime syndicate, followed by her staged death. This…Mandal…is in cahoots with the Commission, getting paid millions for this sham.

'While your mother is being babysat by the mob here, her death is proven in the US by providing DNA evidence and a made-up police report. Around the same time, you get charged and are convicted before turning 27. Then everything goes into their pockets forever. Your mother is free to go for a permanent vacation with a new identity on an island far away from everything—a reward she's waited many years to claim.'

'So even if I go back and claim my right, I'd be considered an invalid?'

'If you'd stayed back and fought the case, maybe we would have had a small chance to win it. I'd made arrangements to pull you out of the country in case you were convicted. Your final hearing is in less than a week, and we have nothing to prove your innocence.'

No fortune cookie could have prepared me for my own future.

My mother never wanted me. I'd lost everything that rightfully belonged to me and I'd soon be a convicted criminal in my country. I wiped the brownie off Akhil's face. At least someone seemed happy with what they had.

'It would be safe to say all is lost then?'

'How can all be lost, sweetheart?' Dad said. 'I just found

you. Don't worry about anything. We have enough money to last a few lifetimes. I made sure of that before I left. How do you think I afforded to have eyes on you all this time? Just pack a lot of sunscreen, and we'll disappear forever.'

I could do with that. Get to be a daughter again. Learn life again. But something gnawed at me; something was missing. 'I don't know, Dad. I feel like nothing in my life has happened out of my own will. I've just been a puppet, playing to the plans of others.'

'Only you can take the accolades, or the blame, for your choices, for who you are,' Dad said. 'The blood in your veins is real. Hell, if you ask me, it's a thick shade of Gladwell. They must have been happy to see you flee the country to save your mother. That made you a fugitive before you even had a chance to fight your case. So they asked the Mandal to play host to you until the verdict was passed back in the States.

'They never expected you to stir their pot. Everything changed when you guys blackmailed them with some information. The news on the street is that the local mob decided to extend your mother's stay against her wishes and those of the Commission... until they get back what you guys have on them. Word also has it they haven't been very hospitable to her since. It seems whatever you have is extremely important to them.'

'Had,' Johnny corrected.

'You lost it?' my father asked.

'We gave it to them,' Johnny said. 'But hopefully we have a copy and know what to do with it. Do we, Kath?'

I nodded and looked back at Dad. 'Why didn't you get in touch with me earlier? Why didn't you tell me you were alive?'

He shifted on the couch until he was next to me and put an arm around my shoulders. 'For your own good. If the

Commission knew I was alive, they would have used you to draw me out and change the trust. Kathy, I've watched you all my life, even though I was very far away. I have pictures of all your birthdays. Even the ones you spent alone. Your graduation. Your PhD. Your successes and your failures. The day you wrote your paper on nanotechnology. The day you walked out of that office, dejected, with a box of personal belongings. The fortune cookies. Your boyfriends and crushes. Your heartbreaks. Your addiction. The fire escape you slept on. The tears that escaped your eyes. I've lived with the helplessness of seeing everything and not being able to do anything. And for that I'm truly, truly sorry. I *am*.'

I had forgiven him even before a single word was spoken between us, when he had removed his scarf. The biggest heist in American history had led me back to him. He offered his hand, and I took it. I wasn't going to let go of him again. But was I willing to let go of my legacy? To accept defeat and live on the run like my father had? *I don't think so.*

'Dad,' I said slowly. 'There might be a way to get back what belongs to us.'

'Oh, crap,' Johnny sighed and looked away. 'Not that look again.'

35 Ruffle All Feathers

✦ Katherine ✦

I deserved sleep. All of us did. But all I did was toss and turn, blaming the damp couch and the uncomfortable pillow; the constant gurgles from the plumbing, the grunts of vehicles outside, the hands of the clock. Too much light. Too little time.

But I knew the fault lay elsewhere—in the deeper echelons of my heart, which pumped furiously. The hustle that travelled across my synapses, in the newly formed distributaries of my nerves. No sleeping comfort could overpower the storm inside me. And I suspected a similar struggle for everyone else in the apartment, the comforts of quieter rooms and cushier beds notwithstanding. It wasn't easy—facing and accepting where we were, the choices we all had made and who we had become.

But we were here, and there was no going back.

We'd blown up a water tank and made it rain money. We'd taken lives. Did it matter who they were—corrupt, murdering men or husbands and fathers?

Were we any different? Or were we just hiding behind a flimsy, fluttering veil of morality? Colours of grey that suited us to be uneasy enough but not remorseful. It comforted me to think I wasn't the only one. And maybe, if all of us were in this together, the company would make my path to hell a little easier.

My dad was here—sleeping in the next room, or at least trying to, like it was just another day. Just when I thought the knots couldn't get knottier, he had walked in with a story that made me see my own life with the eyes of an indifferent observer. I'd laughed a little. Cried some. But mostly, I'd watched myself shuffle and reset to the truth. Maybe a life of no meaning, of living alone and writing fortunes was an easier one.

The light through the curtains grew softer, colder. It was late afternoon, a few hours since everyone had reluctantly agreed to rest for a while. When I told Dad the key to reclaiming what was ours was finding Mom—and hopefully getting her to come back with us, confess and become a witness against the mafia—it had sounded like the perfect plan.

But the more I thought about it, the more holes appeared. Dad was right to say that every hour we spent here, out in the open, made things riskier. That it was wishful thinking of a hopeful daughter to believe Samantha Gladwell would help us. That there were no guarantees we would find her, let alone convince her to do the right thing.

I sighed. Getting up, I walked to the fridge, hoping for a cold one, but found it empty.

'I didn't feel anything.'

Startled, I turned around to find Johnny sitting in a dark corner of the kitchen, a glass of whisky in his hand. A half-empty bottle sat uncapped on the counter.

'Stop creeping up on me like that! I've had enough excitement in the last—'

'I've been sitting here for hours, waiting for you guys to wake up. It's you who just walked in. How the hell am I—'

'Fine.' I sat down next to him and nabbed the glass. 'I was hoping for a beer, but I guess this'll have to do.'

I hadn't gotten a chance to speak with Johnny alone since he'd returned. Shamshu, Rakhi and I had escaped RC and his men the previous evening and made it to our rendezvous point. We'd spent the entire night trying to make sense of the information we'd stolen from the Mandal, praying Johnny had survived the blast.

When he finally returned, sporting a red forehead and my dad's gun at his back, I'd insisted we all get some sleep, that each of us needed to lie in bed and hope to catch a wink. But the truth was that I just needed to be alone, to breathe. To accept that everything happening around me was not just a cocaine-induced hallucination—it was real, and I had to be ready to face it. My father's return had made me selfishly halt our quest to bring down the Mandal, which wasn't fair to Johnny, Shamshu and Rakhi.

'You don't have to drink that.' Johnny tried to take his glass back.

I downed it and cringed. 'So what is it that you didn't feel? The whisky's sting?'

'You know... Sometimes I buy these fake imported dark chocolates. They look exactly like the real thing—the same shiny gold foil, the same perfect little cubes. But when you put them in your mouth, they taste like chalk—anticlimactic and pointless. Watching Debroy die... It didn't make me happy, didn't give me any closure. I thought it would make things easier.'

'Easier comes later. First in line are shame and fear. Then, maybe redemption. Sometimes, if you're lucky, even closure.' I poured myself another drink and gulped it in a go. Those dark chocolates would have been handy to counter the strong malt, fake or otherwise.

'So now you're the undertaker?'

'I did kill someone before you, didn't I?'

'And whatever you felt after that, would you take that deal again?'

'As disgusting as it sounds, I would,' I said, and poured another. 'Bijoy deserved to die. Bloody snake.'

Johnny smiled and reclaimed the glass from me. 'Finding your father instead of your mother turned out to be a good deal?'

I shrugged. 'I don't know. I mean, finding him, knowing he's watched over me and loved me all my life…makes me feel very happy. Very…complete. But the truth about my mother…breaks my heart. Makes me feel like I've lived a lie all these years.'

'Huh… Nothing hurts more than looking back and finding nothing.' He grabbed the bottle and poured himself four fingers. 'I've been there. But if I can overcome it, you can too.'

'Thanks.'

'You think your mother will help?' Johnny asked, pushing his glass towards me.

'The only way to know is by finding her. Given how desperate the Mandal was for the flash drive, she's probably being held against her will now. Maybe she regrets her choices. Maybe there's no island life waiting for her anymore. Maybe, just maybe, she'll realize that running would ruin my life forever and rethink things.

'I have to find her, look her in the eye and ask her if that's what she wants. It's wishful thinking, but that's all I have.'

'Now that they have their flash drive, they'll probably let her go. No point aggravating the situation with their international friends.'

'Which is why I need to move fast.'

'The stubbornness clearly comes from your mother,' Johnny said. 'Your father seems like a pragmatic man.'

'You run away from cops in the dead of the night, escaping death. Then, with no fear of it and nothing to lose, you start and grow an amphetamine business, despite warning and torture from a crime syndicate. When that's not enough, you blackmail them with thin air to multiply your profits. When your bluff is called, you lose your best friend and nearly die yourself but manage to escape, again. But you haven't still had your fill...Jimi be good. You take out one of their leaders, who just happens to be a cop. Then you decide to bring the whole Mandal down. And I'm being stubborn?'

'Touché. But who says there's room for only one?'

'Touché back at ya.' I handed him his glass. One more sip of that and I'd have barley oozing out of my pores. I missed my bourbons. And as terrified as I was to admit it, I missed Manhattan.

'Look... I know how important it is for you to find her,' Johnny said, 'but listen to your father. Leave with him. You found what you were looking for.'

'What's that?'

'Your family. Isn't that what you always wanted?'

'There's merit in that. But then, there was also merit in taking the money from the water tank and disappearing with *your* family instead of seeking revenge. Yet here you are.'

'You're such a pain in the ass.' He got off his chair and walked to the fridge.

'So are you.'

'Listen...' Johnny returned with cubes of ice in his hand, pressing them against his forehead with a grimace. 'We have very little time to act on what we found on that flash drive. Like I said, I've been waiting for you guys to wake up. You just have to tell us what's in there, and we'll take it from there. You don't have to waste any more—'

'Are you kidding me? I'm not going anywhere until we finish what we started. It's the least I can do. For what you did for me. For Rampal. For Imaan… For that child who'll never have a father. My dad wasn't the only family I found here, Johnny. I owe it to you guys. I'll—'

'Then now would be a good time to act.' Shamshu walked in, a pillow in hand.

'How long have you been eavesdropping?' Johnny asked, beads of water dripping down his face as the ice melted.

The door to my father's room opened, and he ambled in, gazing at the ceiling. 'I only heard the merits of walking away from all this.'

'Dad!'

'What?' he said. 'You expect me to sleep on a day like this?' He walked to the kitchen counter and leaned against it, tapping his fingers. 'I could do with a drink too.'

'I heard a little more… Sorry.' Rakhi dragged her feet into the kitchen, switched on the light and started fixing drinks. Akhil followed her in.

'Great. Looks like no one got their beauty sleep,' I muttered.

'Now that we have all the revellers here, let's get the party started,' Johnny said. 'There's a lot I need to catch up on and way more to do. Shamshu, are the people in the shanty okay? Did they get the money?'

'They're fine,' he said. 'A few minor injuries, but nothing serious. The crash happened just in time for us to escape and was just strong enough to do what it was supposed to. A few seconds late and we'd be lamb chops.'

'And the money? Did it get to the right hands?'

'Every last rupee, except what we kept,' Rakhi answered, handing a glass to my father. 'A little dramatic, if you ask me, but it worked. There's more on TV about the "holy rain" than the cops and mafia men buried under the rubble.'

'Wait a minute,' my dad said. 'Kathy, did you make the explosives to blow up the water tank?'

'Well, technically, it was Johnny who made the call and activated the trigger,' I said.

Dad shook his head and gulped his drink down.

'I'm happy to take all the blame,' Johnny offered. 'I hope we found something really important on that flash drive. Or the fireworks were for nothing.'

'We did.' I smiled. 'We definitely did.'

'The likes of which could make RC stop scratching himself?' Johnny asked.

'This will be their kryptonite.'

'What is krypto—' Shamshu started.

'It means we have the queen bee squirming,' I explained. 'If we can trace the money to the right accounts and get this information to the right authorities, this will ruffle *all* feathers.'

'The accounts we've traced so far belong to more than just a few rich, powerful men,' Rakhi said. 'Some senior police officials, an IAS officer, a few ministers in the state, one in the union government and one from the opposition party. It seems everyone is in on this.'

'There's more,' I said, as I stood up and moved to stand next to Dad. The moment I did, he instinctively put his arm around me. I was getting used to the warm fuzzies I got when I was close to him. 'Billions of dollars have been transferred through layers of account until they reach offshore accounts, only to trickle back into the country through hawala networks and even legitimate foreign investments. The files contain not just bank account details and access codes—they map out the entire structure.

'Business plans, addresses, shareholding patterns, shell companies, shady agreements. They show how some key politicians funnel money through real estate deals, buying land from original owners at a fraction of the market prices. They name everyone—government officials, businessmen, a couple of high court judges, clerks and cops. This isn't just the underworld—this is everyone.'

'Amitav Banerjee must have been on this for months. Is there a chance they know we have access to this?' Johnny asked.

'Unlikely. But if I were them, I'd start moving the money around sooner than later, just to be safe,' I said.

'Let's hope it's later,' Johnny said. 'How do we use this information, Kath? Who do we take it to?'

'If this was just corrupt cops and thieving corporate,' I said, 'we could have handed it to the media and hoped the backlash would result in an inquiry. But this... This is way bigger than that. Who knows who owns those media houses and news channels? We have to take this to the right agency.' I paused, then added, 'I could ask Mr Elenburg to contact the US ambassador; they could connect us to the right people.'

'That would be helpful,' Johnny agreed, then turned to Rakhi. 'How long before we stitch up the trails and evidence?'

'At least a day,' Rakhi said.

He scratched the back of his neck. 'Let's hope a day isn't too late.'

Dad looked at me. 'Kathy, if you're going to find your mother, it has to be now—before this goes down. Once the shit hits the fan, if they haven't already let her go, she won't be a priority. Either way, the Commission will know you have something against the Mandal, and they can't afford to have Samantha found. They'll act soon, if they haven't already. I'm going to get IDs and passports made for you. If things go out of hand—'

'Please get one made for Mom as well. I'll text you a photo of her.'

'Kathy, you—'

'Please, Dad. Just do it for me.'

'We've already searched so many places,' Shamshu said. 'Most of the Mandal's guys are off the streets, so it's been impossible to get any new information. We have to be realistic and consider that she's—'

'Someone must have seen her,' I said. 'She'd stand out, just like me. How difficult can it be to notice a blonde woman in Kolkata?'

'Kath, maybe she's no longer here,' Johnny said. 'You have to consider that.'

'I see foreign lady,' Akhil mumbled, unwrapping a chocolate; apparently he'd been listening the whole time.

'I'll put the TV on for him,' Rakhi said. 'Come on, Akhil.'

'Hold on.' I moved in front of him and knelt. 'Akhil, have you seen a foreign lady?'

He nodded.

'Yeah? Where?'

He looked at me, then at the others, eyes wide.

'It's okay, you can tell me,' I reassured him. 'I promise you nothing will happen. C'mon, sweetheart. Tell me where.'

'Where they give me powder and ask me to break house and make holes.'

'Probably a training camp for the kids,' Shamshu said.

'Can you take us there?' I asked.

'I know the place,' he said. 'But I don't want to go there.'

'Okay, you don't have to, I promise. Just tell me—what did this foreign lady look like? How old was she?' I asked.

'She look like you, foreign aunty. She look exactly like you.'

36 Sparks of a Revolution

✦ Katherine ✦

The wail of sirens pierced the hush of the night. We couldn't see them—the throbbing reds of the beacons—but from where we were, near the river in Howrah, we could hear Kolkata's silhouette shifting, shouting.

It was two days after *Dashami*—after the visarjan—when the city had wept and danced and prayed as it carried the goddess to the river. The beats of the dhaak had faded and the idols submerged, but the chants of *'Asche bochor abar hobe'*—the promise of return next year—still hung faintly in the air, like incense refusing to fade. Once the lights dimmed and the pandals emptied, something else had crept in. Something darker.

We sidled through alleys, careful not to run into trouble. We had no time to waste; I had to find my mother before it was too late. Johnny, Shamshu and I hurried between house walls and parked trucks, slipping through the shadows. A gibbous moon showed us the way.

Every few blocks, men scurried, floundering into empty pavilions and open gutters, chased by misdirected bullets that hit lamp posts and burst like momentary fireflies. Like frenzied ants fleeing a crushed nest, men poured out by hundreds, only to be stuffed into police vans.

Across the river, the city lit up, smoke rising through the damp air. Walls crumbled. Roofs caved in. Tall fires raged over the skyline. Flashes of gunshots split the darkness, cars toppled and crashed along the river banks. Shattered windows reflected the inferno as their shards sprinkled down like embers. Searchlights ran amok in the silver sky.

Bathed in the psychedelic orange of racing beacon, the Hooghly flowed gently as the city was cleansed. Not for the first time would it swallow all the blood and gore and move on to the next sin city.

'You got your burning city, Johnny,' I whispered.

'Um…Jimi fucking Hendrix, I did.'

He smiled as we continued to move.

They were everywhere, the cops from the bureau. They stormed all the Mandal hotspots—office campuses, glazed skyscrapers, warehouses, torture houses, slums—and arrested all their men. Even those nestled in the police stations and government apartments. No one was spared. Those who tried to escape encountered fatal metal.

It had only been two days since we handed over the dossier to the right people, but they acted fast. We also sent copies to the media outlets, though only a few smaller ones dared to run it. Within hours, there were sparks of a revolution—people were out on the streets demanding justice. A few ministers of the state resigned. A curfew was imposed. The national channels had no choice but to cover the story as well. The whole country was glued to what hopefully was the beginning of the end.

RC remained at large; I wagered he had hidden himself in one of his horrid trams, dreaming of a clock's mechanism and time's inevitability.

We kept our heads down, avoiding the street riots. When we reached the botanical garden, we looked for the shortest section of the back wall and climbed it. Akhil had shared a patchy description of the place where he had been trained.

'In old palace, where a tree was larger than forest,' he had said.

The description sounded more like a child's fantasy, but as it turned out, Shamshu knew exactly what Akhil was talking about. According to him, there was only one place in Kolkata, maybe even India, where there was a banyan tree so massive it was practically a forest—the botanical garden in Howrah.

I didn't believe such a thing could exist until I saw it.

We landed in a patch of trees so thick that the end of the woods seemed nowhere in sight. 'How far is the tree?' I asked.

Shamshu grinned. 'You're standing under it.'

I looked up and around again. This wasn't just a tree—it was a city of wood. Thousands of thick aerial roots reached down from the heights, plunging into the earth like ancient pillars. They were everywhere, a vast wooden web of twisting limbs and endless branches. Silver moonlight slipped through the cracks, spilling onto the bed of leaves below.

A labyrinth. A fortress. A world of its own.

'We need to keep moving,' Johnny said.

But I couldn't move. I needed to breathe in what I saw; there was so much to take in. 'All this...is one tree? Where's the bark?' I asked.

'It doesn't have any,' Shamshu said.

I glared at them. 'If you guys are trying to spook me, I'm shivering inside already, so cut it out.'

'He's not kidding,' Johnny said. 'The bark of the tree was damaged in a cyclone; they amputated it so the tree could survive. Now it grows without one, like a clonal colony.'

'The tree is spread over two hectares. It makes roots wherever it can to survive...even when it doesn't have an anchor,' Shamshu said.

I marvelled at the peculiarity of the grandeur that surrounded us. 'Just like all of us,' I said.

'The Rockberg House is only a few hundred metres from here,' Johnny said. 'That's the only house on the campus. If there's any place your mother could be, it's there.'

'Is that the old palace Akhil mentioned?'

'Last I remember,' he said, 'it was a rundown, abandoned bungalow, the erstwhile house of a botanist, a herbarium. To Akhil, it might have seemed like a palace. Like I said, we need to keep moving. If the cops have raided this place, you don't want to run into one of them.'

'Or a trigger-happy Mandal member running away from the cops,' Shamshu said.

I nodded. 'Thank you, guys. You didn't have to do this. In fact, you didn't have to do a lot of things that you did for me. I've never had friends like you. Truth is...I've never had *any* friends. In all the despair and hopelessness, I still find a smile inside me, and I owe it to you guys.'

'Of all the places and times, you chose now to get sentimental?' Johnny said.

'I don't know what's on the other side of all this. Better to say it than regret it.'

'Nothing's going to happen. Now let's go find your elusive mother,' Johnny said.

We quickened our pace, pushing through the prop roots, moving towards the bungalow. I thought of what I'd say to my mother—*how* I would say it. Would my anger be misplaced at the moment? Would sympathy work better for my cause? Could I make her not see through me? For all the conspiracies and betrayals, she was still my mother; someone who had watched me grow, even though it had been from a distance.

She had been real, no matter who she was, no matter what my dad had said. She knew me inside out, and my only hope was that it would turn out to be a good thing. Lost in my thoughts, when I finally became aware of my surroundings again, I found myself alone.

'Johnny! Shamshu! Where are you guys? This isn't funny.' My voice was meant to be a loud whisper; at worst a feeble shout. But it turned out to be a futile howl. They were gone, swallowed by the forest of roots.

But there was no time to waste; I had to find my own way to the bungalow. Hopefully they'd be there. I pussyfooted through the dark woods, praying I was heading in the right direction. There were no leading lights or an open sky to walk towards, no lodestar to guide me. For all I knew, I was walking straight into the lap of a Mandal member. But I had to keep walking.

Suddenly, I heard some movement close by, but I wasn't sure of its direction; the crackle of dry leaves grew louder with every step. Was it Johnny? Should I shout out? Then absolute silence took over. A stillness that made my breath sound like a roar. I held it in and froze in place, hoping whatever lurked behind the hanging roots would pass.

Loud footsteps thumped behind me, and an arm grabbed my waist, knocking the wind out of me. Another hand covered my mouth and I was hoisted off the ground, my legs dangling in the air, before slamming me against a root. The hand smelled of gasoline, gunpowder and sweat.

I grappled to break free from my assailant, but he was too strong. It was pointless to waste my remaining breath, so I stopped struggling and hoped a surrender would buy me another, maybe even an escape from the strong clutches.

'Very few things surprise me. But you... You, Ms Gladwell... You really are something.'

That raspy voice was unmistakable.

'Now, if you promise not to make any noise, I could ask my colleague to let go of you,' RC said.

Still pressed against the tree, I nodded.

'Is that a promise?'

'Mmmm.'

'Take your hand off our guest's mouth, Yogi, and let her stand on her feet. But hold on to her, will you? She's a spunky one,' he instructed.

The coarse, rancid hand let go of my mouth, and I gasped for air. I turned to look at RC. 'Where's my mother?'

'Wherever you go, you leave behind ashes, Ms Gladwell,' he said. 'But doing all that just to come right into the lion's den is plain stupid. For your mother? You Americans are strange. All she dreamt about was getting away from all this. From your railroads. From you. She would have, if you hadn't tinkered with business that didn't concern you.'

'Where is she?'

'She's gone. Along with other nonessentials. She's of no use to us; those Americans be damned.'

'Gone where?'

'The same place where you sent my good friend Debroy.'

'You're lying.'

'I have no reason to. As we speak, my men are getting rid of everything in that bungalow. But I do have a use for you. A way to make things right. You'll be my ticket out of here. You see, the Americans have been very nervous ever since we lost you; you and I both have a plane to catch, Ms Gladwell. Very different destinations, though.'

'I'm not going anywhere without my mother.' I tried to wriggle out of my captor's grip with no success.

'Time, Ms Gladwell. I told you, it's the most powerful thing. A tick of the hand changes everything. A minute ago, I was ruined—hunted in my own city, thanks to you and your dwarf friend. The same people who licked my toes are now hungry to have a piece of them. But now, now I have you. And that changes everything.'

A movement above caught my eye.

In the feeble light of the moon, I spotted Johnny crawling on a branch above RC, ready to pounce. All he needed was a few seconds.

'The hand... It's ticked again,' I said. 'Get ready to lose more blood.'

'You American bi—'

'Your clock and your fucking time are over.'

Johnny dropped on to him, locking his arms around RC's neck and dragging him down. They crashed onto the ground, Johnny's grip tightening into a headlock. Yogi let go of me and rushed towards RC, but Shamshu emerged from the roots, a thick branch in his hand. He swung it hard, but Yogi ducked and leapt at Shamshu. They were down on the ground, grappling in a tangle of limbs and crunching leaves. The darkness made it difficult to make out who was winning.

I turned to see a shiny gun in RC's hand. I looked around for a weapon and found Shamshu's stick a few feet away. I sprang to fetch it.

Bang!

I didn't stop to check if I was too late. I grabbed the stick and swung it at RC's head with all my might, praying it landed at the right place.

Thump. Both men went still. I wasn't sure if I'd hit the right man, but I had no time to waste. I hurried towards Shamshu and swung the stick again. It made contact with Yogi's head, then snapped in two. The man slumped in an instant and Shamshu gasped for air. He pushed Yogi off him and rose slowly. I stood still, staring at the pool of blood beneath the man, a broken stick in my hand.

'We're two all,' came a voice form behind me.

I turned around to find Johnny patting dust and leaves off his clothes. My eyes fixed on RC, who lay still on the ground.

'What?'

'Um... Even-steven? That's what you say, right?'

'Yeah...whatever.'

'Are you okay? You don't need to keep gaping at him.'

'Huh? Yeah.'

'Kath. Look at me,' Johnny said.

'I am looking at you.'

'You aren't,' he said. 'Do you want to find your mother?'

'He...he said she's gone.'

One moment, RC was there, rattling about time. Now, time had left him.

'He also said he'd make me a company boss. He's the mafia. Are you going to believe everything he said? Let's go find her. The cops are still clearing out the place. There's a chance she's still there.' He walked towards Shamshu. 'I haven't seen anyone get the better of you, my friend. You're getting old.'

'Not me. *My eyes.* I couldn't see him in the dark. I never miss. Then he plunged at my ribs. I think I broke them again.'

'Good that we had Durga's American avatar with us.' He turned to look at me. 'You need to let go of him, Kath.'

'I'm...just...enjoying my kill; that's all.'

'Tell that to your shaking hands,' he said. He looked at RC, then at me. 'They aren't dead, if that's what you're thinking.'

Blood surged through my ice-cold fingers. I let go of the stick, clenched my hands and glared at Johnny. 'They're not? I didn't kill them?'

'No, but your swings did enough damage. Shamshu, can you find something to tie them to the tree? I'm going to call the cops and share this lottery with them.'

I breathed in. 'They'll make for some interesting prop roots,' I said. 'By the way, the score's three to two, not two all.'

Distant sirens wailed in the air. The cops were not far behind. 'No? How?'

'I saved you from my father as well.'

'He wouldn't have—'

'He's my father. What do you think?' I said. It was Johnny's turn to gape. 'Now let's go. No time to waste.'

37 Mother

✦Katherine✦

I found her. On the top floor of Rockberg House, curled inside a closet. Trembling hands covered her head. She refused to look up, even as gunshots and screams filled the house. The cops were on the ground floor and making their way up, arresting everyone and shooting anyone who didn't comply. Shamshu leaned against the door of the room while Johnny scampered around, looking for an alternate exit.

'Mom, it's me,' I told her. 'It's over. Look at me...look at me!'

She finally did, glaring at me. Her face was pale, her eyes barely open, her crow's feet deeper. 'No, you cannot be here. Get out of my head. Go away!' she said feebly.

'It's okay, Mom. I'm not in your head. You need to stand up. We don't have time.' I offered my hand to her. 'C'mon. Let's go.' She looked at me, then at Johnny and Shamshu. 'It's fine. They're my friends,' I told her. 'I came here to save you.'

My mother reached out slowly, and I pulled her up. She seemed shorter, gaunt. I put an arm around her raw-boned shoulders. 'It's over. I'm here.'

The footsteps and screams outside grew louder; the cops were in the adjoining room.

'I won't be able to hold the door for long,' Shamshu said.

'The backstairs, through the herbarium,' Johnny shouted. 'Let's go.'

As we climbed down, my mom tugged my hand and stopped me. 'Why did you come for me?'

'Because you're my mother.'

38 The Only Thing Real

⁜Katherine⁜

We sat in silence in a hotel room in downtown Kolkata. We didn't have much time for a family reunion, as my trial back home was in four days. Dad stood by the window, looking out. Mom sat back on a couch opposite me, holding a cup of untouched coffee and showing no signs of remorse. It was amazing what a shower and a change of clothes did for her.

I spoke up. 'So much for seeing the beauty in everything, huh, Mom?'

'I'm not going to be lectured by you on who I am,' she said. 'I did what I had to.'

'What you did,' I said, 'was make sure I rot in a jail all my life. Your own daughter. For what? Money?'

'For my own life, my own money and my freedom to do what I wanted to do with it. Who I wanted to *be*. Not the caretaker of a family fortune.' She turned to look at Dad, who was still lost in his thoughts. 'Not a golden statue called Mrs Gladwell.'

'But you cried the day Dad left. I remember my shoulders wet from your tears.'

'They were yours, honey…only yours,' she said. 'I never signed up just to be someone's wife.'

'Not someone's mother either?' I said.

'That's not true. You were the only thing that kept me sane all these years…something that was mine.' She leaned towards me. 'You were the only thing real. The reason I agreed to stay and live a lie for such a long time, even though that was never the plan.'

'Then why?'

'They promised me they wouldn't harm you, that there would be enough money left for you.'

'You cut a deal with the mob and expected them to keep their end of the bargain?' I said. 'They were going to kill you if I hadn't reached in time.'

'You shouldn't have come after me and stepped on their toes.' She sat back and dropped her eyes. 'To be honest, I didn't think you had it in you. I'd imagined you'd finally be happy, having the proverbial diamond spoon on a platinum platter.'

'Sorry to let you down.'

Mom looked up. 'Kath, it was all taken care of. I'd disappear, and you'd have what you wanted. Everyone would be happy. I was family to them. I didn't know they'd back out and—'

'*Family?*' Dad turned back and glared at her.

Mom didn't look at him. 'Well…sort of. My father was a distant cousin of one of the bosses. I never met them or knew them. He'd told me about them when I was a little girl, when he got a telegraph for me as a birthday present, with stories of how it had changed the world.'

'It destroyed our world,' Dad said. 'What my ancestors built with their own hands.'

'I didn't care then,' Mom said. 'And I don't care now.'

'You should have let her be where she was, Kathy. That way we would have seen if she cared.'

'The Commission reached out to me when I lost my parents in a plane crash,' Mom said. 'I was alone, without a home and money. They promised me everything. A house, an education, a good life. But when the time came, I had to be ready. I agreed. For seven years, nothing happened. And then they reached out, telling me I had to meet someone. Marry him for a few years. And for that they'd give me—'

'Hell,' Dad said.

'Arthur, get rid of your anger.' She looked at Dad for the first time. Her silky voice was back. 'It shows that you still care. And honestly, you shouldn't. Our ship never sailed. I was doing a job, nothing more. And I'm done with being Mrs Gladwell.'

'You think I'm angry for what you did to me? I knew about that years back, before I left. I'm furious about what you did to her, Samantha. My daughter. *Your* daughter!'

My mother turned to me. 'And for that I'm sorry. I truly am. All the while, being held a prisoner in that damn house, every second, all I thought about was you, Kath. I didn't regret what was happening to me; I'd made my choice years ago. Its consequences are only mine.'

'Well, those consequences spilled over on to her... But you can still save her.'

'How?'

'By telling the truth,' I said. 'Come back with me to the States. Become a witness and tell the world what you've known all these years. It's the only way I can be saved.'

Mom sniggered. 'Kath, do you know why the Commission decided to be done with me, even though I was family to them?'

'I thought it was the Mandal who wanted to eliminate you because we exposed their secrets,' I said.

'No, it was the other way round. When I tried to escape, the Commission gave the Mandal clear instructions to get rid of me. They didn't do it as they wanted to keep me as leverage against whatever information you and your friends had.'

'You...you tried to escape?'

'When I learnt you were here and causing trouble...that you'd been charged with a serious crime back home. I decided I had to get out. Try and find you. You don't have to believe me. I don't expect you to.'

'I believe you.' I truly did.

'Whatever you had on the mob kept me alive,' my mother said.

'And how do you know all this?' Dad asked.

Mom turned to Dad. 'People talk. The guards talked. So did the workers and other hostages. Yesterday morning, everything changed at that house. The Mandal was burning everything down, clearing the rooms, killing people they didn't trust or need. I hid myself in the closet until Katherine found me. They should have left my daughter alone.' She finally took a sip of the coffee and looked at me. 'So, Kath, you asking me to help you... You're preaching to the choir.'

39 Something to Lose

Johnny

'I see it. You are not ashamed anymore, son.' Naani held my hand and smiled.

Shamshu, Rakhi and I sat at a tea stall in Hazaar Basti, surrounded by our old friends and neighbours. The last few drops of last night's rain trickled from the tarp overhead as the steamy scent of ginger from the boiling kettle filled our noses. Many of the shanty's residents squatted around us, a glass of their morning tea in hand.

Amid clanking hammers and smoky rubble, the rusty walls came down, making way for new foundations. Small trucks squeezed through the narrow lanes, iron rods jutting out of them; some also carried bags of cement and cans of enamel paint. Across the road, the water reservoir was gone, along with the bees.

'It was the last rain of the season,' the man beside me muttered, passing me a glass.

Most of the residents had decided to convert their illegal residences into legitimate homes by buying the land and paying penalties to the municipal corporation. They weren't waiting for the government to pave their roads or plant their trees. They were rebuilding the basti themselves. The asbestos sheets were carried away in lorries, never to be seen again. I caught a glimpse of a ladder missing a few rungs atop such a heap in a truck.

'We'll make a park for the children, and the library will be where your house was,' the man said.

'Do me a favour,' I said, and took a sip of the hot tea. 'Please name it Rampal Sharma Public Library.'

My house. The life I had lived in it. Gone.

I thought back to everything that had led me here? How did a suicidal dwarf bring down a city of 1.5 crore people? It certainly wasn't power. Or strength. I wasn't a trained assassin or a sly businessman. I didn't have any special skills. I was just a coward.

Empty of fear and ready to die, I had nothing to lose. Having long given up on myself, I found it easy to let go of the world. Fear was the stranger who had knocked on my door a few times, but I'd refused to let it in. But now, for the first time in a long while, I felt it—that warm gush that pushes through one's veins, making the heart throb. It told me I had something to lose now, that there was someone to protect—me. I finally mattered to myself.

Thankfully, Rampal wasn't haunting me in my sleep anymore, that rangy bastard. Neither was the little girl in the fire. But there were questions I didn't have answers to. *What next? Where do I go from here?* I couldn't be a nurse anymore, let alone a mini painkiller.

Shamshu had decided he'd return to his village and start an apiary. He had asked me to come along a million times, but I couldn't see myself donning a fencing veil and stealing someone's food.

Rakhi had her own mission. I had helped her initiate the process of adopting the daughter she had given up. She had dragged me to the orphanage, despite my protests. Those places still gave me the chills, but Rakhi never took no for an answer. When we got there, I realized how much I would have missed if I hadn't seen that smile on her five-year-old daughter's face. No amount of money, power or ambition could ever match it.

◆

'What are you going to do?' Shamshu asked me as the three of us walked to meet Kath at her hotel before she left for America with her family.

'Certainly not cooking any more amphetamines or blowing water tanks,' I said.

'Speaking of that... Dr Verma was also arrested,' he said. 'He was merrily cooking meth in one of the Mandal's dens.'

So much for making ten times more money. No more runaway antibiotic prescriptions at that squalid clinic anymore. But a thousand more conspiracy theories concocted by him in prison, for sure.

Rakhi stopped and turned to me. 'I'm thinking of running a few of the pizza delivery outlets,' she said. 'We already have the leases and the scooters. Why don't you join me?'

'I want to leave the city. Leave all this.'

'Leave? Where will you go?' she asked.

'I'm afraid leaving is as far as I've been able to figure out. To be honest, *where* isn't important.'

'You think Kath is doing the right thing by going back?'

'It's highly risky,' I said.

'Shouldn't we try to stop her?' Rakhi asked. 'She's found her father. He has money. She doesn't need more. You should talk her out of it.'

'What would you've done?' I asked her.

She didn't answer, but I knew what she thought. Kath's betting on her freedom for a shot at getting her railroad fortune back was crazy. But she was the same girl who had risked it all by coming here to find her mother in the first place. So no, I wasn't going to try to talk her out of it. Apart from being a futile attempt, it also would be a quarter-hearted one.

I sauntered over those shiny, unmarked, unnamed cobbled bricks. Measuring my future steps, I wondered how far my legs would take me. I didn't have a destination or a path laid out for them, but this much I now knew: my legs, however dwarfed they might be, wouldn't disappoint.

It was time to stride, destinations be damned.

40 Backwards and Ahead

'I can't believe I lost and found so much at the same time,' I said.

'Neither can I,' Johnny murmured.

We stood by the banks of the Hooghly, watching the afternoon sun scatter its golden shimmer on the river's gentle waves. Across the river, a priest prepared for the evening puja.

'Do you realize how bizarre this has been? I mean, what if our rooms in the House of Dolls weren't next to each other? What if we hadn't shared a wall?' I asked.

'You would have burned in the fire, and Bijoy would have killed me in my lab.'

'Not just that, though. Forget if we would have lived or not. This city... It would have stayed the same. Murderous cops would still roam the streets; homes would still be snatched away. People like Rampal and Imaan would lose their lives every day. I certainly wouldn't have saved my mother. Akhil would be lost on the streets instead of being in a good school, away from the madness. You wouldn't have been able to give so much to the people of Hazaar Basti. We made it happen, Johnny. We changed this city. Forever... For good.'

'And now that it's changed, I don't know how to look at it.'

'What's wrong? You should be immensely proud of—'

'I am... I totally am. This is what was missing in my life: significance. And I got it. But now that the show's over, I don't know where to anchor myself.'

'You know, an old professor of mine used to say, "Stop chasing a period. Flow with an ellipsis instead."'

'It's a shame I didn't go to your college.'

'Johnny, you don't need to win over the world. Just a few people. That's enough to last a lifetime. So stop playing for the town. You'll never be able to win it over.'

He grinned. 'But I'd have so much fun trying.'

'So then…now would be the perfect time to ask you…'

'Ask me what?'

I turned to him. 'You know…play for the town. Just a different one. Okay, a very different one.'

'I don't understand.'

'Are you ready to bring down another mob?'

Johnny looked at me for a few seconds, eyes wide open. 'Kath, it's no joke to—'

'I'm not kidding. Look, I couldn't have found my parents without you. And you couldn't have brought down the Mandal without my help. Can you really see yourself stitching wounds and passing gauze pads all your life? You wanted longer shadows… Well, this is it… Another chance to make a difference. To be counted. I know I'll have my back up against the wall the second I land in the US. And this isn't a local city mob that I want to bring down. I don't even know if my mother will be able to put herself on the line for me. Dad can't go back as a Gladwell—he'll be a walking target. Which is why I need you, my friend… Again.'

Johnny stepped closer to the river.

'You're the only one I trust,' I continued. 'Chances are we'll fail against them. But at least we'll have tried. Even if I go to prison, there will be enough in New York for you to make a life for yourself there… So, what do you say?'

'I don't have the papers, the passport. You're leaving today…
I—'

'Here.' I walked closer to him and handed a packet. 'Your passport. With a valid US visa.'

Johnny shifted on his legs, fidgeting with the packet. 'When did you get this done? Those signatures you asked for—they weren't for your papers, were they?'

'They were. And then some.'

'It's too sudden. I don't even have a—'

'You don't need a suitcase to live, Johnny.'

'How were you so sure? Getting a passport made and—'

I shrugged. 'I just was. So what do you say? Ready to change the history of American railroads? Ready to leave this city?'

This city. It wasn't just a city.

Kolkata was a conversation with myself. A celebration of down-in-the-dumps. A victory of failures. A paraphernalia of laughs and giggles and sobs and gallows. Hallucinations and smokes. Fire and water. The cold sweat under my armpits. The hot beads trickling down my face. The ache in my feet from running through its dusty sidewalks and rundown gardens. The chipped columns with their unnamed plaques and unknown capitals. Everything that had burned in the fires. Everything that had survived.

There was no hotel lobby music, no dressed-up greetings by a hotel doorman. I was Kolkata's most perverted voyeur. And I relished every bit of it. The slugs and the slime. Its grind and grime. I'd lost many ways and found better ones without a confounding map. I'd eavesdropped on people singing, arguing, praying and mourning—and I had done some of my own. I had spied on lives and lived off them. And holy mother of Jimi and sweet baby Hendrix, I saw an angel, not too baroque, rise from ruinous flames.

This city. A mirror for those willing to look—inside and out. Backward and ahead. My very own stranger.

But now, it was time to go say hello to an old friend. It was time to get back what rightfully belonged to me.

Acknowledgements

The process of writing my first book, *The Unprodigal*, was one of self-discovery. Stretching to the limits and seeing what stuck, I experimented with thoughts, tested styles and genres. The metamorphosis needed to internalize my skill as a writer was a long one—I had buyer's remorse at times, impostor syndrome all the time. But I got there. Eventually, I found sprinkles of pride and a path forward.

That long-winded road led me to my second work of love and labour, and I am ecstatic to share that this time, I carried none of the earlier baggage. The secret? None. But sheer love for the craft and the willingness to remain a student helped immensely. I dove deeper into the science of storytelling—the textures beneath and the shimmer above. Book after book, there was so much I learnt. One fine day, on the first day of a global pandemic-induced lockdown, I picked up the proverbial pen, confident of the place I was coming from.

My writing process is that of a 'pantser'—someone who writes without a defined plot, letting the story unfold organically. Sort of like flying by the seat of one's pants. I had no idea what I was starting or where it would go, but I trusted my instincts. I was both bystander and puppeteer as the pieces of the puzzle slowly found each other. All I had to do was turn up honest, with no hangovers from the real world. In time, the story discovered me, just as I discovered it.

The Fires We Become has been the most satisfying, moving and complete experience of my writing life. It comes from a sincere love for the world and the emotions that drive us. It is fiery, fast, furious and unapologetically alive. A story we all secretly long to live—and live to tell.

I have my loved ones to thank for this gift:

To Mom—thank you for the immeasurable love you gave me and for always watching over me with those gentle, selfless eyes. Your presence is in every word, every page.

To Dad—thank you for gently nudging me to stay with my passion and never give up. My truest hero.

To Nidhi, my wife—my fiercest critic and greatest cheerleader. I wrote every chapter imagining your reactions—hoping to make you pause, smile and say 'wow'. You have, and always will be, my first reader—the one I picture curled up on a rainy Sunday, paperback in hand, a quiet smile on your face.

To Myra, my elder daughter—when you presented a school project on *The Unprodigal*, the gleam and pride in your eyes pushed me to bring this next one to life. I have yet to meet someone who so effortlessly embodies sensitivity, sincerity and intensity. That you are my daughter is a source of sheer joy. And also, a true test of humility.

To Kimaya, my younger daughter—and the spark behind this book. For five years you have asked me, every couple of weeks, when my next one would be ready. You are a beautiful dynamo—bursting with verve, hugs and life. If only I could be more like you. Thank you for being my truest timekeeper and reality checker.

Who am I to stand in the way if the flight of a father's imagination gives bright, colourful wings to his girls' dreams? Not me. Never me.

To Angela Brown—thank you for your brilliant developmental edit and critique. Angela, a renowned L.A.-based editor, has worked on over 800 books, including titles by *The New York Times* bestselling authors and Oscar-nominated screenwriters. After reading *The Fires We Become*, she wrote: 'Without a doubt, this is the best thriller I've ever edited. This book blew me away! [...] You've created an extremely vivid world that's terrifying but sometimes quite heart-warming.'

Coming from the best in the business, that's affirmation I will cherish forever.

To Pratik, Shalini and Manmeet—thank you for being fantastic beta readers, for your priceless feedback and for being even better friends.

To the entire team at Rupa Publications—thank you for your continued belief in my work.

And, finally, to Paramita—thank you for creating a stunning cover that captures the soul of the story.

So here I am, with a bigger, deeper piece of my heart laid bare. I hope this story gives you something to hold close. I hope it stirs something within you. And most of all, I hope you can imagine the happiness that would bring me.